New York Times bestseller Jill Shalvis is
novels including her acclaimed Lucky
and Cedar Ridge series. The RITA win
Readers Choice winner makes her home near Lake Tahoe.

Visit her website at www.jillshalvis.com for a complete book list
and daily blog, and www.facebook.com/JillShalvis for other news,
or follow her on Twitter @JillShalvis.

Jill Shalvis. Delightfully addictive:

'Packed with the trademark Shalvis humor and intense intimacy, it is
definitely a must-read . . . If love, laughter and passion are
the keys to any great romance, then this novel hits every note'
Romantic Times

'Heart-warming and sexy . . . an abundance of chemistry,
smoldering romance, and hilarious antics' *Publishers Weekly*

'[Shalvis] has quickly become one of my go-to authors of
contemporary romance. Her writing is smart, fun, and sexy, and her
books never fail to leave a smile on my face long after I've closed
the last page . . . Jill Shalvis is an author not to be missed!'
The Romance Dish

'Jill Shalvis is such a talented author that she brings to life
characters who make you laugh, cry, and are a joy to read'
Romance Reviews Today

'What I love about Jill Shalvis's books is that she writes sexy,
adorable heroes . . . the sexual tension is out of this world. And of
course, in true Shalvis fashion, she expertly mixes in humor that has
you laughing out loud' *Heroes and Heartbreakers*

'I always enjoy reading a Jill Shalvis book. She's a consistently
elegant, bold, clever writer . . . Very witty – I laughed out loud
countless times and these scenes are sizzling' *All About Romance*

'If you have not read a Jill Shalvis novel yet, then you really have
not read a real romance yet either!' *Book Cove Reviews*

'Engaging writing, characters that walk straight into your heart,
touching, hilarious' *Library Journal*

JILL SHALVIS

Sweet Little Lies

&

The Trouble With Mistletoe

BOOKS 1 & 2 IN THE HEARTBREAKER
BAY COLLECTION

headline
ETERNAL

Published by arrangement with Avon Books,
an imprint of HarperCollins Publishers

The novels contained in this omnibus, *Sweet Little Lies* and *The Trouble With Mistletoe*, were each published separately by Headline Eternal, an imprint of Headline Publishing Group, in 2016.

First published in this omnibus in 2016
by HEADLINE ETERNAL
An imprint of HEADLINE PUBLISHING GROUP

1

Cataloguing in Publication Data is available from the British Library

ISBN 978 1 4722 4424 6

Offset in 12.65/14.4 pt Times LT Std by Jouve (UK)

Printed and bound in Australia by McPherson's Printing Group

Headline's policy is to use papers that are natural, renewable and recyclable products and made from wood grown in well-managed forests and other controlled sources. The logging and manufacturing processes are expected to conform to the environmental regulations of the country of origin.

HEADLINE PUBLISHING GROUP
An Hachette UK Company
Carmelite House
50 Victoria Embankment
London EC4Y 0DZ

www.headlineeternal.com
www.headline.co.uk
www.hachette.co.uk

MIX
Paper from
responsible sources
FSC   FSC® C001695
www.fsc.org

The paper this book is printed on is certified against the
Forest Stewardship Council ® Standards. McPherson's Printing Group
holds FSC® chain of custody certification SGS-COC-004121. FSC®
promotes environmentally responsible, socially beneficial
and economically viable management of the world's forests

Sweet Little Lies

*To HelenKay Dimon
for being a real friend (the very best kind!)
Also for introducing me to May Chen,
the new love of my life.
Thanks for sharing her.*

*And to May Chen, for bringing back
my love of writing.*

Chapter 1

#KeepCalmAndRideAUnicorn

Pru Harris's mom had taught her to make wishes on pink cars, falling leaves, and brass lamps, because wishing on something as ordinary as stars or wishing wells was a sign of no imagination.

Clearly the woman standing not three feet away in the light mist, searching her purse for change to toss into the courtyard fountain hadn't been raised by a hippie mom as Pru had been.

Not that it mattered, since her mom had been wrong. Wishes, along with things like winning the lotto or finding a unicorn, never happened in real life.

The woman, shielding her eyes from the light rain with one hand, holding a coin in her other, sent Pru a wry grimace. "I know it's silly, but it's a hit-rock-bottom thing."

Something Pru understood all too well. She set a wriggly Thor down and shook her arms to try and bring back some circulation. Twenty-five pounds of wet, tubby, afraid-of-his-own-shadow mutt had felt like seventy-five by the end of their thirty-minute walk home from work.

Thor objected to being on the wet ground with a sharp bark. Thor didn't like rain.

Or walking.

But he loved Pru more than life itself so he stuck close, his tail wagging slowly as he watched her face to determine what mood they were in.

The woman blinked and stared down at Thor. "Oh," she said, surprised. "I thought it was a really fat cat."

Thor's tail stopped wagging and he barked again, as if to prove that not only was he all dog, he was big, *badass* dog.

Because Thor—a rescue of undetermined breed— also believed he was a bullmastiff.

When the woman took a step back, Pru sighed and picked him back up again. His old man face was creased into a protective frown, his front paws dangling, his tail back to wagging now that he was suddenly tall. "Sorry," Pru said. "He can't see well and it makes him grumpy, but he's not a cat." She gave Thor a *behave* squeeze. "He only acts like one."

Thor volleyed back a look that said Pru might want to not leave her favorite shoes unattended tonight.

The woman's focus turned back to the fountain and she eyed the quarter in her hand. "They say it's never too late to wish on love, right?"

"Right," Pru said. Because they did say that. And just because in her own personal experience love had proven even rarer than unicorns didn't mean she'd step on someone else's hopes and dreams.

A sudden bolt of lightning lit up the San Francisco skyline like the Fourth of July. Except it was June, and cold as the Arctic. Thor squeaked and shoved his face into Pru's neck. Pru started to count but didn't even get to One-Mississippi before the thunder boomed loud enough to make them all jump.

"Yikes." The woman dropped the quarter back into her purse. "Not even love's worth getting electrocuted." And she ran off.

Pru and Thor did the same, heading across the cobblestone courtyard. Normally she took her time here, enjoying the glorious old architecture of the building, the corbeled brick and exposed iron trusses, the big windows, but the rain had begun to fall in earnest now, hitting so hard that the drops bounced back up to her knees. In less than ten seconds, she was drenched through, her clothes clinging to her skin, filling her ankle boots so that they squished with each step.

"Slow down, sweetness!" someone called out. It was the old homeless guy who was usually in the alley. With his skin tanned to the consistency of leather and his long, wispy white cotton-ball hair down to the collar of his loud pineapples-and-parrots Hawaiian shirt, he looked like Doc from *Back to the Future,* plus a few decades. A century tops. "You can't get much wetter," he said.

But Pru wasn't actually trying to dodge the weather, she loved the rain. She was trying to dodge her demons, something she was beginning to suspect couldn't be done.

"Gotta get to my apartment," she said, breathless from her mad dash. When she'd hit twenty-six, her spin class instructor had teasingly told her that it was all downhill from here on out, she hadn't believed him. Joke was on her.

"What's the big rush?"

Resigned to a chat, Pru stopped. Old Guy was sweet and kind, even if he had refused to tell her his name, claiming to have forgotten it way back in the seventies. True or not, she'd been feeding him since she'd moved into this building three weeks ago. "The cable company's finally coming today," she said. "They said five o'clock."

"That's what they told you yesterday. And last week," he said, trying to pet Thor, who wasn't having any of it.

Another thing on Thor's hate list—men.

"But this time they mean it," Pru said and set Thor down. At least that's what the cable company supervisor had promised Pru on the phone, and she needed cable TV. Bad. The finals of *So You Think You Can Dance* were on tomorrow night.

"'Scuse me," someone said as he came from the elevator well and started to brush past her. He wore a hat low over his eyes to keep the rain out of his face and the cable company's logo on his pec. He was carrying a toolbox and looking peeved by life in general.

Thor began a low growl deep in his throat while hiding behind Pru's legs. He sounded fierce, but he looked ridiculous, especially wet. He had the fur of a Yorkshire terrier—if that Yorkshire terrier was fat— even though he was really a complete Heinz 57. And hell, maybe he *was* part cat. Except that only one of his ears folded over. The other stood straight up, giving him a perpetually confused look.

No self-respecting cat would have allowed such a

thing. In fact, the cable guy took one look at him and snorted, and then kept moving.

"Wait!" Pru yelled after him. "Are you looking for 3C?"

He stopped, his gaze running over her, slowing at her torso. "Actually," he said. "I'm more a double D man myself."

Pru looked down at herself. Her shirt had suctioned itself to her breasts. Narrowing her eyes, she crossed her arms over her decidedly not DDs. "Let me be more clear," she said, tightening her grip on Thor's leash because he was still growling, although he was doing it very quietly because he only wanted to pretend to be a tough guy. "Are you looking for the person who lives in *apartment* 3C?"

"I was but no one's home." He eyed Thor. "Is that a dog?"

"Yes! And *I'm* 3C," Pru said. "I'm home!"

He shook his head. "You didn't answer your door."

"I will now, I promise." She pulled her keys from her bag. "We can just run up there right now and—"

"No can do, dude. It's five o'clock straight up." He waved his watch to prove it. "I'm off the clock."

"But—"

But nothing, he was gone, walking off into the downpour, vanishing into the fog like they were on the set of a horror flick.

Thor stopped growling.

"Great," Pru muttered. "Just great."

Old Guy slid his dentures around some. "I could hook up your cable for you. I've seen someone do it once or twice."

The old man, like the old Pacific Heights building around them, had seen better days, but both held a certain old-fashioned charm—which didn't mean she trusted him inside her apartment. "Thanks," she said. "But this is for the best. I don't really need cable TV all that bad."

"But the finals of *So You Think You Can Dance* are on tomorrow night."

She sighed. "I know."

Another bolt of lightning lit the sky, and again was immediately followed by a crack of thunder that echoed off the courtyard's stone walls and shook the ground beneath their feet.

"That's my exit," Old Guy said and disappeared into the alley.

Pru got Thor upstairs, rubbed him down with a towel and tucked him into his bed. She'd thought she wanted the same for herself, but she was hungry and there was nothing good in her refrigerator. So she quickly changed into dry clothes and went back downstairs.

Still raining.

One of these days she was going to buy an umbrella. For now, she made the mad dash toward the northeast corner of the building, past the Coffee Bar, the Waffle Shop, and the South Bark Mutt Shop—all closed, past The Canvas tattoo studio—open—and went straight for the Irish Pub.

Without the lure of cable to make her evening, she needed chicken wings.

And nobody made chicken wings like O'Riley's.

It's not the chicken wings you're wanting, a small voice inside her head said. And that was fact. Nope, what drew her into O'Riley's like a bee to honey was the six-foot, broad-shouldered, dark eyes, dark smile of Finn O'Riley himself.

From her three weeks in the building, she knew the people who lived and/or worked here were tight. And she knew that it was in a big part thanks to Finn because he was the glue, the steady one.

She knew more too. More than she should.

"Hey!" Old Guy stuck his head out of the alley. "If you're getting us wings, don't forget extra sauce!"

She waved at him, and once again dripping wet, entered O'Riley's where she stood for a second getting her bearings.

Okay, that was a total lie. She stood there *pretending* to get her bearings while her gaze sought out the bar and the guys behind it.

There were two of them working tonight. Twenty-two-year-old Sean was flipping bottles, juggling them to the catcalls and wild amusement of a group of women all belly up to the bar, wooing them with his wide smile and laughing eyes. But he wasn't the one Pru's gaze gravitated to like he was a rack of double-stuffed Oreo cookies.

Nope, that honor went to the guy who ran the place, Sean's older brother. All lean muscle and easy confidence, Finn O'Riley wasn't pandering to the crowd. He never did. He moved quickly and efficiently without show, quietly hustling to fill the orders, keeping an eye on the kitchen, as always steady as a rock under pressure, doing all the real work.

Pru could watch him all day. It was his hands, she'd decided, they were constantly moving with expert precision. He was busy, way too busy for her, of course, which was only one of the many reasons why she hadn't allowed herself to fantasize about him doing deliciously naughty, wicked things to her in her bed.

Whoops. That was another big fat lie.

She'd *totally* fantasized about him doing deliciously naughty, wicked things to her in bed. And also out of it.

He was her unicorn.

He bent low behind the bar for something and an entire row of women seated on the barstools leaned in unison for a better view. Meerkats on parade.

When he straightened a few seconds later, he was hoisting a huge crate of something, maybe clean glasses, and not looking like he was straining too much either. This was in no doubt thanks to all that lean, hard muscle visible beneath his black tee and faded jeans. His biceps bulged as he turned, allowing her to see that his Levi's fit him perfectly, front *and* back.

If he noticed his avid audience, he gave no hint of it. He merely set the crate down on the counter, and ignoring the women ogling him, nodded a silent hello in Pru's direction.

She stilled and then craned her neck, looking behind her.

No one there. Just herself, dripping all over his floor.

She turned back and found Finn looking quietly amused. Their gazes locked and held for a long beat, like maybe he was taking her pulse from across the room, absorbing the fact that she was drenched and breathless. The corners of his mouth twitched. She'd amused him again.

People shifted between them. The place was

crowded as always, but when the way was clear again, Finn was still looking at her, steady and unblinking, those dark green eyes flickering with something other than amusement now, something that began to warm her from the inside out.

Three weeks and it was the same every single time . . .

Pru considered herself fairly brave and maybe a little more than fairly adventurous—but not necessarily forward. It wasn't easy for her to connect with people.

Which was the only excuse she had for jerking her gaze away, pretending to eye the room.

The pub itself was small and cozy. One half bar, the other half pub designated for dining, the décor was dark woods reminiscent of an old thatched inn. The tables were made from whiskey barrels and the bar itself had been crafted out of repurposed longhouse-style doors. The hanging brass lantern lights and stained-glass fixtures along with the horse-chewed, old-fence baseboards finished the look that said antique charm and friendly warmth.

Music drifted out of invisible speakers, casting a jovial mood, but not too loud so as to make conversation difficult. There was a wall of windows and also a rack of accordion wood and glass doors that opened the pub on both sides, one to the courtyard, the other to the street, giving a view down the hill to the beautiful Fort Mason Park and Marina Green, and the Golden Gate Bridge behind that.

All of which was fascinating, but not nearly as fascinating as Finn himself, which meant that her eyes, the traitors, swiveled right back to him.

He pointed at her.

"Me?" she asked, even though he couldn't possibly hear her from across the place.

With a barely there smile, he gave her a finger crook.

Yep. Her.

Chapter 2

#TakeMeToYourLeader

Pru's brain wondered what her mom would've said about going to a man who crooked his finger at her. But Pru's feet didn't care, they simply took her right to him.

He handed her a clean towel to dry off. Their fingers brushed, sending a tingle straight through her. While she enjoyed that—hey, it was the most action she'd gotten in a very long time—he cleared her a seat.

"What can I get you?" His voice was low and gravelly, bringing to mind all sorts of inappropriate responses to his question.

"Your usual?" he asked. "Or the house special?"

"What would that be?" she asked.

"Tonight it's a watermelon mojito. I could make it virgin-style for you."

He saw God knew how many people day in and day out, and on top of that the two of them hadn't spoken much more than a few words to each other, but he remembered what she liked after a long day at work out on the water.

And what she didn't. He'd noticed that she didn't drink alcohol. Hard to believe that when he had a pub menu, a regular alcoholic beverage menu, and also a special menu dedicated solely to beer, he could keep it all straight. "You kept track of my usual?" she asked, warmed at the idea. Warmed and a little scared because she shouldn't be doing this, flirting with him.

"It's my job," he said.

"Oh." She laughed at herself. "Right. Of course."

His eyes never left her face. "And also because your usual is a hot chocolate, which matches your eyes."

Her stomach got warmer. So did some of her other parts. "The virgin special would be great, thanks."

The guy on the barstool next to her swiveled to look at her. He was in a suit, tie loosened. "Hi," he said with the cheerfulness of someone who was already two drinks into his night. "I'm Ted. How 'bout I buy you an Orgasm? Or maybe even"—wink, wink—"multiples?"

Finn's easy, relaxed stance didn't change but his eyes did as they cut to Ted, serious now and a little scary hard. "Behave," he warned, "or I'll cut you off."

"Aw, now that's no fun," Ted said with a toothy smile. "I'm trying to buy the pretty lady a drink, is all."

Finn just looked at him.

Ted lifted his hands in a sign of surrender and Finn went back to making drinks. Soon as he did, Ted leaned in close to Pru again. "Okay now that daddy's gone, how about Sex On The Beach?"

Finn reached in and took Ted's drink away. "Annnnd you're out."

Ted huffed out a sigh and stood up. "Fine, I gotta get home anyway." He flashed a remorseful smile at Pru. "Maybe next time we'll start with a Seduction."

"Maybe next time," she said, picking one of the sweet, noncommittal smiles from her wide repertoire of smiles that she used on the job captaining a day cruise ship in the bay. It took a lot of different smiles to handle all the people she dealt with daily and she had it down.

When Ted was gone, Finn met her gaze. "Maybe next time?" he repeated.

"Or, you know, never."

Finn smiled at that. "You let him down easy."

"Had to," she said. "Since you played bad cop."

"Just part of the service I offer," he said, not at all bothered by the bad cop comment. "Did you have to cancel your last tour today?"

So apparently he knew what she did for a living. "Nope. Just got back."

"You were out in this?" he asked in disbelief. "With the high winds and surf alerts?"

His hands were in constant motion, making drinks, chopping ingredients, keeping things moving. She was mesmerized by the way he moved, how he used those strong hands, the stubble on his jaw . . .

"Pru."

She jerked her gaze off his square jaw and found his locked on hers. "Hmm?"

A flash of humor and something else came and went in his eyes. "Did you have any problems with the high winds and surf out there today?"

"Not really. I mean, a little kid got sick o

grandma, but that's because she gave him an entire bag of cotton candy and then two hot dogs, and he wolfed it all down in like two seconds, so I'm not taking the blame there."

He turned his head and looked out the open doors facing the courtyard. Dusk had fallen. The lights strung in pretty ribbons over and around the wrought iron fencing and fountain revealed sheets of rain falling from the sky.

She shrugged. "It didn't start raining until I was off the water. And anyway, bad weather's a part of the job."

"I'd think staying alive would be a bigger part of the job."

"Well yes," she said on a laugh. "Staying alive is definitely the goal." Truth was, she rarely had problems out on the water. Nope, it was mostly real life that gave her problems. "It's San Francisco. If we didn't go out in questionable weather, we'd never go out at all."

He took that in a moment as he simultaneously cleaned up a mess at the bar and served a group a few seats down a pitcher of margaritas, while still managing to make her feel like he was concentrating solely on her.

It's his job, her brain reminded her body. But it felt like more.

From the other side of the pub came a sound of a ... floor. Finn's eyes tracked over there.

... waitresses had dropped a dish, and the ... n serving—a rowdy group of young ... ering, embarrassing her further.

... opped over the bar and strode over ... 't hear what he said but the guys at the table immediately straightened up, losing their frat boy antics mentality.

Finn then turned, crouched low next to his waitress, helped her clean up, and was back to the bar in less than sixty seconds.

"You've got an interesting job," he said, coming back to their conversation like nothing had happened.

"Yes," she said, watching as the waitress moved to the kitchen with a grateful glance in Finn's direction. "Interesting. And fun too." Which was incredibly important to her because . . . well, there'd been a very long stretch of time when her life hadn't been anything close to resembling a good time.

"Fun." Finn repeated the word like it didn't compute. "Now there's something I haven't had in a while."

Something else she already knew about him, and the thought caused a slash of regret to cut through her.

Sean came up alongside Finn. The brothers looked alike; same dark hair, same dark green eyes and smiles. Finn was taller, which didn't stop Sean from slinging an arm around his older brother's neck as he winked at Pru. "You'll have to excuse grandpa here. He doesn't do fun. You'd do better to go out with me."

Sean O'Riley, master flirt.

But Pru was a master too, by necessity. She'd had to become well versed in dealing with charming flirts at work. It didn't matter if it was vacationers, tourists, or college kids . . . they all got a kick out of having a female boat captain, and since she was passable in the looks department and a smartass to boot, she got hit on a lot. She always declined, even the marriage proposals. *Especially* the marriage proposals. "I'm flattered," she said with an easy smile. "But I couldn't possibly break the hearts of all the women waiting for their *cocktail* fantasies to come true."

"Damn." Sean mimed a dagger to the heart but laughed good-naturedly. "Do me a favor then, would ya? If you're going to take this one for a spin"—he elbowed Finn—"Show him how to live a little and maybe take him for a walk on the wild side while you're at it."

Pru slid her gaze to Finn, which was how she caught the quick flash of irritation as Sean sauntered off. "You need help living a little?" she asked him lightly. Not easy to do since her heart had started pounding, her pulse racing, because what was she doing? Was she really playing with him? It was a bad idea, the worst of all her bad ideas put together, and she'd had some real doozies over the years.

Don't be stupid. Back away from the cute hottie. You can't have him and you know why.

But the troubling train of thought stopped on a dime when Finn laughed all rumbly and sexy, like maybe he saved it for special occasions.

"Actually," he said, "I've lived plenty. And as for taking a walk on the wild side, I wrote the book on it." He leaned on the bar, which brought him up close and personal. Eyes locked on hers, he stroked a strand of wet hair from her temple.

She went still, like a puppy waiting for a belly rub, staring up at him, her heart still pounding, but for another reason entirely now. "What changed?" she asked, whispered really, because she was pretty sure she knew what the catalyst had been and it was going to kill her to hear him say it.

He shrugged. "Life."

Oh how she hated that for him. Hated it, and felt guilty for it. And not for the first time when she felt overwhelmed and out of her league, she opened her mouth and put her foot in it. "You know, in some circles I'm known as the Fun Whisperer."

He arched a brow. "Is that right?"

"Yep," she said, apparently no longer in control of her mouth. "The fun starts right here with me. I specialize in people not living their lives, the ones letting their life live them. It's about letting stuff go, you see." Seriously. Why wasn't her mouth attached to a shut-the-hell-up filter?

Finn smiled and blew half her brain cells. "You going to teach me how to have fun, Pru?" he asked in that low, husky voice.

Good God, the way her name rolled off his tongue had her knees wobbling. She could see now that his eyes weren't a solid dark green, but had swirls of gold and brown and even some blue in them in the mix as well. She was playing with fire and all her inner alarms were going off.

Stop.

Don't engage.

Go home.

But did she do any of those things? No, she did not. Instead she smiled back and said, "I could knock the ball out of the park teaching you how to have fun."

"I have no doubt," he murmured, and blew all her remaining brain cells.

Chapter 3

#GoBigOrGoHome

It wasn't until Finn shifted away to help one of his servers that Pru let out a shuddery breath. *I'm known as the Fun Whisperer?* She smacked her own forehead, which didn't knock any sense into her. Ordering her hormones to cool their jets, she turned away to take in the rest of the pub.

She was immediately waved over to the far end of the bar, which she'd missed when she'd first come in because hello, she'd honed in on Finn like a homing pigeon.

Informally reserved for those who lived and worked in the building, this end of the bar was instant camaraderie as someone you knew was always there to eat or drink with.

Tonight that someone was Willa, sole proprietor of the South Bark Mutt Shop, a one-stop pet store on the southwest ground-floor corner of the building.

Willa eyed a still very wet Pru and without a word pushed a plate of chicken wings her way.

"You're a mind reader," Pru said and slid onto the seat next to her.

Willa laughed at the squishy, watery sound Pru made when she sat. "When you live in a city that's all hills and rain and soggy rainbow flags you learn really fast what's valuable. An umbrella with all its spokes . . . and a man who believes in happily-ever-afters."

Pru laughed. "Aw. You believe in fairy tales."

Willa smiled, her bright green eyes dancing. If you took in her strawberry red hair cut in layers framing her pretty face and coupled it with her petite, curvy frame, she looked like she belonged in a fairy tale herself, waving her magic wand. "You don't believe the right guy's out there for you?"

Pru took a big bite of a mouth-watering chicken wing and moaned. Swallowing, she licked some sauce off her thumb. "I just think I'd have better luck searching for a unicorn."

"You could wish on the fountain," Willa said.

The fountain in their courtyard had quite the reputation, as the woman she'd seen earlier had clearly known. The 1928 four-story building had actually been built around the fountain, which had been here in the Cow Hollow district of San Francisco for fifty years before that, when the area still resembled the Wild West and was chock-full of dairies and roaming cattle.

Back then only the hearty had survived. And the desperate. Born of that, the fountain's myth went that a wish made here out of true desperation, with an equally true heart, would bring a first, true love in unexpected ways.

It'd happened just enough times over the past hundred plus years that the myth had long since become infamous legend.

A big hand set a mouth-watering looking watermelon mojito mocktail in front of her, the muscles in his forearm flexing as he moved. Pru stared at it for a beat before she managed to lift her gaze to Finn's. "Thanks."

"Try it."

She obediently did just that. "Oh my God," she murmured, pleasure infusing her veins. "What's in it?"

He smiled mysteriously, and something warm and wondrous happened deep inside her.

"Secret recipe," he said while she was still gaping up at him. He turned to Willa. "And your Irish coffee."

Willa squealed over the mountain of whipped cream topping the glass and jumped up to give Finn a tight squeeze.

Pru knew that they were very tight friends and it showed in their familiarity with each other. It didn't seem sexual at all so there was no need for jealousy but Finn definitely let down his guard with Willa. And it was *that*, Pru knew, that gave her the twinge of envy.

Finn waited until Willa sat and attacked her drink before he spoke again. "Your girl Cara tried to con Sean into a drink last night."

Willa, who'd just spooned in a huge bite of the cream, grimaced. She always had three or four employees on rotation at her shop, all of them some sort of rescue, many of them underage. "She have a fake ID?"

"Affirmative," Finn said. "He cut it up on my orders."

Willa sighed. "Bet that went over like a fart in church."

Finn lifted a shoulder. "We handled it."

Willa reached out and squeezed his hand. "Thanks."

Finn nodded and turned his attention back to Pru, who'd sucked down a third of her drink already. "You need your own order of chicken wings?"

What she needed didn't involve calories. It involved a lobotomy. "Yes, please."

"You warming up yet?"

Yes, but that might've had more to do with his warm gaze than the temperature in the room. "Getting there," she managed.

The barest of smiles curved his mouth.

Idle chitchat. That's all this was, she reminded herself. They were just like any other casual acquaintances who happened to be in the same place at the same time.

Except there was nothing casual about her being here. Finn just didn't know it.

Yet.

She'd have to tell him eventually, because this *wasn't* a fairy tale. And she absolutely would tell him. But as a rule, she tended to subscribe to the later-is-best theory.

She realized he was watching her and she squirmed in her seat, suddenly very busy looking anywhere and everywhere except right into his eyes because they made her think about things. Things that made her nipples hopeful and perky.

Things that couldn't happen.

As if maybe he knew what he could do to her with just one look—or hey, it wasn't like her wet white shirt was hiding much—the corners of his mouth quirked.

Which was when she realized that Willa had stopped eating and was staring at the two of them staring at each other. When Willa opened her mouth to say something, something Pru was quite certain she didn't want said in front of Finn, she rushed to beat her friend to it. "On second thought, can I double that order of chicken wings?"

"Sure," Finn's mouth said.

Stop looking at his mouth! She forced herself to look into his eyes instead, those deep, dark, mossy green eyes, which as suspected, was a lot like jumping from the frying pan into the fire. "Um, I think that's my phone—" She started digging through her purse. Wrapping her fingers around her cell, she pulled it out and stared at the screen.

Nothing. It was black.

Dammit.

Finn smiled and walked away, heading back to the kitchen.

"Smooth," Willa said and sipped her Irish coffee.

Pru covered her face, but peeked out between her fingers, watching Finn go, telling herself she was completely nonplussed by her crazy reaction to him, but the truth was she just wanted to watch his very fine ass go.

"Huh," Willa said.

"No," Pru said. "There's no *huh*."

"Oh, honey, there's a *huge* huh," Willa said. "I work with dogs and cats all day long, I'm fluent in eye-speak. And there's some serious eye-speak going on here. It's saying you two want to f—"

Pru pointed at her and snagged the last chicken wing, stuffing it into her mouth.

Willa just smirked. "You know, it's been a long time since I've seen Finn look at a woman like he just looked at you. A real long time."

Don't ask. *Don't ask*—"Why's that?" She covered her mouth. Then uncovered her mouth. Then covered it again.

Willa waited, eyes lit. "Not that *that* wasn't fun to watch, but are you finished arguing with yourself?"

Pru sighed. "Yeah."

"Finn's got a lot going on. Keeping the pub's head above water isn't easy in today's economy. Plus he's slowly renovating his grandparents' house so he can sell it and move out of the city—"

Pru's heart stopped and she swallowed a heavy bite of chicken wing. "He wants to leave San Francisco?"

"To live, yes. To work, no. He loves the pub, but he wants to live in a quieter place and get a big, lazy dog. And then there's his biggest time sink—keeping Sean on the straight and narrow. Add all of that up and it equals no time for—"

"Love?"

"Well, I was going to say getting lucky," Willa said. "But yeah, even less time for love."

Pru turned her head and watched Finn in action, taking care of his employees, his customers, his brother . . .

But who took care of him, she wondered as he worked his ass off, running this entire place and making it look easy while he was at it.

She knew it wasn't about making time. It was about what had happened eight years ago when he'd been just barely twenty-one. Her gut twisted, which didn't stop

her from eating her entire plate of chicken wings when
it came.

An hour later she left the bar warm, dry, and stuffed.
Night had fallen. The rain had tapered off. With the clearing of most of the clouds, a sliver of a moon lit her way.
The courtyard was mostly empty now, the air cool on her
skin. Pots of flowers hung from hooks on the brick walls
and also the wrought iron lining parts of the courtyard.
During the day, the air was fragrant with the blooms but
now all she could smell was the salty sea breeze.

A few people were coming and going, either from the
pub or cutting through for a shortcut to the street and
the nightlife the rest of the Cow Hollow and Marina
area offered. But the sound of street traffic was muted
here, partially thanks to the fountain's water cascading down to the wide, circular copper dome that had
long ago become tarnished green and black. A stone
bench provided a quick respite for those so inclined to
stop and enjoy the view and the musical sound of the
trickling water.

Pru stopped, staring at the coins shining brightly
from the tiles at the bottom of the fountain. What was
it the woman from earlier had said? *Never too late to
wish for love . . .*

On a sudden whim, she went through her purse,
looking for her laundry money. Pulling out a dime, she
stared into the water. *A wish made here out of true desperation, with an equally true heart, will bring a first,
true love in unexpected ways.*

Well, she had the desperation. Did she have the true
heart? She put a hand to it because it did hurt, but that
might've been the spicy chicken wings.

Not that it mattered because she wasn't going to wish for herself. She was going to wish for true love for someone else, for a guy who didn't know her, not really, and yet she owed him far more than he'd ever know.

Finn.

She closed her eyes, sending her wish to . . . well, whoever collected them. The fountain fairy?

The Karma Fairy?

The Tooth Fairy?

Please, she thought, *please bring Finn true love because he deserves so much more happy than he's been dealt.* And then she tossed in the dime.

"I hope you find him."

Pru gasped and whirled around to face . . . Old Guy.

"What's his name?" he asked.

"Oh," she said on a low laugh. "I didn't wish for me."

"Shame," he said. "Though it doesn't really work, you know that, right? It's just a propaganda thing the businesses here in the Pacific Pier building use to draw in foot traffic."

"I know," Pru said, and crossed her fingers. *Please let him be wrong . . .*

"I tried it once," he told her. "I wished for my first love to return to me. But Red's still dead as a doornail."

"Oh," Pru breathed. "I'm so sorry."

He shrugged. "She gave me twelve great years. Shared my food, my bed, and my heart for all of them. Slept with me every night and guarded my six like no other." He smiled. "She'd bring me game she'd hunted herself when we were hungry. She followed me everywhere. Hell, she didn't even mind when I'd bring another woman home."

Pru blinked. "That's . . . sweet?"

"Yeah. She was the best dog ever."

She reached out to smack him and he flashed a grin. "Don't be ashamed of wishing for love for yourself, sweetness," he said. "Everyone deserves that. Whoever he is, I hope he's worthy."

"No, really, it's not—"

"Or she," he said, lifting his hands. "No judging here. We all stick together, you know what I'm saying? Take Tim, the barista at the coffee shop. When he decided to become Tina a few years back, no one blinked an eye. Well, okay, I did at first," he admitted. "But that's only because she's hot as hell now. I mean, who knew?"

Pru nodded. Tina had made her coffee just about every morning for three weeks now, and on top of making the best muffins in all of San Francisco, she was indeed hot as hell. "I'm not wishing for me though. I'm wishing for someone else. Someone who deserves it more than me."

"Well, then," he said, and patted down his pockets, coming up with a quarter, which he tossed in after her dime. "Never hurts to double down a bet."

Chapter 4

#CarefulWhatYouWishFor

Two days later Finn was at his desk pounding the keys on his laptop, trying to find the source of the mess Sean had made of their books while simultaneously fantasizing about one sexy, adorable "fun whisperer," and how much he'd like her to fun whisper him. He was a most excellent multitasker.

He liked that sassy smile of hers. He liked her easygoing 'tude. And he really liked her mile-long legs . . .

He was in the middle of picturing them wrapped around him when he found the problem.

Sean had done something to the payroll that had caused everyone to get fifty percent more than they had coming to them. Finn rubbed his tired eyes and pushed back from his desk. "Done," he said. "Found the screwup. You somehow managed to set payroll to time and a half."

Sean didn't say anything and Finn blew out a breath.

He knew that sometimes he got caught up in being the boss and forgot to be the older brother. "Look," he said, "it could've happened to anyone, don't take it so hard—"

At the sound of a soft snore, Finn craned his neck and swore.

Sean lay sprawled on his back on the couch, one leg on the floor, his arms akimbo, mouth open, dead asleep.

Finn strode over there and exercised huge restraint by kicking his brother's foot and not his head.

Sean sat straight up, murmuring, "That's it, baby, that's perfect—" When he saw Finn standing over him, he sagged and swiped a hand down his face. "What the hell, man. You just interrupted me banging Anna Kendrick."

Anna Kendrick was hot, but she had nothing on Pru Harris. "You're not allowed to sleep through me kicking your ass."

Sean didn't try dispute the fact that Finn could, and had, kicked his ass on many occasions. "Anna Kendrick," he simply repeated in a devastated voice.

"Out of your league. And why the hell don't you sleep in your own office? Or better yet, at home."

Home being the Victorian row house they shared in the neighborhood of Pacific Heights, half a mile straight up one of San Francisco's famed hills.

"I've got better things to do in my bed than sleep," Sean muttered and yawned. "What do you want anyway? I've cleaned my room and scrubbed behind my ears, *Mom*."

"I'm not your damn mom."

This earned him a rude snort from Sean. Whether that was because Finn had indeed been Sean's 'damn mom' since the day she'd walked out on them when they'd been three and ten, or simply because Finn was the only one of them with a lick of sense, didn't matter.

"Focus," Finn said to his now twenty-two-going-on-sixteen-year-old brother. "I found the error you made in the payroll. You somehow set everyone to time and a half."

"Oh shit." Sean flopped back to the couch and closed his eyes again. "Rookie mistake."

"That's it?" Finn asked. "Just 'oh shit, rookie mistake'?" He felt an eye twitch coming on. "This is a damn partnership, Sean, and I need you to start acting like it. I can't do it alone."

"Hey, I told you, I don't belong behind a desk. My strength's in front of the customers and we both know it."

Finn stared at him. "There's more to running this place than making people smile."

"No shit." Sean cracked open an eye. "Without me out there hustling and busting my ass to charm everyone into a good time every night, there'd be no payroll to fuck up."

"You think that's all this pub is, a good time?" Finn asked.

"Well, yeah." Sean stretched his long, lanky body, lying back with his hands behind his head. "What else is there?"

Finn pressed his fingers against his twitching eye so that his brains couldn't leak out, but what did he expect? Back when he'd been twenty-one, he'd been as

wild as they came. And then suddenly he'd found himself in charge of fourteen-year-old Sean when their dad
had gotten himself killed in a car accident. It'd been
hell, but eventually Finn had gotten his act together for
both his own and Sean's sake. He'd had to.

When Sean had turned twenty-one last year, they'd
opened the pub to give them both a viable future. And
if Finn's other goal had been to keep Sean interested in
something, *anything*, he couldn't very well now complain that Sean thought life was all fun and games.

"How about making a living?" Finn asked. "You
know, that little thing about covering our rent and food
and other expenses, like your college tuition? What are
you now, a third-year sophomore?"

"Fourth I think." Sean smiled, though it faltered
some when Finn didn't return it. "Hey, I'm still trying
to find my calling. This year probably. Next year tops.
And then the good times really start."

"As opposed to what you're doing now?"

"Hey, we work our asses off."

"You work part-time at a pub, Sean. By the very
definition of that, you're having fun every single day."

Sean snorted. "Seriously, man, we need to redefine
your definition of fun. You're here twenty-four seven
and you know it. You should've let Trouble show you
what you're missing. She's cute, and best yet, she was
game."

"Trouble?"

"Yeah, man. The new chick. Don't tell me you
weren't feeling her. You made her a virgin version of
our special. You don't do that for anyone else ever."

True. Also true was that he'd been drawn in by Pru's

warm, shiny brown eyes. They matched her warm, shiny brown tumble of long hair, and then there was her laugh that always seemed to prove Pavlov's theory. Except Finn's reaction wasn't to drool when he heard it.

"Did you know she's a ship captain?" Sean asked. "I mean that's pretty badass."

Yeah, it was. She drove one of the fleet ships out of Pier 39 for SF Bay Tours, a tough job to say the least. Finn's favorite part was her uniform. Snug, fitted white Captain's button-down shirt, dark blue trousers that fit her sweet ass perfectly, and kickass work boots, all of which had fueled more than a few dirty-as-fuck day-dreams over the past three weeks.

He'd never forget his first glimpse of her. She'd been moving in, striding across the courtyard with a heavy box, her long legs churning up the distance, that willowy body with those sweet curves making his mouth water. She had her mass of wavy hair piled on top of her head—not that this had tamed the beast because strands had fallen into her face.

Yeah, he'd felt her from day one, and though she often sat at the end of the bar he reserved for his close-knit friends, he hadn't spoken much to her until two nights ago.

"She offered to show you a good time and you turned her down," Sean said, shaking his head in mock sadness. "And you call yourself the older brother. But yeah, you were probably right to turn her down. Would've been a waste of her efforts, seeing as you have no interest in anything remotely resembling a good time."

"I didn't turn her down."

"Flat, dude."

Finn hoped like hell Pru hadn't taken it that way, because he sure hadn't meant it like that. "I was working."

"Always are," Sean said. "Whelp"—he stood and stretched again—"this has been fun, but gotta run. The gang's hiking Twin Peaks today. First to the top gets number one draft pick in our fantasy football league. You should come."

"I won the league last year," Finn said.

"Uh huh. Which means we'd totally try to push you off the trail and sabotage your ascent. So you should definitely come."

"Wow, sounds like a real good time," Finn said. "But there's this . . ." He pointed to his desk and the mountain of work waiting on him.

Sean rolled his eyes. "You know what all work and no play makes you, right?"

"Not poor?"

"Ha-ha. I was going to say not laid."

This was unfortunately true but Finn turned back to his desk. "Kick ass out there."

"Well, duh."

Chapter 5

#DidIDoThat?

Hours later, Finn was still at his desk when Sean sauntered back in, hot, sweaty, and grinning. He helped himself to Finn's iced soda, downing it in three gulps. "Asses have been kicked," he said.

"No way did you beat Archer," Finn said. No one beat Archer at anything physical. The man was a machine.

"Nah, but I got second draft pick."

Annie, one of the three servers coming on shift for the night, stuck her head in. "Already filling up out front," she told them both.

"Got your back, darlin'," Sean said and set Finn's now empty glass back onto his desk. "Always."

Annie smiled dreamily at him.

Sean winked at her and slid out of the office before Finn could remind him of their *no sleeping* with the hired help policy. Swearing to himself, Finn grabbed his iPad and followed. He intended to go over inventory, but was immediately waved to the far end of the bar.

Sitting at it were some of his closest friends, most of them having been linked together in one way or another for years.

Archer lifted his beer in a silent toast. The ex-cop worked on the second floor of the building running a private security and investigation firm. He and Finn went back as far as middle school. They'd gone to college together. It'd been Archer who'd been with him in their shared, tiny frat boy apartment the night the cops had come to the door—not because Finn had been caught doing something stupid, but because his dad had just died.

Next to Archer sat Willa. Bossy as hell, nosy as hell, and loyal as hell, Willa would give a perfect stranger the shirt off her back if Finn and Archer didn't watch her like a hawk.

Spencer was there too. The mechanical engineer didn't say much, but when he did it was often so profound the rest of them just stared at him in shock and awe. Quiet, although not particularly shy or introverted, he'd recently sold his start-up for an undisclosed sum and hadn't decided on his next step. All Finn knew was that he was clearly unhappy.

Since pushing Spence was like trying to push a twenty-foot-wide concrete wall over, they'd all unanimously decided to let it be for now. Finn knew he'd talk about it when he was good and ready and nothing could rush that. For now he seemed . . . well, if not miserable, at least better, and was currently stealing French fries on the sly from Elle's basket.

Elle was new to the group but had fit right in with the exception of Archer. Finn didn't know what was up, but the two of them studiously avoided each other whenever possible. Everyone but Elle was in shorts and tees, looking bedraggled, a little sweaty and a whole lot dusty. Elle hadn't gone on the hike. She didn't do dirt. Or excursion. Dressed to kill as always, she wore a royal blue sleeveless sheath and coolly slapped Spence's hand away from her fries.

He grinned in apology but the minute Elle's back was turned, he stole another. Only Spence could do that and live.

Haley was there too, an intern at the optometrist's shop on the ground floor of the building. But Finn's gaze went directly to the last person sitting there, just as dusty as everyone but Elle.

Pru.

"Got suckered into the hike up Twin Peaks, huh?" he asked.

She smiled the smile of someone who was very proud of herself.

He grinned back. "Number four?" he guessed.

Her smile widened. "Three."

Whoa. Finn turned to Spence, who shrugged. "On the way there, I calculated out who and what everyone's going to pick in the draft," Spence said. "All I needed was the fourth pick, so I didn't see any reason to go crazy out there."

"You did that on the way there," Finn repeated, a little awed.

"Actually, I worked it out in my head before we even left."

Elle looked at Spence. "Remember when you told me to tell you when you were acting like that kid that no one would want to be friends with?"

Spence just grinned and stole another fry.

"She looks so delicate," Willa said and jabbed a thumb in Pru's direction. "Totally thought I could take her." She shook her head. "She wiped the trail with me."

"You do a lot of hiking?" Finn asked Pru.

"Not lately." She lifted a shoulder and sipped at what looked like a plain soda. "I haven't had time," she said demurely. "I'm out of shape."

Archer laughed. "Don't believe that for a second. This girl can move when she's got inspiration, and apparently she takes her fantasy football seriously. You should've seen those long legs in action."

Oh, Finn had. In his sexual fantasies.

"Why didn't you go?" she asked. "Didn't want to show off *your* long legs?"

Archer choked on beer. "I like her," he announced.

Finn didn't take his eyes off Pru. Hers were lit with amusement, which went well with the streak of dirt across her jaw. There was another over her torso, specifically her left breast. "I have great legs," he said.

"Uh huh."

"I do. Tell her," he said to the room.

Spence shrugged noncommittally. "Archer's are better."

Archer grinned. "Damn straight."

Elle let out a rare smile. "I like her too," she said to Archer.

"It's not about my legs," Finn said to Pru. Shit, and now he sounded defensive.

"Maybe you should prove it," she said casually and Archer choked again.

Willa bounced up and down in her seat, clapping. "It's like Christmas!"

"We're keeping her, right?" Spence asked.

"Hey," Sean said, bringing them another pitcher of beer. "If a lady wanted to see my legs, I'd show her. Just sayin'."

Asshole.

Pru turned expectantly back to Finn and he had to laugh. "What, right here?" he asked in disbelief.

"Why not?" she asked.

"Because . . ." Jesus. How had he lost control of this conversation? "I am not dropping trou right here," he said stiffly, and great, because now he sounded like he had a stick up his ass.

"Maybe he hasn't shaved," Willa said. "That'd keep me from dropping trou. I only shaved from my knees down. My thighs are as hairy as a lumberjack's chest, which is why I'm wearing capris and not short shorts. You are all welcome."

Elle nodded like this made perfect sense.

"Gonna have to prove it to the lady," Archer said ever so helpfully to Finn. "Drop 'em."

He was an asshole too.

Willa grinned and tapped her hands on the bar in rhythm and began to chant. "Drop 'em, drop 'em . . ."

The others joined in. Shit. They were *all* assholes.

Pru leaned in over the bar and gave him a come here gesture. He shifted close and met her halfway, stilling when she put her mouth to his ear.

"No one but me can see behind the bar," she whispered.

It took a moment to compute her words because at first all he could concentrate on was the feel of her lips on his ear. When she exhaled, her warm breath caressed his skin and he had to remind himself that he was in a crowded bar, surrounded by his idiot friends.

She smiled enticingly.

"Not happening," he said on a laugh. At least not here, with an audience. He wondered if she'd still be playing with him if they were alone in his bed. Or if that was too far away, his office . . .

Her hair fell into his face and a stubborn silky strand stuck to the stubble on his jaw. He didn't care. She might be streaked with dirt but she smelled amazing.

He was mid-sniff when she whispered, "Fun Whisperer, remember?"

"Maybe I'm commando," he whispered back and was gratified by her quick intake of breath and the darkening of her eyes. "Either way," he said, "I don't drop trou on the first date."

She bit her lower lip and let her gaze drop over him, probably trying to figure out if he was telling the truth about going commando.

Then her phone buzzed and she flashed him a grin as she stepped aside to answer it.

Sean came close and nudged him as they both watched Pru talk into her cell. "That's the woman for you."

"No," Finn said. "She's not. You know I don't date women in the building."

"Which would be a great rule if you ever left the building."

"I leave the building." To get to and from work, but

still. He resented the implication that his life wasn't enough as is.

Elle shoved her glass under Sean's nose. She didn't like beer on tap. "Earn your keep, bar wench."

Sean rolled his eyes but took the glass. "What do you want, your highness? Something pink with an umbrella in it, I suppose?"

"Do I look like a college coed to you?" she asked. "I'll take a martini."

He grinned and shifted away to make it for her.

Willa came around to Finn's side of the bar. She was tiny, barely came up to his shoulder, but she was like a mother cat when riled. He knew better than to go toe to toe with her, especially when she was giving him The Look. But he wasn't in the mood. "No," he said.

"You don't even know what I'm going to say."

"You're going to say I'm being a stupid guy," Finn said. "But newsflash, I am a guy and sometimes we're stupid. Deal with it."

"I wasn't going to say that." She paused when he slid her a look and she sighed. "Okay, fine, I was. But you *are* being stupid."

"Shock," he said.

She put her hand on his arm until he blew out a breath and looked at her again.

"I'm worried about you," she said softly. "You've got yourself on lockdown. I know this place has taken off and you're so busy, but it's like Sean is the one having all the fun with it and you're just . . . letting him. What about you, Finn? When is it going to be about you?"

He turned and watched Sean work his magic charisma on a gaggle of young twenties at the other end of the bar. He'd never gotten to be just a kid. The least Finn could do was let him be twenty-two. "He deserves it."

"And you don't? You're working like crazy and just going through the motions."

True or not, he didn't want to hear it. "You want anything to eat?"

She sighed, getting the message, which was part of why he loved her so much. "No, thanks, I've gotta go. Gotta get up early tomorrow for a wedding. I've got a cake to make and flowers to arrange."

He found a smile. "Another dog wedding?"

In on the joke that she made more money off dog tiaras and elaborate animal weddings than grooming and pet supplies, she laughed. "Parrots."

Finn laughed too and gave her a hug goodnight. As she walked away, his gaze automatically searched for Pru. The gang was all moving to the back room and she was with them, heading for either the pool table or the dartboards. It was tourney night.

He took some orders and flagged down Sean to pass them off. "Fill these for Workaholic, Playboy, and Desperado at your four, five, and six o'clock." He turned and caught Pru staring at him. She'd come back for the bag of leftover chicken wings she'd forgotten.

"Workaholic, Playboy, and Desperado?" she asked.

"Customers," Sean explained.

"We all have nicknames?" she asked.

"No," Finn said.

"Yes," Sean said. And then the helpful bastard pointed out some more in the place. "Klutz, Pee-Dub, and Woodie."

"Pee-Dub?"

Sean grinned. "He's an old friend with a very new wife. He's Pussy-Whipped. PW, which cuts down to Pee-Dub. Get it?"

"I'm sorry to say I do," she said, laughing. "And Woodie?"

Sean smiled. "Would you like me to explain that one to you?"

Finn reached out, put his hand over Sean's face and shoved.

"Hey, she asked," he said, voice muffled.

"What's my nickname?" Pru asked.

Shit. This wasn't going to end well. "Not everyone has a nickname," he said.

She narrowed her eyes. "Spill it, Grandpa."

Sean snorted.

Even Finn had to laugh. "Well it *should* be Pushy."

"Uh huh," she said. "Tell me something I don't know. Come on, what do you two call me?"

"Your first day in the building, it was Daisy," Sean told her. "Because you were holding flowers."

"From my boss for my new place," she said. "What changed?"

"We saw you feeding our homeless guy, so we switched it to Sucker."

"Hey," she said, hands on hips. "He's a nice guy and he was hungry."

"He's hungry because he makes pot brownies," Finn said. "They give him the munchies. And just so you know, we all feed him too. He's got food, Pru. He's just got a good eye for the sweet cuties who are also suckers."

She blushed and he laughed.

"So I'm Sucker? Really?"

"Nope," Sean said. "You're Trouble with a capital T."

Finn shook his head at him. "Don't you have some orders to fill?"

Sean laughed and walked off, leaving him with Pru.

"I'm not a *lot* of trouble," she said.

His gaze slid to her mouth. "You sure about that?"

"Completely." And then she flashed him an indeed trouble-filled smile.

And that's when he knew. *He* was the one in trouble. Deep trouble. "What can I get you?" he asked, his voice unintentionally husky.

"I was sent over here to get a set of darts."

"You play?" he asked, digging some out of a drawer.

"No, but I'm a quick learner. I can do this."

He felt yet another laugh bubble up. "Good 'tude," he said. "Tell Spence to go easy on you, darts are his game. And don't bet against Archer. He grew up a bar rat, you can't beat him."

She bit her lip. "He said he was new at darts."

"Shit," Finn said. "He already conned you, didn't he?"

"No worries," she said. "I've got this."

He watched her go, shook his head, and then got busy making drinks because Sean was very busy flirting with Man-eater at one of the tables, even though she had already eaten him up and spit him out just last month.

When Finn looked up again after fulfilling a bunch of orders, half an hour had gone by and some serious chanting was coming out of the back room.

"Bull's-eye, bull's-eye, bull's-eye . . ."

He whistled for Sean. "Need two mojitos," he said

and dried off his hands before heading out from behind the bar.

"Hey, I'm busy," Sean complained. "Getting some digits over here. Where are you going—Hey, you can't just walk away, you—*Hell*," he muttered when Finn didn't slow.

He entered the back room hoping like hell Archer wasn't taking advantage of Pru. She had a sweet smile, and even though he knew she had a mischievous side and a unique ability to change the energy in a room for the better, she was no match against his friends.

And more had shown up, including some of Archer's coworkers, all of whom were either out of the military or ex-cops. He could see Will and Max up there, both skilled as hell in darts and women.

Shit.

Pru was at the front of the room, at the first of three dart boards. She was blindfolded, dart in hand, tongue between her teeth in concentration as Will spun her around.

Spun her around?

He had time to think *what the fuck* before Will let her go and Pru threw her dart.

And nailed Finn right in the chest.

Chapter 6

#DoNotTryThisAtHome

At the collective shocked gasp of the room, Pru ripped off her blindfold and blinked rapidly to focus her vision. And what she focused in on with horror was the dart stuck in Finn's pec, the quill still quivering from impact.

Archer and Spence had their phones out and were taking pics with big grins but Pru saw nothing funny about this. "Oh my God," she whispered as she ran to him. "*Oh my God.*" Panic blocked her throat as she gripped his arms and stared at the dart. "I hit you!"

"Bull's-eye," he said, looking down at it sticking out of his chest. "Not bad for a beginner."

He was joking. She'd hit him with a dart and he stood there joking. *Good God.* She wished for a big hole to swallow her up, but as already proven, she'd never had much luck with wishes. "I'm so sorry! Do we pull it out? Please, you've got to sit down." She was having trouble drawing air into her lungs. "You need to stay still. You could have a cracked rib or a pierced lung." Just the thought of which had her vision going cobweb-y. "Someone call 911!" she yelled.

Finn calmly pulled out the dart. "I'm fine."

But she wasn't, not even close. The tip of the dart was red. *His blood*, she thought as she felt her own drain from her face.

That's when the red stain began to spread through his shirt, blooming wide. She was living the worst scary movie she'd ever seen. "Oh, God, Finn—" She was freaking out, she could feel herself going cold with fear as she again tried to push him into a chair and put both hands over the blood spot to apply pressure at the same time.

He stood firm, not budging an inch as he captured her hands in his and bent a little to look into her eyes. "Breathe, Pru."

"But I—You—I'm so sorry," she heard herself say from what seemed like a long way off. "I wished for true love, not death, I swear!"

"Pru—"

She couldn't answer. There was a buzzing in her ears now, getting louder and louder, and then her vision faded to black.

Pru came to with voices floating around her head.

"Nice going, Finn. You finally got a good one on the line and you kill her." Archer, she thought.

"She's got a tat," someone else said—Spence?— making Pru realize her shirt had ridden up a little, exposing the compass on her hipbone, the tattoo she'd

gotten after her parents' death, when she'd been missing them so much she hadn't known how to go on without them. The world had become a terrifying place,
and all alone in the world she'd needed the symbol of
knowing which direction to go.

"Finn's more of a piercing kind of guy," Spence said.

"I bet today he's more of a tat guy," Archer said.

"Hell, I'm sold," Spence said.

Pru shoved down her shirt and opened her eyes. She
was prone on a couch with a bunch of disembodied
faces hovering over her.

"She's pretty green," Spence's face said. "Think
she's going to hurl?"

Willa's face was creased into a worried frown. "No,
but I don't think she's moisturizing enough."

"Does she need mouth-to-mouth?" Sean.

"Out. All of you." The low but steely demand came
from Finn and had all the faces vanishing.

Pru realized she was in an office. Finn's, by the look
of things. There was a desk, a very comfortable couch
beneath her, and on the other side of it, a large picture
window that revealed a great view of the courtyard and
the fountain.

She narrowed her eyes at the fountain, sending it
you're dead to me vibes. Because really? She'd wished
for love for Finn and instead she'd stabbed him with a
damn dart.

Gah.

Finn was shoving people out the door. When they
were gone, he leaned back against his desk to look at
her, feet casually crossed, hands gripping the wood on
either side of his hips. He was hot, even in a pose of

subdued restraint as he watched her carefully while she sat up. "Easy, Tiger."

"What happened?" she asked. When she struggled to stand, he pushed off from the desk, coming to her.

Crouching at her side, he stopped her, setting his hands on her thighs to hold her still. "Not yet."

"How did I get here?"

"You fainted," he said.

"I most definitely did not!"

His lips twitched. "Okay, then you decided to take a nap. You weren't feeling the whole walking thing so I carried you."

She stared at him, horrified. "You carried me?"

"That bothers you more than the fainting in front of a crowded bar?" he asked. He shrugged. "Okay, sure, we can go with that. Yes, I picked you up off the floor and carried you. Not that I don't make sure the floors are clean mind you, but there's clean and then there's clean, so I brought you to my couch."

"Ohmigod," she gasped, "I hit you with a dart!"

He was still crouched at her feet. Close enough for her to push his hands from her and start tugging up his shirt, needing to see the damage. "Let me see. I'm a halfway decent medic—which I realize is hard to believe given I ended up on your floor—but I promise, I know what I'm doing." She couldn't shove his shirt up high enough. "Off," she demanded.

"Well usually I like to have a meal first," he said, "and get to know each other a little bit—"

"*Off!*"

"Okay, okay." He reached up and pulled the shirt over his head.

Pru nearly got light-headed again but this time it wasn't the blood. He had a body that . . . well, rocked hers. Sleek and hard-looking, he had broad shoulders, ripped abs, sinewy pecs—one of which had a hole in it an inch from his right nipple. A fact she knew because she'd leaned in so close her nose nearly brushed his skin.

"Feel free to kiss it better," he said.

"I'm checking to see if you're going to need a tetanus shot!" But good Lord, she'd done this to him. She'd put a hole in his perfect, delectable bod—

"Are you going to pass out again?" he asked.

"No!" Hopefully. But to be sure, she sat back. Just for a second she promised herself, and only because replaying the night's events in her mind was making her sweat. "First-aid kit," she said a little weakly.

"What do you need?" he asked, voice deep with concern.

"Not for me, for you!" She sat up again. "You could get an infection, we need a first-aid kit!"

He blew out a sigh, like maybe she was being a colossal pain in his ass. But he rose to his feet and walked toward a door behind his desk. The problem was now she could see his back, an acre of smooth, sleek skin, rippling muscles . . .

He vanished into a bathroom and came back with a first-aid kit, and then sat at her side on the couch. Before he could open it up, she took it from his hands and rummaged through. Finding what she needed, she poured some antiseptic onto a cotton pad and pressed it against the wound.

He sucked in a breath and she looked up at him.

"Getting hit with a dart didn't make you blink an eye," she said. "Neither did ripping it out like a He-man. But this hurts?"

"It's cold."

This got a low laugh out of her. She was trying not to notice that her fingers were pressed up against his warm skin as she held the cotton in place, or that her other hand had come up to grip his bicep. Or that his nipples had hardened.

Or that she was staring at his body, her eyes feeling like a kid in a candy shop, not quite knowing where to land. Those pecs. That washboard set of abs. The narrow happy trail that vanished into the waistband of his jeans, presumably leading straight to his—

"I think I'm all disinfected now," he said, sounding amused.

With a jerky nod, she set the cotton pad aside and reached for a Band-Aid. But her hands were shaking and she couldn't open the damn thing.

His fingers gently took it from hers. Quickly and efficiently, he opened it and put it on himself. "All better," he said and quirked a brow. "Unless . . ."

"Unless what?"

"You changed your mind about kissing it all better?"

That she wanted to do just that kept her from rolling her eyes again.

He laughed softly, which she assumed was because the bastard knew exactly what he did to her.

"So," he said. "You were right. You really do bring the fun. What's next?"

"Hitting you over your thick head with this first-aid kit," she said, closing the thing up.

"You're violent." He grinned at her. "I like it."

"You have a very odd sense of humor." She stood on legs that were still a little wobbly. "I really am sorry, Finn."

"No worries. I've had worse done to me."

"Like?"

"Well . . ." He appeared to give this some thought. "A woman once chucked a beer bottle at my face." He pointed to a scar above his right eyebrow. "Luckily I ducked."

She gaped at him. "Seriously?"

He shrugged. "She thought I was Sean."

"Well that explains it," she said and had the pleasure of making him laugh.

His laugh did things to her. So did the fact that he was still shirtless. "Do you have another shirt?" she asked.

"One without a hole in it, you mean?"

She groaned. "Yes! And without blood all over it." She bent and scooped up his fallen shirt. "I'm going to buy you a new one—" she started as she rose back up and . . . bumped into him.

And his bare chest.

"Stop," he said kindly but firmly as his hands came up to her shoulders. "I'm not all that hurt and you've already apologized. It wasn't even your fault. My idiot brother should never have allowed blindfolded darts. If our insurance company got a whiff of that, we'd be dumped."

But Pru had a long habit of taking on the blame. It was what she did, and she did it well. Besides, in this case, her guilt came from something else, something much, much worse than stabbing him with a dart and she didn't know how to handle it. Especially now that they were standing toe to toe with his hands on her.

Tell him, a voice deep inside her said.

But she was having trouble focusing. All she could think about was pressing her mouth to the Band-Aid. Above the Band-Aid. Below the Band-Aid. Wayyyyy below the Band-Aid . . .

She didn't understand it. He wasn't even her usual type. Okay, so she wasn't sure what her type was exactly. She hadn't been around the block all that many times but she'd always figured she'd know it when she saw it.

But she was having the terrible, no-good, frightening feeling that she'd seen it in the impenetrable, unshakeable, unflappable, decidedly sexy Finn O'Riley.

Which of course made everything, *everything*, far worse so she closed her eyes. "Oh God. I could have killed you."

Just as her parents had killed his dad . . .

And at *that* thought, the one she'd been trying like hell to keep at bay, the horror of it all reached up and choked her, making it impossible to breathe, impossible to do anything but panic.

"Hey. *Hey*," Finn said with devastating gentleness as he maneuvered her back to sitting on the couch. "It's all okay, Pru."

She could only shake her head and try to pull free. She didn't deserve his sympathy, didn't deserve—

"Pru. Babe, you've got to breathe for me."

She sucked in some air.

"Good," he said firmly. "Again."

She drew in another breath and the spots once again dancing in front of her eyes began to fade away, leaving her view of Finn, on his knees before her, steady as a rock. "I'm okay now," she said. And to prove it she stood on her own. To gain some desperately needed space, she walked away from him and walked around his office.

His big wood desk wasn't messy but wasn't exactly neat either, a wall lined with shelves on which sat everything from a crate of pub giveaways like beer cozies and mouse pads, to a big ball of Christmas lights.

Pictures covering one wall. His brother. His friends. A group shot of them on the roof of the building, where people went for star gazing, hot summer night picnicking, or just to be alone on top of the world.

There were a few pics of Finn too, although not many, she saw as she moved slowly along the wall, realizing the pics got progressively older.

There were several from many years ago. Finn in a high school baseball uniform. And then a college uniform. He'd played ball for a scholarship and had been destined for the pros—until he'd quit school abruptly at age twenty-one when he'd had to give everything up to care for his younger brother after the death of his father.

She sucked in a breath and kept looking at the pictures. There was one of Finn and a group of guys wearing no shirts and backpacks standing on a mountaintop, and if she wasn't mistaken, one of them was Archer.

Another of Finn sitting in a souped-up classic-looking Chevelle next to a GTO, a pretty girl standing between the cars waving a flag. Clearly a pre-street-race photo.

Once upon a time, he'd indeed been wild and adventurous. And she knew exactly what had changed him. The question was, could she really help bring some of that back to him, something she wanted, *needed*, to do with all her heart.

Chapter 7

#WafflesAreAlwaysTheAnswer

Finn watched Pru's shoulders tense as she looked at the pictures on the walls, and wished she'd turn his way so he could see her face. But she kept staring at the evidence of his life as if it was of the utmost importance to her. "You okay?" he asked.

She shook her head. Whether in answer to the question or because whatever was on her mind weighed too heavily to express, he had no idea. Turning her to him, he watched as her long lashes swept upward, her eyes pummeling him with a one-two gut punch.

And going off the pulse racing at the base of her throat, she was just as affected by him, which was flattering as hell but right now he was more concerned about the shadows clouding her eyes. "You're worried about something," he said.

She bit her lower lip.

"Let me guess. You forgot to put the plug in your boat and it might sink before your next shift."

As he'd intended, her mouth curved. "I never forget the plug."

"Okay . . . so you're worried you've maimed me for life and I'll have to give up my lucrative bartending career."

Her smile faded. "You joke," she said, "but I *could* have maimed you if I'd thrown higher."

"Or lower," he said and shuddered at the thought.

She closed her eyes and turned away again. "I'm really so very sorry, Finn."

"Pru, look at me."

She slowly turned to face him. There were secrets in her eyes that had nothing to do with the dart thing, and a hollowness as well, one that moved him because he recognized it. He'd seen it in the reflection of his own mirror. Moving in close, he reached for her hand, loosely entangling their fingers. He told himself it was so that he could catch her again if she went down but he knew the truth. He just wanted to touch her.

"I'm sure you have to get back out there—" she started.

"In a minute." He tugged her in a little so that they were toe to toe now. And thanks to her kickass boots, they were also nearly mouth to mouth. "What's going on, Pru?" he asked, holding her gaze.

She opened her mouth but then hesitated. And when she spoke, he knew she'd changed whatever she'd been about to say. "Looks like your life has changed a lot," she said, gesturing to the pictures that Sean had printed from various sources, stuffed into frames, and put out on the shelf in chronological order the day after they'd opened the pub.

When Finn had asked him what the hell, Sean had simply said "not everyone is as unsentimental as you. Just shut up and enjoy them—and you're welcome."

Over the past year new pictures just showed up. More of Sean's doing. Finn got it. Sean felt guilty for all Finn had given up to raise him, but Finn didn't want him to feel guilty. He wanted him to take life more seriously.

"It's changed some," he allowed cautiously to Pru. He didn't know how they'd gotten here, on this subject. A few minutes ago she'd been all sweetly, adorably worried about him, wanting to play doctor.

And he'd been game.

"It looks like it's changed more than some," she said. "The fun pics stopped."

"Once I bought the pub, yeah," he said.

He'd had different plans for himself. Without a maternal influence, and their dad either at work or mean as a skunk, he and Sean had been left to their own devices. A lot. Finn had used those years to grow up as fast and feral and wild as he could. Yeah, he'd been an ace athlete, but he'd also been a punk-ass idiot. He'd skated through on grades, which luckily had come easy for him so his coaches had been willing to put up with his crazy ass to have him on the team. His big plan had been to get drafted into the big leagues, tell his dad to go fuck himself, and retire with a big fat bank account.

It hadn't exactly gone down like that. Instead, his dad had gotten himself killed in a car accident that had nothing to do with his own road rage—he'd been hit by a drunk driver.

Barely twenty-one, Finn might've kept to his plan but Sean had been only fourteen. The kid would've been dumped into the system if Finn hadn't put a lock down on his wild side, grown up, and put them both on the straight and narrow.

It'd been the hardest thing he'd ever done, and there'd been lots of days he wasn't entirely sure he'd succeeded.

"Well I probably should . . ." Pru trailed off, gesturing vaguely to the door. But she didn't go. Instead she glanced at his mouth.

As far as signs went, it was a good one. She was thinking of his mouth on hers. Which seemed only fair since he'd given a lot of thought to the same thing.

"'Night," she whispered.

"Night," he whispered back.

And yet neither of them moved.

She was still staring at his mouth, and chewing on her lower lip while she was at it. He wanted to lean in and take over, nibbling first one corner of her mouth and then the other, and then maybe he'd take a nibble of her plump lower lip too, before soothing it with his tongue. Then he'd work his way down her body the same to every last square inch of her—

"Right?" she asked.

He blinked. So busy thinking about what he wanted to do to her, about the sounds she might make as he worked her over with his tongue, he'd not heard a word she'd said. "Right."

She nodded and . . . walked away.

Wait—what the hell? He grabbed her hand and just barely stopped her. "Where are you going?"

"I just said I really should go and you said right."

Not about to admit he hadn't listened to a word she'd said because he'd been too busy mentally fucking her, he just held onto her hand. "But you're the Fun Whisperer. You have to stay and save me, otherwise I'll go back to work."

"A real wild man," she said with a smile.

He gave another tug on her hand. She was already right there but she shifted in closer, right up against him.

She sighed, as if the feel of him was all she'd wanted, and then she froze. Her eyes were wide and just a little bit anxious now as she stared into his. "Uh oh."

Granted, it'd been awhile but that wasn't the usual reaction he got when he pulled a woman in close. "Problem?"

"No." She bit her lower lip. "Maybe."

"Tell me."

She hesitated and then said, "My mom taught me to show not tell." And then her hands went to his chest, one of them right over the Band-Aid, which she touched gently, running her fingers over it as if she wished she could take away the pain. "I just need to see something . . ."

"What?"

Her gaze dropped to his mouth and again she hesitated.

Tenderness mixed with his sudden pervasive hunger and need, a dizzying combination for a guy who prided himself on not feeling much. "Pru—"

"Shh a second," she whispered. And then closing the gap, she brushed her lips over his.

At the connection, he groaned, loving the way her hands tightened on him. She murmured his name, a soft plea and yet somehow also a demand, and he wanted to both smile and tug her down to the couch. Trying to cool his jets, trying to let her stay in charge, he attempted to hold back, but she let out this breathy little whimper like he was the best thing she'd ever tasted. Threading his fingers through her hair, he took over the kiss, slow, deeper now, until she let out another of those delicious little whimpers and practically climbed his body.

Yeah, she liked that, a whole hell of a lot, and he closed his arms hard around her, lifting her up against him for more. He'd known they had something but this . . . this rocked his world. Hers too because they both melted into it, tongues sliding, lips melding, bodies arching into each other in a slow rhythm.

The door to the office suddenly opened and Sean stood there, face tilted down to his iPad. "We've gotta problem with inventory—" he said, still reading. "Where the hell's the—*Oh*," he said, finally looking up. "Shit. Now I owe Spence twenty bucks."

Finn resisted smashing in his brother's smug smile, barely, mostly because he didn't want to take his eyes off Pru who'd brought her fingers up to her still wet lips, looking more than a little dazed.

Join my club, babe . . .

"Sorry if I interrupted the sexy times," Sean said, not looking sorry at all. He smiled at Pru. "Hey, Trouble."

"Hey," she said, blushing. "I've got to go." She turned in a slow circle, clearly looking for her purse, finding it where he'd dropped it on the couch. She slung it over her shoulder and without actually making eye contact with either of them, said a quick "'night" and headed to the door.

Finn caught her, brushing up against her back. "Let me walk you home—"

"I live only two flights up," she said, not looking at him. "Not necessary."

Right. But it was more than her safety he'd been worried about. She'd been with him during that kiss, very with him, but now there was a distance again and he wanted to breach it.

"If there's any complications from where I tried to kill you," she said to the door. "You need to—"

"I won't. I'm fine." He let his mouth brush her ear as he spoke and he could feel the shiver wrack her body.

"Okay then," she said shakily, and was gone.

Finn turned to Sean.

Who was grinning. "Look at you with all the moves. They grow up so fast."

"You ever hear of a thing called knocking?" Finn asked.

Sean shrugged. "Where's the fun in that?"

"Is everything about fun?"

"Yes!" Sean said, tossing up his hands. "Now you're getting it!"

Finn turned away and eyed the spot between the couch and the desk where he'd just about dragged Pru down to the floor and ended his long dry spell by sinking into her warm, sweet body. "What's the problem with the inventory?"

"It's down, the whole system's down."

Finn snatched the iPad and swiped the screen to access the data. "And you're just now telling me? Are you kidding me?"

"Yes," Sean said.

Finn lifted his head and stared at Sean. "What?"

His brother flashed a grin. "Yes I'm kidding. Funning around. Fucking with your head. I came back here because Archer and Spence sent me in here to spy on you and Trouble. We bet twenty bucks. They thought you might be making a rare move."

Jesus.

"Not me though," Sean said. "I figured you're so rusty you'd need some pointers. And here's your first one—lock the door, man. *Always.*"

Finn headed toward him but Sean danced away with a grin. "Oh and pointer number two—you got your shirt off and that's a good start, but it's the pants that are the important part." He was chortling, having a great ol' time.

Finn smiled at him, shoved him out the door, and slammed it on his smug-ass face.

Then he hit the lock.

"*Now* you lock it?" Sean asked through the wood, rattling the handle. "Hey. You do know I nap on that couch. Tell me you didn't do it on the couch."

Finn turned away and headed to his desk.

Sean pounded on the door once. "You didn't, right?"

Finn put on his earphones and cranked some music

on his phone. And then headed to his desk to wade through the mountain of work waiting on him.

Pru got to work extra early the next morning. It was month end and though Jake did his best to see that his boat captains didn't drown in paperwork, some of it was unavoidable. She wanted to catch up but she hadn't slept well and her eyes kept crossing. Finally, she caved and set her head down on her desk.

Just for a minute, she told herself . . .

Finn pressed his body to hers and she moaned as his hands stroked up her sides, his thumbs brushing over her nipples. She arched into him and he kissed her like it was an art form, like he had nothing more important to do than arouse her and he had all the time in the world to do it. She clutched at him and he ground his lower body into her, letting her feel how aggressively hard he was. Aching for him, she tangled her hands in his hair, kissing him deeper until he groaned into her mouth. "Please," she begged.

"Hell yeah, I'll please." His voice was sexy rough and she held tight, anchoring her hips against his as he slid a hand down her belly and into her panties.

He groaned again and she knew why. She was wet and on fire for him.

Breaking the kiss, he nibbled her ear. "Pru," he said in that deliciously gruff tone. "You have to wake up."

She jerked awake and sat straight up, realizing she'd fallen asleep at her desk doing the dreaded paperwork. "Wha . . . ?" she managed.

Finn was crouched at her side, fully dressed, and breathing a little ragged.

And that's when she realized something else—her hand was stroking what felt like a very impressive erection behind his jeans.

She snatched it back like she'd been burned and he dropped his head and gave a rough laugh. Ignoring how his laugh did funny things to her belly and parts south, she cleared her throat. "Sorry."

"Don't be. Best greeting ever."

"Okay, that was your fault," she muttered, her face heating. "That's what you get for waking me from a deep sleep."

"I'm not sure if you could call that sleep." He lifted his head. He was smiling, the smug jerk. "Jake let me in, pointed me in the direction of your office, which was unlocked. You were moaning and sweaty. I moved in to see if you were okay and you molested me."

She groaned and thunked her head to her desk a couple of times. "Why are you here?" she moaned. "Other than to rudely wake me up from the only action I've had in far too long?"

He laughed. *Laughed.* She gave some thought to killing him but then she realized he was holding a brown bag from which came the most delicious scent.

"Stopped by the waffle shop for breakfast," he said and lifted the bag. "Thought of you."

She went still. "Chocolate and raspberry syrup?" she asked hopefully, willing to let bygones be bygones for a sugar and carb load.

"Of course."

She didn't ask how he knew her kryptonite. Everyone she knew worshipped at the magical griddle inside the magical food cart outside their building that a woman named Rayna ran. Pru snatched the bag from Finn and decided to forgive him. "Do not think that this means we will be reenacting what I was dreaming about."

"Absolutely not," he said.

She paused, her gut sinking to her toes unexpectedly. "Because you don't think of me that way?"

He paused as if carefully considering his next words, and she braced herself. She was good at rejection, real good, she reminded herself.

Apparently deciding against speaking at all, Finn rose to his full height. Since she was still in her chair, this put her face right about level with the part of his anatomy she'd had a grip on only a moment before.

He was still hard.

"Does this look like disinterest to you?"

She swallowed hard. "No."

"Any further questions?"

"Nope," she managed. "No further questions."

Nodding, he leaned over her and brushed his mouth across hers. "Ball's in your court," he said and then he was gone.

Chapter 8

#AllTheCoolKidsAreDoingIt

Pru got up the next morning at the usual time even though it was her day off. She pulled on her tank top and yoga capris and shoved her feet into her running shoes. "I hate running," she said to the room.

The comforter on her bed shifted slightly and she pulled it back to reveal Thor, eyes closed.

"I know you're faking," she said.

His eyes squeezed tight.

"Sorry, buddy, you're coming with me. I ate that entire *huge* waffle Finn brought me yesterday. And I realize you don't care if you can fit into a pair of skinny jeans without your belly rolling over the waistband, and you don't even know who Finn is, but trust me, you wouldn't have been able to resist him or the waffle either."

Thor didn't budge.

"A doggie biscuit," she said cajolingly. "If you get up right now I'll give you a doggie biscuit."

Nothing. This was probably because he knew as well as she did that she was out of doggie biscuits. She would have just left him home alone but the last time she'd done that, he'd pooped in her favorite boots—which had most definitely taken some time and effort on his part.

"Fine." She tossed up her hands. "I'll buy biscuits today, okay? And we'll go see Jake too."

At the name, Thor perked up. He knew that Jake kept dog cookies in his desk so he lifted his head, panting happily, one ear up and the other flopped over and into his eye.

She had to smile. "You're the cutest boot pooper I've ever seen. Now let's hit it. We're going to run first if it kills us."

Thor hefted out a sigh that was bigger than he was but got up. She clipped his Big Dog leash on him, and off they went.

They ran through Fort Mason, along the trail above the water. Not that they could see the water today. The early morning fog had slid in so that Pru felt like she had a huge ball of cotton around her head. They came out at the eastern waterfront of the Port of San Francisco, constructed on top of an engineered seawall on reclaimed land that gave one of the most gorgeous views of the bay.

It was here that Thor refused to go another step. He sat and then plopped over and lay right in front of her feet.

A guy running the opposite way stopped short. "Did you just kill your dog?"

"No, he doesn't like to run," she said.

Clearly not believing her, he started to bend down to Thor, who suddenly found a reserve of energy—or at least enough to lift his head and bare his teeth at the strange man who'd dared to get too close.

The guy jumped back, tripped over his own feet, and fell on his ass.

"Oh my God. Are you all right?" she asked.

He leapt back up, shot her a dirty look, and ran off.

"Sorry," she called after him and then glared down at Thor. "You do know that one of these days someone's going to call animal control on me and get you taken away, right?"

He closed his eyes.

"Come on, get up." She nudged him with her foot. "We've got a little bit more calorie annihilating to do."

Thor didn't budge an inch except to give *her* the low growl now.

"You know what? Fine. We'll risk not fitting into our bathing suits. I don't like swimming anyway," she said, happy enough for the excuse to stop. They walked the rest of the way to the Aquatic Park Pier, which curved out into the bay, giving the illusion of standing out on the water.

A wind kicked up and she was glad to not be out on the water. "Going to be choppy," she said. Which meant at least one person per tour would get seasick. Not that it was her problem. "No throw-up on my calendar today."

Thor, comfy in her lap, licked her chin. He didn't mind throw-up. Or poo. The grosser the better in his opinion. Setting the dog down, she craned her neck and took in the sight of Ghirardelli Square behind them.

It wasn't out of her way to walk over there, but if she did she'd buy chocolate and then she'd have to run tomorrow too. She was debating that when Thor was approached by a pigeon who was nearly bigger than he was.

Thor went utterly still, not moving a single muscle, the whites of his eyes showing.

The pigeon stopped, cocked its head, and then made a faux lunge at Thor.

Thor turned tail and ran behind Pru's legs.

"Hey," she said to the pigeon. "Don't be a bully."

The pigeon gave her a one-eyed stare and waddled off.

Pru scooped up Thor. "I need to get you glasses because you just frightened a full-grown man and then cowered from a bird."

Thor blinked his big eyes at her. "Wuff."

At the sound, the pigeon stopped and turned back. In her arms, all tough guy now, Thor growled.

Pru laughed. "I'm setting you down now, Mr. Badass. We're going to run into work real quick to pick up another box of my stuff—"

Thor cuddled into her, setting his head on her shoulder, giving her the big puppy eyes.

"Oh no you don't with that look," she said. "I'm not carrying you all the way there."

He licked her chin again.

She totally carried him all the way there.

"Jake!" she yelled as she and Thor entered the warehouse on Pier 39 from which SF Bay Tours was run. "Jake?"

Nothing. Besides being her boss, Jake was her

closest friend, and for one week awhile back, he'd also been her lover. They hadn't revisited that for many reasons, not the least of which was because Pru had a little problem. She tended to fall for the guys she slept with.

All two of them.

The first one, Paul, had been her boyfriend for two whole weeks when her parents had died. And since she'd fallen apart and he'd been eighteen and not equipped to deal with that, he'd bailed. Understandable.

Jake had been next. He'd loved her, still did in fact, but he wasn't, and never would be, *in* love with her. And the truth was, she hadn't fallen in love with him either. She actually wasn't sure she was made for that kind of love, receiving or giving. She wanted to be. She really did. But wanting and doing had proven to be two entirely different beasts. "*Jake!*"

"Don't need to yell, woman, I'm not deaf."

With a gasp, she whirled around and found him right there. She hadn't heard him come up behind her, but then again, she never did.

Jake had been in Special Forces, which had involved something with deep-sea diving and a whole lot of danger, and in spite of it nearly killing him, he hadn't lost much of his edge. He hadn't smiled when she'd nearly jumped out of her skin but he'd thought about it because his eyes were amused.

Thor was not. When Pru had jerked, he'd gone off, barking at a pitch that rivaled banshees in heat. "Thor, hush!" she said and turned to Jake, hand to her heart. "Seriously, you take five years off my life every time you do that. And you gave Thor epilepsy."

Jake didn't apologize, he never did. The man was a

complete tyrant. But a softie tyrant, who held out his arms for Thor.

The poor dog was still barking like he couldn't stop himself, eyes wide.

"You're such a pussy," Jake told him.

"Excuse me," Pru said. "You know he can't see very well and you scared him half to death. And hello, he's a *dude*. Which means you two share the same plumbing. So he's not a pussy, he's a big, *male* baby."

"He doesn't have *my* plumbing, chica," Jake said. "I might not have my legs but at least I still have my balls." And with that, he pushed off on his wheelchair, coming closer as he pulled something from his pocket.

A dog cookie.

He held it up for the gone-gonzo dog to see and Thor stopped barking and leapt to him without looking back.

Jake whirled his chair around, and man plus dog took off.

Pru rolled her eyes and followed them past the No One But Crew Past This Door sign, down a hall, then down another to a living area. "We're not staying," Pru said. "I'm just picking up one of the last boxes of my stuff."

"If you'd just use my truck, you could move all your stuff in one fell swoop instead of in a million stages," Jake said. "And I told you I'd help."

"I don't want your help."

He let out a rare sigh and rolled around to face her. "You're still mad that I kicked you out of the nest."

"No." *Yes.*

He caught her hand when she went to walk by him, looking up at her. "You remember why, right?"

"Because your sister's getting divorced and she needs the room you'd lent me here at the warehouse," she intoned.

"And . . . ?"

"And . . ." She blew out a breath. "You're tired of me."

"No," he said gently. "We agreed that I was a crutch for you. That you needed to get out and live your life."

"We?" she asked, her voice a little brittle. Because okay, she wasn't mad at him. She was . . . hurt.

Even as she knew he was right.

They'd been friends since her nineteenth birthday, when she'd applied for a job at SF Tours. He'd just recently left the military and had been through some painful recovery time, and was angry. She'd lost her parents and was equally angry. They'd bonded over that. He sent her for Maritime training and guided her way up the ranks. She couldn't have done it without him and was grateful, but she'd outgrown needing his help on every little thing. "Look," she said. "I'm doing what we both agreed needed to be done. I moved on, I'm getting back on the horse, blah blah."

Jake's mouth smiled but it didn't reach his eyes. "It's more than getting on the damn horse. I want you to want to get back into the game of life."

She sighed. "There's a reason no one plays Life anymore, Jake, the game's stupid. Important life decisions can't be made by a spin of a damn wheel. If it was that easy, I'd spin it right now and get my parents back. I'd make it so that they didn't kill someone else's dad and put all those others in the hospital, changing and ruining people's lives forever. I'd make it so that I could go back a few spaces on the damn board and stay home that night so that no one had to go out and pick me up at a party I should never have sneaked out to in the first place." She let out a rough breath, a little surprised to find out just how much she'd been holding in. Sneaky little things, emotions.

"Pru," Jake said softly, pained.

She pulled her hand free. "No. I don't want to talk about it." She really didn't. It took a lot of time and effort to bury the feelings. Dredging them up again only drove her mad. She moved to leave but Jake wheeled around to stop her exit.

"Then how about we talk about the fact that you've now helped everyone involved that night?" he said. "You sold the Santa Cruz house you grew up in—the only home you ever knew—to be able to put college scholarships in the hands of the two boys of that woman who was hit crossing the street—even though she survived. You even became friends with them. Hell, I now employ Nick in maintenance and Tim said you were helping him find a place to live now that he's out of the dorm—"

"Okay now wait a minute," she said. "I'm not some damn martyr. I sold the house, yes, but I did it because I couldn't handle the memories. I was eighteen, Jake, it was just too much for me." She shook her head. "I didn't give all of that money away. I went to school, I had expenses, I kept what I needed—"

"—Barely. And then there was Shelby, in one of the other cars, remember her? You gave her seed money she needed after her surgery to move to New York like she always wanted."

"I gave her some help, yes," she admitted. "Did you know she still limps?"

"You're still in touch with her?" he asked in disbelief.

She huffed out a breath. "Subject change, please."

"Sure. Let's move on to the O'Riley brothers. You made sure they got your parents' life insurance money, which they presumably used for education and to start their pub. So what now, Pru? It should finally be time to leave the past in the past, but it's not, so you tell me. What's really going on here?"

Yeah, Pru. What was going on? She drew in a breath of air, willing herself not to remember—and grieve— the home she'd sold, everything she'd given up. "He's not happy," she said.

"Who's not?"

"Finn. I want him to be happy."

Jake was shaking his head. "Not your deal."

"But it feels like my deal," she said. "Everyone else is happy, even his brother, Sean. I have to try and help him." Then she told him about the wish and he stared at her like she'd lost her marbles.

"He's going to fall for you," he said. "You know that, right? You have to tell him the truth before that happens, you have to tell him who you are first."

She snorted. "He's not going to fall for me."

Jake smiled, and this time it did reach his eyes. "Believe me, chica, you flash those eyes on him, that smile, some sass . . . he's as good as flat on the ground for you. And you know how I know?"

She shook her head.

"Because I've been there, done that."

"But you didn't stay flat on the ground."

Something flashed through his eyes at that. Regret. Remorse. "That's on me, Pru, not you. And you know it."

Jake didn't do love. He'd told her that going in and he'd never faltered, which wouldn't change the fact that he intended to keep her in his life. He'd proven that by being there for her through thick and thin, and there'd been a whole lot more thin than thick. She'd been there for him as well and always would be. But there were limits now, for both of them.

"Tell me about Finn," he said.

"You already know. He runs O'Riley's. He's loyal to his brother, he's protective and good to his friends, and . . ."

"And?" Jake asked.

And he kisses like sex on a stick . . . "And he works too hard."

"And you think what?" he asked dubiously. "That you're going to change that?"

"He needs a life," she said far more defensively than she'd meant to. "He was robbed of his."

"Not your fault, Pru," Jake said with firm gentleness.

"Well I know that."

"Do you?"

"Yes!" she said, *not* gently.

"Then why are you working your way into his life?"

A most excellent question.

"You didn't work your way into the life of any of the others," he said. "You did what you could and you stayed back, letting them move on without your presence. But not here, not with Finn. Which begs the question, chica—why?"

Again, a most excellent question. But she had the answer for this one, she just didn't want to say it out loud.

Finn was different.

And he was different because she *wanted* him in her life in a way she hadn't wanted anyone for a very long time.

Maybe ever.

"You know what I think?" Jake asked.

"No, but I'm pretty sure you're going to tell me."

"I think, Smartass," he went on undeterred by her sarcasm, "that he's different because you have feelings for him."

No kidding. And she could have added that she was thrown off balance by that very thing. Confused too, because she'd never felt this way about anyone and she didn't want to hurt him. She didn't, but that left her digging a pretty damn big hole for herself. "I said I don't want to discuss this with you."

"Fine. Then discuss it with *him*."

"I will. Soon. But I can't just spit it out, it's a lot to throw at someone. It's only been a few days, I'll get there."

Jake just looked at her for a long beat. "I was at the pub last night."

She froze. "What? I didn't see you."

"I don't see how you could have, since you didn't take your eyes off Finn."

Crap.

"I saw you with him. I saw the look on your face. And I saw the look on his. People are falling, Pru. Denying it is stupid, and one thing you aren't and never have been, is stupid."

"Okay, now you're just being ridiculous." But then she remembered Finn's unexpected kiss, that amazing, heart-stopping, gut-tightening, nipples-getting-happy kiss, and folded her arms over her chest. "*Seriously* ridiculous," she added and then paused. "You really think he could fall for me?"

Jake's eyes softened. "Any guy with a lick of sense would. But chica, you've got to—"

"—tell him, yeah, yeah, I know."

"Before it goes too far," he pressed. "Before you sleep with him."

"I'm not going to—"

Jake held up his hand. "Don't say something that you're going to have to take back, Pru. I was there." He gave her a grim smile. "Don't make me prove how much I love you by going behind your back to protect you by telling him myself."

She stared at him. "You wouldn't dare."

"Try me," he said. "And since I've got you all good and pissed off at me, you might as well remember something else as well. If you sleep with him before everything's square, I'll have to kill him for taking advantage of you when you're still messed up."

"I'm not messed up—" she started and then stopped. Because she was. She was *so* messed up. "Don't even think about interfering. This is my problem to handle." And with that, she strode into what had been her old room, grabbed one of her last boxes of stuff, and turned to go.

"Pru."

She stopped but didn't turn around. Instead she looked down at the box she held. It was labeled PICTURES, and she felt her heart clutch. She'd left this one for nearly last on purpose. Everything in it meant something to her and holding it all in her arms made her heart heavier than the box itself. It was almost more than she could bear, making her wish she'd grabbed one of the other few boxes left, like the one labeled KITCHEN CRAP I PRETEND TO USE BUT DON'T.

"You know I've got your back," Jake said.

She sighed and closed her eyes. "Even if I screw it all up?"

"*Especially* if."

Chapter 9

#RealWorldProblems

In the end, Pru and Thor and Pru's big box of stuff took a cab back to the Pacific Pier building. They had to get out a block early because of traffic, which meant dragging Thor on his leash and carrying the box, which got heavier with each step.

In the courtyard she stopped by the fountain and set the box down for a minute to catch her breath.

Thor plopped down at her feet, panting like he was dying even though he'd barely had to walk at all and he certainly hadn't had to carry a heavy box.

"Hey," she said, "this adulting thing isn't for the faint of heart."

Thor gave the dog version of an eyeroll and huffed out a heavy sigh.

She took pity. "Look, I'm just trying to keep us in shape. Some of us are supposed to be in our prime."

Thor was unimpressed.

She was about to coax him up to her apartment with another bribe when her phone rang. Tim.

She'd met him and his brother Nick after the accident, in the hospital. They'd spent a few days there with their mom, who'd needed surgery to repair her badly broken leg. Michelle had been unable to work for months afterward, a huge strain on the family. They'd lost their apartment and had lived in their car until Pru had been able to sell her parents' house and help.

Michelle had easily accepted her friendship but not the money. In the end, Pru had made an anonymous donation through her attorney. All Michelle knew was that someone in the community had come up with funds to help her and her boys out.

At the time the boys had been in middle school and Pru had been so worried about them. But Nick was working for Jake now and Tim was in college studying to be an engineer.

She was so happy for them.

"Tim," she said when she answered. "Everything okay?"

"That lead you gave me on the apartment near campus, it might pan out," he said excitedly. "They're going to call you as my reference. If we get it, me and my friends will live there together."

"That would be great, Tim," she said.

"You know how hard it is to get a place here," he said. "Almost impossible."

She did know. It'd taken a hell of a long time for her to get into the Pacific Pier building.

"Anyway," he said. "Thanks for the lead. It means a

lot." He laughed a little humorlessly. "We aren't looking forward to living in our cars. Been there, done that."

"No worries," Pru said, her stomach jangling unhappily at the memory. "How's school going?"

"Hard as fuck, but I'm in it," he said. "Gotta go. Talk to you soon."

Pru disconnected and looked at Thor. "We did good. They're going to be okay," she marveled. "All of them." And then she called her contact and put in a second good word for Tim, and was assured they were first in line for the place. It warmed her from the inside out to know it.

Now you need to get okay . . .

But she was working on that. "Come on, let's go."

Thor yawned.

"You know, I could have a cat. A big one who eats little dogs for snacks."

He blinked and she sighed. "Okay, I took that too far. I'm sorry." She crouched down and hugged him in, which he graciously allowed, even giving her a sweet little lick on her cheek. "Love you too," she murmured, kissing the top of his head. "I'm not going to get a cat." She could barely afford to feed the two of them.

She'd never even meant to get a dog at all, but about a year ago, she'd been walking home late one night when she'd heard a funny rumbling sound coming from behind a dumpster. She'd stopped to investigate, but the rumbling had stopped. It was only when she'd started walking again that the rumbling came back.

Pru had walked around the dumpster. Crouching low, using the flashlight on her phone, she'd fallen back on her ass when two glowing orbs had locked in on her.

Scrambling up to run, she realized the rumbling had stopped again and she slowly turned back. Channeling her inner Super Girl, she'd moved closer and had peered down at a scrap of fur surrounding those two huge eyes.

Thor, underfed, filthy, and trembling in terror. It'd taken a bribe to get him out, and another before he'd let her pick him up. All she'd had on her was a granola bar but he'd not been picky. Or dainty. He'd nearly bitten her finger off in his haste to eat.

And Pru, who'd been known to snarl herself when hungry, had fallen in love.

Straightening now with Thor in her arms, her gaze caught on the window across the way.

Finn's office.

The pub wasn't open. The accordion doors were shut and locked, but the morning sun slanted inside. She could see Finn behind his desk, head down. He was either dead, or fast asleep.

Both she and Thor stared at him. "I know," she whispered to her dog. "He's something. But you can't get attached to him, because once I tell him everything, it's over."

Thor set his head on her shoulder. He loved her no matter how stupid she was being.

Leaving her box and Thor—his leash wrapped around a bench—to guard it, she quickly crossed the courtyard to the coffee shop.

Tina stood behind the counter. Tall, curvy, and gorgeous, she had skin the color of the mocha latte she was serving. When it was Pru's turn, Tina smiled. "Your usual?" she asked, her voice low and deep and hypnotic.

"No, this one's not for me," Pru said. "It's for a friend. Um, you don't happen to know how Finn O'Riley likes it, do you?"

Tina smiled wide. "Sugar, he likes it hot and black."

"Oh. Okay, um . . . one of those then."

Tina laughed her contagious laugh and got it ready. When she handed it over, there was a dog biscuit wrapped neatly in a napkin to go. "For Thor," she said. "And how about some advice that you didn't ask for?"

Pru bit her lower lip. Was she that obvious? "Yes, please."

"Two things. First, don't even try to speak to him before he's caffeinated. That man is hot as hell and a great guy, but he's also a bear before his coffee."

"And the second thing?"

"There's no doubt, he's a serious catch," Tina said. "But he's barricaded himself off behind work. So if you want him, you're going to have to show him what he's missing."

"I'm think I'm working on that."

Tina grinned at her. "Because you're the Fun Whisperer?"

Oh, God. "You heard that, huh?"

"Sugar, I hear everything." Tina winked at her, making Pru wonder if that meant that she'd also heard about Pru nearly killing him. Or their first kiss . . .

"Good luck," Tina said. "My money's on you."

Pru took the coffee and dog cookie and headed back through the courtyard. Finn was still asleep. She gave

Thor his treat and put her finger to her lips. "Stay," she said and stepped into the planter that lined the building.

Thor ignored her and attacked his cookie.

Pru, draped on either side by two hydrangea bushes, knocked on Finn's window.

He shot straight up, a few papers stuck to his cheek. His hair was tousled, his eyes sleepy, although they quickly sharpened in on her. His five o'clock shadow was now twelve hours past civilized. And holy cow, he was a damn fine sight.

Before she even saw him coming, he'd crossed his office and opened the window, looking far more alert upon wakening than she'd ever managed.

"What the hell are you doing?" he asked, in the sexiest morning voice she'd ever heard.

"Got you something," she said. "It's not a waffle but . . ." She lifted the coffee and added a smile, trying to not look as if she hadn't just sweat her way through the courtyard with Thor and a heavy box of painful memories—impossible since her shirt was sticking to her and so was her hair. She didn't have to look in any mirror to know that she was beet red in the face, her usual after-exercise "glow."

Finn climbed out the window with easy agility. Pru backed up a step to give him room but he kept coming, stepping right into her space, reaching for the cup like a starved man might reach for a promised meal.

Clearly the man was serious about needing coffee. She stared up at him as he took the cup and drank deeply.

She might have also drooled a little bit.

"Thanks," he said after a long moment. "Most people won't come within two miles of me before I'm caffeinated."

Not wanting to tell him that Tina had already warned her because she didn't want to admit to soaking up info on him whenever and however she could, she just smiled. "How's the hole in your chest?"

He absently reached up and rubbed a hand over his pec, a completely unconscious but very male gesture. "Think I'm going to live," he said.

She eyeballed his hair and the crease on his cheek where papers had been stuck to him. "Living the wild life, huh?"

"The wildest." He looked past her. "So who's the fat cat?"

She turned and followed his line of sight to Thor, who'd curled up in a sunspot next to her box to doze. "I'll have you know that's my fierce, very protective guard dog."

"Dog?"

"Yes!"

He scratched his jaw while eyeing Thor speculatively. "If you say so."

"He protects me," she said. "In fact, he won't let anyone get near me. And don't even think about trying to touch him, he hates men."

"Not me," Finn said. "Dogs love me."

"No, really—" she started but Finn crossed the courtyard and crouched low, holding his hand out to Thor, who had opened his eyes and was watching Finn approach.

"Careful—" Pru warned. "He's like you without

caffeine, only he's like that all the time. He might nip—"

To her utter shock, Thor actually moved toward Finn in a flutter of bravery, his little paws taking him a step closer, his tail wagging in a hopeful gesture that, as always, made Pru's heart hurt.

Then, unbelievably, Thor licked Finn's fist.

"Atta boy," Finn said approvingly in an easy voice full of warmth and affection. "She says you're a dog, what do you think?"

Thor panted happily and rolled over, exposing his very soft, slightly enlarged belly.

"What's his name?" Finn asked, head bent, loving up on her dog.

She glared at Thor. "Benedict Arnold."

Benedict Arnold ignored her completely and she sighed. "Thor."

Finn snorted. "A real killer, huh?"

"Yes, actually, he—"

And that's when Thor strained to reach up and lick Finn's chin. Pru couldn't exactly blame him, she wanted to do the same.

And then . . . her poor-sighted, man-hater of a dog climbed right into Finn's arms and melted like butter on a hot roll. Except minus the hot roll and add a hot guy.

"I can't believe it," she said to herself, watching as Thor settled against Finn's chest like he belonged there, setting his head on Finn's broad shoulder.

"You were saying?" he asked on a soft laugh.

She stared at him, a little dazzled by the laugh. And then there was that stubble and she wondered . . . if he kissed her now and then nuzzled her throat like he had the other night, would it leave a whisker burn?

She wouldn't mind that . . . "Do you have a dog?" she asked.

"No, but someday," he said, reminding her of what Willa had told her, that he wanted a house outside the city and a big dog.

"So what are you doing today?" he asked.

She pointed to the box. "Unpacking some more."

"And you say *I* need a fun whisperer," he teased.

"You were asleep at your desk," she said. "My statement stands. You most definitely need a fun whisperer."

"I'll put fun on my calendar, how's that sound?"

She laughed. "Planning the fun kinda takes the fun out of fun. And anyway, maybe it's also about adventure. Spontaneous adventure."

"I don't know," he murmured, watching her as he still stroked Thor into a pleasure coma. "I can think of a few things that if planned right, would be the epitome of fun *and* adventurous."

She lifted her gaze from her dog's contented face to Finn's and found his eyes warm and lit with something. Amusement? Challenge? "Like?"

He set Thor down, back in the sunspot, and rising to his full height, shifted toward Pru.

She backed up a step, a purely instinctual move because while her body knew how badly it wanted him, her mind was all too well aware that it was a colossally stupid move of the highest order.

He merely stepped forward again, backing her flush to the brick wall lining the courtyard.

Her breathing had gone ragged. Even more so when

he leaned into her with his hands on either side of her head. "You're a contradiction," he murmured. "A push pull."

"Maybe it's because we're oil and water," she managed.

Hands still on her, blocking her escape—not that she wanted to escape those strong arms and that talented mouth—he flashed her a hot look. "Do you want this, Pru?"

She wasn't one hundred percent certain what "this" was, but she *was* one hundred percent certain that she wanted it. And God help her, she wanted it bad, too. When she gave a jerky nod, his hand came up and cupped her jaw, his fingers sliding into her hair, his thumb slowly, lazily, rasping over her lower lip. He watched the movement with a heat that made her legs wobble.

She swallowed hard. "We're in the center of the courtyard."

"What happened to adventurous?" he murmured, his thumb making another slow, intoxicating pass over her lip.

As always, her mouth worked independently of her brain and opened so she could sink her teeth lightly into the pad of his thumb.

He hissed in a breath. The sound egged her on and she sucked his thumb between her lips.

His eyes dilated to black.

Yeah. Suddenly she was feeling very . . . adventurous. Before she could stop herself, her arms encircled his broad shoulders, her fingers sinking into his hair.

This wrenched a low, sexy "mmmm" from him like he was a big, rumbling wildcat. A big, rumbly wildcat who clearly wanted more because he drew her up against him and lowered his lips to hers.

Meeting him halfway, she went up on her tiptoes. He slid a hand up her back to palm the back of her neck, holding her right where he wanted her. Then and only then did his mouth finally cover hers, his kiss slow and sweet.

After, he pulled back and looked into her eyes, smiling at whatever he saw—probably dazed lust. He kissed her again, *not* slow and most definitely *not* sweet this time. Again he ended it too soon but when he lifted his head, the rough pad of his thumb slid back and forth over her jaw while she struggled to turn her brain back on.

"Pru."

And oh, that deliciously rough morning voice. It slid over her like the morning sun, and made her eyes drift shut.

"You take the rugrat," he said. "I'll get your box."

Her eyes flew open. He was holding Thor again. "What?"

"I'll help you upstairs," he said.

Where her bed was. Oh God, had she made her bed? Wait—*was she wearing good panties?*

She mentally shook herself because none of that mattered. You're not going there with him, remember? She couldn't, wouldn't, because she hadn't yet told him who she was. She wasn't ready to do that. Because she knew that once she did, this would be over. He wouldn't want to be friends with the woman whose family had stolen his. He wouldn't want to make her fancy virgin cocktails or pet her silly dog.

Or kiss her stupid . . .

The truth was, he was the best thing to happen to her in a damn long time. And yes, it was selfish. And wrong.

And she hated herself for it.

But she couldn't tell him, not yet. "I've got it," she said. "Really. I'm good."

She just wished she meant it.

Chapter 10

#KarmaIsABitch

It was rare for Finn to find himself on unsure ground. Typically if he needed something, he handled it himself. If he wanted something, he went after it.

He both wanted and needed Pru. That was fact. The knowledge had been sitting in the frontal lobe of his brain and in the bottom of his gut, and also definitely decidedly south of both.

It'd been like that for him since the night she'd walked into his pub dripping wet and smiled that smile at him. And then she'd nailed him with that dart and he'd kissed her, and the problem had only compounded itself.

She drove him nuts, in the very best of ways.

And now she'd brought him a coffee and he'd kissed the daylights out of her again. But this time she didn't seem to want to climb him like a tree. She wanted to escape him.

Badly too, given the sudden panic in her eyes.

It should have been his clue to back off. Walk away.
But he found himself unable to do that.

"How about I just get you upstairs with your stuff," he said, going for as nonthreatening as possible. He bent to put Thor down so he could pick up the box but the dog had other ideas and clung like a monkey. He glanced down. "You sure he's a dog?"

Some of the stress left Pru at that and she laughed a little. "Yes, but whatever you do, don't tell him." She covered Thor's ears. "I think that he thinks he's a grizzly."

Finn met Thor's wary gaze. The little guy really was the most ridiculous looking thing he'd ever seen. Bedraggled, patchy, mud brown fur, he had one ear up and one ear down, a long nose, a small mouth that lifted only on one side like he was half smiling, half smirking, and the biggest, brownest eyes he'd ever seen. Hell, his ears and eyes alone were bigger than the rest of him, and the rest of him didn't weigh as much as a pair of boots. "Little Man Syndrome, huh?" he asked the dog sympathetically.

"He just likes to be carried," Pru said. "He likes to be tall. And he can see better too. Once you pick him up, he won't let you put him down."

Finn tested this theory by once again starting to bend over.

Thor growled. Laughing, Finn tightened his grip on the little guy. "Don't worry, I've got ya," he said and reached to pick up Pru's box with his other hand.

Holy shit, it weighed a ton.

"What are you doing?" Pru asked, crouching at his side. Her voice was tight again. "I said I've got it."

"Pru, it weighs a ton. How far did you carry this thing?"

"Not far," she said, tug-o-warring with him. "Let go—"

"You're as stubborn as Thor, but I'm already here," he said. "Let me help—"

"*No.*" She tried to wrench the box from him, her expression more than a little desperate now, which stopped him in his tracks. Whatever it was in the damn box, she didn't want him to see it, and he immediately backed off—just as she whirled from him. She lost her grip, and the box literally fell apart, the cardboard bottom giving way, the contents hitting the ground.

"Oh no," she breathed and hit her knees on the ground in front of a few old, beat-up photo albums, a few cheap plastic picture frames, and a glass one, which had shattered into a thousand pieces. "It broke," she whispered.

There was something in her voice, something as fragile as the now broken glass frame shattered in shards and pieces at their feet, and it made Finn's chest hurt. Even more so when he saw the picture free of its frame. A little girl standing between two adults, each holding one of her hands.

Pru, he thought, looking into those brown eyes. Pru . . . and her parents?

Her posture said it all as she reached right into the shards of glass for the picture, carefully brushing it clean to hug it against her chest like it meant the entire world to her.

Fuck. "Pru, here, let me—"

"No, it's fine. I'm fine," she protested, pushing his

hands away when he began to gather up the photo albums. "I told you I've got this!"

Thor, soaking up Pru's anxiety, lifted his head and began to howl.

Pru looked close to tears.

Eddie, a.k.a. Old Guy, came out of the alley, presumably to help, took one look at the mess that Finn had found himself in, and did an about-face.

Finn gently squeezed Thor to him. "Quiet," he said in a firm voice.

Thor went quiet.

Pru sucked in a breath, looking surprised right out of her impending tears, thank God. "Stop," he said as she reached into the glass for another picture with absolutely no regard for her own safety. Unable to put Thor down and risk him cutting his paws, he held the dog tight to his chest and reached for Pru's hand with his free one. Pulling her to her feet, he said, "Let's get Thor upstairs and then I'll come back and—"

"I'm not leaving it, any of it."

"Okay, babe, no worries." He whipped out his cell phone and called Archer. No way was Sean awake yet, much less up and moving, but Finn knew he could always count on Archer.

Archer answered with his customary wordy greeting. "Talk."

"Courtyard," Finn said and looked up. Sure enough Archer's face appeared in the second-story window of his office. "We need a box."

"Down in five," Archer said.

He made it in two. Archer set an empty box down

on the bench and reached for Thor, presumably so Finn could handle Pru, but Thor bared his tiny little teeth and growled fiercely.

"Whoa, little dude," Archer said and raised his hands. "I come in peace."

Satisfied he'd protected his woman, Thor went back to cuddling into Finn.

Finn grabbed the box in his free hand and crouched in front of Pru, who had an armful of stuff. "Set everything in here," he said.

She hesitated and he leaned in. "It'll be safer," he said quietly, and she nodded and unloaded her full arms into the box.

Archer had sent a text and Elle showed up with a broom and dust pan, which seemed incongruous to her lacy tee, pencil skirt, and some very serious heels.

"You could've sent someone," Archer said to her.

Elle gave him a don't-be-stupid look and smiled at Pru. "Pretty photo albums. Shame about the frame." She swept up the glass, the line of thin silver hoops clanging on her wrist. "I've got some spare frames I'm not using that would love a home. I'd be glad to give them to you. Is that you and your parents?"

Pru nodded and rose. "Thanks for helping."

"Don't give it another thought," Elle said. "Oh, and it's girls' night out tonight. Karaoke. Doll yourself up, Finn promised nineties glam rock band music." Elle flashed a smile. "My specialty, so just ring if you need something to wear, I've got a closet full."

Archer snorted.

"Okay," Elle said, "so I have two closets full. Eight-ish work for you?"

Pru, looking a little bit dazzled and probably also more than a little railroaded by Elle's gentle but firm take-charge 'tude, shook her head. "I can't sing," she said.

"Nonsense," Elle said. "Everyone can sing. We'll duet, it'll be fun."

Pru didn't look convinced but she did look distracted instead of anguished, and for that Finn was grateful. He brushed a quick kiss on Elle's cheek. "Thanks."

She kissed him back and gave him a look that said *take care of her*, and he knew better than to not do what Elle wanted.

Besides, he wanted the same thing.

A few minutes later he got Pru and Thor upstairs.

"Thanks," she said quietly. "But I'm good from here."

Oh, he got that message loud and clear, but he was still holding both her dog and her box so he stepped into her apartment behind her.

He could see her small kitchen and living room and the wall dividing them that had a square door right in the middle of it. It was a dumbwaiter, which cut through this whole side of the building, a long-ago leftover remnant from when the place had at one time been all one residence belonging to one of the wealthiest, most successful dairy families on the west coast.

Finn knew this only because he'd seen the dumbwaiter in Archer's office. Archer employed guys with major skills and they kept those skills sharp with company-wide training. Once a month that training came in the form of a serious scavenger hunt, and somehow Finn had once ended up one of the things on the list of items to gather.

Archer's idea of funny.

Team One had captured Finn in his sleep once. He'd escaped before they could win though, and he'd been lucky enough to use the dumbwaiter to make his hasty exit. He'd been unlucky enough to end up in the basement in nothing but his boxers, showing up at an illicit poker game between the building's janitor crew and maintenance crew.

He'd joined in and won two hundred bucks, which had kept him from trying to kill Archer.

Pru had the dumbwaiter door latched from her side. Smart girl. That didn't surprise him.

What *did* surprise him was that there was almost no furniture in the entire place.

"Where did you move from?" he asked.

"Not far. Fisherman's Wharf."

"You didn't move your furniture yet?"

"Uh . . ." She headed into her kitchen and was face first into her fridge now, leaving him a very nice view of her sweet ass in her snug yoga capris. "My place there was mostly furnished," she said. "But yeah I have a few things left to move over." Her tank gapped away from her front, affording him a quick flash of creamy, pale skin.

"You work out of Fisherman's Wharf too," he said. "At Jake's charter service, right?"

"Yes." She straightened and faced him. "He's got that huge old warehouse on Pier 39. I both work and lived there."

"With Jake." Wow, listen to him all casual, when his stomach had literally just hit his toes.

"He's got a lot of space. Not all of it is used for business. It's residential too."

Not, Finn couldn't help but notice, exactly an answer. He knew Jake. Knew too a little of the guy's reputation, which was that maybe his legs didn't work, but everything else most certainly did. That guy saw more action than Finn, Archer, Spence, and Sean all together.

Times ten.

"You and him . . . ?" he asked calmly, while feeling anything but.

"Not anymore."

Somehow this didn't make him feel better. He was still holding Thor and the box. Pru came back toward him and took Thor, setting him down, unhooking his leash. Then she turned back to Finn and reached for the new box.

Their hands brushed but he held firm, waiting until her eyes met his. He let his question stand. He had no idea why it mattered to him so much. Or maybe he did. In any case, he was usually good at letting things go, *real* good, but for some reason this wasn't going to be one of those things.

Finally, she blew out a sigh. "Did you think I'd kiss you if I was with someone else?"

"Do you always answer a question with a question?"

Making an annoyed sound, she tugged the box from his arms, her momentum taking her on a half spin from him but at the last minute she whirled back with something clearly on the tip of her tongue.

Problem was, he'd stepped in to follow right behind her. Which was how he ended up with the corner of the box slamming right into his crotch.

Chapter 11

#LoveBites

Pru felt the impact, took in where the box had hit Finn, and staggered back a step in horror. "Oh my God, I'm so sorry! Are you all right?"

He didn't answer. He did however let out a whoosh of air and bent over, hands on his knees, head down.

Good going, Pru. Since you didn't kill him the other night, you went for unmanning him and finishing the job. She quickly set the box down and hovered close, hands raised but not touching him, not sure *where* to touch him. Which was ridiculous. She'd had her tongue halfway down his throat. He'd seen her lose her collective shit over the photograph of her mom and dad . . . "Finn?" she asked tentatively. "Are you okay? *Say something.*"

Head still down, he lifted a finger, signaling he needed a moment.

Going gonzo with all the agitation in the air, Thor

was on a yipping spree, running in circles around them both, panting in exertion.

"Thor, hush!" she said, eyes on Finn.

Thor didn't hush, but she couldn't concentrate on the dog. "I'm so sorry," she said again, finally giving in to the urge to touch Finn, running her hand up and down his back, trying not to notice that under her fingers he was solid muscle. And thanks to his low-riding jeans having slid down his hips when he'd bent over, she could see an inch of smooth, sleek skin and it made her stupid. "I didn't mean to crush your . . . er, twig and berries."

He stilled and then lifted his head. He was pale. No, scratch that, he was green, and maybe sweating a little bit to boot. But he had a funny expression on his face.

Thor was still losing his mind, barking so hard that his upright ear bounced up and down and his floppy ear kept covering his eyes, freaking him out all the more.

"Shh," Finn said to him firmly but not unkindly.

Shockingly, Thor "shh'd."

Finn straightened up a little bit more, but not, Pru couldn't but notice, all the way.

"Twig and berries?" Finn repeated.

"Yeah, um . . ." Pru strained for another reference so that she didn't have to spell it out. "You know, your . . . kibbles and bits."

The corners of his mouth quirked but she wasn't sure if he was mad or amused. "Frank and beans?" she tried.

At that, he out-and-out smiled. "I'm torn between giving you a break and stopping you, or making you go on."

Oh for God's sake. She crossed her arms. "I suppose you have better words."

"Hell yes," he said. "And when you're ready, I'll teach them to you."

Breaking eye contact, she—completely inadvertently, she'd swear it on a stack of waffles!—slid her gaze to where she'd hit him. Did it seem . . . *swollen?* "I've got an icepack if you—"

He choked. "Not necessary."

"Are you sure?" she asked. "Because I really am a good medic, I promise, and—"

He choked off another laugh. "And you're offering to do what, exactly?"

Uh . . . She bit her lower lip.

"Kiss it better?" he suggested in a voice that made her get a little overheated.

Note to self: *not quite ready for prime time with Finn O'Riley.*

He gave her a knowing smirk and moved to the door. Definitely with a slight limp. "You should take Elle up on her offer for a new frame," he said. "That picture clearly means a lot to you and she's got some beautiful things in storage."

And then he was gone.

It was a matter of pride that Finn managed to walk across the courtyard without a limp. Or too much of one anyway. He'd thought about going up instead of down, heading to the roof, the only place in the building that he could go and probably be alone, but he didn't want or need alone time.

Or so he told himself.

"What's up with you, someone knee you in the 'nads?"

He turned his head and found Eddie in his usual place, sitting on a box in the alley. It was a good spot because from there the old man could see both the courtyard and the street.

"Isn't it early for you to be up?" Finn asked him.

"It's trash day."

Finn went through his pockets for extra change. Coming up with a five, he handed it over.

Eddie smiled his gratitude.

When a shadow joined theirs, Finn turned just as Archer appeared silently at his side.

Archer had some serious stealth skills, earned mostly the hard way. He'd lost none of his sharp edges, which considering what he did for a living and the danger he still occasionally faced, was a good thing.

"What happened to your boys?" Archer asked.

Finn resisted the urge to cup his "boys" because they still ached like a son of a bitch from his collision with the corner of Pru's box. "Nothing."

"Maybe he finally got laid," Eddie said to Archer.

Archer's gaze cut to Finn's face. "Nah," he said. "He'd be more dazed. And happy."

Spence joined them. "What's going on?"

"The debate is whether or not Finn got laid," Archer said.

Spence took his turn studying Finn's expression. "He's not happy enough."

"That's what I said." Archer gave a rare smile. "Given how long it's been, I'd assume he'd be doing cartwheels and shit."

Finn took a deep breath as they both laughed at his expression. "How about I *assume* my foot up your ass?"

This only made them crack up harder.

Eddie got himself together first. "Gotta go," he said and headed for the alley. Trash day was his favorite day of the week because he loved nothing more than to go dumpster diving for treasures.

Twice now, the entire building—all fond of Eddie and protective of him as well, had implemented a system where everyone bagged up anything that might be of interest to him separately so that he didn't have to go searching.

And then they discovered that Eddie was dumping out all the bags into the dumpster regardless.

Turns out, Eddie liked the thrill of the find.

"You smell like a skunk," Archer said to Eddie.

Eddie blinked. "Is that right? Well, I'm sure we have skunks around here somewhere."

"You think?" Archer asked casually. "Because I'm thinking it smells like weed."

"Huh," Eddie said. "Good thing you're not a cop these days, huh?"

Oh boy, Finn thought. Even Old Man Eddie knew better than to remind Archer of his cop days, which in turn would remind him why he wasn't one anymore.

Archer's eyes went flat. "You growing?"

"Only exactly what I'm allowed," Eddie said and pulled out a laminated card on a ribbon from beneath his shirt.

"You selling?" Archer asked.

"Sir, no sir," Eddie responded, adding a smartass salute.

Finn and Spence both grimaced. "Man," Spence said. "What have we told you? Archer has *zero* sense of humor."

Eddie grinned. For reasons that Finn had never figured out, Eddie liked to fuck with Archer.

Archer gave a slight head shake, like he was talking himself out of making Eddie disappear. "You know the rec center on Union?" he finally asked.

Eddie nodded. "Past the porn shop but before the COME TO JESUS sign?"

"Yeah," Archer said. "They're having a free meal tonight. Pot roast and potatoes."

"I love pot roast and potatoes," Eddie said.

"You want a ride, come by my office at six," Archer told him.

Eddie grinned at him. "See, I knew you liked me. Though not as much as Finn. Finn gave me five bucks." Eddie looked hopefully at Archer.

Well versed in this game, Archer snorted. "I'll pay you ten if you tell me why lover boy here's limping like he was rode hard and put away wet. I know you know more than you're telling."

"You think he got his knob polished," Eddie said.

Archer flashed another grin. "Yeah."

Finn flipped Archer off, which only made Archer's grin widen.

"I don't know everything," Eddie said. "But I guess I do know some things."

"Such as?" Archer asked.

Eddie held out his hand.

Archer rolled his eyes, fished through his pockets and came up with the promised ten.

"Okay," Eddie said. "I know he went inside Trouble's apartment with her, but only stayed a few minutes. He came back out in this condition. It wasn't long enough for him to get laid . . ." He slid Finn a sideways look. "At least I hope it wasn't. You ain't a quick trigger, are you, boy?"

Spence about busted a gut and handed Eddie another ten. "Totally worth every penny."

Finn shook his head and walked away from those assholes, and he wasn't going back to the pub either. He needed a few hours horizontal on his bed—where he would absolutely not think about how he'd rather be getting his knob polished.

Nineties Karaoke Night cheered Finn up considerably. First Archer bet the gang that Spence couldn't rap "Baby Got Back."

Spence rapped "Baby Got Back." Perfectly. He was in a suit too, evidently fresh from some business meeting.

The ladies went nuts.

In penance, Archer had to sing "I'm Too Sexy" by Right Said Fred.

Shirtless.

The crowd went wild. But even better was what happened when the girls showed up. They walked in together, Elle, Willa, Haley . . . and Pru, all dressed in vintage nineties.

It was a cornucopia of hotness but Finn's gaze went straight to Pru. His heart about stopped. She wore a tight, short, high-waisted denim miniskirt that showed off her mile-long legs to mouth-watering perfection, a cropped white tee with an equally cropped leather jacket that kept giving sneak, tantalizing peeks of smooth, flat belly, and some serious platforms that told him Elle had been in charge. Her hair had been teased to within an inch of its life and she appeared to be wearing glitter as makeup.

Everyone had fun ordering nineties-style cocktails, so he made Pru a special one—a Chocolate Mock-tini. She raved over it so much that everyone else wanted one as well, and it became the night's special.

Eventually the ladies all got up to sing "Kiss" by Prince and brought down the house. Not because they were good. But because they were so bad.

Pru had been right. She couldn't sing. Couldn't dance either. Or keep rhythm. Not that this stopped her or the glitter floating around her in a cloud everywhere she moved.

Finn loved every second of it.

That was until she dragged his ass up on stage and made him do a duet with her. "The Boy Is Mine."

He was pretty sure not a single one of the guys would ever let him forget it either.

Sean bailed shortly after that, a woman on his arm, a smile on his face. Finn was happy for him, but when the night ended and the girls went to leave, he realized he was screwed because he didn't have the option of taking Pru home.

Even if that was only up two flights of stairs.

He had to stay until closing, add up the till, make sure everything got closed and locked up.

Which means he got to watch Pru, his Fun Whisperer, walk out.

She hugged him good-bye, and the feel of her up against him almost had him saying fuck it to the pub. But he couldn't. He showered and hit his bed two hours later. Alone.

And when he woke up the next morning he had glitter all over his pillow.

Chapter 12

#BiteTheBullet

The next few days were busy at work, with Pru's shifts consisting of one cruise after another, but she still had plenty of time to think. A lot.

Karaoke night had been fun. Watching Finn laugh with Archer and Spence had been a highlight for her.

Fun looked good on him. It made her happy to see him happy, and she realized it'd been a good week for her, too. Willa, Elle, and Haley had been so welcoming, taking her in, adding her to their group without hesitation.

It meant a lot. It also meant that she wasn't entirely alone. She knew she had Jake, but he was like a brother at this point. An overprotective, obnoxious one.

You have Finn . . .

Even if she had no idea what to do with him. Although she'd had plenty of ideas the other night.

It turned out that dancing and singing karaoke in

front of a crowd with Finn's eyes on her had been shockingly arousing.

Which apparently had been obvious. Haley had given her a knowing glance at the bar. "You look hungry," she'd said.

"Oh, no," Pru had told her. "I'm fine, I had a plate of chicken wings."

Haley and Willa had laughed.

Even Elle had smiled.

"You're not hungry for food," Elle had informed her, with Curly and Mo nodding their heads in agreement. "You're hungry for a good time. With our boy Finn."

"Well that's just . . . a bad idea," she'd finished weakly. She looked at Willa and Haley for confirmation of that fact.

"Hey, sometimes bad ideas turn out to be the best ideas of all," Willa had said. "Just do it. Have some magical sex. And whatever happens, happens."

What would happen is that Pru would screw up one of the only good things she had going for her right now. "Just do it? That's your big advice?"

"Or in this case, him. Just do him."

Pru snorted.

Willa had turned to Elle and asked, "Think she'll follow my sage advice?"

Elle studied Pru's face carefully. "Hard to say. She's cute and sharp, but she's got some healthy survivor instincts. That might hold her up some."

"Stupid survivor instincts," Willa had said on a sigh.

And Pru agreed. She had some survivor instincts, and they often got in her own way.

"For days a cloud of glitter has been following you

around," Jake said, startling Pru back into the here and now.

"I went to Karaoke the other night," she said. "Rocked it too."

"But you can't sing," Jake said.

"I can totally sing."

He snorted. "And the glitter?"

"It was Nineties Night. This required copious amounts of glitter, which apparently is like the STD of the craft supplies. Once you use it without protection, you can't get rid of it." Pru looked down at herself. "Ever."

"Even Thor's wearing glitter," he said. "You're messing with his manhood."

"Real men aren't afraid of glitter," she said.

"Real men are terrified of glitter."

At the end of the day, Pru collected her dog from Jake's office, where she found him asleep sprawled on top of the desk.

"Seriously?" she asked.

"He likes to see what's going on," Jake said.

And Jake liked the company. She'd almost feel bad about taking Thor away when she'd moved but oh yeah, it'd been Jake's idea for her to go. "I hope he got glitter all over you."

"Hell no," Jake said. "Glitter doesn't dare stick to me. But you've got some on your face."

She couldn't get rid of it. She'd already sent Elle an I-hate-you text. Twice.

"We're going to have to forfeit tonight's game," Jake said. "We're short a player. Trev's out with mono."

She and a group of Jake's other friends and employees

played on a local rec center league softball team. Jake was their coach. Coach Tyrant. "Who gets mono at our age?" she asked.

Jake shrugged. "He's a ship captain, he sees a lot of action."

"I'm a ship captain," she said. "I see *no* action."

"And we both know why," Jake said.

Not going there. "Don't forfeit," she said. "I'll find us a player."

Jake raised a brow. "Who?"

"Hey, I have other people in my life besides you, you know."

"Since when?"

She rolled her eyes and ran out. Well, okay, she didn't run exactly. Thor refused to run. But they walked fast because she had an idea, one that would further her plan to bring Finn more fun.

Of course she'd deviated from the plan a couple of times now, starting with allowing her lips to fall onto his—not once but a holy-cow twice—but she'd decided to give herself a break because he was so . . . well, kissable.

And hey, now she knew that his mouth was a danger zone, she'd just steer clear. Her inner voice laughed hysterically at this, but whatever. She could do it.

Probably.

Hopefully.

In the courtyard, she tied Thor's leash to a bench, kissed him right between his adorable brown eyes and dashed through the open doors of the pub. Breathless, she scanned for Finn, but couldn't find him.

Sean flashed her a smile. "Hey, Trouble." He gestured to her face. "You've got some glitter—"

"I know!"

His smile widened. "Okay then, what can I get you?"

"Finn," she said, and then blushed when he just kept grinning. "I mean, I need to see him. Is he in his office?"

"Nope, boss man isn't in."

She'd never been here when Finn hadn't. "But he's always here."

Sean laughed. "Almost always," he agreed. "But right now, he's . . . well, let's just say he's pissed off at me, so we decided he'd work from the house office so I could live to see another day."

He didn't seem all too worried by this. "I need a favor," she said.

He leaned over the bar, eyes warm. "Name it."

"I need his address."

Sean went brows up. "His address."

"Yes, please."

"You going to show him a good time?" he asked. "Because darlin', he sure could use it."

"I'm on it," she said and then realized what he'd meant, which was not what *she'd* meant. "Wait, that's not—"

"Oh, it's *way* too late," Sean said, laughing his ass off.

"I just need to *talk* to him," she said, trying to regain some dignity.

"Whatever you say." Grabbing a cocktail napkin, he pulled a pen from behind his ear, scrawled an address down, and handed it over to her. "We share a house in Pacific Heights. Less than a mile from here. Go do your thing."

"Which is *talking*," she said.

"If that's what you kids are calling it these days," he said. "Good luck, Trouble."

Not sure why she'd need good luck, she grabbed Thor and headed back out.

Finn lived straight up Divisadero Street, a steep hill that had Thor sitting down and refusing to go another step about a hundred yards in.

Which was a hundred yards past when Pru had wanted to sit down as well. But she scooped the dog up and determinedly kept going, making a quick stop along the way for a spur-of-the-moment gag gift that she sincerely hoped Finn found funny.

By the time she arrived at his house near the top of the hill, she was huffing some serious air. She looked back at the view and was reminded of why she loved this city so much. She could see all of Cow Hollow and the marina, and beyond that, the gorgeous blue of the bay and the Golden Gate Bridge as well.

Worth every second of the walk. Almost. Finn's house was a Victorian-style, narrow row house. The garage was on the bottom floor, two stories above that, with steps leading up to the front door and down to a short driveway—on which sat a '66 Chevelle.

The sexy muscle car's hood was up and a very sexy jeans-covered tush was all Pru could see sticking out of it. She recognized the perfect glutes as Finn's— clearly a sign she'd been ogling said perfect glutes too much. Not that she was repentant in the slightest about this, mind you. In any case, his long denim-covered legs were spread for balance, his T-shirt stretching taut over his flexing shoulder and back muscles and riding up enough to expose a strip of navy boxers and a few inches of some skin.

She tried not to stare and failed. "Hi," she said.

Nothing. He just kept doing whatever it was he was doing under the hood, which involved some serious straining of those biceps.

She moved a little closer. "Finn?"

More nothing, but now she could hear the tinny sound of music and caught sight of the cord from his earbuds.

He was listening to something. Loudly. Classic rock by the sounds of it.

She stared at him, at the streaks of grease on his jeans and over one arm, at the damp spot at the small of his back making his shirt cling to him . . . It was the kind of thing that in the movies would be accompanied by a montage of him moving in slow motion to music, the camera moving in and focusing on that lean, hard body.

Giving herself a mental shake, Pru set Thor down, and holding his leash, shifted even closer to Finn before reaching out to tap him. But at the last minute she hesitated because once again she couldn't figure out where to touch him. Her first choice wasn't exactly appropriate. Neither was her second.

So she settled for his shoulder.

If he'd done the same to her, she probably would've jumped and banged her head on the hood. But Finn had better reflexes, and certainly better control over them. Still cranking on something with a wrench, he simply turned only his head to give her a level stare.

"Hi," she said again and bent over at the waist, hands

to her knees to try to catch her breath. "That's quite a hill."

He reached up and pulled out one earbud. "Hi yourself. Need an oxygen tank?"

"You kid, but I totally do."

"You're still wearing glitter," he said with a smile.

"Five showers since that night," she said, tossing up her hands. "I've taken five showers and it's still everywhere. And Thor has been pooping glitter for days . . ."

Still smiling, he crouched and held out his hand for Thor. "You were quite the show the other night."

She chewed on her lip, not sure if he was teasing or complimenting her or not.

"I could watch you do that every night," he admitted.

"What, make a fool of myself?"

His smile turned into a full-fledged grin. "Sing and dance like no one's watching. *Live* like no one's watching."

And just like that, she melted a little.

Thor was sniffing Finn's hand carefully, cautiously, wanting to make sure this was his Finn, and finally he wagged his tail.

"Atta boy. It's just me." Finn opened his arms and Thor moved in for a hug.

Pru stared at the big, sexy guy so easily loving up on her silly dog and felt her throat go a little tight.

"I know Archer didn't tell you where I live," Finn said, eyes still on Thor. "Or Spence. I mean, Spence would if he thought it was funny but they're both pretty hardcore about having my back."

The hardcore part was undoubtedly true. She'd seen the three guys with each other. There were bonds there that seemed stronger than any relationship she'd ever had, a fact that played into her deepest, most secret insecurity—that she might be unlovable.

"Elle values privacy above everything else," Finn said, "which leaves the busybodies." He was watching her now. "Willa or Haley?" he asked.

"Neither." She hesitated, not wanting to get Sean in trouble.

"Shit." Finn rose, Thor happily tucked under one arm like he was a football. "Eddie?"

"Eddie?" Pru asked, confused. "Who's Eddie?"

"The old guy who enjoys dumpster diving, eating dope brownies, and not minding his own business."

Pru gaped. "I've been feeding him for a month now and he's never told me his name. And I've asked a million times!"

"He likes to be mysterious. And also his brain might be fried from all those brownies. You going to tell me how you found me or not?"

She blew out a breath. "Sean. But he didn't tell me to mess with you or anything," she said hurriedly. "He did it because I have a favor to ask of you and needed to see you in person to do it."

"Sean was at the pub?"

"Yes," she said.

"Working?"

"I think so . . ."

"Huh," he said. "He must have fallen and bumped his head."

"He seemed to have all his faculties about him," she said. "Or at least as many as usual."

Finn snorted and set Thor down. The dog turned in a

circle at Pru's feet and then plopped over with an utter lack of grace.

"I brought you a present," Pru said.

"What?" Finn lifted his gaze from Thor to her face. "Why?"

The question threw her. "Well, partly to butter you up for the favor," she admitted. "I figured if I made you laugh, you'd—"

"I don't need a present to do you a favor," he said, his voice different now. Definitely wary, and something else she couldn't place.

She cocked her head. "You know, presents are supposed to be a good thing."

When he just looked at her, she wondered . . . didn't anyone ever give him anything? And suddenly she wished it was a real present and not a gag gift. But it was too late now so she slipped her backpack off and pulled the bag from inside. Seriously second-guessing herself, not entirely certain of this, not even close, she hesitated.

He took the bag from her and peered inside, face inscrutable.

Nothing. No reaction.

"It's a man's athletic cup," she finally said, stating the obvious.

"I can see that."

"I figured if we're going to hang out together, you might need it."

He stilled and then a low laugh escaped him. "What I need with you, Pru, is full body armor."

True statement.

He lifted his head. "And who says we're hanging out?" he asked, his gaze holding hers prisoner.

She hesitated briefly. "I do."

His eyes never left hers which was how she saw them warm. "Well, then," he said. "I guess it's true."

Their eyes stayed locked, holding for a long beat, and suddenly Pru had a hard time pulling in enough air for her lungs.

"So what's the favor?" he asked.

"I play on a coed softball league. We're short a player tonight and I was hoping—"

"No."

She blinked. "But I didn't even finish my sentence."

"You're short a player for tonight's game and you want me to fill in," he said.

"Well, yes, but—"

"Can't."

She took in his suddenly closed-off expression. "Because . . . you're against fun?"

He didn't react to her light teasing. He wasn't going to play. He clearly had a good reason, maybe many, but he didn't plan on sharing them.

"You should've called and saved yourself a trip," he said.

"I didn't want to make it easy for you to say no."

"I'm still saying no, Pru."

"What if I said I *need* you?" she asked softly.

He paused for the slightest of beats. "Then I'd say you have my full attention."

"I mean *we* need you. The team," she said. "We'll have to forfeit—"

"No."

She crossed her arms. "You said I had your attention."

"You have that and more," he said cryptically. "But I'm still not playing tonight. Or any night."

She knew he was living life carefully, always prepared for anything to go bad. But she knew that wasn't any way to live because the truth was that any minute life could be poof—gone. "Do you remember the other day when you caught me at my worst and saw a few of my demons?" she asked quietly.

"You mean when the picture frame broke."

"Yes," she said, not surprised he knew exactly what she was talking about, that she hadn't been even slightly effective in hiding her painful memories from him.

"You didn't want to talk about it," he said.

"No," she agreed. "And you let me get away with that." She dropped her gaze a little and stared at his torso rather than let him see what she was feeling now. "Whether it was because it doesn't matter to you, or because you have your own demons, I don't know, but—"

"Pru."

Oh thank God, he'd shut her up. Sometimes she really needed help with that. She stared at his neck now, unable to help noticing even in her growing distress and sudden discomfort that he had a very masculine throat, one that made her want to press her face to it and maybe her lips too. And her tongue . . .

"Pru, look at me."

He said this in his usual low timbre, but there was a gentle demand to the tone now that had her lifting her gaze to his.

"It matters," he said. "*You* matter."

This caused that now familiar squishy feeling in her belly, the one only he seemed to be able to evoke. But it also meant that it *was* his demons eating at him and this killed her. "Softball is a problem for you," she whispered.

"No." He closed his eyes for a beat. "Yeah. Maybe a little, by association." He blew out a sigh and turning his head, stared at the sweet car he'd been working on.

Which was when she remembered he'd had to quit playing baseball in college to raise Sean.

God, she was such an idiot.

"You'll have to forfeit?" he asked.

"Yes, but—"

"Shit." He shut the hood of the Chevelle and went hands on hips. "Tell me you guys are good."

She crossed her fingers. "You have to see us to believe it."

Chapter 13

#BadNewsBears

Not ten minutes into the game, Finn stood behind home plate wearing all of the catcher's gear, staring at the team in complete disbelief.

He'd been recruited by a con artist.

He slid his con artist a look. She was playing first base, looking pretty fucking adorable in tight, hip-hugging jeans and a siren red tee with a ragged penny jersey over the top of it, heckling the other team.

She was without a doubt, the hottest con artist he'd ever seen.

"You suck," she yelled to the batter, her hands curved around her mouth.

The batter yelled back, "How about you suck *me*?" And then he blew her a kiss.

Finn straightened to kick the guy's ass but the ref pointed to the batter and then gestured he was out.

"On what grounds?" the guy demanded.

"Being an idiot."

This came from the coach of Pru's team. Jake. He sat at the edge of the dugout, baseball cap on backward, dark lenses, fierce frown . . . a badass in a wheelchair.

With Thor in his lap.

Finn waited for the ump to give Jake a T and kick him out of the game but it didn't happen. Instead, the hitter took one look at Jake, kicked the dirt, and walked back to his dugout.

The next two batters got base hits and both made it all the way home thanks to the fumbling on the field.

Pru's team was the Bad News Bears.

In the dugout between innings, Pru tried to keep morale up, clapping people on the backs, telling them "good job" and "you're looking great out there."

Her rose-colored glasses must also be blinders. Because no one had done a good job and no one had looked great out there either.

At the bottom of the next inning, Finn watched his teammates blow through two strikes in two batters.

The third person up to bat was a twenty-something who had her dark hair up in a high ponytail that fell nearly to her ass. She was teeny tiny and had a sweet, shy smile.

Finn did not have high hopes for her. He might have muttered this under his breath. And Pru might have heard him.

She shot him a dark look. "Positive reinforcement only," she told him. "Or you'll have to go dark."

"Dark?"

"Yeah." She jabbed a thumb toward Jake, who was on the other side of her, watching the field, expression dialed to *irritated* as Thor snoozed on in his lap. "Like Coach Jake," Pru said and turned to her boss. "How are we doing tonight?"

Jake paused as if struggling with the right words. "Fuckin' great," he finally said.

He didn't look great, he looked like he was at stroke level, but Pru beamed at him and then patted his shoulder.

Jake blew out a heavy exhale. "I'll get you back, Prudence."

She gritted her teeth. "We talked about this. You only use my whole name if you want to die. Horribly and slowly."

"Prudence?" Finn repeated, amused by the death glare.

"I know, hard to believe, right?" Jake asked. "It's an oxymoron," Jake said. "She's anything *but* prudent."

Finn smiled. "And the 'they're doing great' part?" he asked *Prudence*. "Are we watching the same game?"

Jake did an impressive eyeroll, slid Pru a glare, and kept his silence, although it looked like it cost him.

"It's called encouragement," Pru said. "And Jake had to go dark, meaning he can't talk unless he's saying something positive, on account of how he used to lower our morale so badly we couldn't play worth anything."

Finn bit back the comment that they couldn't play worth anything now but as the girl at bat stood there letting two perfect strikes go by without swinging and Jake's expression got darker and darker, he nearly laughed.

Nearly.

Because he had no idea how Jake was doing it, keeping his mouth shut. Competition went to the bone with Finn and he was guessing Jake felt the same. "Is she going to swing?" he asked. "Or just keep the bat warm?"

A strangled snort came from Jake, which he turned into a cough when Pru glared at him.

"Abby is Jake's secretary," Pru said. "She's really great."

Finn looked at Jake.

Jake gave a slow head shake.

"What," Pru said, catching it. "She's wonderful! She handles your entire office and she's always sweet, even when you're a total asshole."

"Yes," Jake said. "She's a sweetheart. She's great. In my office and also at handling me, even when I'm a total asshole. What she isn't great at is softball."

"She's learning," Pru insisted.

Abby struck out.

The next batter was a lean and lanky kid, late teens, early twenties maybe.

"Nick," Pru told Finn. "He works in maintenance."

"Pru got him the job," Jake said and Pru shushed him.

Nick strolled out of the dugout, winked at Pru and got a second base hit.

The next batter was a young kid who couldn't have been more than eighteen. She wore thick-rimmed glasses and squeaked at every pitch. She also swung at every ball that came her way and several that didn't.

What she didn't do was connect with a single one. Probably because she kept her eyes closed, which meant that her glasses weren't doing jack shit for her.

Finn tried not to care. It was just a softball game, and a bad one at that, but come on. He looked over at Coach Jake and pointed to their batter. "Mind if I . . . ?"

Jake gestured for him to go ahead, his expression saying good luck.

"Kid," Finn called out.

The kid turned to face him.

"Finn," Pru said warningly but he didn't care. He didn't know how she'd gotten Jake to "go dark" but Finn hadn't made any such promise.

"What's your name?" Finn asked.

"Kasey," the girl said. "I work in accounts receivable."

"You know how to hit, Kasey?"

"Yeah." She paused. "No."

Shit. "Okay, it's easy," Finn said. "You just keep your eyes open, you got me?"

She bobbed her head.

"Make contact with the ball, Kasey. That's all you gotta do."

Kasey nodded again but failed to swing at the next pitch. She turned to nervously eye Finn.

"That's okay," Finn told her. "That was a sucky pitch, you didn't want a piece of that one anyway. The next one's yours." And he hoped that was true.

Pru watched Kasey swing at the next ball and connect.

Finn launched himself off the bench. "Yes!" he yelled, pumping his fist. "That's it, baby, that's it!"

He'd started off not wanting to be here, resenting the game, and yet now he was one hundred percent in it. Even, Pru suspected, having fun. Watching him gave her a whole bunch of feels, not the least of which was happy. She was really doing it, giving him something back.

After Kasey hit the ball, she dropped the bat like it was a hot potato and whipped around to flash a grin Finn's way, executing some sort of very white girl boogie while she was at it. "I did it! Did you see? I hit the ball!"

"Yeah, you did. Now *run*, Kasey!" Finn yelled, pointing to first base. "Run your little ass off!"

With a squeak, she turned and started running.

Finn laughed. He laughed and turned that laughing face Pru's way and she nearly threw herself at him.

"Having fun?" she asked, unable to keep her smile to herself.

"You tell me. *Prudence*."

She was going to have to kill Jake in his sleep.

He grinned at the look on her face and leaned in close so only she could hear him. "You owe me."

"What for?"

"For neglecting to mention that you guys are The Bad News Bears." He glanced at the field and leapt back to his feet, throwing himself at the half wall. "Go, Kasey, go! Go, go, go!"

Pru turned in surprise to see that the shortstop had missed the ball and Kasey was rounding second.

The ball was still bouncing in right field.

"Keep going!" Finn yelled, hands curved around his mouth. "Run!"

Kasey headed toward third.

Finn was nearly apoplectic and Pru couldn't tear her eyes off him.

"That's right!" he yelled. "You run, baby! You run like the wind!"

His joy was the best thing she'd seen all day.

All week.

Hell, all month.

Scratch that, *he* was the best thing she'd seen.

Unbelievably, Kasey made it all the way home and the crowd went wild. Okay, so just their team went wild. Everyone piled out of the dugout to jump on Kasey.

Except Pru.

She jumped on Finn.

She didn't mean to, certainly didn't plan it, her body just simply took over. She turned to him to say something, she has no idea what, but instead she literally took a few running steps and . . .

Threw herself at him.

Luckily he had quick reflexes, and just as luckily he chose to catch her instead of not. He caught her with a surprised grunt, and laughing, hauled her up into his arms. He slid one hand to her butt to hold her in place, the other fisting her ponytail to tug her face up to his.

"Did you see that?" she yelled, losing her ability to self-regulate her voice with the excitement. "It was beautiful, yeah?"

He looked right into her eyes and smiled back. "Yeah. Beautiful."

And then he kissed her, hard, hot, and quite thoroughly.

And far too short. She actually heard herself give a

little mewl of protest when he pulled back and let her slide down his body to stand on her own two feet.

"We're still down by ten runs," he said.

She nodded, but she'd never felt less like a loser in her entire life.

Chapter 14

#TheWholeNineYards

In the end, they lost by five, which Pru actually considered a total win. In the very last inning, she'd dove for a ground ball and slid along the ground for a good ten feet, bouncing her chin a few times while she was at it, but hey, she got the ball.

She also got some road rash.

She hadn't felt it at the time, but by the end of the game when they'd all packed up and were going their separate ways, Pru's aches and pains made themselves known. She slowly shouldered her bag and turned, coming face to face with both Jake and Finn.

Jake—with Thor in his lap—gave her a chin nod. Since their venue was a middle school field only two blocks from his building, they usually walked back together.

Finn didn't give her a chin nod. He just stood there, watching her in that way he had that made her . . . want things, things she wasn't supposed to want from him.

Clearly she needed to work on that.

Jake grimaced. "You're a mess. Let's go, I'll patch you up at the office."

"I'm fine." A big fat lie, of course. Her road rashes were stinging like a sonofabitch. "I'm just going to head home."

Jake slid a look at Finn before letting his gaze come back to her. "You sure that's a good idea?"

Of course it wasn't a good idea. But she wasn't exactly known for her good ideas now was she? "Yep," she said, popping the *P* sound.

"You shouldn't go alone, you might need help."

"I've got her," Finn said.

The two men looked at each other for a long beat. Pru might have tried to mediate the landmine-filled silence between them but her brain was locked on Finn's words.

I've got her . . .

She had long fantasies where that was true . . . She reached to take Thor but Jake shook his head.

"He's coming home with me tonight for dinner. I've got steak."

"Steak?" Pru repeated, realizing she was starving. "But after our games, you usually make hotdogs."

Jake shrugged. "It's steak tonight. I've got enough for you to join, if it's okay with Thor."

Thor tipped his head back like a coyote and gave one sharp "yip!"

Pru spent a few seconds weighing a steak dinner cooked for her versus watching Finn in those sexy butt-hugging, relaxed-fit Levi's of his for a little bit longer. It was a tough decision, but in the end, she took the jeans. "No, thanks."

Jake just gave her a knowing head shake and rolled off.

"Did you just almost trade me in for a steak dinner?" Finn asked.

Pretending she hadn't heard that question, she started walking, but he stopped her.

"You okay?"

"Yeah," she said. "We lose all the time."

"I meant because you used your face as a slip-n-slide on that last play." Earlier, when she'd convinced him to come play, he'd gone inside his house for a duffle bag, from which he'd pulled out his mitt earlier. Now he pulled out a towel and gingerly dabbed it against her chin.

"Ow!" she said.

"But you're fine, right?" he asked dryly.

She removed the towel from her chin, saw some blood and with a sigh put the towel back to her face.

Finn took her bag from her shoulder and transferred it to his, where it hung with his own. "I'll get an Uber."

"I don't need a ride." She started walking, and after a beat he kept pace with her. She worked on distracting herself. The temperature was a perfect seventy-five-ish. The sun had dipped low, leaving a golden glow tipped with orange flame in the west, the rest of the sky awash in mingled shades of blue.

"So what was that about?" Finn asked after a few minutes of silence.

"Nothing. Like I said, sometimes we lose, that's all." Or, you know, always.

"I mean the look Jake gave you."

"Nothing," she repeated.

"Didn't seem like nothing."

"He's got a condition," she said, huffing up the hill. Damn. Why had she said no to getting an Uber again? "You've got to ignore most of his looks."

"Uh huh," Finn said. "What kind of condition?"

"A can't-mind-his-own-business condition." Her aches and pains were burgeoning, blooming as they moved. It was taking most of her concentration to not whimper with each step.

"You sure you're okay?" he asked.

"One hundred percent."

He gave her a once-over, his dark gaze taking in the holes in her knees, and she amended. "Okay, ninety percent," she said and then paused. "Ten at the worst," she amended.

Finn stopped and pulled out his phone.

"We're over halfway there," she argued. "I'm not giving up now."

"Just out of curiosity—do you ever give up?"

She had to laugh. "No," she admitted.

He shook his head, but he didn't ask if she was sure, or try to tell her she wasn't fine. Clearly he was going off the assumption she was an adult.

Little did he know . . .

"Sean plays baseball too," Finn said out of the blue a few minutes later. "He sucks. Sucks bad."

"Yeah?" she asked. "As my team?"

"Well, let's not go overboard."

She took a mock swing at him and he ducked with

a laugh. "In high school, he made it onto his freshman team," he said. "But only because they didn't have enough guys to cut anyone. The painful part was making sure he kept his grades high enough."

Pru hadn't actually given a lot of thought to the day-to-day reality that a twenty-one-year-old Finn would have faced having to get a teenage Sean through high school. There would've been homework to do, dinners to prepare, food shopping needed, a million tiny things that parents would have handled.

But Finn had been left to handle all of it on his own.

Her stomach tightened painfully at all he'd been through, but he was over there smiling a little bit, remembering. "That year half of the JV and Varsity teams got the flu," he said, "and Sean got called up to the semifinals. He sat on the bench most of the game, but at the bottom of the eighth he had to play first base because our guy started puking his guts up."

"How did he do?"

Finn smiled, lost in the memory. "He allowed a hit to get by him with bases loaded."

Pru winced. "Ouch."

"Yeah. Coach went out there and told him if another hit got by him, he'd string him up by his balls from the flagpole."

Pru gasped. "He did not!"

"He did," Finn said. "So of course, the next hit came straight for Sean's knees, a low, fast hit."

"Did it get by him?"

"He dove for it, did a full body slide on his chin while he was at it." Finn gave her a sideways smile. "But he got the damn ball."

"Did he get road rash too?" Pru asked, starting to get the reason for story time.

"Left more skin on that field than you did." Finn grinned and shook his head. "He came through though. Somehow, he usually does."

She loved that the two of them had stuck together after all they'd been through. She didn't know anything of their mom, other than she'd not been in the picture for a long time. Whatever she knew about the O'Rileys was what she'd been able to piece together thanks to the Internet. She'd done her best to keep up by occasionally Googling everyone who'd been affected by her parents' accident—needing to make sure they were all doing okay. When she'd discovered that Finn had opened O'Riley's only a mile or so from where she was living and working, she hadn't been able to resist getting involved.

And now here he was, a part of her life. An important part, and at the thought she got a pain in her heart, an actual pain, because she knew this was all short-lived. She had to tell him the truth eventually. She also knew that as soon as she did, he wouldn't be a part of her life anymore.

"Tonight brought back a lot of memories," he said, something in his voice that had her looking at him.

Regret.

Grief.

"You miss baseball," she said softly.

He lifted a shoulder. "Didn't think so, but yeah, I do."

"Is that why you didn't want to come tonight?"

"I didn't think I was ready, even for softball." He shook his head. "I haven't played since my dad died."

"I'm so sorry." She sucked in a breath, knowing she couldn't let him tell her the story without her telling *him* some things first. "Finn—"

"At the time, Sean was still a minor. He'd have gone into the system, so I came home."

The familiar guilt stabbed at her, tearing off little chunks of her heart and soul. "What about your mom?"

He shrugged. "She took off when we were young. Haven't heard from her since."

Pru had to take a long beat to just breathe. "Sean was lucky to have you," she finally said. "So lucky. I hate that you had to give up college—"

"I actually hated school," he said on a low laugh. "But I really, *really* didn't want to go home. Home was full of shit memories."

Feeling land-locked by her misery, she had to run that through twice. "Finn, I—" She stopped. Stared at him. "What?"

He was eyeing a deli across the street. "You hungry?"

"I . . . a little."

"You ever eat anything from there? They make the most amazing steak sandwiches." He slid her a look. "Don't want you to miss out on steak on my account." He guided her inside where he ordered for them both.

Which was for the best because she couldn't think.

His memories of home were shit? What did that mean?

Finn paid and they continued walking. He was quiet, keeping an eye on her. But she didn't want quiet. "What do you mean home was full of shit memories?"

He took a moment to answer. "You grow up with siblings?" he asked. "Both parents?"

"No siblings but both parents," she said, and held her breath. "Until they died when I was nineteen."

He didn't make the connection, and why would he? Only a crazy person would guess that the two accidents—his dad's and her parents—were the same one.

"That sucks," he said. "Sucks bad."

It did, but she didn't deserve his sympathy. "Before that, it was a good life," she said. "Just the three of us."

"Well, trust me when I say, Sean and I didn't get the same experience."

His body language was loose and easy, relaxed as he walked. But though she couldn't see his eyes behind his dark sunglasses, she sensed there was nothing loose and easy in them. "Your dad wasn't a nice guy?"

"He was an asshole," he said. "I'm sorry he's dead, but neither I nor Sean was sorry to have to finish raising ourselves without him."

She stared at him in profile as she tried to put her thoughts together, but they'd just scattered like tumbleweeds in the wind. All this time she'd pictured his dad as . . . well, the perfect dad. The perfect dad who *her* dad had taken from him and Sean. She let out a shuddering breath of air, not sure how to feel.

"Hey." Finn stopped her with a hand to her arm and pulled her around to face him, pulling off his sunglasses, shoving them to the top of his head to get a better look at her. "You don't look so good. Your cuts and bruises, or too much sun?" he asked, gently pushing her hair from her face and pressing his palm to her forehead. "You're pale all of a sudden."

She shook her head and swallowed the lump of

emotion in her throat. He'd hate her sympathy so she managed a smile. "I'm okay."

He didn't look like he believed her, proven when he switched the deli bag to his other hand and with his free one, grabbed hers in a firm grip. They were only a block from their building at this point, but before they could take another step, Finn stilled and laughed.

Pru looked up to see Spence coming toward them.

Tall and leanly muscled, with sun-kissed wavy hair that matched his smiling light brown eyes, he was definitely eye candy. He wore cargo shorts and an untucked button-down, sleeves shoved up his forearms. He was a genuinely sexy guy, not that he seemed to realize it.

He was walking two golden retrievers and a cat, all three on leashes advertising South Bark Mutt Shop, striding calm-as-you-please at Spence's side.

Spence himself was calm as well, and completely oblivious to the two women craning their necks to stare at his ass as he passed them. He was too busy flipping Finn off for laughing at him.

"I didn't realize you worked for Willa," Pru said. *Or that one could actually walk a cat . . .*

"He doesn't exactly . . ." Finn said.

Spence didn't add anything to this as Finn looked at him. "You're walking a cat. They're going to take away your man card."

"Tell that to the owner of the cat," Spence said. "She asked me out for tonight."

"So now you're using these helpless animals to get laid?"

"Hell yes," Spence said. "And yuk it up now because later I'm going to let Professor PuddinPop here anoint your shoes. Fair warning, he had tuna for lunch and it's not agreeing with him."

"No cats allowed in the pub," Finn said.

"Professor PuddinPop is the smaller retriever," Spence said. "His brother Colonel Snazzypants is a specialist in evacuating his bowels over a wide area. Watch yourself. You've been warned."

"What's the cat's name?" Pru asked.

"Good King Snugglewumps," Spence said with a straight face. "He's actually an emotional support cat, which you look like you could use right now. What the hell happened to you?"

"I slid trying to catch a ball at my softball game," she said.

"With your pretty face?"

"No, that was collateral damage. But I did catch the ball."

"Nice job," he said with a smile and a high-five.

Finn had crouched down low to interact with the animals. The cat was perched on his bent leg, rubbing against him, and both dogs had slid to their backs so he could scratch their bellies.

"The Animal Whisperer," Spence said. "They always gravitate to him." He shook his head at Good King Snugglewumps. "Man 'ho."

Good King Snugglewumps pretended not to hear him.

Finn grinned. "I'm the Animal Whisperer, and Pru here is the Fun Whisperer."

Spence turned to Pru. "How's that going? He learning to have fun yet?"

"He's not much for cooperating."

"No shit." He looked at Finn. "Keep your shoes on, that's all I'm saying."

And then he strode off, two dogs and a cat in tow.

Finn pulled out his phone and snapped a pic of Spence from behind.

Spence, without looking back, flipped him off again.

Still grinning, Finn shoved his phone back into his pocket and reached for Pru's hand. "Let's get you home."

Good idea. In just the minute that they'd stopped to talk, she'd gone stiff, but did her best to hide it. They entered the courtyard and she glanced at the fountain, which, she couldn't help but notice, had not been very busy fulfilling her wish for love for Finn. She sagged behind him just enough that she could point at the fountain and then at her eyes, putting it on notice that she was watching it.

The fountain didn't respond.

But apparently Finn had eyes in the back of his head because he laughed. "Babe, you just gave that thing a look that said you'd like to barbeque it and feed it in pieces to your mortal enemy."

She would. She absolutely would. Hoping for a subject change, she waved at Old Guy, sitting on a bench.

"Eddie," Finn said with a male greeting of a chin jut. "You look better than the other night."

Eddie nodded. "Yeah, it was either a twenty-four-hour flu thing or food poisoning," he said.

"You could stop eating everything everyone gives you," Finn suggested.

"No way! I get good shit, man. Cutie Pie here gives really good doggy bags. Chicken wings, pizza . . ." He looked at Pru. "You know what we haven't had lately?

Sushi—" He broke off, narrowing his eyes. "What happened to you, darlin'? This guy get tough with you? If so, just say the word and I'll level him flat."

Eddie was maybe ninety-five pounds soaking wet and looked like a good wind could blow him over. Finn had at least six inches on him and God knew how many pounds of lean, tough muscle, not to mention a way of carrying all that lean, tough muscle that said he knew exactly what to do with it.

Pru caught him looking at her with a raised brow, like *are you really going to say the word*?

"I roughed myself up," she admitted. "Softball." She started to reach into her pocket for a few dollar bills to give Eddie but Finn put a hand on her arm to stop her. With his other hand he fished something out of his duffel bag.

The third sandwich he'd bought at the deli.

Eddie grinned and snatched it out of thin air. "See? I get good stuff. And you know your way to a man's heart, boy. Mayo?"

"Would I forget? And extra pickles."

"Chips?"

Almost before the word was out, Finn was tossing Eddie a bag of salt and vinegar chips.

Eddie clasped a hand to his own heart. "Bless you. And tell Bossy Lady that I got the bag of clothes."

"Elle?"

Eddie nodded. "She said I was going to catch my death in my wife beaters and shorts, and insisted I take these clothes from her." He indicated his trousers and long-sleeved sweater. It was the surfer dude goes mobster look.

"How do they fit?" Finn asked, smiling, enjoying the old man's discomfort.

Eddie rolled his eyes. "Like a cheap castle—no ballroom."

Finn laughed and reached for Pru's hand again, tugging her toward the elevator.

That's when a whole new set of worries hit Pru. Was he going to come in?

Had she shaved?

No, she told herself firmly. *It doesn't matter if your legs aren't hairy, you are not going there with him.*

At her door, he held onto her hand while rummaging through her bag for her keys, and then opened her door like he owned the place.

But before they could get inside, the door across the way opened and Mrs. Winslow stepped out.

Pru's neighbor was as old as time, and that time hadn't exactly been particularly kind. Still, she was sharp as a tack, her faculties honed by staying up on everything and everyone in the building.

"Hello, dear," she said to Pru. "You're bleeding."

This was getting old. "Skiing accident," she said, trying something new.

Finn flashed her an appreciative grin.

Mrs. Winslow chortled. "Even an old lady knows her seasons," she said. "It's high summer, which means it was softball."

Pru sighed. "Yeah."

"Did you at least win this time?"

"No."

"I think the idea is to win at least sometimes," Mrs. Winslow said.

Pru sighed again. "Yeah. We're working on that." She gestured to Finn at her side, steady as a rock, but looking a little hot and dusty. "I recruited a new player," she said.

"Good choice," Mrs. Winslow said. "He's put together right nice, isn't he."

Pru's gaze went on a tour of Finn from head to toe and back again. Nice wasn't exactly the description she would use. Hot as hell, maybe. Devastatingly, disarmingly perfect . . .

At her close scrutiny, his mouth curved and something else came into his eyes.

Hunger.

"I got a little something delivered today," Mrs. Winslow said. "That's why I've been waiting for you."

"Me?" Pru asked.

"Yes, my package came via your dumbwaiter."

"Why?"

"Because, dear, the dumbwaiter is only on your side of the building."

Okaaay. Pru gestured to her open door. Mrs. Winslow let herself in, unlatched the dumbwaiter door and removed a . . . platter of brownies?

Pru's mouth watered as Mrs. Winslow smiled, gave a quick "thanks" and exited the apartment, heading for her own.

"Those look amazing," Pru said, hoping for an invite to take one.

Or two.

Or as many as she could stuff into her mouth.

"Oh, I'm sorry," Mrs. Winslow said with a negative head shake. "These are . . . special brownies."

Pru blinked and then looked at Finn, who appeared to be fighting a smile. "Special brownies?" she repeated, unable to believe that Mrs. Winslow really meant what she thought she meant.

"Yes," the older woman said. "And you're not of age, or I'd share."

"Mrs. Winslow, I'm twenty-six."

Mrs. Winslow smiled. "I meant over sixty-five."

And then she vanished into her own apartment.

Finn gently nudged Pru into hers, which answered the unspoken question. He was coming in. Into her apartment.

And, if her heart had any say at all, into her life.

Chapter 15

#Doh

Finn dropped both duffel bags and the deli bag on Pru's kitchen counter and then turned to her. "Okay, time to play doctor."

Her entire body quivered, sending "yes please" vibes to her brain. Luckily her mouth intercepted them. "Sure, if I can be the doctor."

His mouth curved. "I'm willing to take turns, but me first."

Oh boy. "Really, I'm fine. I think I just need a shower."

"Do you want something to drink? I could call down to the pub and—"

"No, thanks."

"I wasn't talking about alcohol," he said. "I already know you don't drink."

There weren't many who would so easily accept such a thing without some sort of question. People wanted and expected others to drink socially when they did. Usually whenever she politely declined, the interrogation inevitably started. *Not even one little drink?* Or *what's up with that, are you an alcoholic?*

Pru couldn't imagine actually being an alcoholic and facing that kind of inquisition with class and grace, but the truth was that she didn't drink because her parents had. A lot. They'd been heavy social drinkers. She didn't know if they'd had an actual problem or had just loved to party, but she did know it had killed them.

And that had quenched her thirst for alcohol at an early age.

But Finn didn't push. "How about something warm?" he asked. "Like a hot chocolate?"

She felt her heart squeeze in her chest for his easy acceptance. "Maybe after my shower."

He nodded and leaned back against the counter like he planned on waiting for her. Not knowing how to deal with that, she nodded back and headed for the bathroom. She shut and locked the door and then stared at that lock for a good sixty seconds, because did she really want to lock him out? No. She wanted him to join her, the steam drifting across their wet bodies as he picked her up, pressed her against the shower wall and buried himself deep.

Ignoring her wobbly knees, she left the lock in place, shaking her head at herself. Apparently it'd been too long since her last social orgasm and while she handled her own business just fine, her business was clearly getting bored with herself.

Stripping out of her clothes involved peeling her shirt from the torn skin of her elbows, not a super pleasurable experience. Same for her knees and her jeans. Naked, she took inventory. Two bloody knees, one bloody elbow and a bloody chin.

When she was little and got hurt, her mom would hug her tight and then blow on her cuts and bruises and whisper "see, not so bad . . ."

It'd been a long time, but there were moments like right now where she would've traded her entire world away for a hug like that again. She looked at her bruised, bloody self in the mirror and took a deep breath. "See, not so bad," she whispered and got into the shower.

She made it quick, partly because as she ran soap all over her body, she only ramped herself up, but mostly because her various road rashes burned like hell. But also because as she soaped up, she couldn't help but think of Finn standing in her kitchen, arms casually crossed, pose casual, his mood anything but.

Waiting for her.

Her good parts quivered so she turned the water off, going from overheated to chilled in a single heartbeat. With her bad parts stinging and her good parts throbbing, she stepped out of the shower.

At the knock at the door, she nearly had a stroke.

"How bad is it?" Finn asked through the wood.

She yanked her towel off the rack and wrapped it around herself, her hair dripping along her shoulders and down her back. "Not bad." Her voice sounded low and husky, and damn . . . inviting. She cleared her throat. "Not bad at all."

"I want to see." He tried the handle. "Let me in, Pru."

Her hand mutinied and unlocked the door, but didn't go as far as to actually open it for him. She couldn't because dammit, he was already in. In her head, her veins, *all* of her secret happy places, and, she suspected, her heart.

Finn pushed the door open and stood there, eyes scanning her slowly, his body stilling as he realized she was in just a towel.

He took what looked like a deep breath and stepped the rest of the way in, a first-aid kit in his hand. "Had this in my bag," he said and set it on the countertop to the left of the sink. Turning to her, he put his hands to her waist and lifted her, setting her on the right side of the sink.

Ignoring her squeak of surprise, he opened up his kit, fingered his way through, and came up with gauze and antiseptic. Turning toward her, he sprayed and then bandaged up her elbows, his brow furrowed in concentration as he worked. When he'd finished there, he crouched low.

With another surprised squeak, Pru pressed her legs together and tugged at the bottom of her towel, trying to make sure it covered the goods.

This got her an almost smile as he went about doctoring up both knees, using the spray again, keeping his eyes on his work, his big, strong, capable hands moving with quick, clinical efficiency.

Pru occupied herself and her nerves by watching the way his shirt stretched taut across his shoulders and back, every muscle rippling as he moved. His head was bent to her, his eyes narrowed in concentration, his long, dark lashes hiding his thoughts.

Fine with her, as she was having enough thoughts for the both of them, the number one being—if she relaxed her very tense thighs even a fraction, he'd be able to see straight up to the promised land.

The thought made her dizzy but she told herself it was the spray giving her a head rush.

Because actually, there was something incredibly erotic about that, her being nude beneath the towel and him being fully dressed. But she was all too aware that not only was she a wreck on the inside, she was looking the part.

His concentration shifted from what he was doing, his gaze cutting to hers. Reaching out he brushed his fingers over her cheek. "Why are you blushing?"

"I'm not."

He arched a brow.

"I'm a mess," she blurted out.

He rose at that, brushing his hands from her ankles up the backs of her calves, resting just behind her knees for a beat before giving a little tug, sliding her forward on the counter toward him.

Her legs parted of their own volition and he stepped between them, leaning in close at the same time, his body heat warming her up. His arms slid around her hips, snugging her closer as his lips gently brushed hers. Then those lips made their way along her jawline to just beneath her ear, trailing tiny kisses as he then worked his way down her throat.

"You're beautiful," he whispered. "A beautiful mess."

She choked out a laugh.

"You are," he said against her shoulder now. "So beautiful you take my breath away." Then he lifted his head to look into her eyes letting her see he meant it, entirely.

It'd been a long time since she'd felt beautiful, but she realized that she did. Very much so. She wanted to close her eyes and get lost in that, lost in him, but with one last nip at the sensitive spot where her neck met her shoulder, he shifted his attention to her chin.

She hissed in a breath when he pressed a gauze to it and then held her next breath as well when he leaned forward and kissed her there.

He'd shifted slightly to reach and the rough slide of denim brushed the skin of her bare thighs, making them tremble for more. "What are you doing?" she asked, sounding a little like Minnie Mouse on helium as his mouth and stubbled jaw gently abraded over her skin.

"Kissing your owies," he said innocently, his voice anything but as he continued with his ministrations.

Her traitorous body responded by arching and pressing closer, oscillating her hips to his for the sheer erotic pleasure of hearing him groan.

His mouth brushed her jaw one more time before he met her gaze. "Where else?"

Completely dazed, she shook her head. "Huh?"

"Where else do you hurt?"

She stared up at him. Where else did she hurt? Nowhere, because with his hands and mouth on her, all her pleasure receptors had overcome the pain. But not about to look a gift horse in the mouth, she pointed to her shoulder.

Finn gave it his utmost attention, running his finger over a growing bruise. Then he bent and kissed her there, letting his lips linger a little.

She looked at his mouth on her, those amazing lips pressed to her skin, and shivered.

With a wordless murmur, Finn shifted even closer, his warm, strong arms encircling her so that she could absorb some of the heat coming off him in waves. His long, dark lashes brushed his cheeks when his eyes were closed, like now. He hadn't shaved that morning and maybe not the morning before either. She could feel the prickles of his beard when he turned his head slightly and opened his eyes.

"Where else?" he asked, his voice pure sex.

And here's where she made her mistake. She needed to stay strong, that was all she had to do. But the problem was that she was tired of being strong. And she was having a hard time remembering why she needed to.

"Pru?"

She swallowed hard and pointed to her mouth.

He pulled back, gave her a hot look that melted her bones, and slowly worked his way up her throat with hot, wet kisses. When he got to her jaw, he fisted his hands in her hair and tilted her head right where he wanted her. She felt him open his mouth on her jawline, and with just the tip of his tongue made his way back to her mouth.

Wrapping her arms around his broad shoulders, she moaned and held on tight as he kissed her like maybe she was the best thing he'd ever tasted. And God, the feel of him against her, steady and solid. She didn't know how he did it but even after a long ball game he still smelled amazing. Something woodsy and pure male . . .

Then he pulled back.

Staring up at him, she ached. "Finn?"

"Yeah?"

"Remember how you said the ball was in my court?"

He pressed his forehead to hers for a beat, like he was working on control. She knew she should be as well but she didn't want him to leave, didn't want to be alone in this. "Don't go," she whispered softly.

He opened his eyes, the heat in them nearly sending her up in flames. Nope, she wasn't alone, thank God, because that would really suck. Out of words, she arched into him a little.

He groaned. "Pru."

Afraid the next words out of his mouth would be good-bye, she snuggled in and pressed her mouth to the underside of his jaw in a soft kiss. When he opened his mouth to say something, she took a nibble. At the feel of her teeth on him, he stilled and shuddered, and then his arms tightened on her.

Yes. *This.* It was just what she needed, because here, held by him like this, her guilt, her regret, her fears . . . all of it gave way to this heady, languid sensation of being desired and she didn't want it to stop.

Any of it.

His eyes were deep and intense as he shifted, nudging against the apex of her thighs. Keeping his gaze on hers, he kissed her again, sending licks of fiery desire right through her. Then those hands drifted down to her thighs, his fingers over the terry cloth, his thumbs beneath.

"Is this what you want?" he asked.

She gasped at the sensation of his callused thumbs grazing over her inner thighs, and he caught her mouth with his in a deep, hot, wet kiss as he slipped beneath her towel now, cupping her bare ass in his big hands.

When she was too breathless to hold the kiss, she

broke it off, her head falling back as his mouth skimmed hot and wet down her throat, across her collarbone. Her entire body felt strung too tight, like her skin didn't fit. Impatient, she arched into him again, dragging a rough groan from him.

"Pru." His voice was thrillingly rough, but there was a warning there too. He wasn't going to let this get away from her. She was going to have to say how far they took things.

"I want this," she whispered, clutching at him. "I want . . ."

His mouth was at her ear, bringing her a delicious spine shiver. "Name it."

"You. Please, Finn, I want you."

Raising his head, he stared at her before kissing her again, stroking his tongue to hers in a rhythm that made her hips grind to his. The soft denim of his jeans rasped over the tender skin of her inner thighs and thrilling to it, she wrapped her legs even tighter around him, drawing him closer, the hottest, neediest part of her desperately seeking attention.

Finn said something low and inaudible, and then let out a quiet laugh as he nipped her lower lip, her throat, and then . . . her towel slipped from her breasts.

He'd loosened it with his teeth.

When he put his hot mouth to her nipple, she nearly went over the edge right then and there. He cupped her breasts in his big warm hands, shifting his attention from one to the other, his stubbled jaw gently scraping over her in the most bone-melting of ways, his movements sensual, so slow and erotic she could hardly stand it. "*Finn.*"

He lifted his head and held her gaze while he spread the towel from her, letting it fall to her sides before he worked his way south, lazily exploring every inch of her like he had all the time in the world, humming in pleasure when he found the little compass on her hip. He spent a long moment there, learning her tattoo— with his tongue.

And all she could do was grip the counter on either side of her, head tipped back because it was too much effort to hold it up, her nerve endings sending high bolts of desire through her at his every touch.

She was completely naked to his fully dressed body now. Open, exposed . . . vulnerable in more ways than one. Certainly more than she'd allowed in far too long, although she didn't feel a single ounce of self-consciousness or anxiety about it.

She felt nothing but the sharp lick of hunger and need barreling down on her like a freight train in tune to his clever mouth and greedy hands. She was afraid if he so much as breathed on her special happy place, she'd go off like a bottle rocket.

And then he dropped to his knees.

His hands glided up her inner thighs, holding her open so his lips could make their way homeward bound. About thirty minutes ago she'd thought she needed steak more than anything but it turned out that wasn't true. She needed this, with Finn.

One of their phones buzzed, either hers on the floor in her pants pocket, or his from wherever he had it tucked away. She started to straighten but then his fingers stroked her wet flesh and she forgot about the phone. Hell, she forgot her own name. "Oh God, don't stop. Please, Finn, don't stop . . ."

"I've got you." And then he replaced his teasing fingers with his tongue, giving her a slow, purposeful lick. She whimpered as he continued to nuzzle her, luring her into relaxing again—and then his lips formed a hot suction.

And that was it, she'd become the bottle rocket and was gone, launched out of orbit. Hell, out of the stratosphere. When she came back to planet Earth, she realized she had Finn by the hair, her fingers curled tight against his head, her thighs squeezing his head like he was a walnut to be cracked. "I'm so sorry!" she gasped, forcing herself to let go of him. "I nearly ripped out your hair."

The words backed up in her throat when he turned his head and pressed a soft kiss to her inner thigh, sending her up a very male, very protective, possessive, smug smile. "Worth it," he said, and licked his lips.

She nearly came again. "Please come here."

He rose to his feet and her hands went to his stomach, sliding beneath his shirt to feel the heat of his hard abs. So much to touch, and the question became up or down . . .

His eyes were dark and heated, flickering with amusement as he read the indecision on her face.

"I'm not exactly sure what to do with you," she whispered.

"I could make a few suggestions."

She laughed a little nervously but let her hands glide up his torso, shoving his shirt up as she went. He was so beautifully made . . . "Off," she said softly.

He had the shirt gone in less than a heartbeat and she soaked up the sight of his broad shoulders and chest while her fingers played at the waistband of his jeans. They were loose enough that she could dip in and—

"Oh," she breathed, sucking in a breath as she encountered *much* more than she'd bargained for.

His hot—and amused—gaze held hers. On the surface, he was calm and steady and unflappable as always, but there was an underlying erotic tension in every line of his body, a sense that he was holding back, keeping his latent sexuality in check.

She popped the top button of his Levi's.

And then the second.

And then she'd freed him entirely, pushing his knit boxers aside and all his glory sprung into her hand— and there was a lot of glory. "Finn?"

His voice was rough and husky. "Yeah?"

"I think I figured out what I want to do with you."

It involved the condom that he luckily had in his wallet and her leaning back on the cold tile of her bathroom countertop, but they managed.

And when he slid deep and then grasped her ass in his two big hands and roughly pulled her closer so that he went even deeper, she arched her spine and let her head fall back and felt more alive than she'd felt in far too long. She got chills all over her body and with a wordless murmur, Finn brought her upright so that she was pressed tight to his warm chest. He wrapped his arms around her and she could feel her toes curl. She clenched tight, eliciting a groan from him, and held on. She knew she was digging her nails into his back but she couldn't stop, couldn't breathe . . . "Finn—"

"I know." His hands slid south, cupping her ass, protecting her from the tile. When he did something diabolically clever with those long fingers, she came in a giant, unexpected burst.

From somewhere outside of herself she felt Finn lose control as well. They ended up smashed up against one another, gripping each other hard, faces pressed together, breathing like lunatics.

They stayed like that for a few minutes and then slowly separated. She flopped back against the mirror, not caring that it was chilly against her overheated skin.

Finn sagged against the counter like he wasn't all that sturdy himself. He made quite the sight, shirtless, his jeans opened and dangerously low.

Sexy as hell. She'd do something about it but she felt like a boneless rag doll.

A very sated one. "I'm hoping it was the antiseptic spray," she managed.

"I'm hoping not," Finn said.

She needed to move but couldn't find her limbs to save her life. Finn didn't seem to have the same problem, he used his arms to lean over her and kiss her, eyes open like maybe he was taking her vitals.

She quivered for more. Good God. Since when was she addicted to sex?

Finn caught the look in her eyes and he laughed low in his throat. Sexy as hell. "Give me a minute," he said, voice husky.

She arched a brow, impressed. "Just one?"

"Maybe one and a half," he said, his gaze dropping to her mouth. "Tops."

Her good parts actually fluttered. *Seriously, what was wrong with her?*

"How's the road rash?" he asked, helping her down off the counter and rewrapping her up in the towel.

It took her a moment to get her brain organized enough to even remember what he was talking about. "Good."

"Liar." His voice was quiet and very, very sexy. She wondered if he'd ever considered a side job as a phone sex operator. He'd be fantastic at it. Or maybe he could just read her a book, any book at all . . .

His phone buzzed once more and he blew out a sigh. "That's twice. I'm sorry, I have to look." He pulled his phone from his pocket and glanced at the screen.

A frown creased his brow as he accessed a text.

And then his easy demeanor vanished. He rose to his feet.

"What's the matter?" she asked.

He pulled her towel back around her, tucking it in between her breasts, stopping to brush a sweet kiss to her lips. "I'm sorry. I have to go. Sean's in trouble."

Her heart stopped. "Do you need help?"

"No, I've got it. We've been around this block before, more times than I can count."

"But . . ." She ran her gaze down his body, letting it catch on the unmistakable bulge behind his button fly. "Now?"

"Yeah." He ran the pad of his thumb along her jaw and kissed her again. "Thanks for giving me a taste of you," he murmured against her mouth. "I already want another."

And then he was gone, leaving her sitting there,

mouth open, blinking like a land-locked fish at the open doorway he'd just vanished through.

"I want a taste of you too," she said to the empty void he'd left behind. She looked around her at the steamy bathroom. "I don't even know what just happened," she told it.

But she totally did—she'd just complicated things even more. And in an irreversible way, too.

Dammit, she was supposed to be fun whispering him. Instead, she'd fun whispered herself!

Chapter 16

#MyBad

Finn took the stairs rather than wait for the elevator, and then jogged across the courtyard to the pub, his body practically vibrating with adrenaline.

He could still hear Pru's soft, breathy, whimpery pants in his ear. She'd stilled for his touch like she'd been afraid it would all stop too soon.

She'd even begged him. *Please, Finn, don't stop . . .*

If Sean hadn't called, they'd have moved to her bed by now and be in the throes of round two.

Not once in the past eight years since his life had changed so drastically had he'd had such a wildly hot, crazy sex-capade, but Pru brought it out in him. There was no denying that he felt more alive when he was with her than he'd felt in . . . well, shit.

A fucking long time.

There'd been few opportunities when he was busy

working 24/7 and trying to keep Sean on the straight and narrow.

But Pru had gotten under his skin, and like her, he wanted more. So much more. He wanted to know her secrets, the ones that sometimes put those shadows in her eyes. He wanted to know why she wanted to bring him fun and adventure, but didn't seem to feel like she deserved it as well. He wanted to know what made her tick. And more than anything, he wanted to taste her again.

Every inch of her.

He wanted to see more of her and he had no idea how she felt about that. For the first time in he had no idea how long, he was thinking about more than the bottom line of the pub.

He was thinking about a future, with an adventurous, frustrating, warm, sexy woman he couldn't seem to get enough of.

Skipping the crowded pub, he entered directly into his office, while thumbing through his email on his phone. "So what the hell's so important that—" He broke off as a sound permeated through his thick skull—the soft sigh of a woman experiencing pleasure.

Sexual pleasure.

Jerking his head up, he took in the sight on his couch and whipped back to the door, which he slammed behind him. Grinding his back teeth into powder, he strode around the courtyard to the pub door and went directly to the bar.

Scott, the night's bartender, started toward him but Finn waved him off and grabbed a shot glass to serve himself.

He was trying to lose himself in the happy sounds of the crowd around him, pouring a double when Sean appeared, shirtless, shoeless, buttoning his Levi's.

Behind him was a tall, curvy blonde in a little sundress, her hair tousled, her high-heeled sandals dangling from her hand. Shooting Finn a wry smile, she turned to Sean, ran a hand up his chest and around his neck and leaned in to give him a lingering kiss. "Thanks for a good time, baby." With a last lingering look in Finn's direction, she padded out.

"Fuck," Finn said.

"Exactly," Sean said with a sated grin.

Finn shook his head and headed down the interior hallway to his office.

Sean followed.

"What the hell's the matter with you?" Finn asked.

"Absolutely nothing."

"I'm working real hard here at not chucking this shot glass at your head," Finn said. "You want to come up with better than that and you want to do it quick."

Sean blinked. "What the hell's your problem? Why are you raining on my parade?"

"What the hell's *my* problem?" Finn sucked in a breath for calm. It didn't work. "You texted me that you had an emergency. I dropped everything and race over here to find you fucking some girl on the couch in *my* office."

"I told you, you have the better office."

Finn stared at him, and some of his genuine temper and absolutely zero humor of the situation must have finally gotten through to Sean because he lifted his hands. "Look, you got back here faster than I thought you would, all right? And Ashley just happened to stop by and . . . well, one thing led to another."

Finn tossed back the smoothest Scotch in the place and barely felt the burn. "You told me there was an emergency. That you needed me. Exactly how long did you expect me to take getting here?"

"Longer than sixty seconds," Sean said. "I mean I'm good, but even I need at least five minutes." He flashed a grin.

Finn resisted the urge to strangle him. Barely. "Emergency implies death and destruction and mayhem," he said. "Like, say, our *last* emergency. When dad died."

The easy smile fell from Sean's face, replaced by surprise and then guilt, followed by shame. "Oh shit," he said. "Shit, I didn't think—"

"And there's our problem, Sean," Finn said. "You never do."

Sean's mouth tightened. "No, actually, that's not the real problem. Let's hear it again, shall we? You're the grown-up. I'm just the stupid problem child."

"You're hardly a child."

"But I'm still a problem," Sean said. "Always have been to you."

"Bullshit," Finn said. "Get your head out of your own ass and stop feeling sorry for yourself. Now what the hell's the emergency?"

Sean paused. "It was more of a pub thing," he said vaguely, no longer meeting Finn's gaze.

And a very bad feeling crept into Finn's gut. "What did you do?"

"It's more what I didn't do . . ."

"Spit it out, Sean."

"Okay, okay. But before you blow a gasket, you should know. It's not as bad as the time I nearly burnt the place down by accident. Let's keep it in perspective, all right?"

"Accident?" Finn asked. "You opened the place after hours to have a party with your idiot friends and were lighting Jell-O shots when you managed to catch the kitchen on fire. How exactly is that an *accident*?"

"Well, who knew that Jell-O was so flammable?"

Finn stared at him, at an utter loss. "This is a fucking joke to you, all of it."

"No, it's not."

"Yes, it is. You think I'm just the asshole making you toe the line. I'm trying to give you a life here, Sean, a way to make a living and take care of yourself in case something happens to me."

Sean laughed. *Laughed*. The sound harsh in the quiet room. "You're not dad, Finn. I don't need you to give me a life. I can do that for myself. Contrary to popular belief, I can take care of myself."

"Because you've done a great job of it so far?" Finn asked.

"Fuck you," Sean said and walked out.

"What's the damn emergency?" Finn yelled after him.

But Sean was gone.

This left Finn in charge of the place for the night instead of getting to go back up to 3B where he'd left his mind, and maybe a good chunk of his heart as well.

The next morning was Sunday and despite it being a weekend, Finn was back at the pub. He was working his way through some of the never-ending paperwork that seemed to multiply daily when Sean appeared.

"Where have you been?" Finn asked, hating himself for sounding like a nagging grandma.

Sean ran his hand over his bedhead hair. "Slept on the roof."

Finn shook his head. "Bet you froze your nuts off."

"Just about." Sean paused. "I shouldn't have walked away last night. I'm sorry for that."

"Just tell me the damn emergency already," Finn said.

Sean's jaw went tight, a muscle ticking. A very unusual sight, and a tell that he was actually feeling stressed, something Finn hadn't known his brother could even feel.

Sean pulled two envelopes from his back pocket. "You know how I said I wanted to help you with the business side of things and you said I had to start at the bottom, and I said like the mail room? And you said we don't have a mail room, but yes a little bit like that?"

"It was a joke," Finn said. "Because you think you just jump in but there's a learning curve. So I suggested you start by handling our mail and our accounts payable. And you agreed as long as I didn't come along behind you to check up on you."

"Didn't need dad in the house looking over my shoulder," Sean said.

"Actually, if I'd been dad, I'd have used my fists, or whatever else was handy and just beat the shit out of you," Finn said. "Or have you forgotten?"

Temper flashed in Sean's eyes. Temper, and something else that he got a hold of before Finn could. He didn't speak for a moment, which was rare for Sean. He just stood there, fists clenched at his side, working his jaw muscles. "Fuck it. Fuck this," he finally said and started to turn away but stopped. "No, you know what? Fuck you. Sideways."

"Mature."

But Sean wasn't playing. He shoved a finger in Finn's face. "You think I've forgotten which one of us dad got off on beating up? You think I don't remember at night when I close my eyes that you took it for me, every single time? That I don't know you made sure you were between him and me so I'd be safe? That I survived only because of you? That I'm *still* surviving because of you? You think I don't know that I'm a fuckup who's only here with a semblance of a normal life because you gave it to me?"

Okay, so the something else in Sean's gaze had been grief and remembered horror. And Finn shouldn't have tried to be glib about it, there was nothing glib about how they'd grown up. "I didn't mean to take this there," he said quietly. "You're not a—"

"I forgot to pay our liquor license." Sean's face was hard. Blank. "I forgot and it was due today."

Finn stared at him. "That was the one thing I reminded you of two months ago when you took on the bills."

"The envelope fell behind my desk and got lost. And it wasn't alone. The property tax on the house was back there too and that one's now past due."

"Are you kidding me?"

"Do I look like I'm kidding?" Sean inhaled a deep breath, spread out his arms and shook his head. "See?

You were right. I really am just a fuckup. You should demote me back to—"

"What? Sweep boy?" Finn found his own temper. And hell if he was going to let Sean default to his favorite thing—self-destruction, just because it was easier than growing up. "You wanted to do this, Sean. You wanted in. And now you're telling me what, things are too hard, you're too busy having fun that you can't get your head out of your ass and grow up?"

Sean's eyes narrowed. "Guess so."

Finn stared at him waiting for regret, for an apology, for any-fucking-thing, but nothing came. Just Sean's hooded gaze, body braced for a fight, all sullen 'tude. Finn shook his head. "Fine. You win."

"What does that mean?"

"It means I need some air," Finn said and walked out the door to the courtyard.

It was late morning and unusually warm. Summer was in full swing, which in San Francisco usually meant a sweatshirt sixty-five-ish and fingers crossed for a hope to get into the seventies.

But now, in direct opposition to his mood, it was sunny and warm, and it didn't suit him in the least.

He had no idea where he'd intended to go, only knowing he was going somewhere, needing to vent the ugly inside him, the ugly his dad had bequeathed him.

The gym maybe. He'd go punch the shit out of a bag at the gym.

But to do that, he'd have to walk past Pru standing there watching him, a look on her face that told him she'd heard everything.

Chapter 17

#ThereAren'tEnoughCookiesForThis

Pru stared into Finn's face, wishing like hell she could go back and vanish before he caught sight of her, or barring that, at least do something to ease the pain and anger in his eyes.

"Did you get all of that or do you need me to repeat some of it?" he asked.

"I didn't mean to get any of it," she said. "It was an accidental eavesdrop."

He blew out a sigh, shook his head, and stared over her head at the fountain.

Regret slashed through her. She'd been caught eavesdropping many times, all of them accidental. Once when she'd been young, she'd caught her parents going at it on the dining room table with gusto. It'd been ten o'clock at night and she'd been fast asleep only to wake up thirsty. Not wanting to disturb her parents, she'd made her own way to the kitchen.

At first glance she'd smiled because she'd thought that her dad was tickling her mom. Her mom had loved it when he'd done that, and they'd touched often.

But she'd never seen naked tickling before . . .

Later when Pru had been a teenager, she'd come home from school to find her parents at the table with their neighbor, Mr. Snyder, who was also their accountant, talking about something called bankruptcy. Her mom had been crying, her dad looking shell-shocked.

And then there'd been the night her grandpa had shown up where she'd been spending the night at a friend's. Weird, since she'd called her mom and dad for a ride, not her grandpa. She'd wanted to go home because her friends had decided to sneak in some boys and she hadn't felt comfortable with the attention she'd been getting from one of them. He'd been in her math class, and was always leaning over her shoulder pretending to stare at her work when he was really just staring at her breasts.

The other reason it'd been weird for her grandpa to show up was because she hadn't seen him in years. Not since he and her dad had been estranged for reasons she'd never known. And her dad and her grandpa being estranged meant that Pru was estranged by default.

So why was he at her friend's house?

The night had gone on to become a real-life nightmare, the kind you never woke up from because she'd listened to her grandpa explain to her friend's mom that he'd come to tell his granddaughter that her parents were dead, that her father had been past the legal drinking limit. He'd crossed the center median in the road and had hit another car head on, clipping a second along with the people on the sidewalk.

Pru did her best not to think about that moment, but it crept in at the most unexpected times. Like when she was in the mall and passed by a department store in front of the perfume aisle and caught a whiff of the scent her mom had always worn. Or when sometimes late at night if there was a storm and she got unnerved, she'd wish for her dad to come into her room like he always had, sit on the bed and pull her into his arms and sing silly made-up songs at the top of his lungs to drown out the wind.

Nope . . . eavesdropping had never worked out for her. And when she'd heard Sean and Finn yelling at each other through Finn's open office window, she honestly hadn't meant to listen in. Now she couldn't un-hear what she'd heard. What she *could* do was be there for them. Because this whole thing, their fight, their being parentless, Finn having to raise Sean, all of it, was *her* family's doing. She swallowed hard. "I'm sorry, Finn."

He just shook his head, clearly still pissed off. "Not your fault."

Maybe not directly but she felt guilty all the same. But telling him the truth now when he was already lit up with temper wouldn't help him. It would hurt him.

And that's the last thing she'd ever do.

At her silence, he focused in on her. "How are you doing, are you—"

"Totally fine," she said. "The road rash is healing up already."

Something in his eyes lit with amusement. "Good, but this time I actually meant from when we—"

"That's fine too," she said quickly and huffed out a sigh when he laughed. She looked around for a distraction and saw a couple of women talking about throwing some coins into the fountain. Pru nodded her head over there. "You know about the legend?"

"Of course. That myth brings us more foot traffic than our daily specials."

"You ever . . . ?"

"Hell no," he said emphatically.

She managed a smile. "What's the matter, you don't believe in true love?"

His gaze held hers for a beat. "I try not to mess with stuff that isn't for me."

She couldn't imagine what his growing-up years had been like or the hell he'd been through but she managed a small smile. "Maybe you shouldn't knock something unless you've tried it."

"And you've tried it?" he challenged.

"Oh . . ." She let out a little laugh. "Not exactly. I'm pretty sure that stuff isn't for me either."

His gaze went serious again and before he began a conversation she didn't want to have, she spoke quickly. "I really didn't mean to overhear your fight with Sean. I was just wondering if I could help with whatever was wrong before I went to work."

"What's wrong is that he's an idiot."

"If it helps, I think he feels really bad," she said.

"He always does."

Her heart ached for him as she took in the tension in every line of his body. "You guys do that a lot?" she asked. "Fight like that?"

He slid his hands into his pockets. "Sometimes. We're not all that good with holding back. We sure as hell never did master the art of the silent treatment."

"My family never did either," she said. "Silence in my house meant someone had stopped breathing—thanks to a pillow being held over their face."

Finn gave her a barely there smile, definitely devoid of its usual wattage. "Was there a lot of fighting?" he asked.

"My parents were high school sweethearts. They were together twenty years, most of them spent in a very tiny but homey Santa Cruz bungalow house, where we were practically on top of each other all the time." She sighed wistfully, missing that house so much. "Great house. But seriously, half the time my mom and dad were like siblings, at each other over every little thing. And the other half of the time, they were more in love with each other every day." The ache of losing them had faded but it still could stab at her with a white hot poker of pain out of the blue when she least expected it, like now.

"Sounds pretty good, he said.

"It was." *He'd beaten the shit out of you . . .* The words were haunting her and her gaze ran over Finn's tough, rugged features. It hurt to picture him as a helpless kid standing between a grown man and his little brother, taking whatever punishment had been meant for Sean to spare him the pain of it, and she had to close her eyes against the images that brought.

A hand closed around hers. She opened her eyes as Finn tugged her into him. He stroked the hair from her face and looked down into her eyes. "You sure you're okay?"

He'd just had a huge blowout with Sean and he was

asking about her. She swallowed hard and nodded. It's you—"

He set a finger to her lips. "I'm fine."

The two women at the fountain were laughing and chatting. "Think it's really true?" one of them asked. "If we wish for true love, it'll happen?"

"Well, not with a penny," the other one said, eyeing the change her friend was about to toss in. "How many times have I told you, you can't be cheap about the important stuff."

Her friend rolled her eyes and fished through her purse. "I've got a quarter. Is that better?"

"This is for love, Izzy. Love! Would you buy a guy on the clearance rack? No, you would not."

"Um, I wouldn't buy a guy at all."

"It's a metaphor! You want him new and shiny and *expensive*."

Izzy went back into her purse. "A buck fifty in change," she muttered. "That's all I've got. It's going to have to be enough." She closed her eyes, her brow furrowed in concentration, then she opened her eyes and tossed in the money.

Both women held still a beat.

"Nothing," Izzy said in disappointment. "Told you." She turned away from her friend to stalk off and ran smack into Sean, who'd come out of the pub.

His hands went to her arms to catch from falling to her ass. He looked down into her face with concern. "You all right, darlin'?"

Izzy blinked up at him looking dazed. "Um . . ."

Her friend stuck her head in between them. "Yes,"

she told Sean. "She's okay. She just can't talk in the presence of a hot guy. Especially one she wished for."

He smiled, though it was muted. "You work at the flower shop, right?" he asked Izzy.

She nodded emphatically.

"Well come into the pub and have a drink any time," he said.

Izzy gave another emphatic nod.

"That means yes. And thank you," her friend translated and dragged Izzy away. "Oh-em-gee, the fountain totally works!"

Pru watched them go and had to laugh. Luck was where you made it for yourself and she knew that. She'd wished for love for Finn, and she still wanted that for him but she was realizing that would mean letting him go.

She had to let him go.

Sean looked at Finn. "Need to talk to you," he said.

Finn, face blank, nodded.

"I'll meet you inside," Sean said.

Finn nodded again.

When Sean walked way, Finn turned to Pru.

"Work calls," she said with a small smile.

"Story of my life," he said. "About last night."

Her heart skipped a beat.

"We were onto something."

Her nipples went hard. "Were we?"

"Yeah. And you liked it too."

She felt herself blush a little. "Maybe a little."

"Just a little, huh? Because I still have your fingernail imprints in my scalp." He was out-and-out smiling now, a naughty sort of smile that made her thighs quiver. "I wasn't finished with you, Pru," he said softly. "I had plans."

Oh boy. "Maybe I had plans, too."

"Yeah?" Closing the gap between them, one of his hands went to her hip, the other slid up her back to anchor her to him. "Tell me. Tell me slowly and in great detail."

She laughed and fisted her hands in his shirt, but just before her lips touched his, someone cleared their throat behind them.

"Dammit," she whispered, her lips ghosting against Finn's. "Why do we keep getting interrupted?"

"That is the question," he murmured.

With a sigh she pulled free and turned. "Jake," she said in surprise. "What are you doing here?"

In Jake's lap was a box and on top of that box sat Thor, one ear up, one ear down, his scruffy hair looking even more thin and scruffy than usual, sticking up in tufts on his head.

"Brought you the last box," Jake said. "Never seen anyone stretch a move out so long."

"Yes, well, hiring movers was cut from the budget." Pru scooped up her Thor, kissing him right on the snout. He panted happily, wriggling to get closer, bicycling his front paws in the air, making her laugh and hug him.

"I'm taking him for a grooming at South Bark," Jake said. "He's past due."

"Also cut from the budget," Pru said. But she traded Thor for the box. "Thanks."

"I'll bring him to work when he's finished," Jake said.

And then he didn't roll away.

Pru gave him a long look, but Jake's picture was in the dictionary under *pig-headed* so he didn't budge. "You're going to be late," he told Pru in his boss voice.

With a sigh, she turned to Finn. "I picked up an extra Sunday shift today. I've got to go. Hope you have a good day."

"In case it's our last you mean?"

"You don't think Sean will get the license paid tomorrow?" she asked.

"If he wants to live, he will." But Finn's attention was on Jake.

Pru forced a smile. "Okay, so we're all going off to our own corners now, yes?"

"Go to work, Pru," Jake said.

"Um—"

"It's okay." Finn gave her hand a squeeze. "Knock 'em dead today," he said.

Right. Dammit. With nothing else she could do, she lifted the box of her stuff and walked away from the only two men to have ever earned a spot in her heart. She just hoped they didn't kill one another.

Chapter 18

#BeamMeUpScotty

Finn watched Pru make her way toward the elevator with her box before he turned back to Jake.

Both he and Thor were watching him watch Pru.

Jake was brows up, the picture of nonchalance. "What's going on?"

"Nothing much," Finn said.

Jake took that in and nodded. "You've got an arm on you. The other night at the game you nearly saved our asses—not that anyone could've actually saved our asses."

Finn shrugged. "I played some in college."

"You going to keep playing for us?"

"Depends."

"On what?" Jake asked.

"On if this sudden interest in my ball-playing abilities is in any way related to the woman we both just watched walk away," he said.

"About ninety-nine percent of it, yeah," Jake said.

Okay, so the guy got brownie points for honesty. "Why don't you tell me what you really want to know," Finn suggested.

"I don't want to know anything," Jake said. "I want *you* to know that if you make her so much as shed a single tear, I'll break every bone in your body and then feed your organs to the pigeons. I mean, sure, I'd have to hire it out to do it, but I'm connected so don't think I won't."

Finn stared at him. "You forget your meds or something?"

"Nope."

"Okay, then, thanks for letting me know," he said and turned to go.

Jake rolled into his path. "I'm not shittin' you."

"Also good to know." Finn cocked his head. "I'm going to go out on a limb here and guess that you already had a shot at her and you blew it."

"Why would you think that?"

"Because you just threatened me with death and dismemberment. Only one reason to do that—you fucked up somehow."

Jake stared him down for a minute. He might be in a chair but Finn got the sense he could more than handle himself.

"That might be partially true," the guy finally said.

Finn wrestled with his conscience a moment. "I'd say something helpful here, like it's 'never too late' or 'you can fix any mistake,' because truthfully, I like you. But—"

"—But you like *her* too," Jake said.

"But I like her too," Finn agreed firmly, not willing to back down, feeling a little bit like Thor did about his prized dog cookies. "Much more than I like you."

"It's a bad idea," Jake said. "You and her."

"That's for me and Pru to decide."

Thor jumped down from Jake's lap, walked over to Finn and put his paws on his shins to be picked up—which Finn did.

Then it was apparently Jake's turn to wrestle with his conscience. "What the hell. The damn dog likes you?"

Finn shrugged and gave Thor a quick cuddle before setting him back down on Jake's lap.

Jake muttered something to himself that sounded like "she bit off more than she can chew this time" and turned his chair to roll off.

"Yeah," Finn said to his back.

"Yeah what?"

"Yeah I'm going to keep playing on your team. But I want to buy new jerseys."

Jake rolled back around to face him. "Why?"

Because it would make Pru happy. "You got a problem with SF Tours splashed across everyone's backs in bold letters?"

"Not in the least." Jake paused. "I suppose you also want O'Riley's on there somewhere."

"It'd be nice."

Jake stared at Finn for a beat before nodding. "Our next game's tomorrow night," he said and again he made to leave but didn't. "About Pru and me. We didn't work out for one simple reason."

"What's that?"

Jake looked behind him to make sure Pru wasn't standing there, which normally would've made Finn smile but he wanted to know the answer to this question shockingly bad.

"I made a mistake with her," Jake said, and then grimaced. "Okay, more than one, but the only one you need to know is that she's strong and resilient and smart, so much so that I believed she didn't need anyone, and certainly not me. It must have showed since she called me out on it. She said we couldn't be intimate anymore because I wasn't in love with her and she didn't love me either, at least not in that way. To my shame, I didn't realize that I hurt her by so readily agreeing, by not giving much thought to how she felt about splitting." He paused. "Pru doesn't do casual. She can't. Her heart's too damn big."

"Are you trying to scare me off?"

"Yes," Jake said bluntly. "I hurt her," he said again. "Don't you do the same, don't you even fucking think about it."

"Or the aforementioned death and dismemberment?" Finn asked, only half kidding.

Jake didn't even crack a smile.

Monday morning Pru was waiting outside the county courthouse building, hoping she was in the right place at the right time. When she saw Sean heading for the steps, she pushed away from the wall with relief.

He stopped in surprise at the sight of her. "Hey, Trouble," he said. "What are you doing here?"

"Helping you fix your mess." She smiled at his

confusion. "You here to get the liquor license all square, right?" she asked.

He blew out a sigh, looking disgusted. "Finn told you I screwed up."

"No," Pru said quietly. "He wouldn't. I . . . overheard you arguing."

"Yeah." Sean grimaced and scrubbed a hand down his face. "Sorry. I just hate disappointing him."

"If that's the case, why do you give him such a hard time?"

Sean shrugged. "It's how we show affection."

Pru shook her head with a low laugh. "Boys are weird."

"Hey, at least we don't kick and scratch and pull hair when we fight."

"If that's how you think girls fight, you're with the wrong girls."

He grinned. "You know, I like you, Pru. I like you for Finn. You've got his back. He'd say he doesn't need that but he's wrong. We all need that. He know you're here?"

"No, and he doesn't have to know," she said. "Especially since I'm going to save your ass."

"What do you mean?"

"Follow me." She led him inside the offices, by-passed the public sign-in area and waved through the glass partition to a guy at a desk.

The guy was Kyle, Jake's brother.

Kyle gave her a chin nod and hit a button that had the door buzzing open to them.

"Hey, cutie," he said and took a look at Sean. "What's up?"

"I've got a friend who didn't pay their liquor license bill in time," she said. "What can you do for me?"

"First, tell your friend he's an idiot."

She looked into Sean's tight face. "I think he's aware," she said with a small smile.

"Second, have a seat. You're going to owe me," he told Pru. "Caramel chocolates from Ghirardelli. You know the ones."

"Consider it done," she said and ten minutes later they were back on the front steps of the building.

"You're a lifesaver," Sean marveled. "And a super hero."

"I'll add both to my résumé. Maybe it'll get me a raise."

Sean laughed and hugged her. "Dump my brother and marry me."

She laughed because they both knew he wasn't the marrying type, at least not yet.

There'd been a time where she would've said the same thing about herself, but she knew now that she was changing. A part of her *did* want to let love into her life again. Maybe even have a family someday.

How terrifying was that?

Finn made sure to get to the softball field well before the start of their game.

He had no idea why he was looking forward to it, there were a million things he should be doing instead. But he lowered his sunglasses and scanned the area for Pru.

"She's not here yet," Jake said, rolling up to his side.

"Who?" Finn asked casually.

But not casually enough because Jake snorted.

Giving up on pride, Finn asked, "Is she coming?"

"I'm not privy to her schedule."

"Bullshit."

Jake smiled. "Jealous of me, O'Riley?"

"Do I need to be?"

Jake's smile spread.

Shit.

"Got the new jerseys," Jake said. "You work fast."

Finn shrugged like no big deal. It'd only cost an arm and a leg and a huge favor to get them done in one day.

"I like the SF Tours across the backs," Jake said.

"Good."

"Could've done without the O'Rileys on the breast."

Finn smiled and didn't respond. He was looking forward to seeing his name on Pru's breast.

"What's going on with you two?" Jake wanted to know.

"You ask her?"

"Hell no. I like living."

This gave Finn some satisfaction—that she'd kept what was between them to herself. But then again, that could be because she didn't think there was anything between them.

"I meant what I said yesterday," Jake said.

"About the death and dismemberment?"

"About you and her not becoming a thing."

That's when Finn felt it, a low level of electro-current hummed through him. Turning, he leveled his eyes on Pru and watched as she found him from across the field and tripped over her own feet.

He read her lips and smiled because she was swearing to herself as she picked up speed.

"Sorry I'm late!" she exclaimed breathlessly, like maybe once she'd seen them talking, she'd run over as fast as she could. Hand to her chest, the other holding onto Thor's leash, she divided a look between them. "So . . . what's going on?"

Finn opened his mouth but Jake beat him to the punch. "Game's about to start. Head or tails for home advantage."

Pru slid him a long look and then leveled that same look on Finn, who tried his best to look innocent. And he was actually pretty sure he *was* innocent since he had no idea what was going on any more than she did.

"Tails," she finally said. "It's always tails."

It was heads.

And . . . they had their asses handed to them like last time. But Kasey got a two base hit, and Abby caught a fly ball, and Pru got two base hits.

And once again, Finn had the time of his life.

Afterward, they all made their way back to O'Riley's. Sean immediately pulled him aside.

"Your girlfriend's wearing your name on her breast. Nicely done. You're faster than I gave you credit for, Grandpa."

"The entire team is wearing our logo, not just Pru," Finn said.

"Interesting."

"What?"

"You didn't deny the girlfriend thing," Sean noted.

Finn didn't take the bait and Sean sighed. "Yeah, yeah, you're still pissed off at me. Newsflash, I'm pissed off too."

"I didn't do shit to you."

"I know," Sean said. "I meant I was pissed off at me. For disappointing you."

Finn stilled and then shook his head. "I know you didn't mean to disappoint me."

"But I did. And not only that, I let you down. I let *us* down." Sean paused. "Earlier today, I handled the liquor license problem with Pru's help."

And then Sean told him the entire story of how Pru had been waiting for him and had smoothed the way with ease.

While Finn was still processing that, marveling over the lengths that she'd gone to help without mentioning it or wanting any credit for it, Sean went on.

"After that I went to pay the property taxes. I was there at their offices when they opened at ten."

"Wow," Finn said. "I didn't know you've even seen ten a.m."

Sean shoved his hands into his pocket and looked a little sheepish. "Yeah, I know. It was a first, and believe me it wasn't pretty. And it was worse than having to go to the damn DMV office, too. Got there right on time and had to take a number. Sixty-nine." He flashed a small smile. "I held up my ticket but no one else in the place was amused. The old lady who had number seventy flipped me the bird. She looked like this sweet little old granny and there she was, telling me I'm number one, can you believe it?"

In spite of himself, Finn laughed. "It's true. You are number one."

Sean's smile faded. "I know."

Regret slashed through Finn. "I didn't mean it like that."

"Yeah, you did," Sean said. "And I deserve it. I'm a fuckup, right?"

"Okay, I'm officially taking that back."

For a beat, Sean's expression went unguarded and filled with relief, making Finn feel even worse. There were times, lots of them, when he wanted nothing more than to wrap his hands around Sean's neck and squeeze.

But more than that, he wanted to never be like his dad. Ever. "So . . . how much were the late fees and penalties on the tax bill?"

Sean grimaced. "You remember Jacklyn?"

"The stripper you dated for a whole weekend last year?" Finn asked.

"Exotic dancer. And she doesn't do that anymore."

Oh shit. "Sean, tell me she doesn't now work at the property tax office."

Another grimace. "Well I could tell you that, but it'd be a lie."

Sean had done his charm-the-panties-off-the-girl and then pulled his also usual I'm-moving-to-Iceland. Or maybe it'd been it's-not-you-it's-me. Either way, he'd dumped her. The only reason Finn even remembered was because Jacklyn had then pulled the crazy card.

She'd stalked Sean. It hadn't been all that hard either, Sean had no sense of secret and always put himself out there, one hundred percent. It probably hadn't taken any effort at all for her to find out about the pub.

She'd come in and had climbed on top of one of the tables, stripping and crying at the same time, telling everyone what a scumbag Sean was.

It'd been a spectacle of massive proportions.

"What happened?" Finn asked. "She refused to let you pay up?"

"Not exactly," Sean said.

"Then what exactly?"

Sean looked . . . embarrassed? Impossible, he never got embarrassed. "She said I could renew on one condition," he said. "If I got up on her counter and did a striptease like she'd done at *my* place of work."

"Well, you gotta hand it to her," Finn said. "It's ingenious."

"Diabolical, you mean," Sean said.

"Whatever, but your next sentence better be 'so I totally got up on that counter and did a striptease for her.'"

"Did I mention the place was full?" Sean asked. "And that there were old ladies in there? *Old ladies*, Finn. I took one look at them and things . . . shriveled."

"And?" Finn asked.

"And . . . I didn't want to take my clothes off with shrinkage going on!"

Finn pressed the heels of his hands into his eye sockets, but it didn't work. His brain was still leaking out. Slowly and painfully. "Fine, I'll go down there and talk to her and straighten things out."

"Because that's what you do," Sean said. "You straighten things out. I fuck it all and you come along and clean it back up again, right?"

"Sean—"

"No. I'm done with that shit, Finn," Sean said. "I'm done being the idiot baby brother who needs saving. For once, for fucking once, I want to do the right thing. I want to save you." He shook his head. "No, I didn't get up on the counter. But I apologized to her for being a dick. And then I paid the penalties and late fees, all from my personal account. Our property taxes are current and will stay that way, and it won't happen again."

"Wow," Finn said. "That's great. And thanks." He paused. "From your personal account, huh?"

"Yeah and that hurt, man." Sean rubbed his chest like he was physically pained. "It hurt bad."

Finn smiled. "Also good."

"Now about your girlfriend," Sean said.

Finn raised a brow. He knew Sean was fishing. He had baited the hook and was going to keep saying "girlfriend" until he got a rise out of Finn.

Not going to happen.

"I like her," Sean said quietly.

Again, not what Finn had expected. He'd do just about anything for Sean, and had. But he didn't think he could walk away from Pru.

Not even for his brother.

Sean shook his head. "No, man, I mean I like her for *you*."

The scary part was that they'd finally agreed on something because Finn liked Pru for him too. So much so that at the end of the night—which was really three in the morning, he found himself outside her front door. Not wanting to scare her to death with the late hour, he texted her.

You up?

It took her less than a minute to respond.

Is this a booty call?

He stared down at the words and felt like the biggest kind of asshole on the planet. He was in the middle of texting back an apology when she texted him again.

Cuz I want it to be . . .

He was still smiling when her next text came in:

There's a key hidden on the top of the doorjamb.

He let himself in, crawled into bed with her and pulled her warm, sleeping form in close.

"Finn?" she murmured sleepily, not opening her eyes.

Well, who the hell else? "Shh," he said, brushing his mouth over her temple. "Go back to sleep."

"But there's a man in my bed." She still hadn't opened her eyes, but she did wind her arms around him tight, pressing her deliciously soft curves up against his body, sliding one of her legs in between his. "Mmm," she said. "A *hard* man . . ."

And quickly getting harder. "I didn't mean for this to be a booty call—"

"Finn?"

"Yeah?"

"Shut up." And she rocked against him so that his thigh rasped over the damp heat between hers, taking what she wanted from him.

He loved that she'd figured out that her confidence and belief in herself was as sexy to him as her gorgeous body.

"Mm," she hummed in pleasure, rocking against him, making him even harder. "I wonder what to do about this . . ." she mused.

He rolled, tucking her beneath him, and buried himself deep. "Let me show you."

Chapter 19

#JustLikeThat

Typically as summer progressed and more tourists poured into San Francisco, Pru got buried in work. This summer was no different. She worked long days, during which time she dedicated most of her daydreams to one certain sexy Finn O'Riley and what he looked like in her bed.

And what he did to her in it . . .

"What are you thinking about?" Jake asked her at the end of a shift while she was doing paperwork. "You keep sighing."

"Um . . ." She struggled to come up with something not X-rated. "I'm thinking about how much of a slave driver you are."

"Uh huh," he said, not fooled. "You tell Finn yet?"

"I'm getting there," she said, her stomach tightening in panic and anxiety at the thought.

"Pru—"

"I know, I know!" She blew out a breath. "You don't have to say it. I'm stalling. Big time."

His voice was quiet, almost gentle. "You're really into him."

She closed her eyes and nodded.

His hand slipped into hers and he squeezed her fingers. "You want a chance with him."

She nodded again.

"Chica, to have that chance, you've got to tell him before your window of opportunity closes and things go too far." He waited until she looked at him. "Before you sleep with him or—"

Oh boy.

"—I've got this," she said. "I know what I'm doing."

But they both knew she had *no* idea what she was doing.

That night, Elle and Willa dragged Pru out for "ladies'" night.

They surprised her when they ended up at a lovely spa, snacking on cute little sandwiches and tea before deciding on their individual treatments.

Pru stared at the spa's menu, a little panicked over the luxury that she couldn't really afford.

"It's my treat," Elle said, covering the prices with her hand. "This was my idea. I owe Willa a birthday present."

Willa smiled. "Cuz I can't afford it either."

"But it's not my birthday," Pru said.

"Pretend," Elle said. "I want a mani/pedi and a Brazilian, and I don't like to primp alone."

Which is how Pru ended up with a mani/pedi and her very first Brazilian.

The next day it rained all day long. Pru joked to Jake that after eight long hours on the water—in the rain—she felt like Noah.

Jake felt no mercy at all. "Make the money now, chica. Come wintertime you'll be whining like Thor does for that mini chow across the street, the one who's got fifty pounds on him and would squash him like a grape if given the chance."

So she worked.

At the end of another crazy day, she changed out of her uniform into a sundress and left Pier 39. She was Thor-less. After a stunt where he'd rolled in pigeon poo for some mysterious reason that only made sense to himself, Jake had once again taken him to the South Bark Mutt Shop for grooming.

All Pru wanted to do was to go home and crawl into her bed. For once she was too tired to even dream about having Finn in that bed with her. She wouldn't be able to lift a finger. Or a tongue.

Not that she'd mind if he insisted on doing all the work . . .

But that fantasy would have to wait. She had an errand to run before getting home, hence the sundress. She wanted to look nice for her weekly visit.

She walked up the steps to the home where her grandpa lived and signed in to see him.

Michelle, the front desk receptionist waved at her. Michelle had worked there forever, so they were old friends.

"How is he today?" Pru asked her.

Michelle's easy smile faded. "Not gonna lie, it's a rough one, honey. He's agitated. He didn't like his lunch, he didn't like the weather, he didn't like wearing pants, the list goes on. He's feeling mean as a snake. You want to come back another day?"

But they both knew that the bad days far outweighed the good ones now, so there was no use in waiting or she might never see him. "I'll be fine."

Michelle nodded, eyes warm, mouth a little worried. "Holler if you need anything."

Pru took a deep breath, waved at Paul the orderly in the hallway, and entered her grandpa's room.

He was watching *Jeopardy!* and yelling at the TV. "Who is Queen Victoria, you jackass!" He picked up his cane and waved that too. "Who is Queen Victoria!"

"Hi, grandpa," Pru said.

"No one ever listens to me," he went on, dropping his cane to shake his fist at the TV. "No one ever listens."

Pru moved into his line of sight and picked up the cane for him, wondering if he would know her today. "It's me, Pru—"

"*You,*" he snapped, narrowing his eyes on her, snatching the cane from her hands. "You've got some nerve coming here, Missy, into my home."

"It's good to see you, Grandpa. You sound good, your cold's gone from last week, huh? How are you feeling?"

"I'm not telling you shit. You were a terrible influence on my son. You encouraged him to be a good time, to party, when you knew—" He jabbed the cane at her for emphasis. "It's your fault he's dead. You should be ashamed of yourself."

This hit her hard but she did her best to ignore the hurtful words. "Grandpa, it's Prudence." She purposely kept her voice low and calm so that maybe he would do the same.

No go.

"Oh I knew who you are. I knew you for what you were the first day I saw you," he said, "when Steven first brought you home. He said 'this is Vicky and I love her,' and I took one look into your laughing eyes and I knew. All you wanted to do was have fun and you didn't care what fell by the wayside. Well, I'll tell you what, our business fell by the wayside because he wanted to spend time with you, not that you even noticed. Our business went into the ground because of you, because you didn't care if he had to work—"

"Dad worked," Pru said. "He worked a lot. Mom just tried to get him to enjoy life when she could because he did work so hard—"

"You were trouble with a capital T, that's what you were," he snapped out. "And you still are. Told you that then and I'll tell you again. You're Trouble to the very bone."

She'd frozen to the spot. She'd had no idea that her grandpa had called her mom Trouble, that he thought she'd been a bad influence on her dad simply because she'd wanted him to have a life outside of work.

The irony of this was not lost on her.

What *was* lost on her was how long she must have stood there, mouth open, gaping, letting old wounds reopen and fester because her grandpa grabbed something from the tray by his bed and chucked it at her.

She ducked and a fork skidded across the floor.

"Okay," she said, raising her hands. "That wasn't nice. Grandpa, I'm not my mom. I'm not Vicky. I'm your granddaughter Pru—"

"I don't have a granddaughter!" A piece of toast came hurtling her way, which she also dodged. "You killed him, Vicky. You killed him dead, so go rot in hell."

The words spilled from him, cruel and harsh and this stopped her cold so that she didn't duck quickly enough the next time.

His mug caught her on the cheek.

"Ouch, dammit!" she said straightening, holding her face. "You've got to listen to me—I'm not Vicky!" She went hands on hips. "Grandpa, you are not two years old, you need to stop with the temper tantrums!"

"That's right," he yelled. "I'm not two, I'm a *million* and two. I'm old and alone, and it's all your fault!"

Up until that very moment she'd somehow managed to separate herself from what he was saying, but suddenly she couldn't. Suddenly she wasn't feeling strong and in charge and on top of her life. She was just a girl who'd lost her parents, who had a grandpa whose elevator didn't go to the top floor. She was doing the best she could with what she had, but it wasn't adequate.

She wasn't adequate, as proven by her track record of no one loving her enough to stay with her, and the terrifying thing was, she didn't know how to be more.

"Get out!" he bellowed at her.

Paul appeared in the doorway, looking startled. "What's going on, Marvin?"

"What's going on is you let her in!" And in case there

was any doubt of the "her" in question, her grandpa stabbed a spoon in Pru's direction.

"Okay, now let's just take it down a notch," Paul said, doing his orderly thing, moving between Pru and her grandpa. "Put that utensil down, Marvin. We don't throw stuff here, remember?"

But Marvin couldn't be deterred. "It's her fault! Get out," he yelled at Pru. "Get out and don't come back, you tramp! You son-stealer! You *good for nothing free-loading hussy!*"

Michelle poked her head in, her eyes wide. "Paul, you need help?"

"We're good," Paul said evenly. "Aren't we, Marvin?"

"No, I'm not good! Can't you see her? She's standing right behind you like a coward. Get out!" he bellowed at Pru. "*Get out and stay out!*"

Michelle slipped into the room and put her hand in Pru's. "Come on, honey. Let's give him some alone time."

Pru let herself be led out of the room, heart aching, feeling more alone than she ever had. Her grandpa had never been the best of company but he'd at least been someone who shared her blood, her history . . . and now he wasn't remembering any of that and all she did by visiting him was upset him. She might have to stop coming entirely and then she'd be completely alone.

You already are . . .

She walked home slowly even though it was misting and she was wearing just the sundress and sandals. Her heart hurt. Rubbing it didn't assuage the deep ache that went behind the bone to her wounded soul. She missed her mom. She missed her dad. And dammit, she'd missed feeling whole.

She missed feeling needed. Wanted. Like she was crucial, critical to someone's life. A piece of their puzzle.

Instead she was a tumbleweed in the wind, never anchored. Never belonging to anyone.

With her head down and her thoughts even lower, she nearly ran right into someone on the street. Two someone's, locked in an embrace, kissing as if they were never going to see each other again. The man's arms were locked around the woman, an expression of love and longing on his face as he pulled back, still holding the woman's hands.

Had anyone ever looked at Pru like that? If so, she'd forgotten it, and she didn't think one could ever forget true love. All she wanted, all she'd ever wanted since the day she'd lost her parents, was for someone to care enough to come into her life and stay there.

Her chest tightened and her throat burned, but she refused to give into that. Crying wouldn't help. Crying never helped. All crying did was make the day a waste of mascara. And since she'd splurged on an expensive one this time in a useless effort to give her lashes some volume, she wasn't about to waste it. *Get it together*, she ordered herself. *Get it together and keep it together. You're okay. You're always okay . . .*

But the pep talk didn't work. The lonely still crawled up her throat and choked her.

The man smiled down at the woman in front of him, his gaze full of the love that Pru secretly dreamed of. He took his girl's hand and off they went into the rain, shoulders bumping, bodies in sync.

It broke her heart more than it should have. They were complete strangers, for God's sake. But watching them made her feel a little cold. Empty.

A crack of lightning lit the sky. She startled and then jumped again at the nearly immediate boom of thunder, sharp and way too close. Skipping the wrought-iron entrance to the courtyard, she instead ran directly into the pub.

She stood just inside, her eyes immediately straying to the bar.

Finn stood behind it with Sean, who was addressing everyone in the place, and all eyes were on him.

Except for Pru, who was watching Finn. He stood at Sean's side, his blank face on. Though Pru knew him now, or was coming to anyway, and she could tell by his tight mouth and hooded eyes that he wasn't feeling blank at all.

"So raise your glasses," Sean concluded, lifting his. "Because today's the day, folks, our first anniversary of O'Riley's, which we modeled after our dear departed Da's own pub, the original O'Riley's. He'd have loved this place." Sean clasped a hand to his heart. "If he were still with us—God bless his soul—he'd be sitting right here at the bar with us every night."

The mention of this loss would normally have made Pru's heart clutch because of her family's part in their loss, and there was certainly some of that, but she hadn't taken her eyes off Finn. He wasn't sad. He was pissed. And she thought maybe she knew why.

His dad hadn't been anything like hers. He hadn't cuddled his sons when they'd skinned a knee. He hadn't shown them love and adoration. He hadn't carried them around on his shoulders, showing them off every chance he had.

But for whatever reason, Sean was telling a different story. She had no idea why, but Finn's feelings on the matter were clear.

He hated this toast.

"We miss him every single day," Sean went on and finished up with a *"Slainte!"*

"Slainte!" everyone in the place repeated and tossed back their drinks.

Sean grinned and turned toward Finn. He said something to him but Finn didn't respond because he'd turned his head, and as if he'd felt Pru come in, he'd leveled his gaze right on her.

If she'd thought the oncoming storm outside was crazy, it was nothing compared to what happened between her and Finn every time they so much as looked at each other.

You're trouble with a capital T.

Her grandpa's words floated around in her brain, messing with her head, her heart.

One look into your laughing eyes and I knew. All you wanted to do was have fun and you didn't care what fell by the wayside.

She couldn't do this. She'd thought she was doing the right thing by helping Finn find some fun and adventure in his life but now she knew she wasn't. Worse, she felt too fragile, way too close to a complete meltdown to be here. And yet at the same time, she was drawn, so terribly, achingly drawn to the strength in Finn's gaze, the warmth in his eyes. She knew if he so much as touched her right now, she'd lose the tenuous grip she had on her emotions.

Go. Leave.

It was the only clear thought in her head as she whirled to do just that but Finn's warm, strong arms slid around her, turning her to face him.

He'd caught her.

"I'm all wet," she whispered inanely.

His eyes never left her face. "I see that."

"I'm—" *A mess*, she nearly said but the ball of emotion blocked her throat, preventing her from talking. Horrified to feel her eyes well up, she shook her head and tried to pull free.

"Pru," he said softly, his hand at the nape of her neck, threading through her drenched hair. There were tangles in it but he was apparently undeterred by the rat's nest. Pulling her in slowly but inexorably, his lips brushed her forehead. She could feel his mouth at her hairline as he whispered soothing words she couldn't quite make out.

She melted against him. No other words for it really. He was real. He was solid and whole. He was everything she wanted and couldn't have, no matter how badly she ached for him. She'd already wandered way off the track she'd set for herself, a fact that was now coming back to bite her hard because . . .

Because she was falling for him.

And what made it even worse; her day, her life, this situation . . . was that she not only wanted him in her life, she was desperately afraid and increasingly certain that she *needed* him as well.

She almost cracked at that. Almost but not quite.

But God, she couldn't seem to let him go.

Finn tightened his arms on her, pressing his cheek to the top of her head. "It's okay," he whispered. "Whatever it is, it's going to be okay."

But it wasn't. And she didn't know if she'd ever feel okay again so she pressed her face into his throat and let herself take another minute. Or two.

Or whatever he'd give.

Chapter 20

#HowYouDoin

Finn cuddled Pru into him, alarmed by her pallor, by the way she trembled in his arms, the tiny little quivers that said she was fighting her emotions and losing. Her dress had plastered itself to her delicious curves, her long damp hair was clinging to her face and shoulders.

Pulling back, he took her hand and led her to the bar so he could grab a fresh towel. He started to dry off her wet face and realized it was tears, not rain. "Pru."

"No, it's nothing, really," she said quietly, head down, his fearless fun whisperer . . .

"It's not nothing," he said.

"I just . . . I need to go."

Yeah, not going to happen. At least not alone. Finn turned and jerked his chin at Sean, wordlessly telling him he was in charge of the bar.

Sean nodded and Fin took Pru's hand, leading her down the hallway, not in the least bit sorry for leaving

Sean in the lurch. After that stunt toast Sean had just given, Finn was saving his brother's life by leaving now.

"Finn, really," Pru said. "Really, I'm fine. Really."

"And maybe if you say really one more time, I'll believe you."

She sighed. "But I am fine."

She wasn't but she would be. He'd damn well see to it. He took her to his office.

Thor leapt off the couch where he'd been snoozing, immediately launching into his imitation of a bunny. Bounce, bounce, bounce while bark, bark, barking at a pitch designed to shatter eardrums. "Thor," he said. "Shut it."

Thor promptly shut it and sat on his little butt, which shook back and forth with every tail wag that was faster than the speed of light. The result was that he looked like a battery-operated toy dog.

On steroids.

Pru choked out a laugh and scooped him up. "Why are you here, baby?"

"He got done at the beauty salon and Willa had to go before Jake could pick him up, so I said I'd take him for you."

"It's not a beauty salon," she said, face pressed into Thor's fur, doing a bang-up job at keeping up the pretense of being fine.

"Babe, it's totally a beauty salon," he said. "When I walked in to pick him up, Willa was presiding over a wedding between two giant poodles, one white, one black. The black one was wearing a wedding dress made of silk and crystals."

She slid him a look. No more tears, thank God, but

her eyes were haunted even though she did her best to smile. "Wow," she said.

"Impressed by the lengths Willa's shop goes to make money?" he asked.

"No, I'm impressed that you can recognize silk and crystals."

"Hey, I'm secure in my manhood." He took Thor from her and tucked the dog under an arm. The other he slipped around her waist. "Let's go."

"Where?"

"I'm taking you home. You look about done in."

"I passed done in about an hour ago," she admitted.

They didn't speak again as they crossed the courtyard. But Thor did. He started barking at a pair of pigeons and when Finn gave him a long look, the dog switched to a low-in-the-throat growl.

"They outweigh you," Finn told him. "Pick your battles, man."

The dog was silent in the elevator but that was only because Max, who worked on the second floor in Archer's office, was in it. With his Doberman pinscher Carl.

When Max and Carl got off the elevator, Thor let out a long sigh that sounded like relief, which under better circumstances would've made Finn laugh. "You know your particular breed of mutt was bred to kill Dobermans, right?" he asked the dog.

Thor blinked up at him.

"It's true," Finn said. "They get stuck right here—" He pointed to his throat.

Pru choked out a laugh. "Finn, that's a horrible story!"

He smiled and tugged lightly on a strand of her hair. "But you laughed," he said.

"I laughed because it was a *horrible* story," she said, but was still smiling.

And because she was, he leaned in and kissed her. Softly. "Hey," he said.

"Hey," she whispered back.

He wasn't sure what was going on with her, but it'd only taken one look at her open, expressive face to know she'd somehow been devastated today.

And, given the cut on her cheekbone, also hurt.

Both infuriated him.

The elevator opened and he took Thor's leash in one hand and used the other to guide Pru off. They were in the hallway in front of her door when Mrs. Winslow's door opened.

"Another special delivery?" Pru asked her.

"Not for me," Mrs. Winslow answered. "It's for you."

"Um, I don't eat a lot of special brownies," she said. "No offense."

Mrs. Winslow smiled. "Oh, none taken, honey. I'm just passing the word that there's a little something in the dumbwaiter for you."

"For me? Why?"

"For your bad day," Mrs. Winslow said.

Pru blinked. "How do you know I had a bad day?"

"Let's just say a little birdie looks after all of us," Mrs. Winslow said. "And he let me know to let you know that you're not alone."

"He who?" Pru asked.

But Mrs. Winslow had vanished back into her apartment.

Finn and Pru walked into hers. Finn crouched down and freed Thor from his leash and the dog immediately trotted to his food bowl.

Pru dumped a cup of dry food into it, patted the dog on his head and then went straight to the dumbwaiter.

Finn went to her freezer. He didn't see an ice pack but she did have a small bag of frozen corn. Good enough.

At her gasp, Finn turned to her. She'd pulled out a basket of muffins from the coffee shop. Tina's muffins, the best on the planet.

Finn wrapped the bag of corn in a kitchen towel and gently set the makeshift ice pack to her cheek and then brought her hand up to it. "Hold it here a few minutes," he said.

While she did that, he carried the basket to the kitchen table and they dove into the muffins right then and there.

"Good to have friends in high places," he said instead of asking her about her face, and when she visibly relaxed he knew he'd done the right thing.

Didn't mean he didn't want to kick someone's ass, because he did. Badly.

"It'd be better to know who those friends are," she said, clearly not reading his murderous thoughts. She met his gaze. "Do you know?"

He had an idea but didn't know for certain so he shook his head.

She took another muffin, chocolate chip by the looks of it. "Sean's toast at the pub upset you," she said.

Sitting across from her at her table, with Thor in his lap while he worked his way through a most excellent blueberry/banana muffin, he didn't want to get into Sean's toast. He much preferred to get into whatever had happened to *her*. But he knew that she wasn't going to open up.

Unless he did.

Problem was, he hated opening up. To anyone.

"I'm sorry your dad never got to see the bar and what a success you made of it," she said quietly.

He put his muffin down. "My dad couldn't have cared less what we did with ourselves when we were kids. He wouldn't care what we do now either."

"But Sean said—"

"Sean's so full of shit that his eyes are brown," he said. "My dad never had a pub. Hell, he never even acknowledged he was Irish. My brother perpetuates the lie because he thinks Irish pubs do well and he isn't wrong. We *have* done well but it isn't because we're Irish, it's because we work our asses off."

"You mean you work *your* ass off," she said.

He met her knowing gaze. "I just hate the fraud."

"It's not a fraud if it's true, even a little bit." Reaching across the table, she covered her hand with his. "Stop feeling guilty about something that isn't your fault and isn't hurting anyone. Let it go and enjoy the success you've made of the place, in spite of your father."

He stared at her. "How is it that you're cute, sexy as hell, *and* smarter than anyone I know?"

She gave him a small smile. "It's a gift."

Leaning over the table, he wrapped his fingers around her wrist and pulled the bag of corn from her face. Gently he touched her cheekbone. "You okay?"

"I will be."

Her resilience made him smile. "Yeah?" he asked. "And how's that?"

She shrugged a shoulder. "Well, it's raining, and I love the rain. Someone sent me a basket of muffins, and I love muffins. Thor is actually clean and going to stay that way for at least the next few minutes. I don't have to work until midday tomorrow. And I have company." She smiled. "The good kind." She lifted a shoulder. "It's all good."

She was aiming for light and she'd succeeded. It was how she dealt, he got that. And he was getting something else too—that he could learn a hell of a lot from her.

She rose from her chair and came around the table. She lifted Thor from his lap and set the dog down. Then she climbed into Finn's lap herself and cupped his face.

His arms closed around her and one thought settled into his brain. This feels right.

She feels right.

Chapter 21

#UpShitCreekWithoutAPaddle

Pru lifted her gaze to Finn's, startled by the sudden intensity in his gaze. It said she wasn't alone, that she mattered, a lot.

At least you're not the only one falling . . .

This thought was a cool tall drink of relief immediately followed by a chaser of anxiety.

Because she hadn't meant for this to happen. She hadn't meant for *any* of it; his attention, his affection, his emotional bond . . . and all of it was a secret dream come true for her.

Just as all of it was now a nightmare as well, because how was she supposed to give it up? Give *him* up?

Although the tough truth was, she wouldn't have to. Telling him the truth would accomplish that because *he* would give *her* up once she did.

She'd known they'd be getting to this. She hadn't

missed him looking at her cheek, or the temper that flashed in his eyes whenever he did. "It's—"

"Not nothing. Don't even think about saying it's nothing." His voice was gentle but inexorable steel.

"My grandfather's in a senior home," she said. "Has been for years. I visit him every week but he doesn't always recognize me."

"He hit you?" he asked, his voice still calm, his gaze anything but.

"No." She shook her head. "Well, not exactly."

"Then what exactly?"

"He was trying to get me to leave," she said. "He threw the stuff on his lunch tray at me."

His brow furrowed. "What the fuck?"

"It's that sometimes he thinks I'm my mom," she said. "He didn't like her."

Finn's fingers slid into her hair, soothing, protective, and she felt herself relax a little into his touch.

"Why not?" he asked quietly.

"She . . ." Pru closed her eyes and pressed her face to his throat. "She was a good-time girl. She loved to have fun. My dad loved to give her that fun. We spent a lot of time out on the water and at Giants games, his two favorite things."

He smiled. "And you're still out on the water."

She nodded. "It makes me feel close to them. I used to tell my dad I was going to captain a ship someday, which must have sounded ridiculous but he told me I could do anything I wanted." She paused. "I loved them, very much, but in some ways my grandpa was right. My mom encouraged my dad. The truth is they were partyers, and big social drinkers . . ."

"Is that why you never drink?"

"A big part of it," she admitted for the first time in her life. "Is that weird for you, being with someone who doesn't drink?"

He palmed her neck and waited until she looked at him. "Not even a little bit," he said.

She smiled. "My dad used to say my mom was the light to his dark. He loved that about her. He loved her," she said, her chest tight at the memory of her mom making him laugh. "They loved each other."

There was empathy in Finn's eyes and in his touch. Empathy, and affection, and a grim understanding. He'd had losses too. Far too many.

"I'm glad you have those memories of your mom and dad together," he said. "I know it sucks having them gone, but at least when you think of them, you smile."

Mostly. But not always. Not, for instance, when she thought of how they'd died.

And who'd they'd taken with them . . .

"I'm sorry you don't have those memories," she said quietly.

"Don't be. Because I don't know what I'm missing." He met her gaze. "You had it worse. Your life was a complete one-eighty from mine. You know exactly what you're missing."

And there went the stab to her gut again. "Finn—"

"It's not your fault, Pru. Any of it. Forget it."

As if she could.

He tightened his grip on her. "No more going into your grandfather's room alone. You take an orderly with you, or anyone. Me," he said. "I'll go with you. Or whoever you want, but I don't want you in there with him alone again."

"He's not always that bad—"

"Promise me," he said, cupping her face, taking care with her cheek. "There's only honesty between us, right? We have no reason for anything but. So look me in the eyes and promise me, Pru."

She inhaled deeply, feeling like the biggest fraud on the planet. "I promise," she whispered, hating herself a little bit. "Finn?"

"Yeah?"

Eyes on his, she leaned in close. "Do you remember when you kissed away my hurts?"

"After the first softball game," he said and smiled. "Yeah, I remember. It was a highlight for me." His eyes went smoldering. "Want me to do it again?"

"No, it's your turn," she said. "I'm going to kiss away *your* hurts."

He stilled. "You are?"

"Yes." *Please want me to, please need me to . . .*

A rough sound escaped him then, regret and empathy, making her realize she'd spoken out loud. Closing her eyes, she tried to turn away but his arms tightened around her, his voice low and rough. "I do," he said fiercely. "I'm going to show you just how much I need you. All night long, in fact."

She stared into his eyes, letting the strength in the words, in his body, in his gaze convince her he meant every single word. "The whole night," she repeated, needing the clarification.

"For as long as you need."

Since that was too much to think about, she had to set it aside in her head. Instead she slid her fingers into his hair as his hands caught her, rocking her against her very favorite body part of his. She oscillated her hips, thrilling to the way he groaned at the contact.

No slouch, Finn stroked up her arms, encouraging the spaghetti straps of her sundress to slip from her shoulders. The bodice was stretchy and lightweight and still damp from the rain, which meant it took very little effort for him to tug it to her waist so that her breasts spilled out.

A rough, very male sound of appreciation rumbled up from deep in his throat and his hands went under her dress to cup her ass, pulling her in tighter to him, putting his mouth right at tease-her-nipples level.

He captured one in his mouth and her brain ceased working. Just completely stopped. Probably for the best since she was about to do things with him that she'd told herself she wouldn't do again. "Finn—"

Finn groaned again, a near growl. "Love the sound of my name on your lips," he said and sucked hard, his hands pushing her dress up her thighs as he did.

"Oh no," she said, and right then, with his teeth gently biting down on her nipple and his hands up her dress, he froze.

"No?" he repeated.

"No, as in I'm not going to be the first one naked this time," she clarified. "Why am I always the first one naked?"

"Because you look amazing naked. Here, let me show you—"

"Now just hold on," she said with a low laugh, feeling

dizzy with lust. "Good God, you're potent." She shoved his shirt up his chest and hummed in thrilled delight at the sight of his exposed torso. "Off," she demanded.

He took a hand off her thigh, fisted it in his shirt between his shoulder blades and yanked it over his head, never taking his eyes from hers, immediately going back to the business of driving her right out of her ever-loving mind.

Her hands slid down his bare chest over his abs, which were rigid and taut enough that even though he was sitting, there was no fat ripple. If she didn't want him so badly, she'd hate him for it. She popped open his button-fly jeans and a most impressive erection sprang free into her hands.

He was commando.

"Laundry day," he said.

She stared at him and then laughed. She had him full and hard in her hands, and she was hot and achy and already wet for him, and she was laughing.

"It's not nice to laugh at a naked man," he said, smiling at her, not insulted in the least, the cocky bastard, and it only made her laugh harder.

"I'm sorry," she managed on a snort.

Straightening up, causing those delicious ab muscles to crunch, he nipped her jaw. "You don't look sorry."

She stroked his hard length and her body practically vibrated for him. "I'll work on that," she managed as he pushed up the hem of her sundress.

Her amusement backed up in her throat.

Air brushed over her upper thighs now. Her panties were tiny, enough that when Finn reached his hands around to her ass, there was bare cheek groping.

"Mmm," rumbled approvingly from his throat. His fingers dug in a little, cupping, squeezing, and then slipped beneath the lace, making her quiver.

"Hold this," he said.

She automatically took hold of her own dress at her waist. She felt hot. Achy. *Desperate.* She was already straddling him but his big hands adjusted her legs so that the two of them fit together like two pieces of a puzzle.

"Yeah," he said. "Like that." And then he scraped aside her little scrap of panties and stilled as he got a good look at what he'd exposed.

And that's when she remembered the Brazilian. "It's Elle's fault," she blurted out.

"Oh Christ, Pru." He stroked a reverent finger across her exposed flesh.

Her exposed, *bare* flesh. "She took me and Willa to the spa and—"

The pad of Finn's finger came away wet and he groaned.

"—the next thing I knew . . ." she trailed off when, holding her gaze, he sucked his finger into his mouth. "So . . . you like?" she whispered.

"Love." His hands went to her hips and he lifted her up to the table, plopping her on the wood surface. Then, calm as you please, he scooted his chair in close, draped her legs over his shoulders, lowered his head and . . .

Oh. *Oh.* Her last coherent thought was that maybe Elle had been onto something . . .

"Missed the taste of you," Finn murmured a few minutes later, when he'd rendered her boneless. And not very many minutes either. He shifted back, and afraid he was going away, she made a small whisper of protest and clutched at him.

Flashing her a smile, he reached behind him, pulling his wallet from his back pocket.

"It's a little late to exchange business cards, isn't it?" she asked, trying to make light of their compromising situation because as was already established, her mouth never knew when to stay zipped.

He pulled out a condom.

"Right," she said. Damn, she should have thought of that. Problem was, at the moment, with her dress basically a belt around her waist, exposing all her goodies, she was incapable of thought.

"You take my breath," he said, eyes on her as he tore the packet open with his teeth and then rolled the condom down his length.

She'd never seen anything so sexy in her entire life.

With what looked like effortless strength, he scooped her from the table and lowered her over the top of him, in total control of how fast she sank onto him—which was to say not fast at all. Seemed Finn liked the slow, drive-her-insane grind, and she let out a sound of impatience that made him flash her another smile.

"You think this is funny?" she managed.

"You panting my name, whimpering for more, and trembling for me?" He brushed his stubbled jaw very gently across her nipple and gave her an entire body shiver. "Try sexy as hell."

She was no longer surprised to realize that she felt it. Sexy as hell. It was an utterly new experience for her and she didn't quite know how to rein herself in. So she didn't even try. Instead she went after every inch of him that she could reach, following each touch of her fingers with her mouth. His shoulders, collarbone, his throat . . . God, she loved his throat. But what she loved even more? The rough, extremely erotic sounds she coaxed from him.

"Lift up," he whispered hotly in her ear, and then rather than wait for her to comply, he guided her with his hands on her hips, showing her how to raise up on her knees until he nearly slipped out of her, and then to sink back down, once again taking him fully inside her.

They both gasped as she began to move like that, urged on by his hands, all while their mouths remained fused, kissing hot and deep. When they ran out of air, he wound his fist in her hair and forced her head back, sucking on her exposed throat, his other hand posses-sive on her ass.

Then that hand shifted to the groove between her hip and thigh, his fingers spread wide so that his thumb could rasp over the current center of her universe. She gripped his wrist and held his hand in place.

"You like?" he asked hotly against her ear.

"Just don't stop." Ever . . .

He didn't. He swirled that roughly callused thumb in a very purposeful circle that was exactly the rhythm she needed, making her cry out his name as she came hard.

When she opened her eyes, his were hot and trium-phant, and she wrapped her arms tight around his neck. "It was your turn to go first."

"Always you first," he said and melted her heart.

"I'm not sure that's fair."

He smiled. "Hell yeah, it is. I love watching you come for me." He nipped her chin. "You say my name all breathy and you dig your nails into me. So fucking sexy, Pru."

With a low laugh, she buried her face in his neck.

"That shouldn't embarrass you," he said. "Watching you come makes my world go around."

At the thought, her body clenched around him and he groaned.

"Your turn now," she whispered, and did it again.

"Yeah?"

"Yeah." Empowered, she gave him a little push until he leaned back in the chair. "You just sit there and look pretty," she said. "Let me do the work now."

He flashed her a sexy grin that almost made her come again before he leaned back, clearly one hundred percent good with giving her the reins and letting her have her wicked way with him.

She gave him everything she had, and in the end when he banded his arms around her, his head back, his face a mask of stark pleasure as he shuddered up into her, she felt herself go over again. With him. Into him . . .

It shocked her. A co-orgasm. An *effortless* co-orgasm. She didn't realize it was a real thing. She'd honestly thought it was a myth, like unicorns and good credit ratings.

When she caught her breath and her world stopped spinning out of control she looked at him. Sprawled beneath her, head back, eyes closed, he had a smile on his face.

"Damn," he said. "That just gets better and better."

Dazed, she stood on shaky legs and began to re-arrange her dress. "This isn't anything like what I expected."

He gave a sexy laugh. "Liar."

She froze and looked at him.

"Admit it," he said. "You've wanted me since day one. I sure as hell have wanted you since then."

Laughing at her expression, he pulled her back onto his lap, cuddling her, kissing the top of her head. "You think too much, Pru."

That was definitely also true. She rested her head against his chest and listened to his heartbeat, strong and steady.

"I've got something to say," he murmured, his hands sliding down to palm and then squeeze her ass.

She wriggled a little bit, just to hear that low growl and feel his fingers tighten on her. But while his body was giving her one message, his words gave another.

"You helped Sean out and that means a lot to me," he said.

She froze and lifted her head to look at him. "He told you? He didn't have to do that."

"I'm glad he did. I already knew you're warm and sexy, funny and smart, but what you did, Pru, having his back like that—and by extension, my back as well—that told me everything I need to know about you."

She shook her head. "Anyone would have—"

"No," he said. "They wouldn't. I've got my brother and a select core group of friends that would do anything for me, and that's been it. But now I've got you too. Means a lot to me, Pru. You mean a lot to me."

Oh God. "I feel the same," she whispered. "But Finn, you don't know everything about me."

"I know what I need to."

If only that was true. "Finn—" But before she could finish that statement, the one where she told him the truth, the one that would surely change everything and erase their friendship and trust and . . . *everything*, someone knocked on her door.

"Ignore it," Finn said.

"Pru," came a deep male voice from the other side of her door.

Jake.

Oh, God. *Jake.*

This was bad. Very, very bad. If Jake found Finn here with *that* look on his face, there'd be no holding back the storm. Jake had told her to tell Finn before things went too far, and when Jake told someone to do something, they did it.

But she hadn't.

And things had gone far with Finn. Just about as *far* as a man and a woman could get . . .

She was in trouble. Big trouble. One of the problems with having a wounded warrior as a BFF is that he saw everything as a conflict to fix. She had no doubt he'd take one glimpse at them and very possibly butt his big nosy nose in and enlighten Finn himself.

And that would be bad. Very, very bad. She jumped up and straightened her dress before whirling to Finn. He'd pulled up his jeans, but hadn't fastened them. Nor had he put on his shirt, which meant he sat there in nothing but Levi's, literally, his hair completely tousled from her fingers—bad fingers!—an unmistakable just-got-laid sated expression all over his face.

Not moving.

She waved her hands at him. "What are you doing? Get dressed!"

"Working on it." He stretched lazily, slowly, like he had all the fricking time in the fracking world.

Jake knocked again, annoyance reverberating through the wood. Jake had many good qualities but patience wasn't one of them. "Pru, what the hell are you doing in there—and it'd better not be Finn," he said.

She'd just sent her hands on Finn's chest to give him a little hurry-up nudge, so she had a front-row view of his brows shooting up.

Well, crap.

Then, from outside her door, came the unmistakable sounds of keys rattling, which reminded her of the unfortunate time on moving day when she'd given Jake her damn key. *What had she been thinking?* "You've got to hide!" she whispered frantically to Finn.

"What the hell for?"

With a sound of exasperation she whirled around and eyeballed potential hiding places.

She had little to no furniture.

"Dammit!" Then she focused on the dumbwaiter. Perfect. "Here," she said, opening it and then pushing him toward it. "I need you to get in here for just a minute—"

Finn, solid and steady, didn't move when she'd pushed him. What was it with her and big, badass alphas who only could be budged when they wanted to be budged?

He looked down into her face and seemed to take in her clear panic because he gave a slight head shake. "You've lost it."

"Yes, now you fully understand! I've completely lost it, but to be honest, I lost it a long time ago!"

"I meant me, babe," he said. "I've lost it to even be melted by those eyes of yours, enough that I'll do just about anything for you."

"Good," she said quickly. "Go with that. Please, I can't explain right now, but I need you to hide, for just a minute, I promise."

He shook his head again, muttered some more, something that sounded like "you're a complete dumbass, O'Riley," but then God bless him, he folded up his rangy form in the dumbwaiter.

"Just for a minute," she repeated and slammed the door shut on his gorgeous but annoyed face and turned back to the kitchen—where Finn's shirt and shoes were lying scattered on the floor. *Shit!* She snagged everything up, ran back to the dumbwaiter, opened the door and shoved them at Finn and then slammed the door.

Just as Jake rolled into her kitchen.

Finn sat there in the dumbwaiter, somewhere between pissed off and bemused. And maybe a little turned on, which showed just how messed up in the head he really was.

No one handled him. Ever. And yet Pru just had, like a pro.

Which meant he sat here squished into the dumb-waiter in only his unbuttoned jeans, his shirt in one hand, his shoes in his other, wondering—What. The. Fuck.

He tried to come up with a single reason why, if Pru and Jake were not a thing, that he had to be a dirty little secret. But he couldn't.

And his amusement faded.

Because that's exactly what he was at the moment. Pru's dirty little secret, and while the thought of that might have appealed in fantasy, it absolutely did not hold up in reality.

Not even close.

Leaning in, he tried to catch whatever was going on in Pru's kitchen.

"Why are you breathing like a lunatic?" Jake asked. "And you're all flushed. You sick?"

Try as he might, Finn couldn't catch Pru's response.

But he had no problem catching Jake's next line. "Why is there a pair of men's socks on your floor?"

And that's when the dumbwaiter jerked and went on the move, taking Finn southward.

Chapter 22

#SillyRabbit

"Shit!" Finn had no choice but to hold on as the dumbwaiter began to move, taking him past the second floor, and then the first . . . all the way to the basement. It was a bad flashback to the last time this had happened.

Before he could catch his breath, the dumbwaiter door opened, and yep, he was in the basement. He had an audience too. Luis the janitor, Trudy the head of building cleaning services, Old Guy Eddie, Elle, Spence, and Spence's two buddies Joe and Caleb all sat around a poker table smoking cigars and playing what looked like five-card stud.

They stared at Finn—still in only his jeans, still holding his shirt and shoes—with various degrees of surprise and shock.

Luis didn't even blink, but then again the guy had lost a leg in Vietnam so not much rattled him. He just shook his head. "Some people never learn."

Trudy had been married to Luis—three times. They'd recently celebrated their third divorce, which meant they were already sleeping together again and probably thinking about their fourth wedding. Trudy took in Finn's state of dress—or in this case undress—and her cigar fell out of her mouth.

"Hot damn," she said in a been-smoking-for-three-decades voice. "I didn't even know they made real men that look like that!"

Joe, the youngest one here at twenty-four, who'd MMA-ed his way through college for cash, lifted up his shirt to look down at his eight-pack. "Hey, I'm made like that too."

Spence snorted.

"You're drooling," Elle told Trudy and tossed some money into the pot without giving Finn a second glance.

Finn didn't take this personally. Everyone knew Elle had a thing for Archer. Well, except for Elle herself. And also Archer . . .

Eddie looked at Finn and then pulled the cigar out of his mouth. "You got your wallet on ya somewhere, kid?"

"Yeah," Finn said. Minus his emergency condom . . .

"Well then get over here," Eddie said. "We'll deal ya in on the next round."

Finn looked down at himself. He thought about the night he'd had, how it had started out about as amazing as a night could get, how it'd ended up going south.

Literally.

"I'm raising thirty," Elle said, mind on the game. Not much distracted Elle from her poker game.

"You sure?" Spence asked her.

She narrowed her eyes. "Why wouldn't I be sure?"

Spence just looked at her. He didn't like to waste words but as one of the smartest guys Finn had ever met, he didn't often need them.

Caleb didn't mind using *his* words. "Do you remember the last time we played?"

Elle sighed. "Yeah, yeah, the last time I raised, I ended up signing over my firstborn to Spence. Good thing I'm not planning on having kids." She blew out a breath and folded. "You're right."

"What?" Spence asked, a hand curved around his ear.

"I said you're right!" Elle snapped.

Spence gave a slow smile. "I heard you. I just wanted to hear it again. Can I get it in writing for posterity?"

Elle flipped him off.

This only made Spence grin. "Sticks and stones . . ."

"How about a big, fat loss," Elle griped. "Will that hurt you?" She looked around. "What the hell does a girl have to do to get a drink refill and to keep the game moving?"

Joe scrambled to pour her a drink, infatuation in his gaze. Elle absently patted him on the head and went back to her cards. "You coming or not?" she demanded of Finn.

That was Elle, always on a schedule. With a shrug, he tossed aside his shirt and shoes. What the hell. "Deal me in."

It was three in the morning before Finn staggered home and into bed, where he lay staring at the ceiling.

He'd lost his ass in poker—damn Elle, she had

balls of steel—and afterward he'd dragged himself to the pub to check in and help close. It'd been a busy night, too busy to keep one eye on the door for a certain brown-eyed beauty.

Not that she'd shown up.

Neither had Jake.

Which meant that Finn had ground his back teeth into powder wondering if he'd been played. Or if he was overreacting. Or if he was a complete idiot . . .

It's just that he couldn't stop thinking about how he'd felt buried deep inside Pru, so deep that he couldn't feel regret or pain. Could feel nothing but her soft body wrapped around him, her wet heat milking him dry, her mouth clinging to his like she'd never had anyone like him, ever.

"Shit," he muttered and flopped over, forcing his eyes closed. So she'd wanted to hide what they'd done. So what. He'd had a hell of an incredible time with her and that had been all he'd needed.

Now it was back to the real world.

He'd halfway convinced himself that he believed it when someone knocked on his door.

In Finn's experience, a middle-of-the-night knock on the door never equaled anything good. In the past, it'd meant his dad was dead. Or Sean needed bail money. Or there was a kitchen fire at the pub.

Kicking off his covers, he shoved himself into the jeans he'd left on the floor. As he padded to the door, he shrugged into a shirt, looking out the peephole to brace himself.

It wasn't what he expected.

Instead of a cop, it was a woman. The one woman who had the ability to turn him upside down and inside out. She was in jeans and a tee now, looking unsettled and anxious. Dammit. He pulled back and stared at the door.

"Don't make me beg," Pru said through the wood.

Resisting the urge to thunk his head against the door, he unlocked and opened up.

Pru stared up at him, squinting through the long bangs that hadn't been contained and were in her face. "You left," she said.

"You shoved me in the dumbwaiter."

"You left," she repeated.

He crossed his arms over his chest and refused to repeat himself. She'd stuffed him into the dumbwaiter so she didn't have to reveal to Jake what they'd been up to on her kitchen table. He'd talked himself into filing that away in his head, in a file drawer labeled STUFF THAT SUCKS. He'd thrown away the key.

But apparently he'd forgotten to lock it.

She closed her eyes. "Can I come in?"

"For?"

She opened her eyes and leveled him with those warm brown eyes. "I wanted to apologize."

"Okay. Anything else?"

"Yes." She sighed. "I know this looks bad, Finn, but it's not what you think."

He leaned against the doorjamb. "And what do I think, Pru?"

She put her hands to his chest and gave a little push. A complete sucker, he let her squeeze in past him, taking some sick delight in the fact that she smelled like him.

She strode straight into his bedroom and he followed because he was Pavlov's dog at this point.

She checked out his room, the unmade bed, the moonlight slanting in through his window, casting his mattress in grays and blues. When he came in behind her, she turned to face him and kicked off her shoes.

"We both know what you thought," she said. "But Jake and I aren't a thing. I wasn't hiding you, at least not like that."

"Then like what?"

She held his gaze for a long beat. "I don't always act with my brain. Sometimes I act with my heart, without thinking about the consequences. Jake is my boss and my friend, and he looks out for me."

"He thinks I'd hurt you?"

"No," she said and looked away. "Actually, he thinks *I'll* hurt *you*. And he's probably right."

"You going to break my heart, Pru?" he asked softly, only half joking because what he knew—and she didn't—was that she could absolutely do it if she wanted. She could slay him.

"Actually," she said very quietly. "I'm pretty sure it's going to be the other way around." She reached for him and pushed his still unbuttoned shirt off his shoulders, assisting it back to the floor.

"What are you doing?" he asked.

"What does it look like?" Her fingers drifted down his chest and abs to play with the top button on his jeans.

"You're trying to get me naked."

"Yes," she said. "You going to help?"

Good question. First things first though. He gathered her hands in one of his and cupped her face with the other, tilting it up to his. "You and Jake are—"

"No," she said without hesitation, eyes clear.

He might regret this later but he believed her. "No more hiding, Pru. I won't be anyone's dirty secret, not even yours."

"I know," she said and freed her hands to caress his chest. "We weren't done with each other."

"No?"

She gave a small head shake and let her fingers drift southbound. "Unless . . . you were done with me?"

Not by a long shot. "You're wearing too many clothes," he said and then proceeded to get her out of them. He tugged her T-shirt from the waistband of her jeans and yanked it over her head. Her bra followed the same path and her breasts spilled into his hand, warm and soft, tugging a groan from the back of his throat.

Her hands and mouth were just as busy, landing on whatever they could reach, which at the moment meant she was nibbling at his collarbone, her fingers unbuttoning his Levi's.

Quickly losing control, he crouched in front of her, taking her jeans and panties down with one hard tug. With his face level with one of his favorite parts of hers, he clasped her hips in his hands and tugged her a step closer.

"Oh," she gasped, off balance, sliding her fingers into his hair to steady herself.

But he had her. He had her and he wasn't going to let her fall. He'd had no such luck for himself. He'd already fallen and hard. And feeling his heart squeeze at the thought, he leaned in and put his mouth on her.

Another gasp escaped her lips and his fingers tightened on his hair. "Finn—"

He licked. He nuzzled. He sucked. All while her soft pants and helpless moans and wordless entreaties wormed their way in his ears and through his veins until he didn't know where he ended and she began.

When she came, she came hard and with his name on her tongue. Satisfaction and triumph surged through him at that. When her knees buckled, he rose and scooped her up at the same time, feeling like a super-hero as he tossed her down to his bed.

She bounced once and then he was on her. Maybe a little rougher than she expected because she blinked up at him in surprise as he pinned her to the mattress.

"What are you doing?" she asked, her voice a little hoarse, for which he took full credit.

"Giving you what you showed up here for."

"What if *I* wanted to be in the driver's seat?" she asked.

"Dumbwaiter," he said.

"So . . . this is payback?"

He gathered both of her wandering hands and pinned them to the pillow on either side of her head. "Yes." He nudged her thighs open with one of his and made himself at home between them. "But you can do whatever you want to me in return. Later." He bowed his head and licked his way down her neck. Christ, she tasted good. "Much later."

He'd planned on going slow and savoring all the naked skin against him but as she softened beneath him, wrapping her legs around his waist, he suddenly wasn't interested in slow. He could feel her, hot and wet and ready, and when he slid in deep, they both gasped and instantly combusted with his first hard thrust.

Chapter 23

#CaffeineRequired

That day at work, Pru was going over the schedule for the day when Nick poked his head in from the docks. "Hey," he said. "Got a minute?"

She'd gotten him the job here working for Jake, but they were both always so busy, they didn't often get a chance to talk. "I've got exactly a minute," she said, glancing at the clock and then smiling at Nick. "What's up? How's your mom? How's Tim? I talked to him about a week or so ago."

"Mom's fine," Nick said. "And Tim got that apartment." He smiled. "Thanks to you. Does Jake know he has a saint working for him?"

"Believe me," she said on an uncomfortable laugh. "I'm no saint. And Jake doesn't need to be told otherwise."

"Why? Maybe he'd give you a raise."

"For being a saint? No. Now if I figured out how to clone myself," she said. "He might be so inclined."

Nick gave her a quick, hard hug.

"What's that for?" she asked.

"Everything."

When he'd left, she got a text from Elle that had her staring at her phone, mouth open.

I don't know how or why, but thanks for sending last night's comic relief to poker night.

She stared at the text, horrified. She still couldn't believe she'd done that to Finn.

And that's not the only thing you've done to him . . .

She'd let her emotions get the better of her. That was a mistake, but oh God, what a delicious, sexy, heart-stopping wonderful mistake.

She responded back to Elle with a ? on the off chance she was jumping to conclusions, and Elle was all too happy to explain in her next text:

Biweekly poker night in the basement turned into a peep show when Finn showed up in the dumbwaiter half nekkid. Lucy, you've got some 'splainin' to do.

Her stomach hurt. Her plan to bring Finn a little fun, a little adventure while waiting on the fountain to bring him love, had seemed so simple. Fun and adventure, and maybe even a little walk on the wild side. She honestly hadn't meant to do that in bed.

Or on her kitchen table.

Or in her shower . . .

Oh, God. This whole thing was bad. Very, very bad. And yet it'd all been so heart-stopping good at the same time that she found herself just standing in place at odd moments, her brain glazed over as it ran through erotic, sensual memories like a slide show behind her eyelids. Finn bending her over the end of the bed, his mouth at her ear whispering hot little sexy nothings as he'd teased and cajoled her right out of her inhibitions, his body hard against her.

In her . . .

She blew out a shaky breath. Dangerous thoughts. Because it was her being selfish, and she wasn't going to do that again.

Absolutely not.

Or, you know, as much as she could.

Ugh. She slapped herself in the forehead. *Go back to your plan*, she ordered herself, not giving her inner smart-ass a chance to chime in. No more sexy times, no matter how deliciously demanding he was in bed. And this time, she meant it. One hundred percent. Or at the very least, seventy-five percent.

Certainly no less than fifty percent . . .

Luckily, work was crazy busy and helped keep her mind off all things Finn-related. The weather was warm, which meant that everyone and their mama wanted to get outside. They wanted to be on the water, see Alcatraz, Treasure Island, the Pier 39 sea lions . . .

She was on her second tour of the day when a guy tried to propose to his girlfriend. Unfortunately for him, he apparently hadn't checked out her Pinterest page where she'd pinned pictures of acceptable rings. The proposal went fine until she opened the little black box. It didn't end well, especially since he'd done it in the first five minutes of the two-hour tour, and then had to endure the rest of the ride in frosty silence.

On her last tour, Pru had a bunch of frat boys who kept making jokes, wanting to know if she'd be their captain below deck as well, nudge, nudge, wink, wink, if she'd ever played pirates with her passengers, because they wouldn't mind pillaging and plundering. At that she'd pulled out the baseball bat she kept beneath her captain's chair and asked if anyone needed their balls rearranged or if they wanted to sit down and shut up for the rest of the tour.

They'd gone with sitting down and shutting up.

She'd gotten a call from Jake the second the last of her passengers debarked.

"You have problems with passengers, you let me kick their ass, you don't need to do it," he said. "You're not alone out there, I'm always in your ear."

Literally. They were in constant communication when she was on the water via comms. "Maybe sometimes I want to do my own ass kicking," she said.

"My point is that you don't have to."

"It's a good stress reliever," she said.

"Uh huh. As good as sleeping with the guy you haven't been honest with and then shoving him bareass naked into your dumbwaiter to avoid your ex, your boss, and your best friend?"

The air left her lungs in one big whoosh. "Who told you?"

"Eddie would snitch on his mama for food or cash, you know that."

"And how did Eddie know?" she demanded. "I didn't tell anyone!"

"Didn't have to. Eddie was in the basement at a very intense poker game with a select few when the dumbwaiter opened and out stumbled your boy, pants in hand."

"Shirt!" she yelled. "He had his *shirt* in hand. He was *wearing* his pants!"

"Just tell me you told him."

"I'm working on that."

"Dammit, Pru, it's like you *want* to self-implode your own happiness. Promise me you won't do anything that stupid again until you tell him."

She closed her eyes, knowing he was right. Hating that he was right.

"Pru—"

"—I hear you," she said.

"Promise me. I know you would never break a promise, so right here and now, promise me that—"

"I promise," she said. "I've always intended to tell him and I will. I get that it's been two weeks but I'm working up to it, okay? I'm going to tell him soon as the time is right."

"Just don't miss your window of opportunity, chica, that's all I'm saying."

"I hear you."

They disconnected and Pru closed her eyes. Hard to pretend something hadn't happened when everyone in the free world knew.

She didn't linger after work like she usually did.

Instead she hightailed it out of there. Needing to clear her head, she and Thor walked. Well, *she* walked. Thor got tired about halfway and stopped. He planted his little butt on the sidewalk and steadfastly refused to walk another step.

"You're going to get fat," she told him.

Thor turned his head away from her.

"Come on," she cajoled. "I want to walk out the Aquatic Park Pier and watch the sky change colors as the sun sets."

Thor sneezed and she could have sworn she heard "bullshit" in the sound. And the sad thing was that her dog had more brain cells than she did because he was right.

She was stalling going home. It was just that she'd come to count on Finn's company so much. Too much. He made her smile. He made her ache. He made her want things, things she'd been afraid to want. He made her feel . . . way too much.

Thor hadn't budged so she scooped him up and carried him out to the end of the long, curved pier. She watched the water and thought maybe this wasn't so bad. Yes, she'd made a mistake. She'd been with Finn a few times.

So what.

Other people, normal people, slept with people all the time and she didn't see anyone else angsting over it. For all she knew Finn hadn't given it a second thought, and in fact would laugh off her worries.

But you've slept with him now, as in actually *slept*, snuggled in his arms all night long . . . And that was more intimate than anything else and it changed things for her. "Maybe I'm just being silly," she said hopefully to Thor.

Thor, lazy but utterly loyal, licked her chin.

She hugged him close. "I always have you," she murmured. "You'll never leave me—"

But he was squirming to get down so desperately she did just that. "What's gotten into you?" She stopped when he bounced over to a fellow dog a few feet away.

A small, dainty, perfectly groomed Shih Tzu. The dog stilled at Thor's approach and allowed him to sniff her butt, and then returned the favor while Pru glanced apologetically at the dog's owner.

The woman was in her thirties, wearing running tights and a tiny little running bra, the brand of which Pru couldn't even afford to look through their catalogue.

"Baby," the woman said. "What have I told you? You're a purebred not a disgusting mutt."

"Hey, he's not disgusting, he's just—" But Pru broke off when Thor lifted his leg and peed on Baby.

By the time Pru got to her building, Thor had fallen asleep in her arms, which were nearly dead. Seemed nothing stopped him from catching his beauty sleep, not snooty little dogs with snooty little owners, and certainly not the squealing of said snooty little dogs' owners about the cost of dog grooming and how Pru had let her heathen ruin her "baby."

A low-lying fog rolled in to join dusk as she entered through the courtyard, staying close to the back wall, not wanting to be seen by anyone.

The temps had dropped so she wasn't surprised to

see the wood fire pit lit. She was surprised to see Eddie manning the pit. He waved her over.

Halfway there she realized the entire courtyard smelled like skunk. When she got to Eddie, she pulled the uneaten half of her sushi lunch pack from her bag and gave it to him.

"Thanks, dudette." Pocketing the sushi in his sweatshirt, he poked at the fire with a long stick.

"It's going out," she said.

"I know. I burned it hot on purpose, I had some stuff to get rid of."

"Stuff? Stuff related to the skunk smell?"

He just smiled.

A few minutes went by and Pru realized she was still standing there, now with a wide grin on her face. "I'm starving."

"Me too," Willa said from right next to Pru.

Pru blinked. "When did you get here?"

"A while ago." Willa looked into her face and grinned too. "You're high as a kite."

"What? Of course I'm not," Pru said.

"It's a contact high." Willa looked at Eddie, who had the decency to look sheepish.

"I had some dead seedlings I had to get rid of," Eddie said. "It's fastest to just burn them."

"You can't just burn them out here!" Willa said. "Right, Pru?"

But Pru was feeling distracted. "I need food," she said. "Chips, cookies, cakes, and pies."

"And pizza," Willa said. "And chips."

"I already said chips."

"Double the chips!" Willa yelled to the courtyard

like she was placing an order with an invisible waitress.

Pru laughed at her. "I'm not high as a kite. *You* are."

"No, *you* are."

"No," Pru said, poking Willa in the arm. "*You* are."

"You both are." This was from Archer, who'd appeared in front of them.

"Whoa," Willa said. "The police are here. Run!"

Archer reached out and snagged her hand to keep her at his side. Frowning down at her, he then turned and eyeballed Pru.

She did her best to look innocent even though she felt very guilty. Why, she had no idea.

"Shit," he said in disgust to Eddie. "You got them both stoned out of their minds. What the hell did I tell you an hour ago?"

"You said you'd arrest me if I didn't put out the fire. I'm working on it. It's almost out, dude."

A muscle in Archer's jaw bunched. Willa set her head on his shoulder and looked up at him with a dreamy smile. "Elle's right," she murmured, batting her lashes. "You do look really hot when you're all worked up."

"I'm not worked up—" He broke off and slid her a speculative look. "Elle thinks I'm hot?"

"When you're worked up. When you're not, she thinks you're a stick in the mud."

Archer shook his head and pulled out his phone. "Elle, your girls need you in the courtyard. Now." He slid both Pru and Willa a long look and added, "You're going to want to feed them. Oh, and Elle? Remind me that we have something to discuss."

Willa smacked him. "You can't tell her that I told you that she thinks you're hot!" she hissed.

Archer lifted a finger in her direction and listened to something Elle said. He let out a rare smile. "Yes, that was Willa."

Willa smacked her own forehead. "She's gonna kill me."

Archer disconnected with Elle and pointed at them. "Don't either of you move until she comes and gets you. You hear me?"

"Hear you," Pru said, eyes locked on the pub. The doors were open to the street and the courtyard. The place was full and spilling out sounds of music and laughter.

Behind the bar, Sean and Finn were elbow to elbow, working hard. Finn was shaking a mixer and laughing at something a woman at the bar was saying to him.

Elle appeared in a siren red sheath dress that screamed serious business. Her black heels echoed the statement. "What's going on?" she demanded, hands on hips. "Archer pulled me out of a meeting with the building's board—"

"Was the owner there?" Willa asked. She looked at Pru. "None of us have ever met the owner. He's exclusive."

"*Elusive*," Elle corrected, narrowing her eyes on each of them, and then Eddie.

Who unlike when he'd been dealing with Archer, actually sunk in on himself a little, seemingly sheepish. "I didn't realize," he said.

"Oh for God's sake." Elle took a deep breath and looked a little less uptight. She took another and sighed. "I need pizza."

"Right?" Willa said, grinning.

"Count me in." This was Haley, who arrived from the elevator in her white doctor's coat, looking quite official.

"You're still doctoring," Willa said.

"Nope," Haley said, pulling off her lab coat. "The smoke and commotion drew me down here but I'm done for the day, thankfully. It was a busy one."

"Spence come in for glasses yet?" Elle asked.

Haley bit her lower lip. "I saw him, yes."

"And?" Elle asked. "His eyesight is bad, right?"

"I'm sorry, I can't say," Haley said. "Or HIPAA would drag me away in chains. He'll have to tell you himself."

Elle stared into her eyes and then smiled. "Yeah, he got glasses."

"Damn," Haley said. "I hate when you do that."

"She reads minds," Willa told Pru.

"Like magic?" Pru asked, awed.

"Not magic," Elle said. "You all just wear your every single thought on your sleeves."

"Oh, look at you, dear," Mrs. Winslow said to Pru, coming up to her with a wide smile. "You look amazing."

"Uh . . ." Pru looked down at herself. She was still in her usual work uniform of a stretchy white button-down and navy trousers and boots. "Thanks?"

"Must be all the sexual activity with Finn," the older woman said. "Intercourse does wonders for your skin."

Looking shocked, Willa nearly swallowed her tongue. She turned to Elle, who shrugged.

"You *knew*?" Willa asked.

"When are you going to get it? I *always* know," Elle said.

Pru admired a woman who always had the answers. She really hoped Elle shared some of them because she could really use a few right about now.

"Burgers and hot dogs!" a guy yelled walking through the courtyard. It was Jay. He owned the food truck that usually sat out front, but now he had a tray strapped on him and was making sales left and right like he was going up and down the rows at a baseball stadium. "I've got beef burgers and six inches of prime sausages here! Get 'em while they're hot!"

"Six inches would do me just right," Mrs. Winslow said wistfully. "I wouldn't know what to do with seven or eight."

Try nine, Pru thought and clapped a hand over her mouth to keep from saying it out loud.

"Something you want to share with the class?" Haley asked.

Most definitely not, but the vultures had the scent of roadkill and were circling.

"Oh, she'll talk," Elle said, staring into Pru's eyes. "She'll talk over a loaded pie and a bottle of wine. Girls, let's hit it."

And she walked off.

"She's so badass," Willa whispered, staring after her. "I mean look at that dress. She's badass, kickass, *and* she has a great ass. It's really not fair."

"I can hear you," Elle called out over her shoulder without looking back. She snapped her fingers. "Put it in gear."

And Pru, Haley, and Willa followed after her like puppies on a leash.

Chapter 24

#SuitUp

Pru had no idea how Elle did it, but by the time they got to the street, there was an Uber ride waiting on them.

"Lefty's Pizza," Elle said to the driver.

"I thought you were on a diet," Haley said, climbing into the car.

"Some days you eat salads and go to the gym," Elle said. "And some days you eat pizza and wear yoga pants. It's called balance."

"I always eat pizza and wear yoga pants," Willa said. She gasped. "Does that make me unbalanced?"

"No, actually, it makes you smarter than me," Elle said with a small smile.

Willa sighed. "Or maybe I've just given up on men."

"That's only because you dated a few frogs," Elle said.

"That's an extremely nice way of saying that I'm a

loser magnet. And I couldn't get rid of that one frog either. I still owe Archer for stepping in and pretending to be my boyfriend so he'd back off."

"That's not why he backed off," Elle said. "He backed off because Archer threatened to castrate him if he contacted you again."

Willa gaped. "He did? I was wondering at how easy he made it look."

"And you can make it look easy too," Elle told her. "Next time you want to lose a guy, just tell them 'I love you, I want to marry you, and I want children right away.' They'll run so fast they'll leave skid marks."

Willa snorted. "I'll keep that in mind."

Thirty minutes later they were in a booth, one bottle of wine down, another ready to go, and a large pizza on its way to being demolished. Pru's stomach hurt, but that hadn't slowed her down any.

Willa pulled a book from her purse. "Have either of you been to that new used bookstore down the street from our building?"

"I download my books right to my phone," Elle said. "That way I can read while pretending to listen in on meetings."

"Your boss doesn't mind?" Pru asked.

"My boss knows everything," Elle said. "And one of the things he also knows is that me doing my thing allows him to do his thing."

Made sense.

"Plus, I know where the bodies are hidden," she said.

Probably she was kidding.

"Well, I like the feel of a book in my hand," Willa said and looked at Pru.

"I go both ways," Pru said and then blushed when they all laughed. "You know what I mean."

"I do," Willa said and handed her the book. "Which is why I bought this for you."

Pru eyed the title and choked on a bite of pizza. Willa had to pound her on the back while Pru sucked a bunch of wine down to try and appease her burning throat. No go. *"Orgasms For One?"* she finally managed.

Willa nodded.

"Um . . . thank you?"

"I bought it after you told us that you hadn't dated in a while but before I heard about the dumbwaiter, so . . ."

Pru sighed. "So everyone knows about the dumbwaiter."

"Little bit," Haley said. "What we don't know are the deets."

Elle pointed at Pru. "You. Finn. Go."

"It's . . . a long story."

"I love long stories," Willa said.

Elle just arched a brow. She didn't like to be kept waiting.

"Might as well start talking," Haley told Pru. "She'll get her way eventually, she always does. I've found it's best to give in earlier than later. Besides, I'm tired." She accompanied this statement with a wide yawn.

Pru rubbed her aching stomach. She was starting to feel sick. "Maybe we should postpone this for another day. When I haven't eaten my weight in pizza."

Elle didn't break eye contact with her. She didn't budge a muscle, not even to blink.

Pru sighed. "Fine. Maybe something's happened

between me and Finn, but it's not going to keep happening."

Willa grinned. "So you *did* sleep with him."

"Past tense," Pru said, her gaze still held prisoner by Elle's. "Even if I wish it wasn't." Dammit. "Where did you get this super power?" she demanded. "I need it."

Elle smiled. "I'd tell you but—"

"—But she'd have to kill you," Willa finished on a laugh. "Love it when you say that."

"Except you never let me say it," Elle pointed out.

Pru's stomach turned over yet again and she put a hand on it. "I really don't feel so good."

"Because you're holding back on your new BFFs," Willa said.

"I like you for Finn," Elle said to Pru. "He hasn't chosen anyone in a long time. I'm glad it's you."

"Oh, no. That's the thing," she said. "It's not me. I mean, it was great. He was great. And when I was with him, I felt . . ." She closed her eyes, the memories washing over her. "*Really* great." She could still hear his low, sexy voice in her ear telling her what he was going to do to her, and then his even sexier body doing it, taking hers to places it hadn't been in so long she'd nearly forgotten what it was like to be in a man's arms and lose herself.

"So why is it over then?" Haley asked. "Do you realize how rare 'really great' is? I haven't had 'really great' in so long I don't even know if I'll recognize it."

"You'll recognize it," Elle said, looking at Pru, waiting on her answer.

But Pru didn't answer. Couldn't. Because she hated the reason why. "It's . . . complicated."

"Honey," Elle said with surprising vulnerability and wistfulness in her voice. "The best things always are." She paused. "You'd be really good for him."

Elle wasn't a woman to say such a thing unless she meant it so Pru felt herself warm a little at that. Even if it wasn't true. She wasn't good for Finn. And when he found out the truth about her and who she was, she'd in fact be very bad for him.

"He hasn't dated since Mellie," Willa said thoughtfully. "And she turned out to be—"

"Willa," Elle said quietly. Warningly.

"I'm sorry," she said, not sounding sorry at all. "But I hated her for what she did to him. To him *and* Sean."

"It was a long time ago," Elle said firmly.

"A year. He liked her, a lot. And he got hurt," Willa said. "And you hated her for it too, admit it."

Elle gave a slight head nod. "I would have liked to kill her," she said casually in the way most people would comment on the weather.

"And it changed him," Willa said. She turned to Pru. "Mellie had the dressy boutique here in the building for a while before she sold it. She was wild and fun and gregarious, and she was good for Finn. At first. Until—"

"Willa." Elle gave her a long look. "You're telling tales. He's going to kill you."

"Only if you tattle," Willa said. "Pru needs to know what she's up against."

"What am I up against?" Pru whispered in spite of herself, needing to know.

"Mellie and Sean got drunk one night. And they . . ." She grimaced.

Pru gasped. "No," she breathed. "She slept with his brother?"

"Well, apparently when Finn walked in on them they hadn't quite gotten to home plate but it was close enough."

"Finn walked in on them?" Pru asked, horrified, trying to imagine. She didn't have a sibling, but in her fantasies, if she'd had a sister or brother, they would stand at her back, always. "How awful."

Willa nodded. "It caused a big fight, but they've always fought. Sean had had way too much to drink that night, he was really out of it, and later he kept saying he'd never have made a move on her if he'd been in his right mind. But Mellie wasn't drunk. She knew exactly what she was doing."

"But why would she do that to Finn?" Pru asked.

"Because she'd been after him for a commitment. At that time, he was still finishing up his business degree. She hated that he went to classes early in the morning, studied after that, then handled the business side of O'Riley's, and then often had to work the pub all night on top of that. When he wasn't working his ass off on any of those things, he was dead asleep. He was giving everything one hundred percent, even her, but it wasn't enough. She was bored and lonely, two things that didn't agree with her."

Elle slid Willa a look. "You think he's going to thank you for airing his dirty laundry when he finds out?"

"No, I think he'll put out a hit on me," Willa said. "But he's not going to find out. I'm doing our girl a service here, explaining some things about her man that he's certainly not going to explain to her."

"He's not my man," Pru said.

"He's not going to explain," Willa said to Elle as if Pru hadn't spoken, "because he thinks the past should stay in the past."

"He's not my man," Pru repeated, holding her stomach, which was killing her now.

"The past should *absolutely* stay in the past," Elle said to Willa, something in her voice saying she believed that to the depths of her very soul.

Willa closed her eyes briefly and covered Elle's hand with her own, the two of them sharing a moment that Pru didn't understood. They had history. She got that. They were close friends, and clearly there was a lot about them that she didn't know. Such as what had happened to Elle to make her want her past to stay buried.

Pru didn't have many people in her life. Her own fault. She didn't let many in. It didn't take a shrink to get why. She'd lost her parents early. Her only other living relative often mistook her for devil spawn. There were some school friends she kept in occasional contact with, and she had her coworkers. And Jake.

But it would be really nice to have Willa and Elle as well.

Her stomach cramped painfully again, which she ignored when Willa took her hand.

"I'm trusting you with this, Pru," she said. "Do you know why?"

Unable to imagine, Pru shook her head.

"Because you're one of us now," she said and looked at Elle. "Right?"

Elle turned her head and met Pru's gaze, studying her solemnly for a long beat before slowly nodding.

Willa smiled. "Look at that." She looked at Pru again. "Here's something you might not know. Elle doesn't like very many people."

Elle snorted.

"It's because she's scary as shit," Haley said, drinking the last of her wine.

"Sitting right here," Elle said calmly, glancing at her nails.

Which were, of course, perfect.

Not appearing scared in the slightest, Willa just smiled. "But one thing about her, she never says anything she doesn't mean. And once you're a friend, you're a friend for life." She paused and glanced at Elle, brow raised.

Elle shrugged.

Willa gave her a long look.

Elle rolled her eyes but she did smile. "Friends for life," she said. "Or until you piss me off. Don't piss me off."

A new warmth filled Pru and her throat tightened. "Thanks," she whispered.

Elle narrowed her eyes. "You're not going to cry, are you? There's no crying on pizza night."

"Just got something in my eye," Pru said with a sniff and swiped under her eyes.

Elle sighed and handed her a napkin. "Look, I know I'm a cold-hearted bitch, but Willa's right, you're one of ours now. And we're yours. This is why we're trusting you with Finn. Because he's also one of ours and he means a lot to us."

"Oh no, you can't trust me with him," she said. "I mean—" She shook her head. "It's just that I'm not— we're not a real thing."

"It's cute you think that." Willa patted her hand. "But I've seen you two together."

Pru opened her mouth to protest but the dessert they'd ordered arrived—a pan-size homemade cookie topped with ice cream, and then there was no speaking as they stuffed their faces.

When Pru was done, it came up on her suddenly. Her stomach rolled again and this time a queasiness rose up her throat with it.

Uh oh.

The good news was that she recognized the problem. The bad news was that she was about to be sick. She searched her brain for what she might have eaten and gasped.

Sushi for lunch.

Which meant she'd made Eddie sick too. "I've got to go," she said abruptly. The last time she'd had food poisoning she'd laid on her bathroom floor for two straight days. Privacy was required for such things, serious privacy. Standing on wobbly legs, she pulled some money from her purse and dropped it on the table. "I'm sorry—" She clapped a hand to her gurgling stomach and shook her head. "Later."

She got a cab, but the traffic and the ensuing stop/ start of navigating said traffic just about killed her. She bailed a block early and moved as fast as she could. When she cut through the courtyard of her building, she slid a quick, anxious look at the pub. *Please don't be there, please don't be there . . .*

But fate or destiny or karma, whoever was in charge of such things as looking out for her humility, had taken a break because all the pub doors were still open to the night. Finn stood near the courtyard entrance talking to some customers. And like a beacon in the night, he turned right to her.

She kept moving, her hand over her mouth, as if that would keep her from throwing up in public. If she could have sold her soul to the devil right then to ensure it, she totally would have.

But not even the devil himself had enough power to alter her course in history. She was dying at this point, sharp, shooting pains through her gut combined with an all-over body ache that had her whimpering to herself with each step. Holding back from losing her dinner had her sweating in rivulets.

"Pru," came Finn's unbearably familiar voice— from right behind her.

"I'm sorry," she managed, not slowing down. "I can't—"

"We need to talk."

Yep, the only four words in the English language destined to spark terror within her heart. Talk? He wanted to talk? Maybe when she died. And given the pain stabbing through her with the force of a thousand needles, it wouldn't be long now. Still, just in case, she moved faster.

"Pru."

She wanted to say *look, I'm about to throw up half a loaded pizza and possibly my intestines, and I like you, I like you enough that if you see me throw up that half a loaded pizza, I'll have to kill myself.*

Which, actually, wouldn't be necessary seeing as she was about to die anyway.

"Pru, slow down." He caught her hand.

But the more she put off the now inevitable, the worse it would be. "Not feeling good," she said, twisting free. "I've gotta go."

"What's wrong?" His voice immediately changed from playful to serious. "What do you need?"

What she needed was the privacy of her own bathroom. She opened her mouth to say so but the only thing that came out was a miserable moan.

"Do you need a doctor?" he asked.

Yes, she needed a doctor. For a lobotomy.

With sweat slicking her skin, she ran directly for the elevator, praying that it would be on the ground floor and no one else would want to get on it with her.

Of course it wasn't on the ground floor.

With another miserable moan she headed for the stairwell, taking them as fast as she could with her stomach sending fireballs to her brain and her legs weakened by the need to upchuck.

And oh lucky her, Finn kept pace with her, right at her side.

Which made her panic all the more because seriously, she was on a countdown at this point, T minus sixty seconds tops, and there would be no stopping or averting liftoff. "I'm fine!" she said weakly. "Please, just leave me alone!" She threw her hand out at him to push him away so she could have room in case she spontaneously imploded.

A very real possibility.

But the man who was more tuned into her body than she was had apparently not yet mastered mind reading. "I'm not leaving you alone like this," he said.

She pushed him again from a well of reserved

strength born of sheer terror because she was about to become her own horror show and didn't want witnesses. "You have to go!" she said, maybe yelled, as they *finally* got to the third floor.

Mrs. Winslow stuck her head out her door and gave Pru a disapproving look. "You might be getting some but you're not going to keep getting some if you talk to your man like that. Especially after shoving him into the dumbwaiter the other night."

Oh for God's sake!

How did everyone know about that?

Not that she could ask.

Hell, no. Instead, she stopped and pawed through her purse for her keys before dropping it to scratch and claw at the door like she was being kidnapped and tortured.

Finn crouched down at her feet to pick up her purse and scoop the contests back in. He had a tampon in one hand and Willa's book—*Orgasms For One*—in the other. He should've looked utterly ridiculous. Instead he looked utterly perfect.

"Pru, can you tell me what's wrong?"

"I think she's having a seizure," Mrs. Winslow said helpfully. "Honey, you look a little bit constipated. I suggest a good fart. That always works for me."

Pru didn't know how to tell her she was about to let loose but it wouldn't be nearly as neat as a fart. By some miracle, she made it inside. She was sweating through her clothes by the time she stumbled along without even taking her keys out of the lock, racing to the bathroom, slamming the door behind her.

She had barely hit her knees before she got sick.

From what felt like a narrow, long tunnel, through the thick fog in her head and her own misery, she heard him.

"Pru," he said, his voice low with worry.

From right.

Outside.

Her.

Bathroom.

Door.

"I'm coming in," he said and she couldn't stop throwing up to tell him to run, to save himself.

Chapter 25

#BadDayAtTheOffice

Pru felt one of Finn's hands pull her hair back and hold it for her, the other encircling her, fingers spread wide on her stomach. He was kneeling behind her, his big body supporting hers.

"I've got you," he said.

No one had ever said such a thing to her before and she would have loved to absorb that and maybe obsess over why it meant so much, but her stomach had other ideas. So she closed her eyes and pretended she was alone on a deserted island with her charged Kindle. And maybe Netflix. When she could catch her breath, she brought a shaky hand to her head, which was pounding like the devil himself was in there operating a jackhammer, whittling away at what was left of her brains.

Finn kept her from sliding to the floor by wrapping both arms around her and bringing her gently back, propping her up against him.

"I'm sorry," she managed, horrified that she'd thrown up in front of the hottest man she'd ever had the privilege of sleeping with by accident.

"Breathe, Pru. It's going to be okay."

"Please just leave me here to die," she croaked out when she could, pulling free. "Just walk out of this room and pretend it never happened. We'll never speak of it again."

And then, giving up trying to be strong, she slid bonelessly to the bathroom floor. Her body was hot and she was slick with perspiration. Unable to garner the energy to hold herself up anymore, she pressed her hot cheek to the cool tile and closed her eyes.

She heard water running and squeezed her eyes tight, but that only made her all the dizzier. A deliciously cool, wet washcloth was pressed to her forehead. She cracked an eye and found Finn. "Dammit, you never listen."

"I always listen," he said. "I just don't always agree."

His hand was rubbing her back in soothing circles and she thought she might never move again if he kept on doing that until the end of time. "Why won't you go away?"

When he didn't say anything, she again opened an eye. He was still looking at her with concern but not like she was at death's door. Except if she wasn't dying, that meant she was going to have to live with this, with him seeing her flat on the floor looking like roadkill.

"Do you think you can move?" he asked.

"Negative." She wasn't moving. *Ever.* She heard him on his phone, telling someone he needed something liquid with electrolytes in it.

"Not drinking anything either," she warned him, her stomach turning over at the thought.

He got up and left her, and she was grateful. When he came back in a moment later, she was back to worshipping the porcelain god, trying to catch her breath.

"Any better?" he asked when she was done.

She couldn't speak. She couldn't anything.

He peeled her away from the seat and gathered her in his lap. He laid her head against his shoulder and wrapped his arms around her. "Take a few deep breaths. Slowly."

She tried but she was shaking so hard she thought maybe her teeth were going to rattle right out of her head. Finn wiped the sweat-matted hair from her face and then pressed the cool washcloth to the back of her neck.

It was heaven.

He cracked a bottle of lime-flavored water with electrolytes.

"Where did you get that?" she asked.

"Willa. She has it in her shop. Says she gives it to the nervous dogs after they throw up."

"You told Willa I was throwing up?"

"She's in the kitchen making you soup for tomorrow when you feel better. Elle's bringing her a few ingredients she didn't have."

Pru managed a moan. "I don't want anyone to see me like this."

"You do realize that friends don't actually care what you look like," he said. "Take a sip, Pru."

She shook her head. She couldn't possibly swallow anything.

"Just a sip. Trust me, it'll help."

She did trust him. But drinking anything was going to be a disaster of major proportions.

He was moving her, using his shoulder to hold her head forward. It was take a sip or drown.

She took a sip.

"Good girl," he whispered and let her settle back against him. They sat there, silent, for what seemed like days. Her stomach slowly stopped doing backflips.

"How do you feel?" he asked after a while.

She had no idea.

When she didn't enlighten him, he took the washcloth from her neck, refolded it, and put it against her forehead.

"Eddie," she croaked. "He might be sick too—"

"I've got him covered. Spence is with him but the old guy's got a stomach of iron and doesn't appear to be affected.

She managed a nod, eyes still closed. She must have drifted off then because when she opened her eyes again the light was different in the bathroom, like some time had gone by.

Finn was still on the floor with her, only he was shirtless now, wearing just his jeans.

Oh yeah. She remembered now. She'd thrown up a bunch more times. She had her hands curled around his neck, clutching him like he was her only lifeline.

And he was. She stared at his chest. She couldn't stop herself. No matter how many times she saw his stomach, she wanted to lick it each time.

Not that she wanted to stop there either.

Nope, she wanted to lick upward to his neck and

then trail back down. She wanted to drop to her knees and slowly ease his jeans over his hips and—

"You okay?" he asked. "You just moaned."

Huh. Maybe she really was going to live. She dragged her back to his. His hair was tousled, his jaw beyond a five o'clock shadow, but he still looked hot.

She hated him. "You should go," she said knowing he either had to work or sleep.

He shook his head and brushed his lips over her forehead at the hairline. "It's been a couple of hours since you last got sick," he said. "Sip some more water."

Her stomach was much calmer now, but her head was beating to its own drum. She could feel it pulsating.

"You're dehydrated," he said. "You need the water to get rid of the fever and headache."

Too achy to argue, she nodded. She managed to take a few sips and then her body took over, demanding more.

"Careful," Finn warned, pulling it away when she started to gulp it. "Let's see how that settles first."

"Thor?"

"He's right here, sleeping on my feet. You want him?"

Yes. But she was in bad enough shape to hug him too tight and the last time she'd done that, he'd gotten scared and bit her. She'd stick with just Finn for now. She was pretty sure Finn only bit when naked. Or on really special occasions.

She fell asleep on him again and woke up much later in her own bed. Willa was helping her change.

"That man is gone over you," Willa murmured, tucking Pru into bed.

"It's the damn fountain." Pru had to hold her head

on, keeping her eyes shut even when Willa had paused.

"Fountain?" she asked.

Maybe if Pru hadn't been dying, she wouldn't have answered. "I wished," she said. "I wished for Finn to find love, but the fountain got it all wrong and gave *me* love instead. Stupid fountain. He's the one who deserves it."

"Honey," Willa said softly. "We all deserve love."

Pru wanted that to be true. God, how she wanted that . . .

"And how do you know the fountain didn't get it right?" Willa asked. "Maybe *you're* his true love."

Pru drifted off on that terrifying thought.

"You're going to want to sip some of this."

It was Elle. She sat on the bed at Pru's hip and offered a mug.

"What is it?" Pru asked.

"Only the best tea on the planet. Try it."

"I'm not thirsty—"

"Try it," Elle said again finally. "You're nearly translucent, you need fluids."

So Pru sipped.

"Now," Ella said calmly. "What's this I hear about the fountain and some wish going astray?"

Pru choked on her sip.

Elle rolled her eyes, leaned forward, and pounded Pru on the back.

"Willa told you," Pru said on a sigh.

"Yeah. She's cute but she can't keep a secret. She doesn't mean any harm, I promise. She doesn't have a mean bone in her body. Mostly she's worried about you and thought I could beat some sense into you."

Pru blinked.

"Metaphorically," Elle said. "And plus she wanted to borrow some change so she could go make a wish, seeing how it worked out so good for you."

"The wish was for Finn!"

"Uh huh."

"It was!"

"Well then, I'd say you got a two-fer."

Chapter 26

#WaxOnWaxOff

The next time Pru opened her eyes, the hallway light allowed her to see that someone was sprawled in the chair by her bed. That someone rose when she stirred and sat at her hip.

"How you doing?" Finn asked.

She blinked at the crack of dawn's early light creeping in through the slats of her blinds, casting everything in a hazy gold glow. From outside the window came the early chatter of birds, obnoxiously loud and chipper. She moaned. "I've never figured out if they're happy that it's morning or objecting to its arrival."

Finn smiled. "I vote for objecting."

Her too. He'd changed, she couldn't help but notice. Different jeans, a rumpled black T-shirt. Hair still tousled. Jaw still stubbled. Eyes heavy-lidded. He was without a doubt the sexiest thing she'd ever seen. Which told her one thing at least.

She hadn't died.

He propped her up in her bed, tied her crazy-ass hair back and brought her toast. Cut diagonally. She just stared up at him. Was he a fevered dream? "Tell me the truth," she murmured, her voice rough and haggard. "You're a fevered mirage, right?"

He frowned and leaned over her, one hand planted on the mattress, the other going to her forehead. His frown deepened and he leaned in even closer so that she caught a whiff of him.

He smelled like heaven on earth.

She did *not* smell like heaven on earth, and worse, she felt like roadkill. Like roadkill that had been run over, back upped on, and run over again. Twice.

But not Finn. She pressed in close and plastered her face to his throat at the same moment he pressed his mouth to her forehead.

"You don't feel fevered," he muttered.

"No, that's what happens when things are a mirage. In fact, last night never even really happened."

Pulling back, he met her gaze. "So I suppose you remember nothing."

"Nothing," she agreed quickly. "How could I? Nothing happened."

His lips twitched. "Nicely done."

"Thank you."

He smiled. And then dropped the bomb. "Tell me about the fountain."

"On second thought," she said. "Maybe I actually died. I'm gone and buried . . ."

"Try again."

She looked into his eyes, trying to decide if he knew

the truth about her wish—in which case she might have to strangle Willa and Elle—or if he was just fishing. "Well," she said lightly. "It was built back in the days when Cow Hollow was filled with cows. And—"

"Not the fountain's history, smartass," he said. "I mean why you were muttering about it in your feverish haze."

Huh. So maybe Elle and Willa didn't have to be strangled after all. "I was feverish and delusional," she said. "You need to forget everything you heard. And saw," she added.

"You wished for love on the fountain?" he asked with a whisper of disbelief.

"What does it matter, you don't believe in the myth anyway, remember?"

"That's not an answer," he said.

"I don't believe in the myth either," she said, and he fell quiet, letting her get away with that.

Instead of pushing, he nudged the toast her way. "Eat. And drink. You need to hydrate."

"You sound like a mom."

"Just don't call me grandpa." He got up to go, but she caught his hand.

"Hey," she said. "You went over and above last night. You didn't have to do that."

"I know."

It was hard to hold his gaze. "Thanks for taking care of me."

He just looked at her for a long beat. "Anytime."

By the next day, Pru was completely over the food poisoning and back to work, which was a good thing for several reasons. One, Jake desperately needed her.

And two, she needed to get over throwing up in front of Finn, and short of a memory scrub, working her ass off was the only way to do it. So she buried herself, banning thoughts of Finn, needing to build up her immunity to his sexy charisma.

This worked for two days but then her efforts to lay low failed when he showed up at the warehouse.

He was waiting for her between two tours, propping up a pillar in the holding area where passengers hung out before and after boarding the ships.

"What are you doing here?" she asked, surprised.

"Need a minute with you." He took her hand and pulled her outside. He was in low-slung jeans and a dark green henley the exact color of his eyes. His hair had been finger combed at best and he hadn't shaved, leaving a day's worth of scruff on his square jaw that she knew personally would feel like sex on a stick against her skin.

"You've been avoiding me," he said.

"No, I—"

He put a finger on her lips, his body so close now that she could feel the heat of him, which made her body shift in closer.

Bad body.

"Careful," he said quietly, dipping his head so that his mouth hovered near hers. "You're about to fib, and once you do, things change."

She absorbed that a moment, and wrapping her fingers around his wrist, pulled his finger away from her mouth. "What things?"

His eyes never left hers. "Feelings."

Any lingering amusement faded away because she

knew what he was saying. He didn't believe in lying. Or in half-truths. Or fibs . . . And if he thought she was the kind of woman who did, then his feelings about her would change.

She'd known this going in, of course. What she hadn't known was how strongly it would affect their relationship.

Because he didn't know one important fact.

She'd been lying to him about something since the very beginning. She'd weaved the web, she'd built the brick wall, *she'd* created this nightmare of a problem and she had no idea what to do about it.

"Okay, so I've been avoiding you a little," she admitted, starting with the one thing she did know what to do about.

"Why?"

She stared at him. The truth shot out of her heart and landed on the tip of her tongue. She wanted to tell him. She wanted it out in the open in the worst way. Holding it in was giving her guilt gut aches. But they'd only known each other a few short weeks. She just needed a little bit more time. To charm him. To somehow get him to do what no one else ever had—fall hard enough for her to want to keep her.

No matter that she'd made a huge mistake. She needed to work him into that, slowly. "I'm not good with this stuff," she said quietly. Hello, understatement of the year.

"Going to need you to be more specific."

"I'm not good with . . . the after thing." And so much more . . .

"The after thing," he repeated. "You mean after food poisoning? Pru, who *is* good at that?"

"No. I mean yes, and I don't know. But I was talking about the after sleeping with someone thing."

He looked more than a little baffled, and also somewhat amused. "So having sex isn't the problem, it's that we've actually slept together," he said.

Knowing it sounded ridiculous, she nodded.

She expected him to try and joke that away but he didn't. Instead, he wrapped his big hand up in hers and gave her a crooked smile. "I guess that makes us the blind leading the blind then. I don't do a lot of sleepovers, Pru."

"But you've been in a long relationship before," she said. "With Mellie."

He paused. "Someone's been telling tales."

"It's true though, right?" she asked.

"What is it that you're asking me, Pru?"

Okay, so he clearly didn't want to discuss Mellie. Got it. Understood it. Hell, she had plenty of things she didn't want to discuss either. "I'm trying to say that not only am I not good at sleepovers, I . . . haven't really had any." She bit her lip. Dammit. That made her sound pathetic. She tried again. "It's more that you're my one and only—" Nope, now she was just making it worse. "Okay, you know what? Never mind." She started to walk off. "I'm going back to work."

He caught her and turned her to face him. "Wait a minute."

"Can't," she said. 'I've gotten—"

"Pru," he said with terrifying tenderness as he

bulldozed right over her with his dogged determination, cupping her face. "Are you saying you've never—"

"No, of course I have." She closed her eyes. "It's just been awhile since Jake—and he wasn't a one-night stand. Or even a two-night stand. He was a week-long stand—" She covered her mouth. "Oh my God," she said around her fingers. "Please tell me to stop talking!"

He gently pulled her hand from her mouth. "You and Jake were together only a week?"

"Yes."

"And before that, you'd not been with anyone else?"

"I had a boyfriend in high school," she said defensively.

"But . . ."

"But he dumped me after my parents died," she admitted. "I was a complete wreck, and—"

"That shouldn't have happened to you," he said quietly, stroking her upper arms, his warm hands somehow reaching deep inside her and warming a spot she hadn't even realized was chilled. "That shouldn't have happened to anyone," he said very gently. "So other than your high school asshole boyfriend and one week with Jake, there's been no one else?"

If she'd ever felt more vulnerable or exposed, she couldn't remember it. It was horribly embarrassing, having her sexual history—or lack thereof—laid out, and with it came an avalanche of insecurities. She shook her head and stared at his throat instead of in his eyes, which was easier. Because he had a very sexy throat and—

"Pru. Babe, look at me."

She reluctantly lifted her gaze to his.

"I think I'm starting to understand more about what's going on," he said.

Oh good. Maybe he could explain it to her. That would be supremely helpful.

"What happened between us," he said, "it never occurred to me that you thought it was a one-night stand."

She stared at him, confused. "No?"

"Hell, no," he said. "Not with our chemistry. I knew from the beginning that one night wasn't going to be enough. Or two. Or ten. I thought you knew it too."

She swallowed hard. She did know it. That wasn't the problem. No, the problem was that the time they'd already spent together . . . it had to be enough. It was all she would, could, allow herself. "I didn't allow myself to think that far. Finn—"

"Look, I know we've done things ass-backwards, but I want to fix that." He smiled at her. "Go out with me tonight."

She stared at him. "Like . . . a date?"

"Exactly like a date."

"But—"

His mouth brushed along her jaw to her ear, his words whispered hot against her. "Say 'yes, Finn.'"

"Yes, Finn," escaped her before she could stop herself. Damn. Her mouth really needed to meet her brain sometime. But the truth was, she needed this, needed him. She wanted this moment and she wanted to enjoy it. Selfish as it was, she was going to think about herself for once, just for tonight. Besides, thinking was overrated. "You make it hard to think," she said.

She felt him smile knowingly against her skin. "Pru, I'm going to be so good to you tonight that there'll be no thinking required.

It's a good thing that thinking was overrated.

He picked her up at six. She was nervous as hell, which was silly. It was Finn. And it was just a date.

At a red light, he glanced over at her and flashed a grin. "You look pretty."

She was in a simple sundress and flats. Hair down. "You've seen this dress," she said.

His eyes heated. Clearly he was remembering that it was the dress he'd made her hold at her waist while he'd had his merry way with her. "I know," he murmured. "I love that dress."

She blushed and he laughed softly.

"Where are we going?" she asked, needing a subject change.

"Nervous?"

Yes. "No."

He slid her a knowing glance. "It's a surprise."

That had her worried. But where they ended up made her smile wide and stare at him. "A Giants game?"

"Yeah." He parked at the stadium and pulled her from the car with a smacking kiss. "Okay with you?"

Was he kidding? For a beat, her troubles fell away and she grinned at him. "Very okay."

He brought her hand to his mouth and smiled over their entwined fingers.

She melted.

He fed her whatever she wanted, which was hotdogs

and beer, and they both yelled and cheered the game on to their heart's content.

They sat next to a couple of serious Giants fans who were wearing only shorts—although the girl also wore a bikini top—and their every inch of exposed skin painted Giants orange.

The guy proposed between innings two and three, and it was nothing like the proposal on her ship. When these two hugged and kissed, there was love in every touch—although their carefully painted Giants logo smeared. The orange and white paint mixed into a pale color that actually resembled pink, making them look like a walking advertisement for Pepto-Bismol.

At the bottom of the fourth, the KISS cam panned the crowd and everyone went wild. It stopped on an older couple, who sweetly pecked. Next it stopped on two men who flashed their wedding rings with wide grins before giving the audience a kiss.

Everyone was still cheering when the KISS cam stopped on Pru and Finn. Pru turned to him, laughing, and he hauled her in and laid one on her that made her brain turn to mush and an entire inning went by before her brain reset itself and began processing again.

It was possibly the most fun date she'd been on since . . .

Ever.

After the game, Finn walked Pru to her door. She was a little tipsy so he held her hand, smiling as he listened to her singing to some song in her head that only she could hear.

She had a smudge of orange paint down her entire right side from the woman at the game. It'd drizzled for a few minutes in the eighth inning and her hair had rioted into a frizzy mass of waves.

He wanted to sink his fingers into it, press her back against her door and kiss her senseless. Then he wanted to pick her up so that she'd wrap her long legs around him.

He wanted her. Hard and fast. Slow and sweet. On the couch. In the shower. Her bed.

Anywhere he could get her.

And it wasn't just physical either. He'd told her he didn't think love was for him, but he'd been wrong. At least going off the way his heart rolled over and exposed its tender underbelly every time she so much as looked at him. He wanted to claim her, wanted to leave his mark on her. On the inside. On her heart and in her soul.

But she wasn't ready. She was way behind him in this and he knew that. What they had between them scared her, and more than a little. She needed time, and he could give her that. *Would* give her that.

Even if it meant walking away from her tonight when she was smiling up at him, her eyes shining, her cheeks flushed, happy. Warm.

Willing.

"'Night," he said softly. "Lock up tight."

"Wait." She blinked once, slow as an owl. A tipsy owl. "You're . . . leaving?"

"Yes."

"But . . ." She stepped into him, running her hands up his chest. "Aren't we going to . . ."

He went brows up, forcing her to be specific.

"I thought you'd come in and we'd . . . you know," she whispered, her fingers dancing over his jaw.

Catching her hand, he brought it to his mouth and brushed a kiss over her palm. "No," he said gently. "Not tonight."

"But . . . when?"

"When you're ready to fill in 'you know' with the words," he said.

She stood there, mouth open a little, a furrow between her brows, looking bewildered, aroused, and more than a little off center.

Maybe she wasn't so far behind him after all.

"'Night," he said, cupping her face for a soft kiss. Walking away was one of the hardest things he'd ever done.

When Pru's door closed, another opened and Mrs. Winslow poked her head out. "You sure you know what you're doing?" she asked him.

Hell no, he didn't know what he was doing.

She shook her head at him. "You sure don't know much about women, do you. You can't leave them alone to think about whether they need you, and do you know why?"

He shook his head.

"Because it's only in the moment that a woman will act impulsively. It's all the testosterone and pheromones that pour off you males, you see. Without you right in front of her, that magic stuff wears off and she'll easily remember that she doesn't need you in her life."

"I'm going to hope that's not true," he said.

"You can hope all you want, but you'll be hoping alone in an empty bed."

Chapter 27

#SmarterThanTheAverageBear

Late the next afternoon, Pru was at work wishing she was anywhere but. She was in the middle of an argument with a guy who'd paid for a tour for him and his son the week before, but they hadn't shown up. Now he wanted a refund.

She'd only stepped behind the ticket counter as a favor to one of the ticket clerks who'd had to leave early. This guy was the last person she had to deal with before going home. She'd paused, looking for a credit option on the computer, when he decided she was dicking him around.

"Listen," he bit out. "I'm not going to deal with some homicidal, hormonal, PMS-y, minimum-wage chick who doesn't give a shit. I want the supervisor. Get him for me."

"Actually," she said. "You've got a supervisor right

here. And no worries. I was homicidal hormonal last week. This week I'm good. Even nice, if I say so myself."

He didn't smile. He was hands on hips. "I want my money back."

Pru's gaze slid to the person who'd just come in behind him. Finn. He stood there quietly but not passively, watching. Pru turned back to Pissy Man and pointed to the large sign above her head.

No refunds.

The guy leaned in way too close. "Do you have any idea who I am?"

An asshole? A thought she kept to herself because she was busy noticing that Finn shifted too, until he was standing just off to her left, body language signaling that while he was at ease, he was also ready to kick some ass if needed.

She'd thought of him today. A lot. Last night after he'd left, she'd nearly called him a dozen times. He wanted words and she had them. She wanted to say "please come back and make love to me."

Because if she knew one thing, it was that what they'd done together wasn't just sex.

Dammit.

For now, her cranky customer was still standing there with a fight in his eyes. "I'm in charge of the budget for the city's promo and advertising department," he told her. "We make sure that your entire industry is listed in all the Things to Do in San Francisco guides. Without me, you'd be cleaning toilets."

Okay, now that was a bit of a stretch. "Listen, it

wouldn't matter if you were POTUS. There are no re-funds. I can get you a credit for another tour but you have to be patient with me while I figure out—

He slammed a hand down on the counter, but she didn't jump. She'd dealt with far bigger assholes than this one. Before she could suggest he leave, Finn was there.

He'd moved so quickly she never even saw him coming as he stepped in between her and the guy. "She said no refunds and offered you a credit," Finn said. "Take it or leave it."

"Leave it," the guy snapped.

"Your choice," Finn said. "But unless there's something else you'd like to say, and fair warning, it'd better be 'have a nice day,' you need to go."

The guy stared down Finn for the briefest of seconds before possibly deciding he liked his face in the condition it was in because he strode out without another word.

"Seriously?" Pru asked Finn.

He shoved his hands into his pockets. "What?"

"I had that handled."

He slid her a look. "You're welcome."

She let out a short laugh. "I was handling myself just fine." Always did, always would. Having been on her own for so long, she really didn't know any other way.

And yet he'd been there for her. When she'd been lonely. When she'd been sad. When she'd been sicker than a dog.

Whenever she'd needed.

"Pru," he said, "that guy was a walking fight. Where the hell's Jake?"

"Off today, and I didn't need him. It's not like he

was going to take a swing at me. The only thing he was swinging was a poor vocabulary and a small dick."

His mouth twitched. "Okay, I stand corrected."

"And?"

"And what?" he asked.

"And you're sorry for stepping in and handling my fight for me?"

He just looked at her.

Nope, he wasn't sorry for that. Good to know. She took a longer look at his face and realized that not only wasn't he sorry, he looked a little tall, dark, and 'tude ridden. She'd seen him mad several times now so she recognized the stormy eyes, tight mouth, and tense body language. "So how's your day?"

He lifted a shoulder.

Okay. She reached out and put a hand on a very tense forearm. "Are you okay?" she asked quietly. "Because it doesn't feel like you are."

"I'm fine."

She gave him an arched brow.

He shrugged. "I just hate pushy assholes who think they can push someone around to get what they want."

She stared up at him, once again reminded that she wasn't the only one in this relationship-that-wasn't-happening with demons. "Because of your dad?"

"Maybe," he admitted. "Or maybe because I spent a good portion of my youth protecting Sean. He was a small, sickly kid with a big, fat mouth. It wasn't easy to watch his back and keep him safe because he attracted assholes and bullies." He scrubbed a hand down his face. "I guess I still get worked up about that. I saw that guy being aggressive with you and I wanted . . ."

"To protect me," she said softly.

"Yeah." He gave her a half grimace, half smile. "Not that you can't do it yourself, but emotions aren't always rational."

With her hands still fisted in his shirt, she gave a gentle tug until he bent enough that she could kiss him softly. And then not so softly. "I know," she whispered. She kissed him again.

"What was that for?" he asked when she pulled free, his voice sexy low and gruff now.

"For being the kind of guy who can admit he has emotions."

He cupped her face. "We don't have to tell anyone, right?"

She smiled. "It'll be our secret." But then her smile faded because she wasn't good at secrets.

Or maybe she was too good at them . . . "I'm not helpless," she said. "I want you to know that."

"I do know it." He paused, looking a little irritated again. "Mostly."

"Good," she said. "Now that's settled, you should know, the caveman thing you just pulled . . . it turned me on a little bit."

He slid her a look. "Yeah?"

"Yeah."

Looking a little less like he was spoiling for a fight, his hands went to her hips and he pulled her in tighter.

What the hell was she doing? Clearly, she wasn't equipped to stay strong, and who could? The guy was just too damn potent. Too visceral. Testosterone and pheromones leaked off of him. She dropped her head to his chest. "Ugh. You're being . . . you."

"Was that in English?"

"This is all your fault."

"Nope. Definitely not English."

"You're being all hot and sexy, dammit," she said. She banged her head on his chest a few times. "And I can't seem to . . . not notice said hotness and sexiness."

He smiled. "You want me again."

Again. *Still* . . . She tossed up her hands. "You wear your stupid sexiness on your sleeve and you don't even know it."

His smile widened. "All you have to do is say the word, babe. Or preferably words. Dirty ones are encouraged."

When she blew out a sigh, he laughed.

"You really can't say the words, can you," he said, sounding way too amused about that, the ass. He flung an arm around her. "Cute."

Cute? She had mixed feelings about that. On the one hand, she'd rather he found her unbearably sexy. But on the other hand, he was already more than she could handle. Maybe cute was just right.

She gave him a push and strode around, locking up.

He followed, still looking pretty damn smug, waiting patiently.

"Where do you want to go?" he asked.

"Who says I'm going anywhere with you?"

"Your body."

She realized she'd plastered herself to his front again. "You're not working tonight?"

"Later. I worked all day and have a full crew on now. They'll be fine for a few hours on their own."

Oh God. How was she going to resist? "Are you

going to take me out on another date and then dump me at the door?"

"Depends."

"On?" she asked.

He just smiled mysteriously as he slid his fingers into her hair, letting his thumb stroke once over her lower lip so that it tingled for a kiss.

His kiss.

He wanted her to say the words and she knew what words too. *Make love to me . . .*

"You've got choices," he said. "You can pick a place, or let me surprise you."

His bed. She picked his bed.

She retrieved Thor from his nap spot in Jake's office and then Finn drove them out of there, his hands as sure on the wheel as they always were on her body.

Stop looking at his hands!

He took her for drinks at a cute place in the Marina, where they sat at a small table on the sidewalk with Thor happily at their feet watching the world go by.

Finn paid. He always paid. And he was sneaky about it too. She never even saw the check before he had it handled.

After, they headed to Lands End, a park near the windswept shoreline at the mouth of the Golden Gate Bridge.

The three of them followed a trail along a former rail bed to the rocky cliffs that revealed a heart-stopping, stunning three-hundred-and-sixty-degree vista of the bay. The wild blue ocean below was dotted with white-caps thanks to the heavy surf of the early evening.

"Wow," she whispered. "Makes you realize that the

whole world isn't centered around your own hopes and dreams."

He looked out at the view. "What are your hopes and dreams?"

She glanced at him, startled.

"I know you love being a boat captain," he said. "But what else do you want for yourself? To own your own charter business? To have a family?"

He was serious, so she answered truthfully. "I do love my job but I don't want to run an empire or anything. I'm happy doing what I do. And . . ." Her heart was suddenly pounding. "I do want a family." Because his eyes felt like mirrors into her own soul, she turned to the water again. "Someday," she whispered.

His hand slipped into hers, warm and strong.

She held on and breathed for a moment. "And you?"

"I love my job too," he said. "And I want to keep the pub for as long as it works. But I don't want to live in the city forever. I want a family too, and I'd rather have a yard and a street where they can ride their bikes and have other kids nearby . . ."

She smiled. "You want a white picket fence, Finn?"

"It doesn't have to be white," he said and made her laugh.

And yearn . . .

Thor enjoyed himself thoroughly, chasing after squirrels until one of them turned on him and chased him right back into Pru's arms.

Finn shook his head. "He's missing something."

"He doesn't have the killer gene," she admitted, giving the mutt a squeeze.

"I was thinking balls . . ." But he took Thor and

carried him for her, letting the dog nuzzle at the crook of his neck.

Pru rolled her eyes, but inside, secretly, she wanted to nuzzle there too.

"Look," Finn said, grabbing her hand with his free one, pointing with their joined fingers to the hillside below of cypress and wildflowers every color under the sun.

"Wow," she whispered. "Gorgeous."

"Yeah," he said, looking at her.

She laughed. "That's cheesy."

He grinned. "You liked it."

"No, I didn't."

He peered at her over his dark sunglasses, letting his gaze slip past her face.

She followed his line of sight and realized that her nipples were pressing eagerly against the thin white cotton of her shirt. "That's because I'm cold," she said and crossed her arms over her chest.

He laughed. "It's seventy-five degrees."

"Downright chilly," she said, nose in the air.

Grinning, he reeled her in, and with Thor protesting between them, he kissed the living daylights out of her.

Then he tugged her down the trail, heading for the epic ruins of Sutro Baths.

She'd never been here before. Even better, they were alone. Pru had no idea why, maybe because it was the middle of the week, or just late enough in the day, but they had the place to themselves.

They walked through the ruins and Finn showed her a small, rocky cave. It was cool inside. Quiet.

Finn brought her over to a small opening that allowed

her to see out to the rocky beach. Standing inside the cave, surrounded by the cavernous rock and way-too-sexy man, she could not only see the water but feel it in the cool mist that blew into the cave and stirred the hair at her temple.

Thor wriggled to be freed and Finn set him down, where he immediately scampered to a pile of rocks to explore.

This left Finn's hands free to tug Pru into him. "I should probably admit," he said, his mouth at her ear, "being alone in here is giving me ideas."

She bit her lower lip. Her too!

Laughing quietly at her expression, he fisted one hand in her hair. The other slid down and squeezed her ass. "You too?"

Okay, yes, so maybe she had a secret fantasy about doing it somewhere that they could maybe get caught, but she wasn't about to tell him so. Absolutely not. "I have a secret fantasy about doing it somewhere where we could maybe get caught," she said. *Dammit, mouth!*

His grin was fast and wicked, assuring her he was absolutely up for the challenge. She laughed again, nervously now. "But I'm pretty sure it's just a fantasy," she said quickly, putting her hands on his chest to keep him at arm's length.

Or to keep him close. She hadn't quite decided.

The hand on her ass shifted up a little and then back down, slipping inside the back of her pants. "How sure is pretty sure?" he asked, his fingers stroking the line of her thong, but before they could slip beneath, she laughed again and pulled free.

"Pretty, *pretty* sure," she said shakily.

His gaze slid down her body. "I suppose you're cold again."

Well aware that her greedy nipples were still threatening to make a break right through the material of her shirt, she scooped up Thor and clutched him to her chest.

Thor seemed to give her a long look like *please don't make me wait while you two do disgusting things to each other.* "Don't worry," she muttered to the dog. "I've got a handle on things now."

"I've got something you could get a handle on," Finn said.

She rolled her eyes. "Weak."

"It's not weak."

She laughed. "I remember."

"So if we're not making fantasies come true, how about dinner?" he asked.

Dilemma. She couldn't take him home, she'd sleep with him again. "Pizza," she said, thinking a crowded Italian joint should be safe enough.

"Sold," Finn said.

They left the cave and walked along the rocky beach for a few minutes. The tide was out, the water receded a hundred yards or more it seemed. Pru managed to trip over a rock and then her own two feet, dropping Thor's leash to catch herself. So naturally Thor took off directly toward the waves at the speed of light, barking the whole way.

"Thor!" she yelled. "He can't swim," she told Finn. "Sinks like a stone."

"Trust me, he'll swim if he has to."

But she couldn't be so calm. Her baby was racing

right for the waves. She started after him much slower, having to be careful on the rocks.

"Don't worry," Finn said. "He'll be back as soon as his paws get wet."

But Thor hit the water and kept going, right into a wave. And then the worst possible thing happened.

He vanished.

"Oh my God." Pru took off running down the rocky beach, heading directly for the spot where Thor had vanished. She kicked off her sandals and dove in.

The next wave crashed over her head and smashed her face into the sand. Gasping, she pushed upright, swiping the sand from her face to find . . .

Thor sitting on the shore staring at her, his tail whipping back and forth, his mouth smiling wide, proud of himself. Dripping wet, he barked twice and she'd have sworn he said, "Fun, right?"

Finn laughed and picked the dog up. Thor wriggled to get free but Finn just tucked the dripping wet, very-proud-of-himself dog beneath one arm and reached for Pru with the other, a wide smile on his face.

Pru went hands on wet hips. "Are you laughing at me? You'd better not be laughing at me."

"I wouldn't dream of it."

She narrowed her eyes.

Finn did his best to squelch his smile and failed. "I told you he'd be fine."

"Uh huh."

His laugh drifted over her. "I'm guessing that this time you really are cold instead of just pretending to be."

She looked down at her shirt. Yep, plastered to her

torso and gone sheer to boot, making her look more naked than she would be without a stitch of clothing. She narrowed her eyes at him but he just kept smiling. So she took a step toward him with the intention of wrapping her very wet self around him until he was just as wet as she.

But he dodged her and held up a hand. "Now let's not get crazy—"

She flung herself at him. Just took a running step and a flying leap.

He was a smart enough man to catch her, and in spite of the fact that it meant she drenched him with seawater, he hauled her in and held her close.

"Got you," he said, and melted away her irritation in a single heartbeat. Because he always did seem to have her, whether it was soothing her after *she'd* hit *him* with a dart, or when she'd been upset about her grandpa, or sick with food poisoning . . . He had her. Always.

It was as simple and terrifying as that.

Chapter 28

#SliceOfHumblePie

Finn bundled both the wet dog and the even wetter woman into his car. He pulled a blanket from his emergency kit and tucked it around them.

"I'm f-fine," Pru said, teeth chattering, lips blue.

Uh huh. In other words, "back off, Finn." Not likely. But he wasn't surprised at the attempt. Every time they got too close she seemingly regretted their time together.

He regretted nothing. Not the way she'd felt in his arms and not the way he'd felt in hers. From the beginning, there'd been a shocking sense of intimacy between them, one that had momentarily stunned him, but he'd gotten over it quickly.

He wanted even more but he was smart enough to know a reticent woman when he saw one. She was still unsure. She needed more time.

And he'd already made the decision to give it to her.

"Your teeth are going to rattle right out of your head," he said, cranking up the heat, aiming the vents at her.

Clearly freezing, she didn't utter a word of complaint. Instead she seemed much more concerned that he would skip the afore-promised pizza. "It takes calories to keep yourself warm," she said. "Pepperoni and cheese calories. A lot of them."

"I'll call it in and have it delivered while you shower," he assured her.

"No!" She paused, clearly searching for a reason to ditch him. "Lefty's won't deliver."

"Then we can call Mozza's," he said.

She managed a derisive snort in between shivers. "Mozza's isn't real pizza."

"Okay." He pulled into the back lot of Lefty's. "Stay here, I'll just run in and get it real quick."

But she was right behind him, emergency Mylar blanket wrapped around her and all.

Waiting in line, he slid her a look. "You didn't trust me to pick the right pizza."

"Not even a little bit."

Lefty was taking orders himself, he loved people. Smiling broadly at Pru, he said, "Hey there, cutie pie. What happened, you get pitched overboard? Not a good day for a swim, it's kinda brisk."

"Don't I know it," she muttered. "I had to save Thor. Life or death situation."

Finn grinned and Pru turned a long look his way, daring him to contradict her story.

Finn lifted his hands in surrender and Lefty went brows up. "Sensing a good story here. Someone start talking."

"Would love to," Pru said. "But you've got a long line waiting, so—"

"They'll wait." Lefty set his elbows on the counter and leaned in. "Is it as good as you trying to kill our boy here with a dart?"

She whirled on Finn. "You know that was an accident! You've been telling people I tried to kill you?"

Lefty laughed. "Nah, he didn't say a word. Never does. Willa told me. Oh and Archer's guys too, Max and the scary-looking one with the tattoo on his skull."

Pru smacked her forehead. "How is it possible that the people in our building gossip more than a bunch of guys in a firehouse?"

"Don't you mean a bunch of girls in junior high?" Lefty asked.

"No," she said, glowering. "Girls have got nothing on guys when it comes to gossip." She sent a long look at Finn, daring him to disagree.

"One hundred percent true," he said and paid for their food. And then because she seemed skittish about going back to her place, he brought her and Thor to his.

As they got out of the car, Pru muttered something that sounded an awful lot like "just keep your clothes on and you'll be fine."

Finn hid his grin. "Problem?" he asked her.

She scowled. "Just hungry."

He let them inside. His phone buzzed an incoming call from Sean and he turned to Pru. "Help yourself to my shower to get warmed up."

When she'd shut herself in his bathroom, he answered his phone.

"We're filled to capacity," Sean said.

"Great. And?"

"And," Sean said, sounding irritated. "We need you."

"You're fully staffed. The pub doesn't need me."

There was a silence, during which Finn could hear Sean gnashing his teeth together. "Okay, I need you," he finally said, not sounding all that happy about the admission. "There's a bachelorette party here and the bridesmaids are *insane*, man. They've pinched my ass twice. I've also got a birthday party for some guy who's like a hundred and he's got a bunch of old geezers with him and they're doing shots. What if one of them ups and croaks on us? And then there's the fact that Rosa's sick and says she has to go home early. Code for her boyfriend doesn't have to work tonight and she wants to go see him."

Finn heard the shower go on down the hall. He hadn't had a woman here in this house . . . ever. Not once. The relationships in his life had all been short-lived ones, all existing away from home. He tended to keep his personal life out of his sex life.

And his personal life hadn't been a priority, in any sense of the word. His brother and the pub had been his entire world for a damn long time, which meant that Pru had been right when she'd told him that first night in the bar that he hadn't been living his life. It had been living him.

He wanted to change that. He wanted what he'd been missing out on. He wanted a relationship.

And he wanted it with Pru.

"Are you even listening to me?" Sean asked, clearly pissy now. "I need you to get your ass down here and help me with this shit."

"No," Finn said. "You're in charge."

"But—"

"Figure it out, Sean," Finn said and disconnected. He filled a bowl of water for Thor, and since the little guy was looking a little waterlogged, he wrapped him up in a blanket and made him comfortable on the couch.

Thor licked Finn's chin and closed his eyes, and was snoring in thirty seconds flat.

"If only your owner was as easy to please," Finn said.

Thor smiled in his sleep and then farted.

Pru stood under Finn's heavenly shower until she'd thawed. Then she wrapped herself up in one of his large, fluffy towels and went looking for him, hoping he had a pair of sweats she could wear while her clothes dried.

She found Thor asleep in the middle of Finn's comfy-looking couch. The sliding glass door was open so she left the dog to his nap and poked her head out. The deck there was small and cozy and completely secluded by the two stucco walls on either side.

There was a tiny table, two chairs, and an incredible view of Cow Hollow, and beyond it, the Golden Gate Bridge and the bay.

Finn came out. She heard him set the pizza and drinks on the table and then he came up behind her where she stood hands on the railing staring out at the view. His hands covered hers. She could feel the warmth of his big body seeping into her. And something else. Hunger. Need. He always invoked those emotions in her, and if she was being honest, far more too. "I was hoping to borrow some of your clothes," she managed.

"Anything."

He had her caged in and she liked it. When he lowered his head to nuzzle the side of her throat, she nearly turned into a happy little kitten and began to purr.

"I like you like this," he said huskily. "Just warm, soft, delicious, naked woman in my towel."

"How do you know I'm naked under here?" she heard herself ask daringly.

Taking the challenge, he slid a hand up her thigh, letting out a low, sexy, knowing laugh when she squeaked.

"*Clothes*," she demanded.

"Sure." But instead of backing off, he lifted a hand to point to Fisherman's Wharf, where if she squinted, she could just make out Jake's building. "Sometimes I stand right here and look for you," he said.

She closed her eyes and let her body follow its wishes, which meant she rested her head back against his chest.

Finn brushed the hair from the nape of her neck and slid his mouth across the sensitive skin there, giving her a full body shiver of the very best kind.

"You always smell so damn good," he murmured against her skin, his mouth at her jaw now while his hands slid over her body, revving her engines, firing up all her cylinders. "And now you smell like me. Love that. You make me hungry, Pru."

"Good thing we have pizza," she said breathlessly.

"It's not pizza I'm hungry for." His hands skimmed over her towel-covered breasts, skipping her nipples which were dying for his attention.

She made a little whimper of protest and felt him smile against her neck.

"You're teasing me," she accused.

"No, if I was teasing you, I'd do something like this . . ." And he dragged hot, openmouthed kisses down her throat, his hands continuing to tease until she whimpered in frustration. "*Finn.*"

"Tell me."

Stay strong, Pru. "I need you," she whispered. "I need you so much."

"Right back at you, Pru." And then he whipped her around and lifted her up onto the rail. "Hold on tight," he said against her throat.

Not having a death wish, she threw her arms around his neck. This had the towel loosening on her. But left with the choice of holding onto it or Finn, she did what any red-blooded, sex-starved woman would do—she let the towel fall.

Finn kissed her and then pulled back just enough to take a good, long look at her, letting out a rough groan. "You take my breath, Pru. Every fucking time. You're so beautiful."

She opened her mouth to tell him ditto but his mouth covered hers before she could speak as his hands began a full assault on her now naked body. It took him only a few beats to have her writhing under his ministrations, straining for more, and his hot gaze swept over her, heating her up from the inside out. "You're not cold?"

He was really asking this time and she managed to shake her head. "Not even a little."

With a smile, his mouth worked its way south-ward. As for Pru, she kept a monkey-like grip on him, her head falling back. "Oh my God," she whispered. "We're *outside.*"

His mouth curved against her bare shoulder. "Do you want me to stop?"

"Don't you dare—" She broke off and sucked in a breath as he gently captured her nipple with his teeth.

Mindless now, she rocked up into him. "Please don't let go of me."

"Never." He sucked her into his hot mouth making her moan and clutch at him. He had one arm tight to her back while his free hand danced its way up the inside of her thighs. The flat of the railing that she was balanced on wasn't quite as wide as her ass but he had her, and in spite of joking that she didn't trust him to pick the pizza, she did.

Truth was, she trusted him one hundred percent, with her pizza, with her body, and if she was being honest, with her heart too.

It was a shocking thought but she didn't have the brain power to lend to it at the moment. She was far too busy being taken apart by Finn's fingers as they stroked knowingly over her. But in the vague recesses of her mind, she was aware that if she trusted him one hundred percent, she needed to trust him with the facts of who she was.

And she would. It was just that things between them had heated up so quickly and unexpectedly in their short time together, and had become so unexpectedly complicated. She wanted to tell him everything, and soon. But it hadn't really been all that long—only been two weeks—and she needed a little more time to figure it all out first.

The early evening's breeze floated over her bare skin, along with Finn's heated gaze. Every inch of her was crying out for his touch, needing him more than she'd ever needed anything in her life. "*Finn.*"

"Don't let go of me," he said and tugged a gasp from her when his fingers went from teasing to driving her right to the edge, moving in beat with her heart. Suddenly she no longer cared if she was in danger of plummeting to her death because she was too busy coming apart.

When she could hear past the roar of her own blood in her ears, she hoped like hell that his neighbors hadn't been able to hear her cries. "Were we loud?" she whispered.

He grinned. "We?" he asked, laughing when she smacked him in the chest.

He caught her hand, kissed her palm, and then tore open a condom packet. Protecting them both, he plunged into her as his mouth claimed hers again.

Good God. She wasn't going to die from a fall. She was going to die of pleasure, right here . . .

Chapter 29

#HoustonWeHaveAProblem

The week went by in a blur for Pru. It was a rare blue moon–two full moons in the same calendar month—so SF Tours held a special moonlit cruise week.

Which meant that Pru and the other boat captains worked during the day, crashed for a few hours on whatever horizontal surface they could find in the building, and then went back out at night on the water.

This went on for three days.

On the fourth day, she crawled home and into bed right after grabbing dinner—Frosted Flakes. But she came awake some time later in her dark bedroom to find someone in it with her. Then that someone pulled his shirt over his head and shucked his jeans.

She'd recognize that leanly muscled bod anywhere and swallowed hard at the gorgeous outline of him bathed in nothing but moonlight. It didn't matter how many times she saw him in the buff, he never failed to steal her breath. With her still blinking through the dark trying to see his every sexy inch, he slipped beneath the covers with her.

Naked.

"Chris Pratt?" she asked. "Is that you?"

"You don't need Chris Pratt," Finn said as he pulled her into a heated embrace.

He was damp and chilled. "Hey!" she complained.

"It's raining sideways," he explained, wrapping himself around her. "Nasty storm. Your bed was closer than mine. And mine was missing something."

"What?"

"You."

Aw. Dammit. "How did you get in?" she asked. "I mean, your hands are magic but not *that* magic."

"Your hidden key." His magical hands began stroking her, while at the same time he pressed hot kisses against the back of her neck. "Do you mind?"

She loved being in the circle of his arms. Loved the way he touched her so knowingly and sure, and since he was actually licking her now, she couldn't concentrate on anything beyond his tongue. Did she mind? "Only if you stop."

His hands were hypnotic, his palms a little rough with calluses, his long talented fingers tracing over her breasts, teasing her nipples.

One thing she'd come to know about him, he was incredibly physical. Whenever they were together like this, he wanted to touch and taste and see . . . everything. There was no hiding, not that she could remember to. He was an incredibly demanding lover, but also endlessly patient and creative. She never knew exactly what to expect from him but he always left her panting for more. "Aren't you tired?" she asked.

"I can sleep when I'm dead." He slipped his fingers inside her panties to cup and squeeze her ass, and then wriggled them to her thighs.

And she was a goner.

"Missed this," he murmured in her ear.

She'd been hoping for sleep. Now she hoped for this to never end. "It hasn't been all that long," she managed. "A few days."

"Four. Too long." Her T-shirt and panties vanished and then his hand was back to its serious business of driving her out of her mind. In less than a minute she was thrusting against his fingers. And in the next, she came so fast her head was spinning.

"God, I love watching you come," he said, and then proceeded to show her what a true force of nature could accomplish.

Mother Nature had nothing on him.

Later Pru lay in Finn's arms, her head on his shoulder, her face pressed into his throat, knowing by the way he was breathing that he was out cold, dead asleep. Poor baby, being a sex fiend was exhausting.

He'd left work and had come here, to her. And there in the dark, she smiled, her body sated, her heart so full she almost didn't know what to do with herself.

Had she ever felt like this? Like she just wanted to climb into the man next to her and stay there?

Being with Jake had been good. She'd had no

complaints, but she wasn't for him. When they'd split, he'd moved on with shocking ease.

And in truth, so had she.

But it'd left her feeling just a little bit . . . broken, and more than a little bit unsure about love in general.

But then Finn O'Riley had come into her life. She knew that she had no business feeling anything for him at all. But apparently, some things—like matters of the heart—not only happened in a blink but were also out of her control.

She felt her heart swell at just the thought and before she could stop herself, she mouthed the words against his throat. "I love you, Finn."

She immediately stilled in shock because she hadn't just mouthed the words, she'd actually said them.

Out loud.

She remained perfectly frozen another beat, but Finn didn't so much as twitch.

It took a while but eventually she relaxed into him again, and there in the dark, told herself it was okay. He didn't know.

He didn't know a lot of things . . .

The panic that was never far away these days hit her hard. She'd been telling herself that she'd waited to tell him the truth in the hopes he'd understand better once he knew her. But deep down, she wasn't sure she'd done the right thing. Telling him now was going to be harder, not easier.

And the outcome felt more uncertain than ever.

As always, Pru woke up just before her alarm was due to go off at the shockingly early hour of oh-dark-annoying-thirty. But this time it wasn't thoughts of the day ahead that woke her. Or the knot of anxiety wrapped in and around her chest.

It was the fact that she was wrapped around a big, strong, warm body.

Finn had one hand tangled in her hair and the other possessively cupping her bare ass, and when she shifted to try and disentangle herself without waking him, he tightened his grip and let out a low growl.

Torn between laughing and getting unbearably aroused—seriously, that growl!—she lifted her head.

And discovered she wasn't the only one wrapped around Finn like a pretzel.

Thor was on the other side of him, his head on Finn's shoulder, eyes slitted at her.

And she did laugh then because it'd been Thor who growled, not Finn. "Are you kidding me?" she whispered to her dog. "He's *mine*."

But no he's not, a little voice deep inside her whispered. *He doesn't yet know it but you wrecked this—long before it'd even begun.*

Pru told the little voice to *shut up* and concentrated on Thor. "I found him first," she whispered.

Thor growled again.

Thor didn't look impressed in the least. She opened her mouth to further argue but Finn spoke, his voice low and morning gruff. "There's plenty of me to go around."

Pru felt the pink tinge hit her cheeks and she shifted her focus from Thor to Finn.

Yep. He was wide awake and watching and, if she had to guess, more than a little amused that she'd been willing to fight her own dog for him.

"He's mine?" Finn repeated.

"It's a figure of speech." She grimaced at the lameness of that but he smiled.

"I like it," he said. "I like this. But mostly, I like where we're going."

If she could think straight, she'd echo that thought, but she couldn't think straight because every moment of every single day she was painfully aware she'd built this glass house that couldn't possibly withstand the coming storm . . .

"Pretty sure I just lost you for a few beats," Finn said quietly, eyes serious now, dark and warm and intense as he ran a finger along her jaw. "Was it what I said about liking where we're going thing?"

She tried to play this off with her customary self-deprecatory humor. "Since where we're going is always straight to bed, I can't do much complaining about that, can I," she said in a teasing voice, desperately hoping to steer the conversation to lighter waters, because one thing she couldn't do was have the talk with him while naked in his arms.

But she should have known better. Finn couldn't be steered, ever.

"This is more than that," he said, voice low but sure, so sure she wished for even an ounce of his easy confidence. "A lot more."

His gaze held hers prisoner, daring her to contradict him, and she swallowed hard. "It's only been a few weeks," she said softly.

"Three," he said.

"It just seems like we're moving so fast."

"Too fast?" he asked.

She gnawed on her lower lip, unsure how to answer that. The truth was, she'd already acknowledged to herself how she felt about him. And another truth—she wouldn't mind moving along even faster. She wanted to leap into his arms, press her face into his neck, and breathe him in and claim him as hers.

For always.

But she'd gone about this all wrong, and because of that she didn't have the right to him. Not even a little.

His fingers were gentle as they traced the line of her temple. "Babe, you're thinking too hard."

She nodded at the truth of this statement.

"You're scared," he said.

Terrified, thank you very much. She nodded again.

"Of me?"

"No. *No*," she said again, firmly, cupping his face. "It's more than I'm scared of what you make me feel."

He didn't seem annoyed or impatient at her reticence. Instead he kept his hands on her, his voice quiet. "I'm not saying I know where this is going," he said. "Because I don't. But what I do know is that what we've got here between us is good, really good."

She nodded her agreement of that but then slowly shook her head. "Good can go bad. Fast." As she knew all too well.

"Life's a crap shoot and we both know it," he said. "More than most. But whatever this is, I can't stop thinking about it. I can't stop wanting more. I think we've got a real shot, and that doesn't come around every day, Pru. We both know that too." He paused. "I want us to go for it."

Heart tight, she closed her eyes.

He was quiet a moment, but she could feel him studying her. "Pru, look at me."

She lifted her gaze and found his still warm, but very focused. "Say the word," he said seriously. "Tell me that this isn't your thing, that you're not feeling it, and I'll back off."

She opened her mouth.

And then closed it.

His fingers on her jaw, his thumb slid over her lower lip. "You're the self-proclaimed Fun Whisperer," he said. "You're the one preaching about getting out there and living life. So why are you all talk and no go, Pru? What am I missing?"

She choked out a laugh at his sharpness and dropped his head to his chest.

"Tell me what you're afraid of," he said.

Her words came out muffled. "It's hard to put words to it."

He wasn't buying it and slid his hands into her hair and lifted her face. "Fight through that," he said simply. "Fight for me."

Of course he'd say that. It was his MO. Want something? Get it. Make it yours. Go for it, one hundred percent.

Which brought home one hard-hitting point—she needed to adopt that philosophy and do what he'd said, fight for what she wanted. Fight for him.

She'd left her cell on the kitchen counter the night before and from down the hall, it rang. She ignored it but once it stopped, it immediately started up again. Not a good sign so she slid out of bed. Realizing she was very, very naked, she bent to pick something from the pile of discarded clothes and heard a choked sound from the bed.

She turned and found Finn watching her every move, eyes heavy-lidded but not with sleepiness.

He crooked his finger at her.

"Oh no," she said, pointing her finger back at him. "Don't even think about waving your magic wand and—" Shit. "I didn't mean *wand* as in . . ." Her gaze slid down past his chest and washboard abs to the part of him that never failed to be happy to see her. "You know."

He burst out laughing. "Babe, if my 'wand' really was magic, then you'd be on it right now."

She felt herself blush to the roots, which only seemed to amuse him all the more. She actually took a step toward him when her phone rang yet a third time. With a sigh, she slipped his shirt over her head and padded out of the room.

Three missed calls, all from Jake. She tapped on the voicemail he'd just left, hitting speaker so she could make some desperately needed coffee as she listened.

"You're either still sleeping or hell, maybe you're out playing fairy godmother before work," he said, sounding disgruntled. "I heard from a little birdie that you got Tim a place to live."

Damn. Not a little birdie at all. Nick had spilled the beans on her. Again.

"I don't know how long you intend to go around fixing wrongs that aren't yours to fix," Jake said. "But at some point you're going to have to let go. You know that, right? You can't go on keeping track of everyone from the accident and righting their worlds. The seed money for what's-her-name—"

"Shelby," she said, as if Jake could hear her.

"Then there was the place to live for Tim. The job for Nick. And how about what you did for F—"

At the sound behind her, Pru hit delete at the speed of light.

Because she knew the rest of Jake's sentence.

The beep of Jake's message being deleted echoed in the room as she turned to face Finn, wearing only his jeans, unbuttoned.

"What was that about?" he asked.

"Oh . . ." She waved her hand. "You know Jake, sticking his nose into everything."

"Sounds like he thinks you're the one sticking your nose into everything."

She took a deep breath. *Be careful. Be very careful unless you're ready to give up the fantasy right here, right now.* It needed to be done. She knew that now more than ever. She'd do it tonight after work, when they had time to talk about it. *And after you figure out how to make him realize you'd only meant to help.*

Even if in her heart she knew that was no way to make him understand. He was smart and resourceful and sharp, and he was standing there steady as a rock.

Her rock.

Waiting for answers.

"I do tend to stick my nose into things," she said as lightly as she could. "I've got to get to work . . ."

"Or you need to change the subject."

Her smile faded. "Or that."

"You know . . ." He stepped into her, slid his hands to her hips and ducked his head to meet her gaze. "You once told me I needed to let stuff go."

She choked out a low laugh and stared at his Adam's apple. "Haven't you heard, swallowing your own medicine is the hardest thing to do?"

He wrapped her ponytail around his fist and gently tugged until she looked up at him. "What's going on, Pru?"

"What's going on is that I need to get ready for work—"

"In here." He slid his free hand up and tapped a finger over her temple.

She managed another smile. "You'd be surprised by how little's going on in there—"

"Don't," he said quietly. "If you don't want to do this, you only have to say so."

She hesitated and he took a step back. "Wow," he said, looking like she'd sucker punched him.

"No," she said. "I—"

He'd already turned and headed into her bedroom. She started to follow, but he came back out again, holding his shoes. Still no shirt, since she was wearing it. "Finn."

He headed to the door.

"Finn."

He stopped and turned to her, eyes hooded.

"Can we talk about this tonight?"

"Sure. Whatever." He started to leave but stopped and muttered something to himself. He then came at her, hauled her into his arms and kissed her. When his tongue stroked possessively over hers, her knees wobbled, but far before she was ready, he let her go.

He stared down at her for a beat and then he turned and left, shutting the door quietly behind him.

She moved to the door and put her hands on it, like she could bring him back.

But it was far too late for that.

Chapter 30

#JustTheFactsMa'am

Outside Pru's front door, Finn stopped and shook his head. She was holding back on him, big time. But he knew something else too.

So was he.

Because as long as she wasn't one hundred percent in, it felt . . . safe. The crazy thing was that he wanted her to be one hundred percent in. He wanted to do the same.

But he wasn't going to beg her. He wanted her to come to him on her own terms. Until she did, he could hold back that last piece of his heart and soul and keep it safe from complete annihilation.

He was good at that.

He dropped his shoes to the floor and shoved his feet into them. He'd just bent over to tie them when Mrs. Winslow opened her door.

"Whoa, good thing my ovaries are shriveled," she

said. "Or you'd have just made me pregnant from that view alone."

Finn straightened and gave her a look that made her laugh.

"Sorry, boy," she said. "But you don't scare me."

With as much dignity as he could, he hunkered down and went back to tying his shoes, attempting to keep his ass tucked in while doing it.

When he'd finished, he stood up to his full height to find her still watching. "You're a nice package and all," she said, "but I like 'em more seasoned. Men are no good until they're at least forty-five."

"Good to know," he muttered and started down the hall.

"Because until then," she said to his back. "They don't know nothing about the important things. Like forgiveness. And understanding."

He blew out a breath and turned to face her. "You're trying to tell me something again."

"Now you're thinking, genius," she said. "If you were forty-five or older, you'd have already picked up on it."

He went hands on hips. "Got a busy day ahead of me, Mrs. Winslow. Maybe you could come right out and tell me what it is you want me to know."

"Well, that would be far too easy," she said and vanished inside, shutting her door on him.

Finn divided a look between her door and Pru's before tossing up his hands and deciding he knew nothing about women.

Finn strode into the bar. His morning crew cleaners Marie, Rosa, and Felipe all lifted their heads from their various tasks of mopping and scrubbing and blinked.

Shit. He forgot that he was making the morning walk of shame.

Shirtless.

It was Felipe who finally recovered first and gave a soft wolf whistle. "Nice," he said with an eyelash flutter and a hand fanning the air in front of his face.

Finn rolled his eyes in tune to their laughter. Whatever. He strode to his office and—as a bonus annoyance—found Sean asleep on his damn couch.

In Finn's damn spare shirt.

He kicked his brother's feet and watched with grim satisfaction as Sean grunted, jerked awake, and rolled off the couch, hitting the floor with a bone-sounding crunch.

"What the fuck, man?" Sean asked with a wide yawn.

"I need my shirt."

"I'm in it," Sean said. Captain Obvious.

Fine. Whatever. Finn slapped his pockets for his keys. He'd just drive home real quick and—

His keys weren't in his pockets. Probably, given his luck, they were on the floor of Pru's bedroom. He walked out of his office and strode through the pub.

"Just as nice from the rear," Felipe called out.

Finn flipped him off, ignored the hoots of laughter, and hit the stairs, knocking on Pru's door.

From behind him he heard a soft gasp and a wheeze. Craning his head, he found Mrs. Winslow once again in her doorway, this time with two other ladies, mouths agog.

"You were right," one of them whispered to Mrs.

Winslow, staring at Finn. She was hooked up to a portable oxygen tank, hence the Darth Vadar–like breathing.

"I haven't seen hipbones cut like that in sixty years," the other said in the same stage whisper as her friend.

"You realize I can hear you, right?" Finn asked.

The women all jumped in tandem, snapping their gazes up to his. "Oh my god, he's *real,*" the woman with the oxygen tank said—wheezed—in awe.

Mrs. Winslow snorted. "You'll have to excuse them," she said to Finn. "They probably need their hormone doses checked."

Finn decided the hell with waiting on Pru to answer her door. He'd slept with her. He'd tasted every inch of her body. She'd done the same for him. So he checked the handle, and when it turned easily in his palm, he took that as a sign that the day had to improve from here.

When Finn had left, Pru stood there in the kitchen, shaken. She grabbed her phone because she needed advice. Since she was still wearing only Finn's shirt, she propped her phone against the cereal box on the counter so that when the FaceTime call went through to Jake, he'd only see her from the shoulders up.

No need to set off any murder sprees this morning.

When he answered, he just looked at her.

"Hi," she said.

"Hi yourself. You think I don't know your thoroughly fucked face?"

She did her best to keep eye contact. "Hey, I don't point it out to you when *you* get lucky."

"Yes you do. You march your ass into my office, pull out your pocketknife, and make a notch on the corner of my wood desk."

"That's to make a point," she said.

"Which is?"

"You get lucky a lot."

He arched a brow. "And the problem?"

Well, he had her there. "I need your advice."

"Why now?"

"Okay, I deserve that," she said. "But remember when you were worried that Finn was the one who would get hurt?" She felt her eyes fill. "You were off a little."

"Ah, hell, Pru," he said, voice softer now. "You never did know how to follow directions worth shit."

She choked out a laugh. "I know this is a mess of my own making, I totally get that." She closed her eyes. And I've got no excuse for not finding a way over the past few weeks to tell Finn sooner." Well, she did sort of have one—that being she was deathly afraid to lose him when she'd only just found him.

Not that Finn would take any comfort from that.

Jake sighed. "Chica, the mistake's been made. Shit happens. Just tell him. Tell him who you are and who your parents were. Get past it. Stop hiding. You'll feel better."

No, she wouldn't. Because she knew what came next.

Finn would be hurt.

She'd been so taken aback by the speed of events between the two of them, at how fast things had gotten out of her control, that she was scared. Terrified, really.

Because hurting him had been the last thing she'd ever wanted. She opened her mouth to say so but at the sound of footsteps coming toward the kitchen, not hurried or rushed or trying to be stealthy, she whirled around, already knowing who she'd be facing.

Finn, of course. Still shirtless, face carefully blank, he strode to the table and picked up his forgotten keys.

Shit.

God knew how long he'd been there or how much he'd heard. It was impossible to tell by his expression since he was purposely giving nothing away.

Which really was her answer.

He'd heard everything.

"Finn," Jake said, taking in his shirtless state with a slight brow raise.

"Jake," Finn said, either not noticing the unspoken question from Jake or ignoring it completely.

Then they both looked at Pru, to their credit both doing so with a mix of affection and concern. With good reason, as it turned out, because she suddenly felt like she was going to be sick.

Go time, she thought.

"Pru," Finn said quietly. Not a question really but a statement. He wanted to know what was going on.

Oh God, this was going to suck. And the worst part was she'd started all of this with the best intentions. All she'd ever wanted was to fix a wrong that had been done to him, a terrible wrong that she regretted and had carried around until she'd been able to do something about it.

And she'd righted wrongs before, successfully too. But she'd crossed the line this time and she knew it.

And now she had to face it head on.

"Trust him, chica," Jake said from her phone. "He deserves to know and you deserve to be free of this once and for all. If he's who you think, it'll be okay."

And then the rat fink bastard disconnected.

"Pru?" Finn brought up his free hand and slid his fingers along her jaw, letting them sink into her hair. His expression was wary now, but that didn't stop him from standing in her space like they were a couple. An intimate one.

Her heart tightened. It'd been everything she'd ever wanted.

Only a few moments ago he'd been looking morning gruff and deeply satisfied. Now there was something much more to his body language and—Oh good Lord. He had a bite mark just to the side of his left nipple. She felt the heat rise up her cheeks.

"I have another on my ass," he said, his tone not its usual amused or heated when discussing their sex life. "We'll circle back to that. Talk to me, Pru."

Her heart was pounding, her blood surging hard and fast through her veins, panic making her limbs weak. She looked at her phone but Jake was long gone and in the reflection of the screen she could see herself.

She hadn't gotten away from last night unscathed either. There was a visible whisker burn on her throat and she knew she had a matching mark on her breasts.

And between her thighs.

Finn had brought her pleasure such as she'd never known, both in bed and out.

And now it was over . . . "I'm so sorry," she said. "I've kept something from you."

"What?" There was some wariness to his tone now, though he still spoke quietly. Willing to hear whatever she had to say.

She immediately felt her blood pressure shoot through the stratosphere.

"Just tell me, Pru."

Well, if he was going to be all calm and logical about this . . . She inhaled a deep breath. "It's about my parents. And their accident."

His eyes softened with sympathy, which she didn't deserve. "You never say much about how it happened," he said. "I haven't wanted to push. You don't push me on my dad's shit and I appreciate that, so—"

"It was a car wreck." She licked her suddenly dry lips. "They . . . caused other injuries." She paused. "Life-altering injuries."

His eyes never left hers. "And?"

"And I . . . got involved."

"You've been . . . helping them?"

"Yes, but only in the smallest of ways compared to the damage my parents caused."

He looked at her for a long moment. "That's got to be painful for you."

"No, actually, it's healing."

He looked skeptical.

"I had to," she said softly. "Finn, my parents are the ones in the car who killed your dad."

His brow furrowed. "What are you talking about? The man driving the car that hit him was some guy by the name of Steven Dalman."

"My dad," she said quietly. "My mom never took his last name. Her family was against the match every bit as much as his. She gave me her name, not his . . ." She trailed off when Finn abruptly turned from her.

He shoved his fingers into his hair and didn't say a word. She wasn't even sure if he was breathing, but she couldn't take her eyes off him. Off the sleek, leanly muscled lines of his bare back. The inch of paler skin low on his waist where his jeans had slipped.

The tension now in every line of his body.

She tried to explain. "I just wanted . . ."

Finn whipped back around. "Want what? To satiate your curiosity? See if Sean and I were as devastated as you? What exactly did you want, Pru?"

"To make it better," she said, throat tight. "That's all I've ever wanted, was to make it better. For both of you, for everyone who my dad . . ." She covered her mouth.

Destroyed.

"I see," he said quietly. "So that's what I was to you, another pet project like the others you collected and fixed their broken lives."

"No, I—"

"Truth, Pru," he said, voice vibrating with fury. "You owe me that."

"Okay, yes, I needed to help everyone however I could. I needed to make things right," she reiterated, swallowing a sob when he shook his head. She was losing him. "So I did what I could."

"I didn't need saving," he bit out. "Sean and I had each other and we were fine—" He stilled and his eyes cut to hers, sharp as a blade. "It was you. You got us that money that was supposedly from a community fundraiser. Jesus, how did I not guess this before?" His gaze narrowed. "Where did that money come from?

Is that why you sold your childhood home? To give it to us?"

"No, the money from the house went to the others. For you and Sean, I used my parents' life insurance policy."

He stared at her. "Fuck," he said roughly and turned to go.

She managed to slide between him and the door. "Finn, please—"

"Please what?" he asked coldly. "Understand how you very purposely and calculatedly came into my life? Moved into this building? Sat in my pub? Became my friend and then my lover? All under the pretense of wanting me, while really you were just trying to assuage some misguided sense of guilt." He stopped and closed his eyes for a beat. "Jesus, Pru. I never even saw you coming."

Having her crimes against him listed out loud made her feel sick to her soul. "It wasn't like that," she said.

"No? You sought me out, decided I needed fixing, slept with me, probably had a good laugh over me telling you how much you meant to me . . . all without telling me why you were really here—to ease your damn conscience." He shook his head. "Hope you got everything in that you wanted because we're done here."

"No, Finn. I—"

"Done," he repeated with a terrifying finality. "I don't want to see you again, Pru."

And then he walked out, breaking the heart she hadn't even realized she had inside her to break.

Chapter 31

#MissedItByThatMuch

Weighted down by so many emotions that she couldn't name them all, Pru called in sick, letting Jake think she'd gotten her period and had debilitating cramps.

Since she'd never used such an excuse before, had in fact never missed work at all, she didn't feel in the least bit sorry.

Her ovaries had to be good for something, right?

She marathoned *Game of Thrones* and never left the couch. Every time her mind wandered to Finn, her heart did a slow somersault in her chest, her lungs stopped working, and her stomach hurt, so she did what anyone would do in the throes of a bad breakup.

She ate.

The next morning she was jerked out of her stupor when someone knocked on her door. She blinked and looked around. She was still dressed, still on her couch, surrounded by empty wrappings of candy bars and other varieties of junk food—the evidence of a pity party for one. She grabbed her phone but there were no missed calls, texts, or emails from Finn.

And why would there be? He'd been pretty clear.

He didn't want to see her again.

The knock came again, less patient now. She got to her feet and looked out the peephole.

Willa, Elle, and Haley.

Elle was front and center, her eyes on the peephole.

"I'm not feeling very sociable," Pru said. "In fact, I'm feeling pretty damn negative and toxic so—"

"Okay, listen, honey," Elle said. "Life sucks sometimes. The trick is not letting negative and toxic feelings rent space in your head. Raise the rent and kick them the hell out. And I've brought help in that regard." She lifted a bag.

Tina's muffins.

Pru opened the door.

Elle handed her the bag.

Haley handed over a very large coffee.

Willa smiled. "My job is to be supportive and get you to talk."

"Way to be subtle," Elle said.

Ignoring that, Willa hugged Pru. "Okay, so I missed the subtle gene," she said. "But you should know, we are unbelievably supportive."

"Even if I screwed up?"

"Even if," Willa said.

"I'm not going to talk about it," Pru warned, barely able to talk past the lump in her throat. "Not now. Maybe not ever."

Seemingly unconcerned by this, they all moved into Pru's apartment and eyed the scene of the crime.

Willa picked up an empty bag of maple bacon potato chips. "They make bacon chips?" She looked into the empty bag sadly. "Damn, I bet they were amazing."

"How did you know something was wrong?" Pru asked with what she thought was a calm voice.

"Because you missed Eighties Karaoke and didn't answer any of our calls last night," Elle said. "And you'd told me you wouldn't miss it unless Chris Evans came knocking at your door." She looked Pru over, her rumpled sweats and what was undoubtedly a bad case of bedhead hair. "And I think it's safe to say that didn't happen."

"It could have," Pru muttered and set the coffee down to dive into the bag of muffins. She started with a chocolate chocolate-chip.

Haley reached to put her hand in the bag and Pru clutched it to her chest with a growl that rivaled Thor's.

Haley lifted her hands. "Okay, not sharing. Got it." She turned to Elle and Willa. "I think we've verified the breakup rumor."

Pru froze. "There's a breakup rumor?"

Willa lifted her hand, her first finger and thumb about an inch apart. "Little bit."

Pru sank to the couch, still clutching her muffins. "I'd like to be alone now."

"Sure," Elle said. "We understand." And then she sat on one end of the couch and picked up the remote to turn the volume up. "Season three, right? Love this show."

Eyes on the screen, already enraptured, Haley sat on the other end.

Pru opened her mouth to complain but Willa took the floor, leaning back on the couch, leaving a spot right in the middle for Pru.

She blew out a breath and in the respectful silence that she appreciated more than she could say, she wasn't alone at all.

Two days later Pru walked to work. In the rain. She knew she was bad off when Thor didn't complain once. He did however, keep looking up at her, wondering what their mood should be.

Devastated. That was the current mood. But she didn't want to scare him. "We're going to be okay."

Thor cocked his head, his one stand-up ear quivering a little bit.

He didn't believe her.

And for good reason. She hadn't slept. She'd called in sick again and Jake had let her get away with that.

Until this morning. He'd called her at the crack of dawn and said, "I don't care if your uterus is falling out of your body, take some Midol and get your ass into work. Today."

She wasn't surprised. And to be honest, she was ready to get back to it after a two-day pity party involving more ice cream than she'd eaten in her twenty-six years total. She'd run out of self-pity stamina. Turned out it was hard to maintain that level of despair.

So with it now at a dull roar, she'd showered and dressed and headed to work. "I just feel . . . stupid," she told Thor. "This is all my fault, you know."

"Honey," a woman said, passing her on the sidewalk. "Never admit that it's all your fault." She was wearing the smallest, tightest red dress Pru had ever seen, and the five-inch stilettos were impressive.

"But this time it really is," Pru told her.

"No, you're misunderstanding me. Never admit it's your fault, *especially* when it is."

The woman walked on but Thor stopped and put his front paws on Pru's leg.

She picked him up and he licked her chin.

Her throat tightened. "You love me anyway." She hugged him, apparently squeezing too tight because he suffered it for about two seconds and then growled.

With a half laugh and half sob, she loosened her grip. When she got to work, she walked straight through the warehouse to the offices. She passed those by too and headed back to the area where Jake lived.

He was lifting weights, the music blaring so loud the windows rattled. She turned off the music and turned to face him.

"You okay?" he asked, dropping the weights, turning his chair to face her, his face creased in worry.

She'd planned what she would say to him. Something like *I know, you told me so, blah blah blah, so let's not talk about it, let's just move on.* And she opened her mouth to say just that but nothing came out.

"What's going on?"

She burst into tears.

Looking pained, he stared at her. "Did you forget the Midol? Because I bought some, it's in my bathroom. I've had it for over a year, I've just never figured out how to give it to you without getting my head bit clean off."

She threw her purse at him. "I didn't get my damn period!"

"Oh shit," he said, blanching. "Oh fuck. Okay, first I'll kill him and then—"

"No!" She actually laughed through her tears. "I'm not pregnant."

He let out a long breath. "Well, Jesus, lead with that next time."

Pru shook her head and turned to go, but he was faster than her even in his chair. He got in front of her and blocked the door.

"Talk to me, chica," he said.

"You done being a stupid guy?"

"I'll try to be." He said this quite earnestly, his gaze on hers. "You did tell him then."

She nodded.

"And . . . it went to hell?" he guessed.

"In a hand basket," she agreed.

"I'm sorry."

She shook her head. "Don't be. I was a dumbass. I should have told him from the get-go like you said a million times."

Jake let out a rare sigh. "Look, chica, yeah, you made a mistake. But everything you did was for the right reasons. You should feel good about that. You set out to help everyone from the accident and now you can say you did that. In a big way. In a much bigger way than anyone else I know would have."

She thought about it and realized she did feel good about that part. "So it's mission accomplished," she said softly.

"Yeah." He smiled. "Proud of you."

The words were a balm on her broken heart. The ache didn't go away and she wasn't sure if it ever would.

Loss was loss, and Finn no longer being in her life was a hard pill to swallow. But she'd survived worse and she'd come back from rock bottom.

She could do it again.

Well . . . next time maybe tell him who she was before sexy times and getting hearts involved . . .

The first two days were a complete blur to Finn. On day three, he stood in his shower contemplating the level of suckage his life had become until the hot water ran out. He stood there as it turned cold and then icy, completely forgetting that they were on a water watch and he'd pay a penalty if he went over his allowed usage for the month.

He was sitting on his couch staring at the still-off TV when Sean called. "I'm taking tonight off," Finn said.

"Oh, hell no you're not," Sean said. "Three fucking nights in a row? I can't do this by myself, Finn. This is a damn partnership and you need to start acting like it."

Finn dropped his head, closed his eyes, and fought the laugh. "Are you throwing my words back in my face?"

"Hell yes." Sean paused. "Is it working?"

"I think you owe me more than a few nights."

Sean blew out a breath. "Yeah." He paused again, this one a beat longer. "What's wrong?"

"Nothing."

"Bullshit," Sean said. "You take time off never. Let me guess. You're . . . running away from home? No, it's worse than that. Shit. Just tell me quick, like ripping off a Band-Aid. You're dying?"

"I'm not dying. Jesus, you're such a drama queen."

"Right, then what?" Sean demanded. "Are you dumping me, is that it?"

Finn pinched the bridge of his nose. Sean's greatest fear was being dumped, and to be fair, he'd earned that particular anxiety the hard way from their parents. Pulling his head out of his own ass was hard but Finn managed for a second to do just that. "I can't dump you," he said, "you're my brother."

"People dump their family all the time," Sean said, and then paused. "Or they just walk away."

Finn softened and let out a sigh. "Okay, so yeah, I suppose I *could* dump you. And don't get me wrong, there are entire days where I'd like to at least strangle you slowly. But listen to me very carefully, Sean. I've honestly never, not once, wanted to dump you from my life."

There was a long silence. When Sean finally spoke, his voice was thick. "Yeah?"

"Yeah. I'd do anything for you. And I'll never walk away from you." And up until a few days ago, he'd have given Pru that very same promise.

And yet he had walked away from her.

At that thought, the first shadow of doubt crept in, icy tendrils as relentless as the afternoon fog.

"Are you going to tell me what's up?" Sean asked. "If it's not me and the pub's okay, then what? You mess up with Pru or something?"

"Why would you say that?" Finn demanded.

"Whoa, man, chill. It's a matter of elimination. Other than work, there's nothing else that could get to you like this. So what happened?"

"I don't want to talk about it."

Sean was quiet a second. "Because of Mellie? I apologized for that like a thousand times but I'll do it again. I was an asshole and an idiot. And drunk off my ass that night. And it was a long time ago. I'd never—"

"This has nothing to do with Mellie," Finn said.

"Then what? Because Pru's pretty damn perfect."

Finn sighed. Not perfect. But perfect for him . . . "Why does it have to be anyone's fault?"

Sean laughed wryly. "It's just the way of the world. Men screw up. Women forgive—or don't, as the case often goes."

Finn blew out a breath. "I walked away. I had my reasons but I'm not sure I did the right thing." It was a hell of an admission considering he rarely second-guessed himself.

"If I've learned one thing from you," Sean said, "it's to suck it up and always do the *right* thing. Not the easy thing, the right thing."

Finn managed a short laugh. "Listen to you, all logical and shit."

"I know, go figure, right? So . . . you going to do it? The right thing?"

Finn sighed. "Who are you and what have you done with my brother?"

"Just hurry up and handle it and get your ass back to work."

"There he is."

Chapter 32

#TakeMeToYourLeader

When Finn finally made his way to the pub that night, he stood in the middle of the bar as music played around him. His friends and customers were all there having fun, laughing, dancing, drinking . . .

The pub was a huge success, beyond his wildest imagination. He'd never really taken the time to notice it. But he was noticing now that his heart had been ripped out of his chest by a gorgeous dynamo of a woman with eyes that sucked him in and held him, a sweet yet mischievous smile that had taken him places he'd never been . . . then there was how he'd felt in her arms.

Like Superman.

And he'd dumped her. Roughly. Cruelly. And her crime? Nothing more than trying to make sure he was okay after a tragedy that hadn't even been her fault. Not in the slightest.

Hating himself for that, he stopped right in the middle of the place. He wasn't in the mood for this. He needed to think, needed to figure out what the hell to do to alleviate this pain in his chest and the certainty that he'd walked away from the best thing that had ever happened to him.

But everyone was at the bar, waving at him. Bracing himself for the inquisition, he headed that way.

"Rumor is that you've been a dumbass," Archer said.

Finn stared at him. "How the hell did you know—"

"The girls and I stopped by Pru's place," Willa said. "Is she okay?"

"She looks and sounds like her heart's been ripped out." Willa met his gaze. "She'd clearly been crying."

Shit.

Elle squeezed his hand. "Whatever you did, it's not completely your fault. You're a penis-carrying human being, after all. You're hard-wired to be a dumbass."

"Sit." Spence kicked out a barstool for him and poured him a beer from the pitcher in front of them.

Finn took a second look at him. "You're wearing glasses."

Haley grinned proudly. "Do you like them? I picked them out for him."

"No, you didn't," Spence said. "I did."

Haley patted him like he was a puppy. "You were impatient as always and grabbed the first pair off the display you could. It took you less than two seconds. I waited until you'd left and put them back and picked you out a better pair that would better suit your face."

Spence pulled his glasses off and stared at them. "I liked the other pair better."

"Yeah?" Haley asked. "What color were they?"

Spence paused. "Glasses color."

Haley rolled her eyes. "Just like a man," she said to Will and Elle, who nodded.

Archer shook his head at Spence. "This is why you're single."

"You're single too," Spence said.

"Because I want to be."

Spence closed his eyes. "We were going to rag on Finn, not me. Let's stick with the plan."

"Right," Archer said and looked at Finn. "Tell us all how you messed up so we can point and laugh."

"And then fix," Willa said, giving the others a dirty look as she patted the empty seat. "Come on now, don't be shy. Tell us everything."

"Yes," Ella said. "I want to hear it all, because that girl? She's not just yours, Finn. She's ours now too."

"She's not mine," Finn said.

Everyone gaped at him.

Elle narrowed her gaze. "Does this have anything to do with that wish she made for you on that damn fountain? You know about that, right?"

Finn blinked. "She wished for *me*?"

"Have you ever heard of being gentle?" Archer asked Elle. "Even once?"

Elle sighed. "Okay, so he didn't know. Sue me." She shot Archer a dirty look. "And like you know the first thing about being gentle."

"Didn't know what exactly?" Finn demanded, refusing to let them go off on some tangent. "Someone needs to start making sense or I swear to God—"

"She made a wish for you to find true love," Willa

said. "I was never clear on why she wished for you and not for herself. Probably because that's who she is, down to the bone."

Spence sucked in a breath. "I've been by that fountain a million times. It never once occurred to me to make a wish for someone else. That's . . ."

"Selfless," Willa said. "Utterly selfless. And, by the way, it's also something that *none* of us would've thought to do. So it's not just Spence here who's an insensitive ass."

"Thanks, Willa," Spence said dryly.

She turned expectantly to Finn. "So? What happened?"

A terrible knot in his chest twisting, Finn snatched Spence's beer and knocked back the rest of the glass, not that it helped.

"Sure, help yourself," Spence muttered.

Everyone was looking at Finn, waiting.

He shook his head. "I can't. It's . . . private. What happened between us stays between us."

"Hey, this isn't Vegas," Spence said, and earned himself a slap upside the back of his head by Elle.

"Do you love her?" Willa demanded of Finn.

At the question, that knot in his chest tightened painfully. "That's not the problem. She . . . kept something from me."

"That sucks," Archer said, as Finn knew, understanding all too well the power of secrets and how they could destroy lives.

"No," Elle said, glaring at Archer. "No, you don't get to blindly side against her. She maybe had her reasons. Good ones," she said very seriously.

Something they knew that Elle understood *all* too well. She had secrets too, secrets they kept for her.

Archer met Elle's gaze and something passed between them. The fight might have ratcheted up a notch but Willa, always the peacemaker, spoke up. "Do you love her?" she repeated to Finn firmly.

Finn's mind scrolled through the images he had. Pru coming into the pub drenched and still smiling. Pru dragging him away from work to a softball game. Comforting him after a fight with Sean. Clutching a photo of her dead parents and still finding a smile over their memory. She'd brought a sense of balance to his life that had been sorely missing. It didn't matter whether she was standing behind the controls of a huge boat in charge of hundreds of people's safety or diving into a wave to save her dog, she never failed to make him feel . . . alive.

Just a single one of her smiles could make his whole day. The sound of her laugh did the same. And then there was the feel of her beneath him, her body locked around his when he was buried so deep that he couldn't imagine being intimate with anyone else ever again . . .

"Yes," he said quietly, not having to speak loud because the entire group had gone silent waiting on his answer. "I love her."

"Have you told her?" Willa asked.

"No."

"Why not?"

"Because . . ." Yeah, genius, why not? "And exactly how many people have *you* told that to?" he asked.

"Good one, going on the defensive," Elle said, not looking impressed.

Willa agreed with an eyeroll. "I mean I get that when you're playing sports or bragging to the guys and you need a six-foot-long dick," she said. "But this is Pru we're talking about."

"Six-foot-long dick?" Spence asked, grinning.

Willa waved him off and spoke straight to Finn. "Whatever she kept to herself, you did the same, Finn. You always do, even with us. You held back. You think she didn't feel that? Pru keeps it real and she's tough as nails, but she lost her family," she said, unknowingly touching on the very subject of the breakup. "She lost them when she was only eighteen and it left her alone in the world. And as you, more than anyone else knows all too damn well, it changes a person, Finn. It makes it hard to put yourself out there. But that's exactly what she does every single day without complaint, she puts herself out there."

I love you . . . Pru had whispered those words to him when he'd been drifting off to sleep that last night, and he'd told himself it was a dream. But he knew the truth. He'd always known.

She had more courage than he'd ever had.

"So presumably there was a fight," Elle said. "And then what? She walked?"

"And you let her?" Willa asked in disbelief. "Oh, Finn."

"You can fix it," Haley said softly. "You just go to her and tell her you were wrong."

Archer, eyes on Finn, put his hand on Haley's, stopping her. "I have a feeling we've got things backwards," he said.

"Ohhhh," Willa said, staring at Finn. "*You* walked."

Finn nodded. He'd walked. And she'd let him go without a fight.

Not that he'd given her any choice with the *I don't want to see you again* thing . . . *Fuck*. Willa was right. He'd been wielding around a six-foot dick, which made *him* the six-foot dick.

Willa looked greatly disappointed. "I don't understand."

Finn shook his head. "I know. But I'm not going to tell you more." He might have turned his back on Pru, but he wouldn't have these guys doing the same. She deserved their friendship. She deserved a lot more than that, but he was still so angry and . . . *shit*. Hurt. He pushed away from the table. "I've gotta go."

He hoped to be alone but Sean followed him back to his office. "What aren't you telling me?" he asked. "What is it she did that was so bad?"

Finn shook his head.

"Just tell me," Sean pushed. "So I can tell you that you're being an idiot and then you can go make it right."

Finn stared at him. "What makes you believe that this can be made right?"

Sean lifted a shoulder. "Because you taught me that love and family is where you make it, with who you make it. And even in this short amount of time, Pru's become both your love and your family."

That this was true felt like a knife slicing through him. "Sean, her parents were the ones in the car that killed dad. Her dad was the drunk driver."

Sean stared at him. "Are you shitting me?"

"I couldn't have made that up if I'd tried."

Sean sank to the couch. "Holy shit."

"Yeah. Listen, this stays right here in this room, yeah?"

Sean lifted his gaze and pierced Finn. "You're protecting her."

"I just don't want to hurt her," he said. At least not more than he already had . . .

"No, you're protecting her." Sean stood again. "The way I bet she was trying to protect you when she didn't tell you who she was."

Finn shook his head. "What are you saying?"

"That *you're* the dumbass, not her." Sean shook his head. "Look, I've got to get back out there. One of us has to have their head in the game, and trust me, no one's more surprised that it's me." He stopped at the door and turned back. "Listen, I get that you're too close to see this clearly, but take it from someone who lost as much as you did in that accident . . . we didn't lose shit compared to what Pru lost. She doesn't deserve this, not from you. Not from anyone."

And then he let himself out and Finn was alone. He went to his desk and pushed some paper around for half an hour, but it was useless. He was useless. He'd just decided to bail when Archer walked right in. "Ever hear of knocking?"

Archer paced the length of the office and then came to him, hands on hips.

"*What*?" Finn asked.

"I'm going to tell you something," Archer said. "And I don't want you to take a swing at me for it. I'm feeling pissed off and wouldn't mind a fight, but I don't want it with you."

Shit. "What did you do?" Finn asked wearily.

Archer grimaced. "Something I once promised you I wouldn't."

Finn stared at his oldest and most trusted friend in the world and then turned to his desk and poured them both some whiskey.

Archer lifted his glass, touched it to Finn's, and then they both tossed back.

Archer blew out a breath, set the glass down and met Finn's gaze. "I looked into her."

Archer had programs that rivaled entire government computer systems. When he said he'd looked into someone, he meant he looked *into* them. Inside and out. Upside down and right-side up. When Archer looked into someone, he could find out how old they were when they got their first cavity, what their high school P.E. teacher had said about them, what their parents had earned in a cash-under-the-table job four decades prior.

Archer didn't take this power lightly. He had a high moral code of conduct that didn't always line up with the rest of the world, but he'd never—at least not to Finn's knowledge—looked into his friends' pasts or breached their privacy.

He had, however, looked into Willa's last boyfriend, but that had been for a good reason.

"When?" Finn asked.

Archer gave him a surprised look. "Shouldn't the question be *what*? As in what did I find out?"

"You know who she is."

"Yes," Archer said. "Do *you*?"

"Why the fuck do you think I'm standing here by myself?" Finn asked.

Archer looked away for a beat and then brought his gaze back. "There's stuff you might not know."

"Like?"

"Like the fact that she's spent her life since the accident trying to right that wrong to everyone who was affected. That she, anonymously through an attorney, gave every penny she was awarded in life insurance to the victims of that accident, including you and Sean. She not only kept zero for herself, she sold the house she was raised in and used that money to help as well. She kept nothing, instead dedicated the following years to making sure everyone else was taken care of, whatever it took. She helped them find jobs, stay in college, find a place to live, everything and anything that was needed."

Finn nodded.

"You know?" Archer asked in disbelief. "So what happened between you two? She came clean and . . ."

"I got mad that she lied to me."

"You mean omitted, right? Because not telling you something isn't lying."

Finn swore roughly but whether that was because he was pissed or because Archer was right, he wasn't sure. "It was more than that. She had plenty of opportunities to tell me. If not when we first met, then certainly after we—"

Archer let that hang there a moment. "I'm thinking she had her reasons," he said quietly. "And it wasn't all that long. What, three weeks? Maybe she was working her way up to it."

Finn shook his head.

"Look, I'm not excusing what she did," Archer said. "She should've told you. We both know that. But we also both know that it's never that easy. She had a lot working against her, Finn. She's alone, for one. And she's got the biggest guilt complex going that I've ever seen."

Finn swore again and shoved his fingers in his hair. "She shouldn't feel guilty. The accident wasn't her fault."

"No," Archer said. "It wasn't. So I'm going to hope like hell you didn't let her think it was, no matter how badly she stepped on your ego."

"That's completely bullshit. This isn't about my ego."

"Your stupid pride then," Archer said. "I was with you when your dad died, don't forget. I know how your life changed. And I realize we're talking about a soul here and I don't like to speak ill of the dead, but you and I both know the truth. Yours and Sean's life changed for the better when your father was dead and buried."

Finn let his head fall back and he stared at the ceiling.

"You know what I think happened?"

"No," Finn said tiredly, "but I bet you're about to tell me."

Archer smiled grimly, and true to his nature, didn't hold back. "I think you fell and fell hard, and then you got scared. You needed an out and she gave it to you. Hell, she handed it to you on a silver platter. Well, congrats, man, you got what you wanted."

At his silence, Archer shook his head and headed for the door. "Hope you enjoy it."

Finn sat there stewing in his own frustration, both bad temper and regrets choking him. Enjoy it? He couldn't imagine enjoying anything, ever again. He looked around him. In the past, this place had been his home away from home.

But that feeling had migrated to Pru's place two floors up.

Just as his emotions had migrated to the same place, over softball, darts, hikes, and long conversations about what they wanted out of their hopes and dreams, often chased by the best sex he'd ever had.

He hadn't realized just how far gone he was when it came to her. Or how lost in her he'd allowed himself to become.

But he was. Completely lost in her, and lost without her.

He hadn't seen that coming. He'd assumed they'd continue doing what they'd been doing. Being together. Hell, it'd been so easy it'd snuck up on him.

And he'd fallen, hard.

That wasn't the surprise. No, that honor went to the fact that in spite of what she'd done, he was *still* in love with her.

And, he suspected, always would be.

Chapter 33

#LifeIsABowlOfCrazy

Pru was up on the roof with Thor, watching the fog roll in when she felt someone watching her. "I'm not going to jump, if that's what you're worried about," she said.

Archer stepped into her line of sight and crouched at her side. "Of course you're not, you're stronger than that."

She felt a ghost of a smile cross her lips. "You sure about that?"

"Very."

She turned her head and met his gaze, and saw that he knew everything. She sighed. "For what it's worth, I realize that I should've told him from day one, but I thought if he knew, he wouldn't give me the time of day and I wanted to help him."

"He doesn't like help."

"No kidding."

Archer smiled. "Finn's got the world in black or white. Like . . . the Giants or Dodgers. Home grown or imported. Us or them. For me, and for you too, I suspect, it's not so simple. He's a smart guy, though, Pru. He figures things out. He always does, in his own time."

She shook her head, kissed the top of Thor's, and rose. "That's sweet of you to say, but he won't. And I don't expect him to. I made a mistake, a really big one. And sometimes we don't get second chances."

"You should," Archer said.

"He's right." This was from Willa, who appeared from the fire escape and came over to them. "Everyone deserves a second chance."

"Where's Elle?" Archer asked.

"She couldn't climb the fire escape in her heels and she refused to leave them behind. She's taking the elevator."

Spence showed up next. He came from the fire escape like Willa and held Pru's gaze for a long beat before nodding and stepping out of the way, making room for the person hitting the rooftop right behind him.

Finn.

He climbed over with agility and ease and dropped down, coming straight for Pru without a glance at any of his closest friends.

Pru's heart stopped. Everything stopped including her ability to think. She took a step back, needing out of here. She wasn't ready to face him and pretend to be okay with the fact that they were nothing to each other now.

"Wait," Finn said, reaching for her hand. "Don't go."

God, that voice. She'd missed him so very much. Feeling lost, she looked at the others, who'd backed off to the other side of the rooftop to give them some privacy. "I need to go," she whispered to Finn.

"Can I say something first?" he asked quietly. "Please?"

When she nodded, he gently squeezed her hand in his. "You told me you made a mistake and that you wanted to explain," he said. "And I didn't let you. That was my mistake, Pru. I was wrong. We each made mistakes, not just you. And I get that we can't pretend that the mistakes didn't happen, but maybe we can use them to cancel each other out."

Her heart was a jackhammer behind her ribs, pounding too fast for her veins to keep up with the increased blood flow. "What are you saying?"

"I'm saying that I forgive you, Pru. And in fact, there was never anything to forgive. Can you forgive me?"

The jackhammer had turned into a solid lump, blocking her air passage. "It's . . ." She shook her head and tried desperately to keep hope from running away with her goose sense. "It can't be that easy," she whispered.

"Why not?" He reached for her other hand, taking advantage of her being stunned into immobility to tug her into him. Toe to toe now, he cupped her jaw. "Our last night together, you said something to me when I was drifting off." His gaze warmed. "You said it and then I felt your sheer panic, so I let it go. Or that's what I told myself. But the truth is that I was just being a coward."

She had to close her eyes at his gentle touch because just the callused pads of his fingers on her felt so right she wanted to cry.

"I love you, Pru," he said quietly but with utter steel.

Her eyes flew open and her breath snagged in her lungs. She hadn't realized how badly she'd needed to hear those words but . . . "Love doesn't fix everything," she said on a hitched breath. "There are rules and expectations in a relationship. And there are some things you can't take back. What I did was one of those things."

He shook his head. "Life doesn't follow rules or expectations. It's messy and unpredictable. And it turns out love is a lot like life—it doesn't follow rules or expectations either."

"Yes, but—"

"Did you mean what you said?" he asked. "Do you love me, Pru?"

She stared up at him and swallowed hard, but her heart remained in her throat, stuck there with that burgeoning hope she hadn't been successful at beating back. "Yes," she whispered. "I love you. But—"

"But nothing," he said fiercely, eyes lit with relief, affection. *Love.* "Nothing else matters compared to the fact that I managed to get the most amazing woman I've ever met to fall in love with me."

She slowly shook her head. "I'm not sure you're taking my concerns seriously."

"On the contrary," he said. "I'm taking you and your concerns *very* seriously. What you did was try to bring something to the life of two guys you didn't even know. You set aside your own happiness out of guilt and regret, when you had nothing to feel guilt and regret for. You lost a lot that day too, Pru. You lost more than anyone else. And there was no one to help you. No one to try to make things better for you."

Her throat closed. Just snapped shut. "Don't," she managed to whisper. "We can't go back."

"Not back, then. Forward." He gently squeezed her fingers in his. "I was wrong to walk away, so fucking wrong, Pru. What we had was exactly right and I'm sorry I ever made you doubt it."

Eyes still closed, she shook her head, afraid to hope. Afraid to breathe. He brought their entwined hands to his heart so that she could feel its strong, steady beat, as if he was willing his calm confidence about his feelings for her to soak in.

She let it, along with his warmth, appreciating more than she could say what his words meant to her. She hadn't realized how much she'd needed to hear him say he didn't blame her, that she had nothing to feel guilty for . . . It was as if he'd swept up all her broken pieces and painstakingly glued them back together, making her whole again. "Finn—"

"Can you live without me?" he asked.

Her eyes flew open. "What?"

"It's a simple question," he said. "Can you live without me?"

She stared past him at the others. Elle had arrived and maybe they were on the other side of the rooftop, but they were making absolutely zero attempt to hide the fact that they were hanging on every word.

"Pru," he said quietly.

She met his gaze again, chewing on her lower lip.

"Not talking?" he asked. "Fair enough. I'll go first. I can't live without you. Hell, I can't even breathe when I think about you not being in my life."

"You can't?"

"No." He gently squeezed her. "I live pretty simply, always have. I've got these interfering idiots—" He gestured to his friends behind them.

"Hey," Spence said.

"He's right," Willa said. "Now shh, I think we're getting to the good stuff."

Finn shook his head and turned back to Pru. "I thought they were all I needed and I felt lucky to have them. But then you came into my life and suddenly I had something I didn't even realize was missing. Do you know what that was?"

She shook her head.

"It's you, Pru. And I want you back. I want to be with you. I want you to be mine, because I'm absolutely yours. Have been since you first walked into my life and became my fun whisperer. And you can't tell me it's too soon for a relationship because we've been in one since the moment we met. We're together, we're *supposed* to be together. Like peanut butter and jelly. Like French fries and ketchup. Like peaches and cream."

"Like titties and beer," Spence offered.

Archer wrapped his arm around Spence's neck and covered the guy's mouth with his hand.

"No," Pru said.

Finn stared at her. "What?"

"No, titties and beer don't go together," she said. "But also no, I can't live without you either."

Finn stared at her for a beat, his eyes dark and serious and full of so much emotion she didn't know how to process it all. And then suddenly he smiled the most beautiful smile she'd ever seen. He took her hand, brought it to his mouth and brushed a kiss over her fingers before hauling her up against him.

"You ready for this?" His voice was rough, telling her how important this was. How important *she* was.

"For you?" she whispered against his jaw. "Always."

Epilogue

#YouHadMeAtHello

Two months later . . .

Finn let out a long breath as he parked. Santa Cruz was south of San Francisco and thanks to traffic, it'd taken them over an hour to get here. He got out of the car and came around for Pru.

"Keep the blindfold on," he said, as he'd been saying the entire drive.

Her fingers brushed over the makeshift blindfold—a silk handkerchief that they'd played with in bed the night before—and smiled. "I'm hoping we're heading toward a big cake."

"I told you to aim higher for your birthday."

"Okay," she said. "A nice dinner first and *then* a big cake."

"Higher," he said.

She let their bodies bump and she rubbed her hips suggestively to his. "Dinner, cake, and . . . that weekend away you promised me?" she asked hopefully.

"Getting warmer." He gripped her hips, holding her close enough that she could feel exactly what she did to him.

She smiled warmly, sexily, gorgeous . . . his everything. "Can I peek yet?"

His gut tightened as he turned her so that she faced the small Santa Cruz beach cottage in front of them. "Okay," he said. "You can look."

Pru tore off the blindfold and blinked open her big eyes, which immediately widened as she gasped. She stared at the place in front of her and then turned her head and stared at him for a beat before swiveling back to the house. "Oh my God," she breathed and put a hand to her chest. "This is—was—my parents' house. Where I grew up."

"I know," he said quietly.

Pru stared at the tiny place like it was a sight for sore eyes, like it was Christmas and Easter and every other holiday all in one. "I haven't been here in so long . . ." She looked at him again. "It's ours for the weekend?"

He took both of her hands in his so that she faced him. "The owners had it in a beach rental program." He slipped a key into her right hand.

"You rented it for me?" she breathed.

"Yes." He paused. "Except I didn't rent it. I bought it. It's in your name now, Pru."

Her mouth fell open. "What?"

"The owners live on the other side of the country. They instructed the management program to sell it if the opportunity arose." His heart was pounding and he hoped like hell he'd done the right thing here, that she would take it in the spirit he intended. "The opportunity arose."

Looking shaky, she took the few steps and unlocked the front door. Then she stepped inside. He followed, slowly, wanting to give her time if she needed it.

The place was furnished. Shabby beach chic. Tiny kitchen, two tiny bedrooms, one bathroom. He already knew this from his previous visit to scope everything out, but he followed as Pru walked through, quiet, eyes shuttered.

The postage-stamp-size living room made up for its tininess with the view of the Pacific Ocean about three hundred feet down a grassy bluff.

Pru walked to the floor-to-ceiling windows and looked out.

Finn waited, willing to give her all the time she needed. He was prepared for her to be mad at him for overstepping, but when she turned to him, her eyes didn't hold temper.

They held emotion, overfilling, spilling down her cheeks.

"Pru." He stepped toward her but she held up a hand.

"Finn, I can't accept this. We're just dating, it's not right—"

"Yeah, about that just dating thing." He tugged her into him—where he liked her best. Cupping her jaw, he tilted her face to his. "I don't want to just date anymore."

She blinked. "You bought me a house and now you're dumping me?"

"I bought you a house and now I'm asking you to take us to the next level."

She just stared into his eyes in shock and he realized something with his own shock. "You expected me to change my mind about you," he said.

She shook her head. "More that I'm afraid to want more from you. I don't want to be greedy."

Finn cupped her face, keeping her chin tilted so that she had to look at him. He needed her to see how serious he was. "Pru, don't you get it yet? I'm yours until the end of time."

She relaxed against him with a small smile. "Okay, that's good," she said a little shakily. "Seeing as I want whatever of you that you're willing to give me."

He let out a low laugh. "Everything. I want to give you everything, Pru."

Her eyes shined brilliantly. "You already have," she whispered and tugged his mouth to hers, kissing him with all the love he'd ever dreamed of and more. So much more.

When they broke for air, her eyes were still a little damp but also full of affection and heat. Lots of heat. "Did you really mean *everything*?" she asked.

"Everything and anything." To prove it, he pulled a small black box from his pocket where it'd been sitting for a week and flipped it open.

With shaking fingers, she took out the diamond ring. "Oh my God."

"Is that 'oh my God yes I'll marry you, Finn O'Riley?'" he asked.

She both laughed and cried. "Did you doubt it?"

"Well, I still haven't heard 'yes, Finn.'"

With a laugh, she leapt into his arms and spread kisses over his jaw to his mouth. "Yes, Finn!"

Grinning, he slid the diamond ring onto her finger.

She admired her hand. "So how pushy would it be of me to ask for something else right now?"

"Name it," he said.

She put her mouth to his ear. "I'd like some more of what you gave me last night. Right here, right now."

Remembering every single hot second of last night, he smiled. "Yeah?"

"Yeah." She bit her lower lip again, which didn't hide her smile. "Please?"

"Babe, anything you want, always, and you don't even have to say please."

The Trouble With Mistletoe

To my Oldest, who isn't that old—
and let's not forget I had her when I was twelve,
so I'm not that old either—
for tirelessly walking me around San Francisco
every time I needed to see
something for this book.
I'm so proud of you.
XOXO forever.

Chapter 1

The sun had barely come up and Willa Davis was already elbow deep in puppies and poo—a typical day for her. As owner of the South Bark Mutt Shop, she spent much of her time scrubbing, cajoling, primping, hoisting—and more cajoling. She wasn't above bribing either.

Which meant she kept pet treats in her pockets, making her irresistible to any and all four-legged creatures within scent range. A shame though that a treat hadn't yet been invented to make her irresistible to *two*-legged male creatures as well. Now *that* would've been handy.

But then again, she'd put herself on a Man-Time-Out so she didn't need such a thing.

"Wuff!"

This from one of the pups she was bathing. The little guy wobbled in close and licked her chin.

"That's not going to butter me up," she said, but it totally did and unable to resist that face she returned the kiss on the top of his cute little nose.

One of Willa's regular grooming clients had brought in her eight-week-old heathens—er, golden retriever puppies.

Six of them.

It was over an hour before the shop would open at nine a.m. but her client had called in a panic because the pups had rolled in horse poo. God knew where they'd found horse poo in the Cow Hollow district of San Francisco—maybe a policeman's horse had left an undignified pile in the street—but they were a mess.

And now so was Willa.

Two puppies, even three, were manageable, but handling six by herself bordered on insanity. "Okay, listen up," she said to the squirming, happily panting puppies in the large tub in her grooming room. "Everyone sit."

One and Two sat. Three climbed up on top of the both of them and shook his tubby little body, drenching Willa in the process.

Meanwhile, Four, Five, and Six made a break for it, paws pumping, ears flopping over their eyes, tails wagging wildly as they scrabbled, climbing over each other like circus tumblers to get out of the tub.

"Rory?" Willa called out. "Could use another set of hands back here." Or three . . .

No answer. Either her twenty-three-year-old employee had her headphones cranked up to make-me-deaf-please or she was on Instagram and didn't want to lose her place. *"Rory!"*

The girl finally poked her head around the corner, phone in hand, screen lit.

Yep. Instagram.

"Holy crap," Rory said, eyes wide. "Literally."

Willa looked down at herself. Yep, her apron and clothes were splattered with suds and water and a few other questionable stains that might or might not be related to the horse poo. She'd lay money down on the fact that her layered strawberry blonde hair had rioted, resembling an explosion in a down-pillow factory. Good thing she'd forgone makeup at the early emergency call so at least she didn't have mascara running down her face. "Help."

Rory cheerfully dug right in, not shying from getting wet or dirty. Dividing and conquering, they got all the pups out of the tub, dried, and back in their baby pen in twenty minutes. One through Five fell into the instant slumber that only babies and the very drunk could achieve, but Six remained stubbornly awake, climbing over his siblings determined to get back into Willa's arms.

Laughing, she scooped the little guy up. His legs bicycled in the air, tail wagging faster than the speed of light, taking his entire hind end with it.

"Not sleepy, huh?" Willa asked.

He strained toward her, clearly wanting to lick her face.

"Oh no you don't. I know where that tongue's been." Tucking him under her arm, she carted him out front to the retail portion of her shop, setting him into another baby pen with some puppy toys, one that was visible to street traffic. "Now sit there and look pretty and bring in some customers, would you?"

Panting with happiness, the puppy pounced on a toy and got busy playing as Willa went through her opening routine, flipping on the lights throughout the retail area. The shop came to life, mostly thanks to the insane amount of holiday decorations she'd put up the week before, including the seven-foot tree in the front corner—lit to within an inch of its life.

"It's only the first of December and it looks like Christmas threw up in here," Rory said from the doorway.

Willa looked around at her dream-come-true shop, the one finally operating in the black. Well, most of the time. "But in a classy way, right?"

Rory eyed the one hundred miles of strung lights and more boughs of holly than even the North Pole should have. "Um . . . right."

Willa ignored the doubtful sarcasm. One, Rory hadn't grown up in a stable home. And two, neither had she. For the both of them Christmas had always been a luxury that, like three squares and a roof, had been out of their reach more than not. They'd each dealt with that differently. Rory didn't need the pomp and circumstance of the holidays.

Willa did, desperately. So yeah, she was twenty-seven years old and still went overboard for the holidays.

"Ohmigod," Rory said, staring at their newest cash register display. "Is that a rack of penis headbands?"

"No!" Willa laughed. "It's reindeer-antler headbands for dogs."

Rory stared at her.

Willa grimaced. "Okay, so maybe I went a little crazy—"

"A *little*?"

"Ha-ha," Willa said, picking up a reindeer-antler headband. It didn't look like a penis to her, but then again it'd been a while since she'd seen one up close and personal. "These are going to sell like hotcakes, mark my words."

"Ohmigod—don't put it on!" Rory said in sheer horror as Willa did just that.

"It's called marketing." Willa rolled her eyes upward to take in the antlers jutting up above her head. "Shit."

Rory grinned and pointed to the swear jar that Willa had set up to keep them all in line. Mostly her, actually. They used the gained cash for their muffins and coffee fix.

Willa slapped a dollar into it. "I guess the antlers do look a little like penises," she admitted. "Or is it peni? What's the plural of penis?"

"Pene?" Rory asked and they both cracked up.

Willa got a hold of herself. "Clearly I'm in need of Tina's caffeine, *bad*."

"I'll go," Rory said. "I caught sight of her coming through the courtyard at the crack of dawn wearing six-inch wedge sneakers, her hair teased to the North Pole, making her look, like, eight feet tall."

Tina used to be Tim and everyone in the five-story, offbeat historical Pacific Pier Building had enjoyed Tim—but they *loved* Tina. Tina rocked.

"What's your order?" Rory asked.

Tina's coffees came in themes and Willa knew just what she needed for the day ahead. "One of her It's Way Too Early for Life's Nonsense." She pulled some more cash from her pocket and this time a handful of puppy treats came out too, bouncing all over the floor.

"And to think, you can't get a date," Rory said dryly.

"Not *can't* get a date," Willa corrected. "Don't want a date. I pick the wrong men, something I'm not alone in . . ."

Rory blew out a sigh at the truth of that statement and then went brows up when Willa's stomach growled like a roll of thunder.

"Okay, so grab me a muffin as well." Tina made the best muffins on the planet. "Make it two. Or better yet, three. No, wait." Her jeans had been hard to button that morning. "Crap, three muffins would be my entire day's calories. One," she said firmly. "One muffin for me and make it a blueberry so it counts as a serving of fruit."

"Got it," Rory said. "A coffee, a blueberry muffin, and a straitjacket on the side."

"Ha-ha. Now get out of here before I change my order again."

South Bark had two doors, one that opened to the street, the other to the building's courtyard with its beautiful cobblestones and the historical old fountain that Willa could never resist tossing a coin into and wishing for true love as she passed.

Rory headed out the courtyard door.

"Hey," Willa said. "If there's any change, throw a coin into the fountain for me?"

"So you're on a self-imposed man embargo but you still want to wish on true love?"

"Yes, please."

Rory shook her head. "It's your dime." She didn't believe in wishes or wasting even a quarter, but she obediently headed out.

When she was gone, Willa's smile faded. Each of her three part-time employees was young and they all had one thing in common.

Life had churned them up and spit them out at a young age, leaving them out there in the big, bad world all alone.

Since Willa had been one of those lost girls herself, she collected them. She gave them jobs and advice that they only listened to about half the time.

But she figured fifty percent was better than zero percent.

Her most recent hire was nineteen-year-old Lyndie, who was still a little feral but they were working on that. Then there was Cara, who'd come a long way. Rory had been with Willa the longest. The girl put up a strong front but she still struggled. Proof positive was the fading markings of a bruise on her jaw where her ex-boyfriend had knocked her into a doorjamb.

Just the thought had Willa clenching her fists. Sometimes at night she dreamed about what she'd like to do to the guy. High on the list was cutting off his twig and berries with a dull knife but she had an aversion to jail.

Rory deserved better. Tough as nails on the outside, she was a tender marshmallow on the inside, and she'd do anything for Willa. It was sweet, but also a huge responsibility because Rory looked to Willa for her normal.

A daunting prospect on the best of days.

She checked on Six and found the puppy finally fast asleep sprawled on his back, feet spread wide to show the world his most prized possessions.

Just like a man for you.

Next she checked on his siblings. Also asleep. Feeling like the mother of sextuplets, she tiptoed back out to the front and opened her laptop, planning to inventory the new boxes of supplies she'd received late the night before.

She'd just gotten knee-deep in four different twenty-five-pound sacks of bird feed—she still couldn't believe how many people in San Francisco had birds—when someone knocked on the front glass door.

Damn. It was only a quarter after eight but it went against the grain to turn away a paying customer. Straightening, she swiped her hands on her apron and looked up.

A guy stood on the other side of the glass, mouth grim, expression dialed to Tall, Dark, and Attitude-ridden. He was something too, all gorgeous and broody and—hold up. There was something familiar about him, enough that her feet propelled her forward out of pure curiosity. When it hit her halfway to the door, she froze, her heart just about skidding to a stop.

"Keane Winters," she murmured, lip curling like she'd just eaten a black licorice. She hated black licorice. But she was looking at the only man on the planet who could make her feel all puckered up as well as good about her decision to give up men.

In fact, if she'd only given them up sooner, say back on the day of the Sadie Hawkins dance in her freshman year of high school when he'd stood her up, she'd have saved herself a lot of heartache in the years since.

On the other side of the door, Keane shoved his mirrored sunglasses to the top of his head, revealing dark chocolate eyes that she knew could melt when he was amused or feeling flirtatious, or turn to ice when he was so inclined.

They were ice now.

Catching her gaze, he lifted a cat carrier. A bright pink bedazzled carrier.

He had a cat.

Her entire being wanted to soften at this knowledge because that meant on some level at least he had to be a good guy, right?

Luckily her brain clicked on, remembering everything, every little detail of that long ago night. Like how she'd had to borrow a dress for the dance from a girl in her class who'd gleefully lorded it over her, how she'd had to beg her foster mother to let her go, how she'd stolen a Top Ramen from the locked pantry and eaten it dry in the bathroom so she wouldn't have to buy both her dinner and his, as was custom for the "backward" dance.

"We're closed," she said through the still locked glass door.

Not a word escaped his lips. He simply raised the cat carrier another inch, like he was God's gift.

And he had been. At least in high school.

Wishing she'd gotten some caffeine before dealing with this, she blew out a breath and stepped closer, annoyed at her eyes because they refused to leave his as she unlocked and then opened the door. Just another customer, she told herself. One that had ruined her life like it was nothing without so much as an apology . . .

"Morning," she said, determined to be polite.

Not a single flicker of recognition crossed his face and she found something even more annoying than this man being on her doorstep.

The fact that she'd been so forgettable he didn't even remember her.

"I'm closed until nine." She said this in her most pleasant voice although a little bit of eff-you *might've* been implied.

"I've got to be at work by nine," he said. "I want to board a cat for the day."

Keane had always been big and intimidating. It was what had made him such an effective jock. He'd ruled on the football field, the basketball court, *and* the baseball diamond. The perfect trifecta, the all-around package.

Every girl in the entire school—and also a good amount of the teachers—had spent an indecent amount of time eyeballing that package.

But just as Willa had given up men, she'd even longer ago given up thinking about that time, inarguably the worst years of her life. While Keane had been off breaking records and winning hearts, she'd been drowning under the pressures of school and work, not to mention basic survival.

She got that it wasn't his fault her memories of that time were horrific. Nor was it his fault that just looking at him brought them all back to her. But emotions weren't logical. "I'm sorry," she said, "but I'm all full up today."

"I'll pay double."

He had a voice like fine whiskey. Not that she ever drank fine whiskey. Even the cheap stuff was a treat. And maybe it was just her imagination, but she was having a hard time getting past the fact that he was both the same and yet had changed. He was still tall, of course, and built sexy as hell, damn him. Broad shoulders, lean hips, biceps straining his shirt as he held up the cat carrier.

He wore faded ripped jeans on his long legs and scuffed work boots. His only concession to the San Francisco winter was a long-sleeved T-shirt that enhanced all those ripped muscles and invited her to BITE ME in big block letters across his chest.

She wasn't going to lie to herself, she kind of wanted to. *Hard.*

He stood there exuding raw, sexual power and energy—not that she was noticing. Nor was she taking in his expression that said maybe he'd already had a bad day.

He could join her damn club.

And at that thought, she mentally smacked herself in the forehead. No! There would be *no* club joining. She'd set boundaries for herself. She was Switzerland. Neutral. No importing or exporting of anything including sexy smoldering glances, hot body parts, *nothing.*

Period.

Especially not with Keane Winters, thank you very much. And anyway, she didn't board animals for the general public. Yes, sometimes she boarded as special favors for clients, a service she called "fur-babysitting" because her capacity here was too small for official boarding. If and when she agreed to "babysit" overnight as a favor, it meant taking her boarders home with her, so she was extremely selective.

And handsome men who'd once been terribly mean boys who ditched painfully shy girls after she'd summoned up every ounce of her courage to ask him out to a dance did *not* fit her criteria. "I don't board—" she started, only to be interrupted by an unholy howl from inside the pink cat carrier.

It was automatic for her to reach for it, and Keane readily released it with what looked to be comical relief.

Turning her back on him, Willa carried the carrier to the counter, incredibly aware that Keane followed her through her shop, moving with an unusually easy grace for such a big guy.

The cat was continuously howling now so she quickly unzipped the carrier, expecting the animal inside to be dying giving the level of unhappiness it'd displayed.

The earsplitting caterwauling immediately stopped and a huge Siamese cat blinked vivid blue eyes owlishly up at her. It had a pale, creamy coat with a darker facial mask that matched its black ears, legs, and paws.

"Well aren't you beautiful," Willa said softly and slipped her hands into the box.

The cat immediately allowed herself to be lifted, pressing her face into Willa's throat for a cuddle.

"Aw," Willa said gently. "It's alright now, I've got you. You just hated that carrier, didn't you?"

"What the ever-loving hell," Keane said, hands on hips now as he glared at the cat. "Are you kidding me?"

"What?"

He scowled. "My great-aunt's sick and needs help. She dropped the cat off with me last night."

Well, damn. That was a pretty nice thing he'd done, taking the cat in for his sick aunt.

"The minute Sally left," Keane went on, "this thing went gonzo."

Willa looked down at the cat, who gazed back at her, quiet, serene, positively angelic. "What did she do?"

Keane snorted. "What *didn't* she do would be the better question. She hid under my bed and tore up my mattress. Then she helped herself to everything on my counters, knocking stuff to the floor, destroying my laptop and tablet and phone all in one fell swoop. And then she . . ." He trailed off and appeared to chomp on his back teeth.

"What?"

"Took a dump in my favorite running shoes."

Willa did her best not to laugh out loud and say "good girl." It took her a minute. "Maybe she's just upset to be away from home, and missing your aunt. Cats are creatures of habit. They don't like change." She spoke to Keane without taking her gaze off the cat, not wanting to look into the dark, mesmerizing eyes that didn't recognize her because if she did, she might be tempted to pick one of the tiaras displayed on her counter and hit him over the head with it.

"What's her name?" she asked.

"Petunia, but I'm going with Pita. Short for pain in the ass."

Willa stroked along the cat's back and Petunia pressed into her hand for more. A low and rumbly purr filled the room and Petunia's eyes slitted with pleasure.

Keane let out a breath as Willa continued to pet her. "Unbelievable," he said. "You're wearing catnip as perfume, right?"

Willa raised an eyebrow. "Is that the only reason you think she'd like me?"

"Yes."

Okay then. Willa opened her mouth to end this little game and tell him that she wasn't doing this, but then she looked into Petunia's deep-as-the-ocean blue eyes and felt her heart stir. *Crap.* "Fine," she heard herself say. "If you can provide proof of rabies and FVRCP vaccinations, I'll take her for today only."

"Thank you," he said with such genuine feeling, she glanced up at him.

A mistake.

His dark eyes had warmed to the color of melted dark chocolate. "One question."

"What?" she asked warily.

"Do you always wear X-rated headbands?"

Her hands flew to her head. She'd completely forgotten she was wearing the penis headband. "Are you referring to my reindeer antlers?"

"Reindeer antlers," he repeated.

"That's right."

"Whatever you say." He was smiling now, and of course the rat-fink bastard had a sexy-as-hell smile. And unbelievably her good parts stood up and took notice. Clearly her body hadn't gotten the memo on the no-man thing. Especially not *this* man.

"My name's Keane by the way," he said. "Keane Winters."

He paused, clearly expecting her to tell him her name in return, but she had a dilemma now. If she told him who she was and he suddenly recognized her, he'd also remember exactly how pathetic she'd once been. And if he *didn't* recognize her then that meant she was even more forgettable than she'd thought and she'd have to throw the penis headband at him after all.

"And you are . . . ?" he asked, rich voice filled with amusement at her pause.

Well, hell. Now or never, she supposed. "Willa Davis," she said and held her breath.

There was no change in his expression whatsoever. Forgettable then, and she ground her back teeth for a minute.

"I appreciate you doing this for me, Willa," he said.

She had to consciously unclench her teeth to speak. "I'm not doing it for you. I'm doing it for Petunia," she said, wanting to be crystal clear. "And you'll need to be back here to pick her up before closing."

"Deal."

"I've got a few questions for you," she said. "Like an emergency contact, your driver's license info, and"—God help her, she was going to hell if she asked this but she couldn't help herself, she wanted to jog his memory— "where you went to high school."

He arched a brow. "High school?"

"Yes, you never know what's going to be important."

He looked amused. "As long as I don't have to wear a headband of dicks, you can have whatever info you need."

Five extremely long minutes later he'd filled out the required form and provided the information needed after a quick call to his aunt—all apparently without getting his memory jogged. Then, with one last amused look at her reindeer antlers a.k.a. penis headband, he walked out the door.

Willa was still watching him go when Rory came to stand next to her, casually sipping her coffee as she handed over Willa's.

"Are we looking at his ass?" Rory wanted to know.

Yes, and to Willa's eternal annoyance, it was the best ass she'd ever seen. How unfair was that? The least he could've done was get some pudge. "Absolutely not."

"Well we're missing out, because *wow.*"

Willa looked at her. "He's too old for you."

"He's thirty. What," she said at Willa's raised brow. "You've got the copy of his driver's license right here on the counter. I did the math, that's not a crime. And anyway, you're right, he's old. Really *old.*"

"You do realize I'm only a few years behind him."

"You're old too," Rory said and nudged her shoulder to Willa's.

The equivalent of a big, fat, mushy hug.

"And for the record," the girl went on, "I was noticing his ass for *you*."

"Ha," Willa said. "The devil himself couldn't drag my old, dead corpse out on a date with him, even if he is hot as balls. I gave up men, remember? That's who I am right now, a woman who doesn't need a man."

"Who you are is a stubborn, obstinate woman who has a lot of love to give but is currently imitating a chicken. But hey, if you wanna let your past bad judgment calls rule your world and live like a nun, carry on just as you are."

"Gee," Willa said dryly. "Thanks."

"You're welcome. But I reserve the right to question your IQ. I hear you lose IQ points when you get old." She smiled sweetly. "Maybe you should start taking that Centrum Silver or something. Want me to run out and get some?"

Willa threw the penis headband at her, but Rory, being a youngster and all, successfully ducked in time.

Chapter 2

#OpenMouthInsertFoot

Two mornings later, Willa's alarm went off at zero dark thirty and she lay there for a minute drifting, dreaming . . . thinking. When Keane had returned for Petunia the other night, she'd been with a client so she hadn't had to deal with him.

But she'd made sure to look her fill.

And that bothered her. How could she like looking at him so much? Maybe it was because he was so inherently male and virile he could've walked right off the cover of *Alpha Male* magazine, if such a thing had existed.

The thing was, she wasn't supposed to care what he looked like, or how sexy his low-timbered voice was, or that he was taking care of his aunt's cat in spite of not liking said cat.

Because hello, ditched for the dance . . .

"Gah," she said to her bedroom and rolled over, sticking her head beneath her pillow.

She was too busy for a guy. Any guy. She had work and work was enough. She loved having the security of a bank account, when once upon a time she'd had nothing of her own and only herself to rely on.

She was proud of how far she'd come. Proud to be able to help kids who were in the same situation she'd once been in.

When her alarm went off, she jerked awake and groaned some more but rolled out of bed, blinking blearily at the clock.

Four in the morning.

She hated four in the morning as a general rule but today was an early day. She needed to hit the flower market and get some shopping done for an event she had going that night and also for her upcoming in-store Santa Extravaganza pet photo shoot, an annual event where customers would be able to get their pet's photo taken with Santa. It was a big moneymaker for her, and half of the profits went to the San Francisco animal shelters.

She dragged a grumpy Rory with her, where they bought supplies for the night's event, the photo booth, *and* additional foliage to boot.

"What's all that for?" Rory asked.

"More Christmas flavor."

Rory shook her head. "You've got a serious problem."

"Tell me something I don't know."

They got back to the shop by six thirty a.m. and

went to work. Sitting cross-legged on the counter of her shop with a sketch pad, Willa mapped out the evening's event, a wedding she'd been hired for as a wedding consultant, designer, and officiator.

For two giant poodles.

At seven on the dot, her friends Pru, Elle, and Haley showed up with breakfast, as they did several times a week since they all lived or worked in the building. Currently they were decimating a basket of Tina's muffins before scattering for their various jobs for the day. Haley wasn't yet in her lab coat for her optometrist internship upstairs, and had cute bright red spectacles perched on her nose. Pru wore her captain's attire for her job of captaining a tour boat off Pier 39. Elle was the building's office manager and looked the part in a cobalt blue suit dress with black and white gravity-defying open-toe pumps.

Willa looked her part too. Jeans and a camisole top despite the fact that it was winter. She kept her shop warm for the animals and her arms bare for when she was bathing and grooming.

The current discussion was men, and their pros and cons. Pru had a man. She was engaged to Finn, the guy who ran the Irish pub across the courtyard, and a really good guy along with being one of Willa's closest friends. So needless to say, Pru sat firmly on the pro side. "Look," she said in her defense of love. "Say you really need some orgasm RX, you know? If you're in love with someone, he'll go down on you and expect nothing back because he knows you'd do the same for him. Love is patient, love is kind." She smiled. "Love means oral sex without the pressure to reciprocate."

"Love is keeping batteries in your vibrator," Elle told her and the rest of them laughed, nodding. They all had a long list on the con side for men. Well, except for Haley, who dated women—when she was so inclined to date at all.

Although Willa had to admit, she did like the idea of orgasm RX . . .

"Yes, but what about spiders?" Pru ask. "A man will get the spiders."

There was a silence as the rest of them contemplated this unexpected benefit to having a man.

"I learned to capture and safely relocate," Haley finally said. "For Leeza."

Haley's last girlfriend had been a serious tree hugger. And a serial cheater, as it turned out.

"I just use the long hose on my vacuum cleaner," Elle said, looking smug. "No awkward morning-after conversation required."

"This is about Willa today so don't get me started on you," Pru told her. "You and Archer cause electric fires to break out when you so much as pass by each other. Remind me to circle back to that."

Elle shrugged it off. "You've heard of opposites attract?" she asked. "Well me and Archer, we're a classic case of opposites *distract*. As in we don't like each other."

They all laughed but choked it off when Elle gave them each a glacial look in turn.

Okay, so everyone knew she had a secret thing for Archer—except Elle herself apparently.

Well, and Archer . . .

Willa was just grateful to not be the center of attention anymore, although she wished they'd go back to
the fascinating morning-after discussion because she
hadn't had a lot of awkward morning afters. She tended
to complicate her bad choices in men by sticking too
long instead of running off. Maybe that was where
she'd always gone wrong. Maybe next time she was
stupid enough to give another guy a shot, it would be
a strictly one-time thing. And then she'd run like hell.

"Tell me the truth," Pru said. "When it comes to me
waxing poetic about mine and Finn's relationship, on
a scale of one to that friend who just had a baby and
wants to show you pics for hours, how annoying am I?"

Willa met Elle's and Haley's amused gazes and they
each murmured a variation of "not that bad."

Pru sighed. "Shit. I'm totally that new mom with
baby pics."

"Hey, knowing it is half the battle," Elle offered and
being a master conversation manipulator, looked at
Willa. "Tell us more about this guy with the cat."

"I can tell you he's hot," Rory said as she walked
by carrying a case of hamster food. "Like *major* hot.
And also Willa remembers him from high school. He
stood her up for some dance, but he doesn't remember
it or her."

"Well how rude," Haley said, instantly at Willa's
back, which Willa appreciated.

"I don't think he was being rude," Rory said. "Willa
had been bathing puppies and looked like a complete
train wreck, honestly, all covered in soap suds and

puppy drool and maybe some poop too. Even you guys wouldn't have recognized her."

"I looked how I always look," Willa said in her own defense. "And that part about high school was confidential."

"Oops, sorry," Rory said, not looking sorry at all. "I'll be in the back, grooming Thor."

Thor was Pru's dog, who had a penchant for rolling in stuff he shouldn't, the more disgusting the better. Pru blew Rory a grateful kiss and turned to Willa. "So back to hot-as-balls guy. More info please."

Willa sighed. "What is there to say? We went to school together and he never noticed me back then either so I should've known."

"How well did you know him?" Elle asked, eyes sharp. She was the logical one of the group, able to navigate through any and all bullshit with ease.

"Obviously not well," Willa said, hunching over her sketch pad.

"Hmm," Elle said.

"I don't have time to decipher that hmm," Willa warned her.

"You remember when Archer and Spence threatened to castrate your ex?"

Spence and Archer were the last members of their tight gang of friends. Spence was an IT genius. Archer an ex-cop. The two of them together had some serious skills. And yes, they'd stepped in when Willa had needed them to. "That was different," she said. Ethan had been an asshole, no doubt. "Keane's never going to be an ex, asshole or otherwise, because we're never going to be a thing. Now if we're done dissecting my life, I've got a lot to do before tonight's wedding."

She'd stayed up late working on the tuxes her client wanted the poodles to wear. Yes, tuxes. Just because she was in on the joke that South Bark Mutt Stop made more money on tiaras and weddings and gimmicks than actual grooming or supplies didn't mean she couldn't take the wishes of her clients seriously.

And hey, who knew, maybe if she ever got pets of her own other than the fosters she sometimes took in, and if she had more money than she knew what to do with, she might want a wedding for her dogs too. Although she sincerely doubted it. In her world, love had always been fleeting and temporary—sort of the opposite of what all the pomp and circumstance of a wedding conveyed.

Still, game to believe in lasting love as a possibility, at least for others, Willa dropped the giant poodle faux tux front over her own head and looked in the mirror. "What do we think?"

"Very cute," Pru said. "Now jump up and down and do whatever it is dogs do to make sure it holds up."

Willa jumped up and down like she was a dog in a show, holding her hands out in front of her, wrists bent as she hopped around to get the full effect of the tux. The girls were all still laughing when someone knocked on her front door.

Once again it was ten minutes before nine and in mid–dance step Willa stilled, experiencing a rush of déjà vu. The look on everyone's faces confirmed what she needed to know. Still, she slowly turned to the door hoping she was wrong.

Nope.

Not wrong.

Keane Winters stood at the door, watching her.

"Perfect," she said, her dignity in tatters. "How much do you think he saw?"

"Everything," Elle said.

"You should get the door," Pru said. "He looks every bit as hot as Rory said, but he also looks like he's in a rush."

"I'm not opening the door," Willa hissed, yanking off the tux front. "Not until you guys go. Go out the back and hurry!"

No one hurried. In fact, no one so much as budged.

Keane knocked for a second time and when Willa turned to face him again, he went brows up, the picture of gorgeous impatience.

"Well, honestly," Pru said. "Do men learn that look at birth or what?"

"Yes," Elle said thoughtfully. "They do. Willa, honey, don't you dare rush over there. You take your sweet-ass time and make sure to swipe that panic off your face and smile while you're at it. Won't do you any good to let him know he's getting to you."

"See," Willa said to Haley and Pru. "At least one of you isn't influenced by dark, knowing eyes and a darker smile and a pair of ohmigod-sexy guy jeans."

"Okay, I didn't say that," Elle said. "But I'm not so much influenced as curious as hell. Get the door, Wills. Let's see what he's made of."

"He just saw me dancing like a poodle," she said.

"Exactly, and you didn't scare him off. He's got to be made of stern stuff."

Willa sighed and headed to the door.

Again Keane held the pink bedazzled cat carrier, which should have made him look ridiculous. Instead it somehow upped his testosterone levels. His sharp eyes were on her but they turned warm in a way that melted her right through her center as she moved toward him. She stopped with the glass door between them, hands on hips, hoping she looked irritated even if that wasn't quite what she was feeling.

His gaze lowered from her face to run over her body, which gave her another unwelcome rush of heat. Dammit. Now she was irritated *and* aroused—not a good combo.

His mouth quirked at the saying on her apron that read *Dear Santa, I Can Explain.*

Drawing a deep breath, she opened the door. "You've got Petunia again. I hope that means your great-aunt Sally isn't still sick."

He looked surprised that she'd remembered his aunt's name, or that she'd care. "I don't know," he said a little gruffly. "She left me a message saying that I was in charge for the rest of the week but for two days now Pita's been happily destroying my job-site. I'm throwing myself on your mercy here. Can you help?"

Wow. He must be really desperate since he was actually asking and not assuming. But since Petunia was a sweetheart, she knew she'd do it.

"I'll even tell you where I went to high school," he said, adding a smile that was shockingly charming.

Wow. He hadn't lost his touch when it came to turning it on. "Not necessary," she said, painfully aware of their audience.

Keane's attention was suddenly directed upward, just above her head. She followed his line of sight and found a sprig of mistletoe hanging from the overhead display of small, portable doggy pools. *Mistletoe? What the hell?* She glanced behind her and what do you know, suddenly Rory and Cara were a flurry of movement racing around looking very, *very* busy. "When did the mistletoe go up?" she asked them. "And why?"

"FOMO," Cara said from behind the counter.

"Fear of missing out," Rory translated. "She was hoping a hot guy would come in and the mistletoe would give her an excuse."

Willa narrowed her eyes and her two soon-to-be-dead employees scattered again.

"Interesting," Keane said, looking amused.

"I'm not kissing you."

His mouth curved. "If you take Pita for the day, *I'll* kiss *you*."

"Not necessary," she said, gratified no one could see her heart doing the two-step in her ears. "I'll take Petunia for the day. No kiss required or wanted."

Liar, liar . . .

Keane stepped inside. And because she didn't step back far enough, they very nearly touched. His hair was a little damp, she couldn't help but notice, like maybe he'd just showered. He smelled of sexy guy soap, a.k.a. amazing. He wore faded jeans with a rip along one thigh and another long-sleeved T-shirt with *SF Builders* on the pec, so her guess that he was in construction seemed correct.

He also was covered in cat hair.

From right behind him one of her regulars came in. Janie Sharp was in her thirties, had five kids under the age of ten, worked as a schoolteacher and was continuously late, harried, exhausted, and desperate.

Today, her three youngest were running around her in circles at full speed, screaming as they chased each other while Janie held a fishbowl high, trying to avoid spilling as she was continuously jostled. "I know," she yelled to Willa. "I'm early. But I'll have to kill myself if you don't help me out this morning."

This was a common refrain from Janie. "As long as you don't leave your kids," Willa said. Also a common refrain. At the odd sound from Keane, she glanced over at him. "She's only kidding about killing herself," she said. "But I'm not kidding about her kids."

Janie nodded. "They're devil spawn."

"Names?" Keane asked.

Janie blinked at him as if just seeing him for the first time. Her eyes glazed over a little bit and she might've drooled. "Dustin, Tanner, and Lizzie," she said faintly.

Keane snapped his fingers and the kids stopped running in circles around Janie. They stopped making noise. They stopped breathing.

Keane pointed at the first one. "Dustin or Tanner?"

"Tanner," the little boy said and shoved his thumb in his mouth.

Keane looked at the other two and they both started talking at once. He held up a finger and pointed at the little girl.

"I'm an angel," she said breathlessly. "My daddy says so."

"Did you know that angels look out for the people they care about?" Keane asked her. "They're in charge."

The little girl got a sly look on her face. "So I getta be in charge of Tan and Dust?"

"You *look out* for them." He turned his gaze on the two boys. "And in turn, you look out for her. Nothing should happen to her on your watch, ever. You get me?"

The two boys bobbed their heads up and down.

Janie stared down at her three quiet, respectful kids in utter shock. "It's a Christmas miracle come early," she whispered in awe and met Keane's gaze. "Do you babysit?"

Keane just smiled and for a moment, it stunned the entire room. He had a hell of a smile. One that brought to mind hot, long, deep, drugging kisses.

And more.

So much more . . . *"No,"* Willa said and took Janie's fishbowl. "You're not giving your kids to a perfect stranger."

"You got the perfect part right," Janie murmured and shook it off. "Okay, so we're going to Napa for an overnight. Can I leave you Fric and Frac?"

"Yes, and you know I'll take very good care of them," Willa promised and gave Janie a hug. "Get some rest."

When Janie was gone, Keane went brows up. "Fish? You board fish?"

"Babysit," she corrected, eyes narrowed. "Are you judging me?"

He shook his head. "I just brought you the cat from hell. I'm in no position to judge."

She gave a rough laugh and his gaze locked on her mouth, which gave her another quick zap of awareness.

"Thanks," he said. "For taking Pita today. It means a lot."

From behind the counter came a low "aw" and then a "shh!" that had her sending her friends a "shut it" look.

Keane swiveled to look too but as soon as he did, Elle, Pru, and Haley suddenly had their heads bowed over their phones.

Rory came through carrying another case of feed and took in Willa and Keane's close proximity. "Nice," she said. "I'm happy to see you came to your senses and gave up the no-men decree."

Willa narrowed her eyes.

"Oh, right," Rory said, slapping her own forehead. "Keep that to yourself, Rory. Almost forgot."

Keane slid Willa an amused look. "No-men decree?"

"Never you mind." She set the fishbowl on the counter and reached for Petunia. "You know the deal, right?"

"You mean where I pay double for being an ass and you pretend not to like me?" He flashed a lethal smile. "Yeah, same terms."

"I meant be here before closing." She sighed. "And I'm not going to bill you double."

His smile turned into a grin. "See? You *do* like me."

And then he was gone.

Willa turned to her friends and employees, all of whom were watching him go.

"That's a really great ass," Pru said.

"I agree," Haley said. "And I don't even like men."

Willa shrugged. "I didn't notice. I don't like him."

Everyone burst out laughing.

"We'd correct you," Elle said, still smiling, "but you're too stubborn and obstinate to see reason on the best of days and I don't think this is one of those . . ."

Yeah, yeah . . . She narrowed her eyes because they were still laughing, clearly believing she was totally fooling herself about not liking Keane.

And the worst part was, she knew it too.

Chapter 3

#BahHumbug

Keane Winters was used to crazy-busy and crazy-long days. Today in particular though, thanks to subcontractors not doing what they'd been contracted to do and the weather going to hell in the way of a crazy thunderstorm that intermittently knocked out electricity. And let's not forget the time-and-money-consuming detour to replace his phone and laptop thanks to his aunt's cat. At least she *looked* like a cat but Keane was pretty sure she was really the antichrist.

His phone buzzed and he dropped his tool belt to pull it from his pocket. One of his guys had sent him a link from the *San Francisco Chronicle*.

> Keane Winters, one of this year's San Francisco's People to Watch, is a self-made real estate developer on the rise . . .

He supposed the self-made part was true. Currently in the middle of flipping three properties in the North

Bay area, he'd been putting in so many hours that his core team was starting to lag. They all needed a break, but that wasn't happening anytime soon.

Winters specializes in buying up dilapidated projects in prime areas and turning them into heart-stopping, must-have properties. He doesn't find any use for sentimentality, ruthlessly selling each of them off as he completes them.

Also true. Financially, it didn't pay to hold on to the projects. There'd been a time not that long ago when he'd *had* to sell each off immediately upon completion or end up bankrupt. And yeah, maybe he'd lucked into that first deal, but there'd been no luck involved since. He was a risk taker and he knew how to make it pay off. As a result, he'd gotten good at burying sentimentality, not just with the properties he developed, but in his personal life too.

And as far as that personal life went, he'd been walking by South Bark after getting his coffee every morning for months and it'd never once occurred to him to check out the shop. He hadn't had a dog since Blue, who he'd lost the year before he'd left home, and he sure as hell wasn't in a hurry to feel devastated from loss like that again anytime soon.

Or ever.

But then his great-aunt Sally had dropped off Pita and he'd met the sexy owner of South Bark. Keane had no idea why Willa seemed irritated by the mere sight of him, but he felt anything *but* irritated by the sight of her. He thought maybe it was her eyes, the brightest green eyes he'd ever seen, not to mention her temperament, which appeared to match her strawberry blonde hair—way more strawberry than blonde.

He walked through the top floor of his favorite of his three current projects, Vallejo Street. The other two—North Beach and Mission Street—were purely strategic business decisions and would go right on the market the minute he finished them.

Buy low, renovate smart, sell high. That'd been his MO, always.

But the Vallejo Street house . . . He'd picked up the 1940 Victorian for way too much money five years ago on the one and only whim he could remember ever having. But he'd taken one look at the neglected old house and had seen potential in the three-story, five thousand square feet, regardless of the fact that it'd been practically falling off its axis.

Since then, he'd had to get into other projects fast and hard to recoup the lost seed money, and had worked on Vallejo Street only as time allowed.

Which was why it had taken so long to get it finished, or very nearly finished anyway. For the past year, the bottom floor had been serving as his office. He'd been living there as well. All that would have to change when he got it on the market, something he needed to do, as selling it would give him the capital for new projects.

He walked to one of the floor-to-ceiling windows and looked out. The day's light was almost gone. The city was coming to life with lights, backdropped by a view of the Golden Gate Bridge and the bay beyond that.

"Dude." This from Mason, his right-hand guy, who stood in the doorway. "We need to get the guys in here this week to help work on the loft since you and your little height phobia can't—Are you listening to me?"

"Sure," Keane said to the window. He could see the Pacific Pier Building and pictured Willa in her shop wearing one of her smartass aprons, running her world with matching smartass charm.

Someone snorted. Sass. His admin had come in too, and no one cut through bullshit faster than Sass.

"He's not listening to me," Mason complained.

"Not a single word," Sass agreed.

Keane's phone beeped his alarm. "Gotta go," he said. "I've got ten minutes to pick up Pita before South Bark closes."

"I could go get her for you," Sass offered. "What?" she asked when Mason's mouth fell open. "I offer to do nice stuff all the time."

"You offer to do nice stuff *never*," Mason said.

"All the time."

"Yeah? Name *one*," Mason challenged.

"Well, I wanted to smack you upside the back of your head all day," she said. "And I resisted. See? I think that was exceptionally nice."

Keane left while they were still arguing. It would take him less than five minutes to walk to South Bark but Pita wouldn't appreciate the chilly walk back, so he drove. Parking was the usual joke, so that by the time he got a spot twenty minutes had gone by.

He walked through the courtyard, taking a moment to admire the gorgeous architecture of the old place, the corbeled brick and exposed iron trusses, the large picture windows, the cobblestone beneath his feet, and the huge fountain centerpiece where idiots the city over came to toss a coin and wish for love.

All of it had been decorated for the holidays with garlands of evergreen entwined with twinkling white lights in every doorway and window frame, not to mention a huge-ass Christmas tree near the street entrance.

But that wasn't what stopped him. No, that honor went to the wedding prep going on. Or at least he assumed it was a wedding by the sheer volume of white flowers and lights, the ivory pillar candles set up in clusters paired with clove-dotted oranges and sprigs of holly running along the edge of half of a very crooked archway—

He stopped short as it fell over.

"Crap!"

The woman who yelled this had strawberry blonde hair, emphasis on strawberry.

Willa squatted low over the fallen pieces of the archway trying to . . . God knew what.

"Shit. Shit, shit, shit," she was muttering while shaking the hell out of the screw gun in her hand. "Why are you doing this to me?"

"It's not the screw gun," he said, coming up behind her. "It's operator error."

She jerked in response and, still squatting, lost her balance and fell to her butt. Craning her neck, she glared up at him. "What are you doing creeping up on me like that?"

He reached a hand down to her and pulled her to

her feet. And then grinned because she was wearing another smartass apron that read *OCD . . . Obsessive Christmas Disorder.*

With a low laugh for the utter truth of that statement, he took the screw gun from her.

"It's broken," she said.

He inspected it and shook his head. "No, you're just out of nails." He crouched, reaching for more from the box near her feet to reload the screw gun.

Since she was still just staring at him, he turned his attention to what she'd been doing. "You realize that this archway is only going to be three feet high, right?"

"That's perfect."

"In what universe is that perfect?" he asked.

"In the dog universe. It's a dog wedding."

That had him freezing for a beat before he felt a smile split his face.

She blinked. "Huh."

"What?" Did he have chocolate on his teeth from the candy bar he'd inhaled on the way over here, the only food he'd managed in the past four hours?

"You smiled," she said, almost an accusation.

"You've seen me smile."

"Not really, not since—" She cut herself off and took the gun from him. "Never mind. And thanks."

"There's really going to be a dog wedding? Here, in the courtyard?" he asked.

"In less than an hour unless I screw it all up. I'm the wedding planner." She paused as if waiting for something, some reaction from him, but he managed to keep his expression even.

"You're not going to laugh?" she asked. "Because you look like the kind of guy who would laugh at the idea of two dogs getting married."

"Listen," he said completely honestly. "I'm the guy who needed a fur-sitter because he was terrorized by a ten-pound cat, so I'm not throwing stones here. Speaking of which, where is the little holy terror?"

"She's in my shop safe and sound with plenty of food and water, napping in the warmest spot in the place— between Macaroni and Luna."

He must have looked blank because she said, "The two other pets I'm babysitting today. Well technically Cara, one of my employees, is doing the babysitting at the moment."

"I hope you aren't attached to those other pets," he said. "Because Pita will tear them up one side and down the other."

Willa merely laughed and pulled her phone from one of her apron pockets, a few dog treats cascading out as well, hitting the cobblestone beneath their feet.

With an exclamation, she squatted down to scoop them up at the same time that Keane did, cracking the bottom of his chin on top of her head.

This time they both fell to their butts.

"Ow!" she said, holding her head. "And I'm so sorry, are you okay?"

He blinked past the stars in his vision. "Lived through worse," he assured her, and reached out to gently rub the top of her head. Her hair was soft and silky and smelled amazing. "You?"

"Oh, my noggin's hard as stone, just ask anyone who knows me," she quipped.

Their gazes met and held and he realized that their legs were entangled and was struck by the close proximity and the unbidden and primal urge he had to pull her into his lap.

Clearly not on the same page, she picked up her phone and went back to thumbing through her pics. *"Ha,"* she exclaimed triumphantly. *"Here."* She leaned in to show him her phone's screen, her arm bumping into his. When he bent closer, her hair brushed against his jaw, a strand of it sticking stubbornly to his stubble.

"See?" she asked.

He blinked away the daze she'd put him in and realized she was showing him a pic of the front room in her store. And just as she'd said, there in front of a holly-strewn fake mantel lay a huge pit bull and a teeny-tiny teacup . . . piglet. Entwined.

Between them was a familiar-looking white ball of fluff with the black face of his nightmares. And that nightmare's face was pressed trustingly to the pit bull's. For a long beat Keane just stared at it. "Photoshop, right?" he finally asked. "Just to fuck with me?"

She laughed, and he found himself smiling at just the sound. But soon as he did, her amusement faded, almost as if she'd just reminded herself that she didn't like him. Standing, she turned away. "Well, finally."

"What?"

"Archer and Spence are here."

"The dogs?"

"No, two of my best friends."

"I met your best friends," he said. "They were the ones who watched our conversation this morning like we were a Netflix marathon, right?"

"I have a whole gang of BFFs," she said. "Archer and Spence are on wedding security detail tonight." The cell phone on her hip rang. She looked at the screen and swore.

"The antichrist committed murder, didn't she," he guessed.

"No, of course not! I've got a cake emergency."

"Well I can't compete with that. Go ahead," he said. "I'll build the dog archway."

She hesitated. "It has to be perfect."

Keane had built houses from the ground up and she was questioning his ability to put together an archway. For dogs. "Cake emergency," he reminded her.

"Shit. Okay . . ." She looked at him very seriously. "Do you need any help?"

He stuck his tongue in his cheek. "I'm pretty sure I can handle it."

Looking torn, she blew out a sigh. "Okay, if you're sure. And . . . thanks."

He merely waved Ms. Doubtful One off, though he wasn't above watching her rush away. Yeah, his gaze locked on her sweet ass in those snug skinny jeans tucked into some seriously kickass boots. He was still watching, neck craned to catch the last of her as he turned back to his work and . . . nearly plowed into two guys standing there shoulder to shoulder staring at him. The two who Willa had pointed out as Archer and Spence.

Neither spoke.

"So . . . you guys here for the bride or the groom?" Keane asked.

No one blinked.

"It's a joke," Keane said. "Because the groom and the bride are dogs. See, it's funny."

Neither smiled.

"Tough crowd," he muttered.

"We're here for Willa," one of them said. The bigger, more 'tude-ridden one, who looked like he'd seen the darker side of the world and maybe still lived there. The other guy was leaner but just as fit, his eyes assessing Keane with careful interest.

"Hey." This was Willa herself, yelling from the other side of the courtyard's fountain. "Play nice!" She pointed at her two friends. "Especially you two."

Spence and Archer busted out sweet-looking smiles for her and added cheerful waves. Then the minute she turned away, they went back to deadpan staring at Keane.

"Okay, great talk," he said. "I'm going to build this dog gazebo now. You can either stand there or give me a hand."

The bigger guy spoke. "The last guy she went out with played games with her head." His tone was quiet, his gaze direct and steady.

The other guy, clearly the more easygoing of the two, nodded. "They never did find the body, did they?"

The other guy slowly shook his head.

Okay then. "Good to know," Keane said lightly but suddenly he was feeling anything but light. He didn't like the thought of anyone screwing with Willa. Still fixated on that, he turned his back on her bodyguards and got to work. When he straightened to hoist the arch, suddenly there were four extra hands—both guys lending their strength to the cause.

Still not talking.

After that they were apparently a threesome and recruited as such to be the official setting-up-chairs committee. One hundred and fifty chairs to be exact.

For a dog wedding.

The three of them were hot and sweaty in no time even with the cold December air brushing over them.

"At least it's easier than that time she made us help her do that South Beach wedding, remember, Arch?" the leaner guy asked, giving Keane his first clue on which was Archer and which was Spence.

Archer just grunted as he lined up the last row, his gaze drifting to the edge of the courtyard where Elle stood in a siren red dress working both a cell phone and an iPad.

Spence followed his friend's gaze. "How is it she never gets dirty or sweaty?"

Archer shook his head. "Dirt and sweat don't stick to Elle; she isn't human."

Spence laughed. "So she's still mad at you then."

"She's always mad at me."

"You ever figure out why?"

Archer didn't answer.

Willa came up with three bottles of water. "Chilly night," she said.

Keane, who'd been still getting the occasional frosty looks from Spence and Archer, snorted.

Willa took this in and then looked at them each in turn. "What's going on?"

No one said a word.

She reached up and grabbed Spence by the ear. He manfully winced instead of yelped. "What the hell, Wills."

"What's the weird vibe? What's going on?"

Spence carefully pried her fingers from his ear. "Why didn't you twist off Archer's ear?"

"Because Archer's probably wearing two guns and a knife," she said.

Keane glanced over at the guy. Archer's body language hadn't changed. He was deceptively casual, his gaze hard and alert. Military or law enforcement, he figured.

Willa went hands on hips.

Archer didn't cave, but Spence did. "We were just making sure this one passed muster after Ethan—" He broke off at the look on Willa's face.

Keane had two older sisters. They'd mostly ignored him unless he'd put himself in the line of fire. During those times, their gazes had shot out promised retribution that might or might not include maiming and torturing. Death was a given.

Willa had the look down.

"This one?" Willa repeated. "Oh my God."

Spence opened his mouth but Willa shook her head and pointed at him.

"No," she said. "You know what? This is really all my own fault."

"No, it's not," Archer said firmly. "Ethan was an asshole serial creeper—"

"I meant it's my fault that I'm friends with you two!" And then without so much as glancing over, she jabbed a finger in Keane's face, nearly taking out an eye. "He isn't a date," she said. "He isn't a future date. And he sure as hell isn't a *past* one."

Keane opened his mouth but then shut it again. This was the second time now she'd referred to a past between them. He was so busy mentally rewinding the conversation that he nearly missed Spence and Archer taking off. He didn't, however, miss Spence's sympathetic glance as he left.

"Listen," Willa said when it was just the two of them. "I'm grateful for your help, very grateful actually, but—"

"How do you know I'm not a future date?" Well, hell, he hadn't realized that had bugged him so much.

Willa looked just as flabbergasted. "I just know," she finally said. "I—" She broke off when a little boy not more than four years old tugged on her apron. She immediately smiled, a warm, sweet smile that dazzled Keane more than it should as she hunkered low to be eye-to-eye with the kid.

"Hey, Keller." She straightened his mini tux jacket. "You look handsome tonight."

"My daddies say they're ready."

"Perfect, because so are we."

Keller tipped his head way back to look up at Keane. "You're wearing funny shoes for a wedding."

"They're work boots," Keane told him. "And speaking of footwear, yours are on the wrong feet."

Keller looked down at his shoes and scratched his head before tipping his head up again. "But I don't have any other feet," he finally said.

Fair enough, Keane thought but Willa helped the kid sit down and fix his shoes. Then she went back to being an adorable but utter tyrant, bossing everyone into doing her bidding. No one complained. In fact, everyone seemed happy to jump to her every command.

He could use her on his jobsites.

Ten minutes later the wedding was taking place, complete with marriage certificates that each dog put a paw print on, and a video recording by Rory. There'd apparently been a registry as well because a stack of wrapped gifts from South Bark sat on a table.

"I've just run out of those bedazzled leashes," Willa was saying to someone, consulting an iPad after the ceremony. "But I'll be happy to take an order."

Yeah, Keane was starting to see a whole other side to Willa and her entrepreneurial skills. And he had to admit, he liked this side of her. She was smart as hell, but surrounded by all the fluff as she was, she'd nearly fooled him.

After, when the crowd thinned and then dissipated altogether, he stuck around and helped her with the takedown.

"This isn't necessary," she said.

"Because I'm not a present or future?"

She gave him a long look and then turned to struggle with the archway.

Moving in close to help, he reached around her to add his strength to separate the two pieces of the arch.

Her back to his front, she stilled, and so did he because a zap of what felt like two hundred volts of electricity went straight through him.

"What was that?" she whispered, not moving a single inch.

He'd given this some thought so he had a ready answer. "Animal magnetism."

She unfroze at that, slipped out from beneath his arms to face him. "Oh no. No, no, no. That's one thing we absolutely do *not* have."

He laughed a little because apparently she'd given it no thought at all. Not super great on the ego. "You really going to tell me you don't feel it?"

She chewed on that for a moment. "I'm telling you I don't *want* to feel it," she finally said.

Welcome to my club, he thought.

Chapter 4

#FactsJustGetInTheWay

The days that followed the wedding blurred together for Willa, swamped as she was with the early holiday rush. Not that she minded since the shop, like always, filled all the holes inside her, the ones her rough early years had left.

Yep, she was completely fulfilled.

But then she'd seen Keane Winters and something had happened, something weird and unsettling. He made her realize that she hadn't plugged all her holes at all, that there was at least one still open and gaping inside her.

With a groan, she got up to face her day. Her apartment was also in the Pacific Pier Building, four flights up from her shop. The place was small but cozy. The living room and kitchen were really all one room, divided by a small bar top. On the wall between her living room and short hallway that led to her bedroom was a small door that opened to a dumbwaiter, a throwback to the days when this building was one very large ranching family's central compound. That was back in the late eighteen hundreds, when there'd still been actual cows in the Cow Hollow district of San Francisco.

The dumbwaiter door was locked now but sometimes mysterious gifts ended up in there for her, like cookies or muffins. And then there was the time Archer had a training exercise for his men in the guise of a scavenger hunt, and one of the items required to obtain had been Finn, who'd ended up stuck in the dumbwaiter while making a run for it.

Archer's idea of funny.

In any case, there was nothing in there now no matter how much she wished for some muffins, so she showered and dressed. Today's work uniform consisted of her favorite pair of jeans, which only had one hole in a knee, and another lightweight camisole. She topped that with an easy-to-remove sweater for grooming clients.

She wasn't surprised when she got to work and the knock came on her shop's door at ten minutes before opening. Nor was she surprised at the traitorous leap her pulse gave. It'd been two weeks since Keane had shown up that first morning. Since then, there'd been no rhythm or reason to the days he came in. Sometimes he'd show up for a few days in a row and then nothing for another few days. Whenever she asked about his aunt, he got a solemn look on his face but shook his head. *"Not better yet,"* he always said.

Willa hated to admit she had an ear cocked every

morning, wondering if she'd see him. Hated even more that she always put on mascara and a lip stain just in case. As his knock echoed in the shop, she forced herself to remain still.

"You're going to want a look at this," Elle said from Willa's right. She was leaning against the front counter sipping her hot tea. The kind she ordered in from England because she was a complete tea snob.

"Nope, I don't," Willa said. She didn't have to look because she knew what she'd see—some version of Hot Builder Guy with those T-shirts that stretched taut over his broad shoulders, emphasizing a whole lot of muscles apparently gained the old-fashioned way—by sheer manual labor. His hair would be carelessly tousled, like he hadn't given his looks a second thought. And why should he? When you looked like that, you didn't even need a damn mirror.

"He looks good in clothes," Elle said appreciatively. "I'll give him that. Let him in, Willa."

"I just poured my milk," she complained.

"Yes, and I'm totally judging you based on your choice of plain Cheerios, you unfrosted weirdo." Elle's gaze hadn't left the front door. "But holy cow hotness, Batman, really, you want to see this."

"Why?"

"He's in a suit, that's why. My eyes don't know what to do with themselves."

Willa whipped around so fast she gave herself whiplash.

Keane's sharp eyes were scanning the store. When they settled on her, she felt it all the way from her roots to her toes and some very special spots in between. Every. Time. "Damn."

"Told you," Elle said. "I thought you said he was a carpenter of some sort."

"He listed himself as self-employed on my forms when he left Petunia that first day," she murmured, unable to tear her gaze off him standing there looking like God's gift.

If God's gift came carrying a pink bedazzled carrier . . .

"I can't decide which is the hotter look for him," Elle said. "Hot and suited up, or hot and in Levi's."

"It might be a draw," Willa admitted.

"So you *do* like him," Elle said triumphantly.

"No, but I'm not dead. I mean look at him."

"Believe me," Elle said. "I'm looking. So are you really going to stand there and tell me you're still not moved by him at all?"

"Hello, did you miss the part where he not only stood me up, he also doesn't remember doing it?" Willa asked.

"And are you missing the part where that happened a long time ago?" Elle asked. "Because he totally stepped in and helped you at that wedding. Is it possible you're overdramatizing?"

"I'm not overdramatizing, I *never* overdramatize!" Willa stopped talking as she realized she was waving her arms, spoon in the air and everything. "Fine. It's my red hair. You can't fight genetics."

"Uh-huh." Elle's expression softened. "Honey, I know your past wasn't exactly easy, but I think you've got him all tangled up in that emotional landmine. And before you tell me it's none of my business, you should know that I'm only saying so because I get it, I really do."

Willa sighed because she knew Elle did. She'd had an even rougher time than Willa, and she hated that for the both of them. "Getting stood up like that by him during that particular time in my life was . . . memorably traumatic," she said. "So yeah, there's no doubt I'm projecting. But you remember the torture of high school, right? Or maybe you don't, maybe you were popular like Keane was. I, on the other hand . . ." She shook her head. "I was invisible," she admitted. "And it really messed with my self-esteem."

Elle's smile faded. "Okay. So we stay mad at him then."

Willa's heart squeezed. "Thank you," she said and moved toward the door.

Keane's morning had started at dawn and had already been long, involving a near brawl with an engineer, kissing up to a client who couldn't make up her mind to save her own life, and a way-too-long meeting with the interior decorator for North Beach, who loved to hear himself talk. Now as he stood at South Bark's locked door, he had twenty minutes to get back for another meeting.

Willa took her sweet-ass time opening up, and when she did, she stared at him like she'd never seen him before.

"Keane?" she asked, whispered really, as if she wasn't quite sure.

"Yeah." *Who the hell else?*

"Just checking." Her gaze ran over him slowly. "I thought maybe you had a twin or something."

"Yeah, and the cat hates both of us."

She laughed. It was unexpected, to say the least, and he stared at her. Her bright green eyes were lit up, her smile more than a little contagious. He didn't have time for chitchat but when it came to this woman, he couldn't seem to help himself. "I'm not kidding," he said.

"I know," she said. "That's why it's so funny." Her jeans were worn and faded and fit her petite curvy body like a beloved old friend. He loved her little top, which read *Naughty AND Nice* across her breasts and had teeny-tiny straps and was thin enough to reveal she was both wet and chilly.

Her strawberry blonde hair was in wild layers, some of them in her eyes, and she knew exactly why he was there but she went brows up, wanting him to ask. This should've annoyed the hell out of him but instead he was amused. "Tell me you have time for Pita today," he said, doing their usual dance, willing to beg if he had to. Yesterday Pita had used a very expensive set of blueprints as her personal claw sharpener an hour before a meeting in which he'd needed those plans.

"You changed your work uniform," she said instead of answering. "You're in a suit."

"A necessary evil today."

"You look . . . different."

Torn between satisfaction that she was noticing his looks at all and unexpected annoyance that she'd judged him by his clothes, he didn't answer right away.

Being judged wasn't exactly a new thing for him. He'd been judged by his parents as a kid for not being solely academic. He'd been judged in school for not being just a jock or an academic, but somewhere in the middle, and as a result, he worked hard to fit in anywhere and was proud of his ability to do so. "You judging me by my clothes?"

"Not even a little bit," she said in a tone that he'd heard before, the same tone that again suggested he should know what the hell she was talking about.

"Okay," he said. "I cave. I want to buy a vowel."

She glanced over her shoulder at Elle, who lifted a shoulder. "Give him hell, honey," she said and hopped off the counter, leaving out the courtyard-side door.

Keane didn't have time for this. "What am I missing?" he asked, determined to figure out why she'd twice now referred to a past. And suddenly an odd and uncomfortable thought came to him. "Do we know each other or something?"

"Why?" she asked, eyes suddenly sharp. "Do you remember me from somewhere?"

"No."

Willa stared at him for a long beat and then shook her head. "No, we don't know each other. At all. And to be clear," she added, those brilliant eyes narrowed now, "I liked you better as a carpenter." With that, she took Pita from him and walked away.

At two minutes past six that evening, Keane flung his truck into park and jogged in the pouring rain across the street to South Bark.

The front door was locked, lights off—except for the strings and strings *and strings* of Christmas lights wound through the inside of the shop, making it look like the North Pole at Christmastime.

On steroids.

And crack.

The sign read CLOSED but there was a piece of paper attached to it that said:

Unless you're an extremely rude person who's late in picking up their precious bundle of love, use the back door.

Gee, he thought dryly, who could she possibly be referring to . . . ? He strode through the courtyard and entered the back door to South Bark to find Willa up to her elbows in suds, bathing a huge Doberman.

"Who's a good boy," Willa was saying to the dog in a light, silly voice that had the dog panting happily into her face. "That's right," she cooed, "you are, aren't you? Aren't you a good boy?"

"Well I don't like to brag," Keane said, leaning against the doorjamb. "But I do have my moments."

She jerked and whirled around to face him. "I didn't hear you come in." She looked him over. "You changed."

He looked down at his jeans and long-sleeved T-shirt. "I ended up working on some electrical for a good part of the day until the storm hit," he said. "I didn't want to accidentally electrocute myself in a suit and make things easy for the undertaker."

She didn't smile. "You were working on electricity in these conditions?"

"The job doesn't always wait for good weather. And no worries, I haven't accidentally electrocuted myself in years."

She didn't respond to this but drained the tub and wrapped Carl in a huge towel. She attached his lead to a stand. "Give me a second," she said to Keane and vanished into the hallway.

She didn't go far because he heard her say, "Need a favor, can you finish up with Carl for me?"

"Depends." Rory's voice. "Is his owner here?"

"Max?" Willa asked. "No, he's with Archer on a job but he'll be here soon to pick up Carl, who just needs to be dried and combed through. Why? Is there a problem with Max?"

"No," Rory said quickly. Too quickly. "Fine," she said on a sigh. "I can't stop thinking about him."

"And I can't stop thinking about grilled cheese," Willa said.

Rory laughed. "That would be a lot easier." She paused. "He asked me out again."

"I see," Willa said, her voice softer now. "Honey, he's one of the good guys. Archer wouldn't have him on his team otherwise."

"My radar's still broken."

"Well, I get that," Willa said commiseratively and then the two of them walked back into the room.

Rory rolled up her sleeves. "I've got this." She smiled at Carl. "And you're a far better date than the marathon of *American Horror Story* I was planning anyway." She kissed the dog right between the huge, pointy ears.

Carl licked her face from chin to forehead, making the girl laugh.

Willa gestured for Keane to follow her down that hallway to what looked to be her office.

Pita was sprawled on her back across a wood desk, all four legs sticking straight up in the air like she'd been dead and stiff for days.

Keane stopped short in shock.

Not Willa. She laughed and moved to the desk to tickle Pita's belly.

The cat yawned wide and stretched, rubbing her face up against Willa's wrist, and a ridiculous sense of relief came to Keane.

He didn't have to call Sally and tell her that Pita was dead. At least not tonight.

"Daddy's come to pick you up," Willa said, nuzzling the cat.

"Funny," Keane said and noticed the empty fishbowl next to Pita. "Were you fish sitting again?"

"Was," she said and let out a slow, sad breath. "I've been letting Petunia have the run of the place because she's so sweet and the customers love her, but I turned my head for a few minutes to assist Rory with some grooming and . . ." She swallowed hard. "I think Petunia was hungry."

His heart stopped. "Jesus. Are you kidding me?"
"Yes."

He blinked at her. "What?"
"Yes, I'm kidding you."

He just stared at her. "That was mean."

"Don't be late again," she said, but damn if her smug smile wasn't lighting up his rough day like nothing else had. How she managed to do that while irritating the shit out of him at the same time was anyone's guess. "I'm sorry I was late, I'll pay late fees."

Willa shook her head. "It was only a few minutes and you were working on electricity. I wouldn't have wanted you to rush and get zapped."

"Aw," he said. "More proof that you do care about me."

"I care about the paycheck."

He laughed. "Duly noted." He knew he should get Pita and leave. He was starving, he still had paperwork to tackle, and certainly she had things to do too, but he didn't make a move to go.

They were still staring at each other when a woman stuck her head in the office. Keane recognized her as Kylie, one of the woodworkers who ran Reclaimed Woods, a shop across the courtyard that created gorgeous homemade furnishings. He'd bought several things from her in the past year. He smiled in greeting as he realized she had a very tiny dog's head peeking out the breast pocket of her denim jacket.

"Hey, Keane," she said and Willa looked surprised that they knew each other. "He's a customer," Kylie told her. "A good one. Listen," she went on in a rush, her hand cupping the puppy's head protectively. "I'm watching this little guy for a friend."

"Adorable," Willa said, moving closer to touch. "Breed?"

"Hard to say, he's only three weeks old. He's still bottle-fed too, but I'm thinking Chihuahua."

Not what Keane was thinking, not with those paws that were nearly bigger than his ears.

"It's too cold for him, I think," Kylie said. "He shakes all the time. I'm worried he's going to rattle the teeth right out of his head. All two of them."

"I've got just the thing." Willa pulled what looked like a stack of tiny doll sweaters from a bin by her desk.

"You're a lifesaver," Kylie said, taking four, one of which was a Santa costume. "Bill me." She turned to Keane. "When you get a chance, stop in. I just finished that reclaimed wood furniture set you saw me working on, what, six months ago now?"

"I will."

She flashed a smile, blew a kiss to Willa for the sweaters, and then was gone.

Willa slid him a look as she opened her laptop and hit some keys. "I saw the look on your face when you saw the dog sweaters. I make more money on dog sweaters, bedazzled collars, tiaras, and dog weddings than I do from anything else."

"You make money however you make money, Willa. It's a good thing."

She paused and looked at him for a long beat, like she was testing his genuineness.

"When I saw you in action at that wedding," he said, "I was impressed. People and animals are important to you and you run a really smart business from that."

"Animals ground me," Willa said quietly. "But yeah, I did my homework before I opened this place to make sure I could make a living at it. It's turned out better than my wildest dreams."

"You should be proud of yourself and what you've built here."

She paused, looking a little startled, like maybe no one had ever said such a thing to her before. And then she abruptly changed the subject, like she'd just realized she was being nice. "Any news on your aunt?"

He shook his head. "I'm not sure." It was a hell of a thing to have to admit because he was a guy who prided himself on always having the answers, or at least being able to get them. But the truth was, as it pertained to his family, he'd never known much.

He also hadn't given it a lot of thought until Sally had shown up on his doorstep just over two weeks ago now, leaning on a cane with one hand, her other clutching Pita's pink carrier. He'd taken the cat because she'd seemed so frail and worried, and he'd wanted to alleviate some of her stress.

He'd never expected to *still* have the cat.

Willa scooped Pita up from the desk and the damn cat nuzzled right into her neck. And for the first time in his life, Keane found himself jealous of a cat. "Seriously, what's your secret with her? You wear tuna as perfume?"

Willa laughed, a soft musical sound, and nuzzled the cat right back. "Let's just say I speak her language."

"Yeah? What language is that?"

"Something a man like you wouldn't understand." She kissed Pita's face and gently coaxed her into the carrier. "The language of loneliness."

Keane felt something shift in his chest and go tight. "You might be surprised."

She stared at him for a beat and then suddenly got very busy, zipping up the carrier, looking anywhere but at him, and he realized she was embarrassed. He slid his hand over hers, stilling her movements. "Have dinner with me."

She blinked in surprise.

Yeah, he was just as surprised.

"I'm sorry," she said haltingly. "I shouldn't have—Honestly, I wasn't angling for a date—"

"I know," he said. "But I'm standing here because I want to keep talking to you, only my stomach is growling and demanding sustenance. Come on, Willa. We're both off work and neither of us are wearing wedding rings. Let's go eat."

She stared at him. "Just like that?"

"Just like that."

"It doesn't seem like a smart idea," she said.

"Why not?"

She hesitated and he wanted to ask her about what Archer and Spence had alluded to that night, about her ex being a complete asshole, but that was none of his business. It didn't mean that he didn't want to hunt up the guy and teach him a lesson.

Or two.

"Lots of reasons," she finally said.

"Name one."

She opened her mouth and then closed it. "I can't really seem to come up with a single reason."

"Because there isn't one," he said. "Look, if I was Elle, would you go out to dinner with me then?"

"Of course. She's my friend."

"And Spence? Or Archer? If I was one of them, would you eat with me?"

"Again," she said, eyes narrowing. "Yes."

"But not me."

"No."

He took the cat carrier from her hands and set it on her desk. Then he stepped in so that they were toe to toe and dipped down a little to look right into her eyes.

She sucked in a breath. And that wasn't her only reaction either. Her pupils dilated and her nipples went hard against the thin material of that cute little shirt with the cute little straps.

She'd been very busy distracting him with her sharp tongue and quick wit, so he'd almost missed it. But this insane attraction he had for her? *She felt it too.* "Tell me what to do here," he said quietly. "I know you're hungry. I can hear your stomach growling louder than mine."

She slapped her hands over her lower belly, her fingers first bumping into his abs, which jumped at her touch.

"Dammit," she said, her eyes wide on his, the pulse at the base of her throat going batshit crazy. "It's a noisy beast."

"So let me feed it," he said.

"Maybe I don't like you."

"Maybe?"

"Haven't yet decided," she admitted.

Never one to back away from a challenge, he smiled. "So you'll let me know. You ready?"

When she still hesitated, he gently rasped the pad of his thumb over the pulse point on her throat. "Do I make you nervous, Willa?"

She lifted her chin. "Of course not," she said, her mouth so close to his that he couldn't help but stare at it, gripped by a driving need to cover it with his.

"Especially," she added softly with a light of mischief in those green depths, "since I could knee you in the family jewels right now if I needed to."

"I appreciate your restraint," he said. "Can we go get food now?"

"I guess."

He laughed. "Don't overwhelm me with enthusiasm."

"Just don't . . . read anything into this," she said.

He looked into her eyes and yeah, saw definite attraction for him. Reluctant attraction.

He'd take it.

He scooped the carrier in one hand and grabbed hers in his other.

"Afraid I'll change my mind?" she asked, looking amused.

"More afraid you'll carry out that threat to my family jewels."

Her startled laugh warmed him to his toes. *Game on,* he thought. Even if he had no idea what that game was.

Chapter 5

#TheFirstCutIsTheDeepest

Willa had no idea what the hell she thought she was doing agreeing to go out with Keane for dinner, but apparently her feet knew because they took her back into the grooming room to tell Rory.

The girl was crossed-legged on the floor in front of Carl, brushing him. Sitting facing her, Carl's head was higher than Rory's but he sat still happily, smiling.

Carl loved attention, all of it.

"I'm heading out," Willa said.

"Thanks for the newsflash."

"I'm going with Keane."

Rory froze. Only her eyes swiveled to Willa. "Has hell frozen over?"

Willa sighed. Given that all her current feelings for Keane were mixed up with her past feelings for him, she could hardly explain it to someone else much less herself. "It's just dinner."

"Uh-huh," Rory murmured, stroking an ecstatic Carl. "Remember you're the one who said the devil himself couldn't drag your cold, dead corpse out on a date with Keane even if he was hot as balls."

"Shh!" Willa took a quick look behind her but thankfully Keane hadn't followed. "It's all very . . . complicated."

"Complicated," Rory repeated, amused. "Maybe we should have the birds-and-bees talk, like you always try to have with me when I'm attracted to the wrong-for-me guys."

"Funny," Willa said. The fact was, both of them were attracted to the wrong men, *still*.

But Rory was on a roll, ticking off points on her fingers. "No sleeping with him on the first date, no matter how amazing he kisses—"

"Oh my God, keep your voice down!" Willa looked behind her again. "I'm not going to sleep with him on the first date." Even if the low, sexy tone of his voice did very interesting, *very* distracting things to her body. Nope, she wasn't going down that road because that road led to her downfall every time. This was just dinner, that was it. It was the only way she could ensure her emotional security. No more falling for a guy too quickly. Nope. Not gonna happen.

Rory wasn't done reciting the notes. "A public setting, don't take your eyes off your drink, and don't have more than one."

Any humor in this reversal of roles faded fast at that as the conversation took a turn she hadn't expected but should have. Neither of them would ever forget the night Rory had become a part of Willa's life.

Rory had been in the foster system for ten years when she turned eighteen and had been set loose into the big, bad world all on her own.

And oh how well Willa knew the feeling. It'd felt like she was being thrown away.

Rory had met a guy at a bar who'd seemed fun, gregarious, and charismatic. She'd somehow missed his stalker, predator characteristics.

Willa had been on a walk through the Marina Green one night when she'd found Rory in the park, sick as a dog from the drug that had been dumped into her drink. Willa had taken her to the hospital, helped her recover from the events she couldn't even remember, given her a job, and basically bullied her back to life.

Willa knew that Rory felt like she owed her for all that but she didn't. She also knew that Rory would do absolutely anything for her, which she took very seriously. She had to. Because once upon a time she'd been that lost little girl too.

Rory was watching her, her eyes giving away her worry.

"I'll be fine," Willa said. "Really."

Just then came a single knock on the back door. Max stood there in cargoes, work shirt, and full utility gear, looking pretty badass, clearly coming in off a job for Archer. "Hey," he said, eyes tracking straight to Rory. "How's it going?"

Since Rory had apparently swallowed her tongue,

Willa smiled at him. "Great. Rory's just finishing up Carl." She looked at Rory. "Lock up for me?"

Still silent—hugely unlike her—Rory nodded.

Willa thought maybe she was missing a piece of the puzzle here but she couldn't very well ask Rory with Max standing tall and handsome right there, his eyes also holding secrets. Willa gave Carl a kiss on the head and then the same to Rory, making the girl laugh.

"Just go already," Rory said, looking embarrassed.

"Be safe," Willa said to her.

"I'll make sure of it," Max said and Willa met his serious gaze.

Yep. Definitely missing a piece of the puzzle. "Thanks."

He nodded and five minutes later she and Keane walked out to his truck. He set the cat carrier carefully in the backseat like maybe it was a ticking bomb but made her smile when he hesitated and then locked a seatbelt around it.

When he caught her watching, he shrugged. "She's just ornery enough to knock herself off the seat and die and then come back to haunt me, so I'm taking all necessary precautions." He opened the passenger door for her but caught her before she could slide in. "You're cold."

Actually, she was freezing. "I forgot my jacket this morning—No, don't give me yours," she said when he made to take his off.

So instead he spread it open and wrapped as much of it around her as possible. Chest to chest, thighs to thighs . . . and everything in between mashed up against each other all cozy like.

Except it didn't feel cozy.

It felt . . . sexy as hell.

It would've taken more control than she had to keep her hands to herself. She wrapped herself around him, letting her fingers trail up the sculpted muscles of his back.

At her touch, his gaze met hers, dark and heated. Oh boy. She was in trouble here, and she forced herself to back away and get into her seat.

A minute later, he'd rounded the front of the truck and slid in behind the wheel. He craned around to eyeball Pita like she was a pissed-off rattlesnake.

Willa laughed and Keane turned all that concentrated hotness on her. "What?"

"I'm picturing Petunia coming back from the dead to haunt you."

With a small smile, he leaned in close and slid his fingers along her jaw. "You think that's funny?"

"I'd do the same thing."

His mouth quirked. "Revengeful, huh?"

"Absolutely."

His fingers still on her jaw, he let his thumb slide lightly over her lower lip, making it hunger for a touch.

His touch.

No, make that his mouth. She wanted his mouth on hers and wasn't that just annoying as hell. "This isn't happening," she said out loud, because surely that would make it true.

"What isn't?" he asked. "Dinner with me despite you saying that the devil himself couldn't drag your cold, dead corpse out on a date with me, even if I was . . . how did you put it? Hot as balls?"

"I didn't say that!" She felt her face flush. She was doing her best to desperately hold on to her resentment over their past, but even she could admit she was quickly losing the battle here, to curiosity.

And lust.

"If you're going to eavesdrop," she said with as much dignity as she could, which wasn't much, "at least get your facts straight."

He just laughed, a sexy sound that woke up all her happy spots, damn him. And he knew it too. She sunk in her seat a little, crossed her arms over her chest and looked out the window. "Be amused all you want, I'm holding firm."

He didn't look worried.

Which in turn worried her.

They made a stop on Vallejo Street, at the top of the hill lined with beautiful old Victorians. Here the houses were big and gorgeous and expensive. The one in front of them had some scaffolding wrapped around it, which didn't take away from the absolutely gorgeousness of the place.

"Wait here," Keane said and reached behind him to grab the cat carrier. "I'm just going to run the antichrist inside before we go so she doesn't have to sit in the truck during dinner."

"You live here?"

"It's one of my renovation projects. It's also my office and where I temporarily park my head at night."

"It's beautiful," she breathed, unable to take her eyes

off of it. "One of the most beautiful homes I've ever seen."

He smiled. "Thanks but you should've seen it when I first got ahold of it several years ago. You wouldn't have given it a second look." He started to get out of the truck but then hesitated. "You'll still be here when I get back, right?"

She wanted to see inside that amazing house. "You could take me with you to guarantee it."

"I trust you," he said.

She didn't buy that for a second. What she did buy was that he didn't want her to go inside. "You leave dishes in the sink?" she asked. "Clothes all over the floor? Or maybe you've got someone in there waiting on you . . ." She was just joking but she didn't like thinking it could be true.

"You mean a woman?"

Well when he said it like that, it did sound dumb. "Never mind," she said. "Do what you have to do."

He stilled a beat and then set the carrier down again and leaned in close to her. With one hand on the headrest at the back of her head and the other on the seat at her opposite hip, he caged her in, his face an inch from hers.

Smiling.

The ass. He was temptation personified and he knew it. And also, he smelled good. She had no idea how he'd managed to work all day long doing what he did and still smell amazing, but he did. She closed her eyes, making herself sit still instead of doing as she wanted—which would've been smushing her face into the crook of his neck and inhaling him like she was a third grader with a bottle of glue.

"You want to come upstairs, Willa?" he asked, voice pure sex.

What she wanted was to put her hands back on his chest now that she knew it was as hard as it looked. Instead she gripped either side of her seat with white knuckles. "Of course not."

"I think you do. I think you want something else too."

"What I want," she said as coolly as she could, "is dinner as promised."

"Liar," he chided softly.

"Well that's just rude, calling your date a liar."

"So it *is* a date." His tone was very male and very smug. It should've pissed her off but instead it did something hot and erotic to her insides.

Clearly knowing it, he smiled at her and then dragged his teeth over his lower lip as he contemplated her.

Gah. She wanted to do that. And she wanted to do more too. She wanted him shockingly badly and suddenly she couldn't remember why she shouldn't. She tried to access her thought processes on the subject but her brain hiccupped and froze. Which surely was the only reason she let go of the death grip on her seat, slid her fingers into his hair, and . . . brushed her mouth over his.

He didn't move, not a single muscle, but when she pulled back, his eyes had gone dark as night, piercing her with their intensity.

"Don't read that the wrong way," she whispered.

"Is there a wrong way to take it when a beautiful woman kisses you?"

"Um . . ."

He laughed low in his throat, like maybe she delighted him, and then he mirrored what she'd done. He slid his hands up her throat and into her hair, intensifying the pleasure already wreaking havoc inside her body so that desire laced its way from her chest to her stomach, and then much lower.

"Um . . ."

His lips curved. "You said that already."

She laughed nervously, feeling sixteen and stupid all over again, but seriously, if his voice got any lower she was going to embarrass herself here. It was so deep and husky that she could *feel* his words. "I . . ."

He waited for her to speak but honestly, she had nothing. Not a single thought in her head.

He smiled, a wicked, naughty smile, and the hand in her hair slowly pulled her head back. And then he lowered his perfect mouth to hers in a devastatingly slow and unhurried kiss, sealing his lips to hers as one powerful arm curled around her hip to keep her in place.

Pulsing waves of heat unfurled inside of her and she gave a helpless moan, prompting him to tighten his grip on her and deepen the connection with a better angle and a lot more tongue.

She'd started this, she'd been in charge, but she was no longer even remotely in control. For a beat she let her fingers wander, eliciting a rumbly groan from deep in his throat, the sound incredibly erotic. Then she pulled back and stared up at him.

"I have no idea what I did to deserve that," he murmured quietly, stroking a finger along her temple. "But I'm going to drop Pita off now before this goes too far."

Their gazes held and she could see the humor shining in his, crinkling at the edges. Right, she thought. Good. One of them could still think.

"Okay?" he asked, which was when she realized she had two fistfuls of his shirt, holding him to her.

"Sure." She made herself loosen her grip, smoothing out the wrinkles she'd left, and again she could feel his tight abs through the cotton. Very tight.

She wanted to lick him like a lollipop.

But he didn't want this to go too far. Not with her. She needed to remember that. Maybe she should write it down so she didn't forget. She was nodding to herself like a bobblehead when he said her name and then waited until she looked at him.

"Not that I don't want it to go too far," he said, his gaze revealing heat and the raw power she was getting used to seeing in those dark depths when he looked at her. "But not in my truck, Willa. Not with you." He got out of the car and waited while she did the same. Then he picked up the carrier with Petunia in it and with his other hand, grabbed hers.

"It's okay," she said quickly. "I can wait here."

"Don't chicken out now," he said, looking amused. "You can satiate your curiosity and check to make sure I'm not double booked tonight all at the same time."

She tried to pull free of his grip, but he had her, and she laughed a little to herself—*the sexy jackass*—as he nudged her inside ahead of him.

She immediately forgot why she was mad. The main level was rich with Victorian architectural details: beautiful trim, a crafted stairway with ornate wood railings and stairs. Gorgeously charming light fixtures hung in the entry and living room, paying homage to the period style of the home.

"Wow," she murmured, taking in the surprisingly wide-open space that was still liberally protected from the renovation with tarp runners across the hardwood floors. She could see into the open kitchen and den as well as the still unfinished loft above and to the left. The dining room and living area were clearly being used as office space.

What she didn't see was a single Christmas decoration. "You said you live here?" she asked.

"Temporarily."

"There's no holiday decorations."

"No." He couched low to set down the carrier and unzipped it. Rising to his full height, he stared down at the thing, hands on hips as if braced for warfare. "I have three projects going right now. This is one of them."

She looked around in marvel. "How did you get started doing this?"

"The short of it is that I begged, borrowed, and stole the money for the first fallen property and then kicked some serious ass to not lose my shorts over the deal."

"Fallen?" she asked.

"In that first case, a foreclosure. I slapped some lipstick on it and quickly turned it around for a small profit, emphasis on *small*." He gave a quick smile. "I got better as time went on."

"Someone had to walk away from their home?" she asked. "And you gained from that?"

"They chose to walk," he said pragmatically. "The bank wanted their money back. I ate mac and cheese for an entire year to make it work."

Okay, she got that. Because as he'd told her, you make money however you make money. She took in the gorgeous, incredible details of his work and marveled at his talent. "It's amazing."

"You wouldn't have said so if you'd seen it before," he said. "It was just about a complete teardown. I've had this place the longest. It's taken the most work of any other project. I really need to get it on the market, should've already done it by now."

She was boggled. "How could you get rid of this place? You put such heart and soul into it."

"It's worth a lot of money," he said, not giving a lot away although there was something to his body language, the set of his wide shoulders maybe, that told her she wasn't getting the whole story.

"The profit will go into my next project," he said.

And yet he hadn't sold it. Possibly it meant too much to him, and she could certainly see why. "Maybe you're attached to it," she said.

He shook his head in surprise. "I don't get attached."

She looked at him. "Ever?"

"There's no place for it in my world."

"Huh," she said, thinking of all of *her* attachments. Her friends, who were also her family. Rory, Cara, and all the others she hired and took on. "I get attached to everything and everyone," she admitted.

"No kidding."

This took her aback. "What does that mean?"

He glanced at her and laughed softly. "I've seen you in action, Willa. It seems that once you make a friend, you keep them until the end of time. Same thing with animals. I'm pretty sure you've never met a two-legged or four-legged creature you don't fall for. You collect hearts and souls like most women collect shoes."

"Hey. I collect plenty of shoes." And anyway, he was only partially right. Maybe she did collect hearts and souls, but she didn't keep them. Being a foster kid had taught her that all too well. You only borrowed the people—and animals—you loved. You didn't get to keep them.

Even when you wanted to.

"I really do love this place," she murmured, turning in a slow circle. "It's so warm and welcoming. If this house was mine, I'd never leave it."

"That's the thing, it's not my home, not really."

"Where is your home then?" she asked.

He paused. "I've not really settled on one yet." He looked around as if seeing it for the first time. "If I was ready, I'd want it to be a place like this but for now it's just where I sleep and work. I've got some small finish work to get to yet before I can put it on the market."

She watched him as he spoke. He'd turned to watch the carrier but that wasn't what grabbed her attention and held.

No, it was that he wasn't buying what he was trying to sell her. Whether he really was done with the property or not, she had no idea, but she had the feeling he wasn't *ready* to be done.

Maybe . . . maybe he could get attached to things after all. Things like this house. And . . . her.

This wayward, out-of-nowhere thought set off all her inner alarms. She had to work at keeping her face blank through her panic. This wasn't going to happen. She wouldn't allow it. Not here, not with him, because she knew from experience that once the pit bull that was her heart snapped its jaws onto something, it took a miracle to let go.

Chapter 6

#HitMeWithYourBestShot

While Willa stood there reeling a little bit about her unwanted feelings for Keane, the world kept spinning on its rotation, completely oblivious to her unhappy epiphany.

It was her greatest wish that Keane would remain oblivious as well, which meant that she had to be careful because he wasn't the sort of guy to miss much.

Or anything.

Luckily, Petunia chose that moment to stroll out of her carrier, nose in the air, tail swishing prissily back and forth, her entire demeanor projecting Queen Bee.

Until she saw Willa. Then she immediately let out a happy chirp and trotted over, her tubby belly swinging to and fro as she wound herself around Willa's legs, purring.

"Ingrate," Keane said mildly.

Willa relaxed a little. Okay, they were moving

on. This was good. This was *great,* and she let out a long breath that caught in her throat at Keane's next words.

"What's the matter?"

"Nothing."

His expression was doubtful. "It's something. Something's different. Is it the house somehow, or the kiss?"

Oh for God's sake. Most men were oblivious. Why had she had to kiss the one who wasn't?

No, they most definitely did not need to talk about it.

Petunia, clearly tired of humans, stalked off and Willa watched her go, wistful. Why wasn't she a cat? *Why hadn't she stayed in the truck?*

"Willa."

"Um . . . hold on a sec, my phone's going off." She pulled it from her pocket like she'd just received an important text. She brought up a new message and quickly typed.

Her:
Alskjfa;oiw;af;o3ij;asjfe

She got an immediate response.

HeadOfAllTheThings:
Are you just texting me gibberish so you look busy
in front of someone you don't want to talk to again?
Who is it this time, that UPS guy with gingivitis?

Willa started to thumb in a response, but Keane came up behind her, *right* behind her, and even though he wasn't actually touching her, she could feel his heat, the tempered strength in his big body, and she got a rush so strong her knees wobbled.

Her phone pinged another incoming text and assuming it was Elle teasing her, she ignored it. But behind her Keane wrapped his fingers around her wrist and brought the screen up so that they could see the readout.

It wasn't Elle.

AssholeExDONOTAnswer:
Miss you.

"I especially like your contact name for him," Keane said. "The infamous Ethan?"

Willa nodded dully because really she was just stunned to hear from the guy at all after so much had happened. Ethan had started off so normal but he'd slowly morphed into a possessive, jealous, angry guy. It'd happened gradually enough that at first she thought she was overreacting. She'd reminded herself he'd been good to her, and as a people pleaser she'd doubled her efforts to make him see he had nothing to worry about.

Classic mistake.

When he'd blown up at her at the pub one night for dancing with Finn and tried to physically haul her out of the place, she'd taken a stand. Actually, she'd tossed a drink in his face and he'd screamed like a baby.

That's when he'd been ejected from the pub by Archer.

And then Willa had ejected him from her life.

The next day she'd found her cash drawer in the shop

emptied of three hundred bucks and a stack of her gift cards verified and missing.

For a long time she'd blamed herself and then she'd found her mad and had ached for an apology. But that ache had faded, replaced with some hard-won maturity. She no longer was that same woman who'd give a perfect stranger the shirt off her back. Nope, she'd care for a perfect stranger's cat though, and at that thought, she snorted.

"It's funny?" Keane asked.

"Not funny ha-ha. More like"—she mimed a gun with her first finger and thumb, bringing it up to her temple—"blow my brains out funny."

Keane didn't look amused. "This is the serial creeper, right?"

Since he seemed more than a little tense all of a sudden, she smiled to show him she wasn't bothered by this blast from her past. Hell, she was getting used to it. "Give me a sec?"

He nodded but didn't go away. Okaaay. So she composed her answering text with an audience:

> The person you're trying to reach has forwarded this text to the police, who are still trying to locate you. Please text your current addy and place of employment to make it easy for them but know it's not necessary as this was a felony case and they'll be tracking you down by triangulation of your cell-phone pings.

She felt Keane, a big, strong presence at her back. "Exactly what did this guy do to you?"

Nothing she wanted to get into right now. Or ever. "Nothing but live up to the contact name I gave him."

"I especially like the cell-phone-ping thing," Keane said.

She laughed a little. "I don't actually know if that's a thing. I saw it on *Criminal Minds* once and it stuck with me."

"Nice." His voice was warm and approving. "Now forward the text to the cops like you said."

She grimaced. "I was actually just fibbing about that part. But I did promise Archer I'd let him take care of it personally if Ethan contacted me again. Archer used to be a cop and he hasn't lost any of his skills." She craned her neck and met Keane's gaze. "I think he's been really looking forward to this."

"Good. Forward the text."

"Now?"

"Now."

Okay then. She forwarded the text to Archer. "Feel better?" she asked as her phone buzzed with Archer's immediate response:

On it. Don't worry.

"Yeah," Keane said. "I feel better."

They left the house, with Willa giving it a final look back as they walked out to his truck. It felt a little silly to fall for a house but that's what she'd done.

Keane drove to the Embarcadero. It had a view that eclipsed any other place in the city, at least in Willa's opinion. They walked along the water and stopped to take in the heart-stopping view of the bay.

"Thought we'd eat here," Keane said of the Waterfront Restaurant behind them.

She hesitated. "When you said 'let's get some food,' I thought we'd get a burger or a taco," she said. "I don't think I'm dressed for this."

He let his gaze run over her, taking in her sweater and skinny jeans. She'd need to lose ten pounds before she could get anywhere even close to skinny.

"I like what you're wearing," he said. "You're beautiful."

This actually left her speechless.

"And anyway, I'm hungry for more than just a quickie."

She stared at him. "Is that a double entendre?"

"Actually, it might have been a triple entendre."

She laughed and looked at the restaurant front. She'd walked by the place enough times, always drooling over the great view and menu, but she'd never actually been inside.

Turned out, the food was fantastic.

And so was the company, dammit.

As they ate, they watched the moon hang above the water. A salty breeze brushed through the outside patio, mingling with the warm air coming out of the standing heaters beside every dining table.

It was unexpectedly . . . romantic. So much so that she had to keep reminding her hormones to take a chill pill, not that they listened. She was far too attracted to Keane for her own good. He was smart, funny, sexy . . . At some point she came up with the brilliant idea to concentrate on what she *didn't* like. "Why aren't there any holiday decorations up at your place?" she asked.

"Because you bought out all the decorations in the entire city."

Okay, so she had to laugh at that. "Elle thinks my shop looks like Christmas and New Year had a baby who threw up on everything."

He smiled and she thought *bingo,* something else she didn't like about him—he didn't appreciate her admittedly obsessive need to celebrate the holidays, supersize style.

"It could've been worse," he said. "I didn't see Santa himself represented anywhere in your shop."

"He's coming soon," she admitted. "I'm doing a Santa Extravaganza. Customers bring their pets in to be primped and then can get into a photo booth with Santa."

"Nice. Love your entrepreneurial spirit." He smiled. "So do you go nuts for all the holidays or just Christmas?"

Because the question was genuine and there didn't seem to be any sense of mocking in his dark gaze, she answered with more honesty than she'd intended. "Yes, all the holidays. It's a holdover from when I was a kid and didn't always get to celebrate them."

His smile faded as he looked at her and she suddenly developed a fascination with her last sip of wine.

"Parents not into the holidays?" he asked.

She shrugged. "My dad got himself killed while hunting with his buddies when I was two. My mom was young when she had me, too young. She's . . . not really cut out for parenting."

An understatement. She'd gotten better over the years, enough to call and check in once in a while.

And ask for money.

Keane slid his hand to hers on the table and gently squeezed her fingers. "I'm glad you treat yourself to the holidays then. So does Father Time come on New Year's?"

"No," she said on a laugh and then admitted the rest. "But Cupid comes on Valentine's Day."

He stared at her and then burst out laughing, a sound she was all too quickly becoming addicted to. Damn. She quickly wracked her brain to come up with more things she didn't like about him. Such as he seemed unwilling—not incapable, which would've been different, but *unwilling*—to get attached to Petunia. Also, he clearly didn't fully appreciate her holiday decorating skills. And then there was the fact that he kissed like sex on a stick—No, wait. That was a pro not a con.

"How about you?" she asked. "What's your take on holidays?"

"I don't have a reason as good as you do for going one way or the other," he said. "I was a late-in-life unhappy surprise to a couple of college professors who'd already raised two daughters. They were really into their work. Holidays got in the way of that work."

Well that sounded lonely. And sad. "So you didn't get to celebrate much either?" she asked, suddenly feeling . . . small. Back in school she'd judged him for being a jock, when maybe sports had been all he'd had.

And if that thought didn't open up a whole big can of worms . . .

"No, not much celebration at the Winters's house," he said. "And you didn't want *my* pity, Willa, so don't you dare give me any. I didn't know any different. It didn't bother me."

"But . . ." She swallowed the rest of that sentence because he was right. He'd treated her pride with respect and she needed to do the same. "Do you all keep in touch?"

"Not as much as we should." Regret slashed through his features. "I hardly even knew I had a great-aunt Sally until she showed up on my doorstep just over two weeks ago now."

Willa had spent a few years searching for long-lost family to no avail. She was riveted by this peek into Keane's life. "Really?"

"Yeah. She's my grandma's sister," he said, "and apparently there was some big feud fifty years ago involving the two of them falling for the same man."

"Wow. Who ended up with the guy?"

"My grandma," he said. "And then I guess she caught her sister flirting with him and accused Sally of trying to steal him out from right beneath her nose. It divided the family."

"That's awful."

"I'm pretty sure even without the scandal, we'd have all drifted apart," he said. "We're not much for emotion, us Winterses. We like to keep it all closed off and we're good at it."

She shook her head because though she knew he believed that, she'd seen him display emotion, plenty of it. Frustration and exhaustion when he'd first brought her Petunia. Anger, though he'd done his best to hide it from her, when she'd gotten the text from Ethan.

And then there'd been the sheer blast of passion and heat when he'd kissed her.

Yeah, he felt plenty. He just didn't like it.

And that she could understand. She didn't like it when emotions got the better of her either. The difference between him and her was that he could zip them up and walk away.

She wasn't made like that.

After dinner, they walked some more, ending up inside the colorful and packed Marketplace in the Ferry Building. She bought a loaf of fresh bread and Keane picked up what looked like an expensive whiskey. When she started to panic that the evening was feeling way too much like a real date, she pretended to be shocked at the time and suggested she had to get home.

Keane gave no indication of being annoyed or disappointed, just took her hand and walked her back to his truck. When he drove around the block of her building, making her realize he was looking for a parking spot, the facts sunk in.

One, his five o'clock shadow had a shadow and made her physically ache with yearning to feel it brush over her skin.

Two, he had a bottle of alcohol.

Three, he was clearly planning to walk her up to her apartment.

It all added up to an uncomfortable truth—if he so much as looked at her mouth in that innately masculine, watchful way of his, she'd probably jump his sexy bones.

"Don't worry about finding a spot," she said quickly, reaching for the door handle as he slowed down, his gaze on a car up ahead that was getting ready to pull out. "I can get out right here." She smiled at him brightly and hoped the whites of her eyes weren't showing, revealing her panic. "Thankssomuchfordinner," she managed and hopped out.

"Willa. Wait—"

But nope, she couldn't. She needed to get the heck out of Dodge before she did something incredibly stupid. So she ran into the courtyard of her building without looking back.

It was second nature to slow at the fountain and search her pockets. Dog treats. Her keys. And *yes,* a nickel, which she tossed into the water to make her usual wish.

Old Man Eddie, the homeless guy who lived in the alley, poked his head out. He was sitting on his box between two Dumpsters—his favorite spot because from his perch he could see both the courtyard and the street. He was always chipper and smiling, but tonight his smile was devoid of its usual wattage.

"Any of your wishes come true yet?" he asked.

"Not yet. Are you okay?"

He lifted a shoulder. "Waiting for my holiday cheer to kick in."

A lot of people in the building took turns making sure Eddie had everything he needed, but mostly it was Spence, herself, and Elle in charge. They'd tried getting him into a shelter several times but he preferred his alley. She peered over and could see why he hadn't found his holiday cheer yet: it was dark and dank. "Brought you dinner," she said and handed him her doggie bag. "Lobster linguine. Bad for our diet, but totally amazing."

"Thanks, dudette. What's the hurry? Bad date?"

"Worse," she said. "*Great* date."

Clutching the leftovers, he nodded like he got it all too well. "Thanks for dinner. Think I'll walk to the Presidio first though. All the Victorians are decorated with wreaths and lights, and some of them have baskets of candy out."

"Be safe," she said and watched him go, her own problems dissolving as her mind raced to find a way to help Eddie find his cheer.

And then it came to her.

Changing directions, she ran to her shop. Quickly letting herself in, she pulled down a string of lights that she'd put up along her checkout counter. She grabbed an extension cord and her staple gun too. Less than three minutes later she was in Eddie's alley, stapling the string of lights above his spot—between the two Dumpsters.

Stepping back, she eyed her work. The lights lit the alley up in brilliant colors, warming the area and giving some cheer to it as well. Nodding in satisfaction, she left.

When she exited the elevator on the fourth floor five minutes later she was shaking with cold and so deep into her own thoughts that the tall, built shadow of a man standing there scared her nearly out of her own skin.

"Dammit, Keane," she gasped, hand to her heart. "You startled me."

"Did you really just decorate the alley for the homeless guy that lives there?" he asked.

"Maybe. And his name is Eddie."

Keane's eyes were warm and went a long way toward heating her up. So did his smile.

"Are you laughing at me?" she asked.

"I'd never laugh at a woman who decorates dark alleys and carries a mean stapler gun at crotch level."

She looked down at the tool in her hand and rolled her eyes. "The alley looked lonely."

"You mean Eddie looked lonely and you wanted to do something for him."

That too.

He tipped her face up and she found his eyes more serious now. "You're pretty amazing," he said. "You know that?"

She squirmed a little bit at the unexpected praise but he didn't give her any room. "If I ask you a serious question, Willa, will you give me an honest answer?"

She hesitated. "Maybe." And maybe not . . .

"Why don't you want to like me?"

She blinked. "What?"

"You heard me. I'm missing something, something big I think. No more playing, Willa; tell me. You gave up the right to keep it a secret after you kissed me."

"You kissed me back," she whispered.

"Yes, and I'm going to kiss you again soon as you finish talking."

"No, actually, you're not." She drew in a shaky deep

breath, held it for a minute, and then let it go in one long shudder. "Fine, I'll tell you the truth," she said, tired of holding it in anyway. "But just remember, you asked."

He nodded.

"We went to high school together for a year." Once that escaped, the rest came out really fast, as if that could help ease the reliving of the humiliating experience. "You were the popular jock and I was . . . a nobody. You stood me up for my first—and last—dance." Just saying it out loud made her mad all over again. "And then to add insult to injury, you don't even remember."

He just stared at her. "Run that by me one more time. Slower. And in English."

"No," she said, turning to her front door. "I'm not going to say it again. It was hard enough to live with and even harder to say it the one time."

He caught her and with gentle steel pulled her back around and pressed her up against the hallway wall. Hands still on her arms, he leaned in, holding her there. "Why don't I remember you?"

"Because you're an ass?" she asked sweetly, pushing ineffectively at his chest. "Back up."

"In a minute." He wasn't going to be distracted. "You weren't in any of my classes."

"No. I was a freshman when you were a senior. There was a Sadie Hawkins dance and you were the only guy in the whole school I wanted to go with. I was new there so I didn't have friends to talk any sense into me. I caught you coming out of one of your football practices and I thought . . . Well, never mind what I thought. You were in a hurry, which I didn't realize until I stopped you." She squeezed her eyes shut as remembered humiliation washed over her. "I spoke too fast then too. Way too fast. You had to ask me to repeat the question. Twice."

He let out a breath, closed his eyes, and dropped his forehead to hers. "Tell me I was nice about it. Tell me I wasn't a complete eighteen-year-old dick."

"You don't get to ask that of me," she said and gave him another push. "Because I was so forgettable that you don't even remember me."

"Yeah, so I was a complete eighteen-year-old dick," he muttered. *"Shit."* He tightened his grip on her when she tried to break free. "Listen to me, Willa, because I want to make something perfectly clear here." He opened his eyes and held hers prisoner. "You're the most unforgettable person I've ever met."

She let out a soft sigh of unintentional need because pathetic as it was, the words felt like a balm on her raw soul. "Don't—"

"Tell me what I said to you that day."

"You said 'sounds cool.'" She dropped her forehead to his chest. "And I practically floated home. I didn't have a dress. Or shoes. Or money to get into the dance. I had to beg, borrow, and steal, but I managed to do it, to get myself together enough that I'd be worthy of a date with Keane Winters."

A rough sound of regret escaped him. "I had a real problem with girls back then," he said. "I didn't know how to say no."

"Cue the violins."

He grimaced. "I know. But there were these sports groupies and—"

"Oh my God." She covered her ears. "Stop talking! I don't want to know any of this."

"I'm just saying that they used to hang around outside of practice and then jump us when we left the locker room. If you were there, I probably thought you were one of them."

Willing to concede that this might actually be true, she lifted a shoulder but managed to hold on to most of her mad. "You should have known by taking one look at me that I wasn't a damn groupie."

"You'd think. But eighteen-year-old guys are assholes." He looked genuinely regretful. "Tell me the rest."

"Nothing more to tell. You didn't show. And you never so much as looked at me again."

"Willa—"

"End of story," she said. "Both back then and now." She ducked beneath his arms and fumbled for her keys, practically falling into her apartment. She shut the door harder than was strictly necessary and didn't know if she was disappointed or relieved when he didn't even attempt to follow her.

Chapter 7

#FallenAndCantGetUp

Keane woke up to a heavy pressure on his chest that felt like a heart attack—no doubt the result of wracking his brain all night long, trying to remember Willa from high school.

To his chagrin, he still couldn't.

He'd been telling her the utter truth when he'd said that a lot of girls had waited on the players after practices. He'd ignored most of them and when they'd refused to be ignored, he'd flashed a smile and done his best to flirt his way to the parking lot rather than hurt anyone's feelings.

So it killed him that he'd hurt Willa.

But the truth was, he hadn't given a lot of thought to how any of those girls had taken his ridiculous and stupid comments designed to help him escape. It hadn't been until he'd gotten to college that he'd lost some of his shyness around women.

Okay, all of it.

He'd met his first real girlfriend—Julie Carmen—his freshman year and they'd gotten serious fast, fueled by the sheer, mind-numbing hunger of eighteen-year-old lust.

By the end of that first year, he was no longer thinking with his head, at least not the one on top of his shoulders. For the first time in his life he had someone so into him that she wanted to spend every waking moment with him, and he'd gotten off on that. He'd wanted to marry her, ridiculous as that sounded now. He'd told himself to play it cool, to hold back, but he had no real experience with that and ended up blurting it out at a football game over hot dogs and beer.

Real smooth.

Julie had been cool about it and he'd been . . . happy, truly happy for the first time in his life. That had lasted two weeks until she'd dumped him, saying she'd only been in it for a good time and because he had a hot body, and she was sorry but he wanted way more from her than she could give.

He hadn't reverted to his shyness around women. Instead he'd accepted that he wasn't good with or made for long term, a fact made easy to back up since he had no desire to give his heart away again.

But one-night stands . . . he'd gone on to excel there, for quite a few tumble-filled years. Until now, in fact. Willa was unlike any woman he'd ever met. She was passionate, smart, sexy . . . and she made him laugh.

And her smile could light up his entire day.

He wasn't actually sure what to do with that, but he knew he wanted to do something.

The weight on his chest got heavier. Yep, probably a heart attack. Well, hey, he'd nearly made it to thirty and it'd been a pretty good run too.

No regrets.

Well maybe one—that he wouldn't get to kiss Willa again or see that soft and dazed look on her face after he did, the one that said she wanted him every bit as much as he wanted her.

The pressure on his chest shifted, getting even heavier now. He opened his eyes and nearly had a stroke instead of a heart attack.

Pita was sitting on his ribcage, her head bent to his, nose to nose, staring at him.

"Meow," she said in a tone suggesting not only that she was starving, but that he was in danger of having his face eaten off if he didn't get up and feed her.

Remembering Willa's admonishment that he hadn't tried to connect with the damn thing, he lifted a hand and patted her on the head.

Pita's eyes narrowed.

"Right, you're a cat not a dog." He stroked a hand down her back instead and she lifted into his touch, her eyes half closed in what he hoped was pleasure.

"You like that?" he murmured, thinking *middle ground!* So he did it again, stroked her along her spindly spine for a second time.

A rumble came from Pita's throat, rough and

uneven, like a motor starting up for the first time in a decade.

"Wow," he said. "Is that an actual purr? Better be careful, you might start to almost like me."

On his third stroke down her back, she bit him. Hard. Not enough to break the skin but she sank her teeth in a bit and held there, her eyes narrowed to slits.

"Still not friends," he gritted out. "Noted. Now let go." When she didn't, he sat up and dislodged her, and with an irritated chirp, she leapt to the end of the bed, turning her back on him and lifting her hind leg, going to work cleaning her lady town.

He looked down at his hand. No blood, good sign. He slid out of bed and . . .

Stepped in something disgustingly runny and still warm. Cat yak. He hopped around and swore the air blue for a while and then managed to clean up without yakking himself.

Barely.

He found the little antichrist sitting up high on the unfinished loft floor, peeking over the edge down at where he stood in the kitchen.

"Are you kidding me?" he asked.

"Mew."

Shit, she was stuck. There was a ladder against the wall because Mason had been working up there this week. Keane, hating heights, had avoided going up there at all and had absolutely no idea how she'd managed to climb the construction ladder in the first place.

Blowing out a sigh, he climbed up halfway and held out his arms. "Come on then."

Pita lifted a paw and began to wash her face.

He dropped his head and laughed. What else could he do? Clearly the cat didn't give a shit that he had a height phobia. And yeah, it was a ridiculous phobia for a builder to have but that didn't change a damn thing.

He glanced down—oh shit, he hated that—and assured himself it was only eight feet. Then he kept going. "Cat," he said at the top and reached for her.

She jumped, but not for him. Instead she hit the ladder over his shoulder, lithely running past him like she was Tinker Bell complete with wings.

From the top, Keane looked down and felt himself start to sweat. Grinding his back teeth, he climbed down and found Pita staring disdainfully at her food bowl, which was still full from last night.

This got his attention. "You didn't eat? Since when don't you eat?"

She swished her tail and gave a "mew" that he figured translated to *that shit is for cats and I'm a Queen Bee, remember?*

He took a closer look and realized she seemed a little thin, at least for her, which concerned him in a way her attitude hadn't. He'd called Sally three times this week alone but hadn't gotten a return call. What if Pita wasted away and died before Sally came for her? How would he explain that?

Worried, he went hunting through his admittedly not well-stocked cabinets and found a can of tuna. *Score.* "Cats love tuna," he told Pita. "Willa says so."

Pita just stared at him censurably with those deep blue eyes.

Finding a can opener took a while, making him re-alize something a little startling. He'd lived here for going on six months now and though it was by far his favorite property he'd ever owned . . . he'd not ever really moved in. Yes, he had all his stuff here but that wasn't much. He'd moved around frequently over the years, from one property to the next as he fixed them up and sold them, so he'd gotten good at traveling light.

Maybe too good.

Once he got his hands on a can opener, he waved it triumphantly at Pita, who looked distinctly unim-pressed. He opened the can and dumped it into another bowl and set it in front of her.

She froze and then sniffed it with the caution of a royal food-taster.

"It's albacore," he said. "The good stuff."

She gave it another brief sniff and then turned and walked away.

He stared after her. "Seriously? You lick your own ass but turn your nose up at fucking tuna?"

He was still staring after her in disbelief when his cell phone rang. "Keane Winters," he snapped, not reading the display. "Cat for sale."

There was a long pause.

"Hello?" he said.

"Are you selling *my* cat?" came a soft and slightly shaken older woman's voice.

Shit. His great-aunt Sally. "Sorry, bad joke," he said and grimaced, shoving his free hand through his hair. "And am I ever glad to hear from you. I've been calling—"

"I know." Her voice sounded a little faint. "I'm out front, may I come in?"

"Yes, of course." Was she kidding? She was here to pick up Pita and for that he'd roll out the red carpet. "You didn't have to call first—"

"I didn't want to interrupt any . . . meetings you might have had. With women."

He choked back a laugh as he moved through the house toward the front. What was it with people thinking he had a lineup of chicks every night? "I'll make sure to keep all the women locked up in the bedroom while you're here," he said.

She gasped in his ear.

"I'm kidding, Aunt Sally. It's just me." Not that he wouldn't mind having Willa sprawled out in his bed right about now . . .

He opened the door. Sally was bundled up in a thick coat, hat, scarf, gloves, and boots, and since she was under five feet tall, she looked a bit like a hobbit. Hat quivering, she walked ahead of him into the foyer and then stopped abruptly, her back to him as she studied his place.

"It's beautiful," she said softly. "You do beautiful work. I never understood your parents' contempt for what you do with your bare hands."

Leaving him stunned, she called for the cat. "Petunia, darling, come to Mommy."

Pita came running, eyes bright, a happy chirp escaping her, the same sound she used with Willa too.

Old woman and cat had a long hug and then his aunt finally straightened slowly, her back still to him.

There was an awkward silence that he had no idea how to broach. It was safe to say he didn't know his own parents all that well. Yes, they'd raised him. Somewhat. But the truth was he'd been a latchkey kid who'd spent most of his time at sporting events, with friends, or in front of a gaming system. When he'd turned eighteen and moved out, there'd been a blast of overwhelming relief from his parents. They'd been virtual strangers to each other and in the years since they hadn't gotten to know each other any better.

He knew his aunt even less. "How are you feeling?" he asked.

She was silent for a long moment. "Do you ever have regrets about our family?" she asked instead of answering. "How little we all bother with each other?"

One thing the Winterses didn't do was discuss feelings. Ever. In fact, they buried them deep and pretended they didn't exist. So he stared at her stiff spine, an uncomfortable feeling swirling in his gut.

She sighed. "Right. Listen, I'm sorry about this, Keane."

Oh shit. "Tell me what's wrong."

She stayed where she was but he realized her shoulders were a little slumped as she pulled open her large handbag. From it, she pulled out a plastic Ziploc baggie filled with what were unmistakably cat toys. "For Petunia," she said.

"But—"

"And I've got her special blankie too. She'll need it for nap times."

"Aunt Sally." Gently he turned her to face him. "What's going on?"

"I can't take her back yet." Her rheumy blue eyes went suspiciously watery. "I need you to keep her a little bit longer. Do you think you can do that without selling her?"

"I was kidding about that." Mostly. As for the question of could he handle Pita . . . He'd handled a lot of shit in his life so theoretically he could handle one little cat.

And then there was the built-in bonus—he'd have a reason for Willa to let him back into her shop, and yeah, he was pretty sure he needed to give her a reason. "Talk to me."

"It's nothing for you to worry about." She reached up to pat his head like he was a child, but being a whole lot shorter than him she had to settle for an awkward pat to his forearm. "I'm having some cat food delivered," she said. "Petunia needs routine."

"And what do you need?"

She inhaled a shaky breath. "I need to make this transition as easy as possible for her."

Keane took her small, frail hand in his much bigger one. "Done. But now you, Aunt Sally. What can I do for you?"

There was another long pause and then a suspicious sniff, and in the way of men everywhere the world over, his heart froze in utter terror.

"I didn't know you as a child," she said quietly. "And that was my own doing. Nor did I bother with you when you got older, not until I needed you anyway. And that's also my shame." She squeezed his fingers. "You're a good man, Keane Winters, and you deserved better from me. From all of us. I've got no right to ask this of you, but please. *Please* take care of my baby."

And then she was gone.

He turned and stared down at the cat, who stared right back. "I think we're stuck with each other now."

Her eyes said she was unimpressed. And then she turned and, with her tail high in the air, stalked off.

"No more yakking in my bedroom, you hear me?" he called after her.

And shit, now he was talking to a cat. Shaking his head at himself, he shoved his feet into his running shoes—his *new* running shoes since Pita had taken a dump in his beloved, perfectly broken-in ones two weeks before—and hit the concrete.

He didn't have a set route. Running was for clearing his brain, and he let his feet take him where they wanted to go. Sometimes that was along the Embarcadero, or through Fort Mason. Or the Presidio, or the Lyon Street steps.

Today it was Cow Hollow.

He wanted to talk to Archer, wanted to make sure he was doing something about Ethan contacting Willa. All Keane knew of Archer was that the guy clearly took care of his own, and he did consider Willa one of his own. He'd seen that firsthand at the dog wedding.

Keane didn't expect Archer to be at work this early. He assumed he'd have to leave a message. But when he got to the Pacific Pier Building and took the stairs to Archer's second-floor offices, Archer was standing in the front room with Elle, the both of them staring down at an iPad screen together. There were two other men, one younger with a Doberman at his side, the other dressed like he'd just come back from a takedown, complete with more than one gun. He was talking when Keane entered, pointing at the iPad as if explaining something.

Archer lifted his head, eyes intense and hard. Whatever he'd been looking at had pissed him off. It clearly wasn't a good time but Keane didn't care. "About that text Willa got last night from her asshole ex," he said.

Archer exchanged a long look with the other men. "Taken care of," he finally said.

"Take care of how?" he wanted to know. "She shouldn't have to deal with him. I want to make sure she doesn't have to."

"She won't," Archer said grimly. "He won't contact her again."

Keane waited for a better explanation, but apparently Archer didn't feel the need to explain himself.

Elle shook her head at Archer and turned to Keane. "Good morning, by the way. And this is Joe," she said of the guy all weaponed up. "He's Archer's second in command. And Max," she said of the younger guy. "And this handsome four-legged guy"—she patted the huge dog on the head—"is Carl. And what Archer meant to say is that he and Max got Ethan. And because he had a warrant out for his arrest for being rough with other women and also stealing from them as well, they put his pansy ass in jail."

Keane's jaw was so tight he could barely speak. "When?"

"About an hour after she sent me the text last night," Archer said.

Elle smiled a little tightly but her eyes were warm. "As you know, Willa is incredibly special, to all of us. We've got her back." She paused. "And it's nice to know that you do as well. Isn't it, Archer?"

Archer slid her a look. She gave him one back, prompting him to blow out a sigh. "Yeah," he said and then his eyes hardened again. "Don't fuck it up. Don't fuck her up."

"Okay then," Elle said cheerfully. "Moving on. Welcome to the gang, Keane. You're one of us now, right, Archer?"

"As long as he doesn't fuck it up," Archer repeated.

Keane held the guy's gaze and gave a short nod. He wouldn't fuck it up. He couldn't.

Because he already had.

Back outside on the sidewalk, he stood in the early-morning dawn, a thick layer of fog casting everything in blues and grays. The lights were on inside Willa's shop, though the sign on the door said CLOSED.

He could see in the windows, see movement past the bright string of holiday lights and boughs of holly. Willa was there.

In another man's arms.

Chapter 8

#TisTheSeason

Willa had slept like crap. She wanted to blame it on the sheer amount of food she'd inhaled at dinner last night with Keane but even she, a woman who knew the value of putting her head in the sand once in a while, couldn't fool herself.

It hadn't been dinner. It was Keane: his smile, his eyes.

His kiss . . .

It was also the sombering certainty that he couldn't—or wouldn't—get any more attached to her than he had anything else in his life. Not his family, his work, Petunia . . .

And certainly not her.

She rolled out of bed and showered and since she'd run out of coffee, skipped makeup. No need to risk poking out an eye with a mascara wand when she had only major catastrophic medical insurance.

She ran down the four flights of stairs and called it exercise, entering her shop with three minutes to spare before a longtime client showed up. Carrie had standing reservations for one-day-a-week babysitting services for Luna, her new teacup piglet, and Macaroni, her "baby," a.k.a. sixty-five-pound, sweet-as-pie pit bull.

Thirteen-year-old Macaroni had arthritis, no teeth, questionable bowel control, and hip dysplasia, but he was pure heart. So much so that Carrie hadn't been able to put him down as her family had been gently suggesting.

Macaroni loved Willa and the feeling was mutual. He was a lot of work but he was absolutely the high-light of her week.

Except Carrie didn't show up. Figuring she was just running late, Willa began working on setting up the Santa Extravaganza Photo Booth for the upcoming weekend. She lost track of time until Spence appeared with two coffees in hand looking unaccustomedly solemn.

Spence was the brain of their gang. Quiet but not even remotely shy, he'd been recruited for a government think tank right from college—which he'd finished with a mechanical engineering degree at age eighteen. He'd never said much about that job but he'd hated it. A few years later he and some of his coworkers had gone to work for themselves. Last year they'd sold their start-up and struck gold. Willa had no idea if he'd gotten a penny or a million bucks; he never talked about it.

Since then he hadn't found his next thing. They all

knew he was unhappy and hated that for him, but if Spence didn't want to talk, Spence didn't talk. He'd been keeping busy with a variety of things and one of them was that he showed up at her shop several times a week to handle her pet-walking duties for her, which she loved. Nothing like a sexy geek to help increase business.

In fact, he was closer to Carrie and her pets than Willa since Carrie was dating one of Spence's ex-partners. "Come in," Willa called out to him. "Macaroni isn't here yet."

"I know." Spence came closer, set down the two coffees, and reached for her hand. "Honey, Macaroni passed away this morning."

Willa felt her heart stop, just stop. "Oh no," she breathed and pressed a hand to her chest, not that it alleviated any pain. "How?"

"In his sleep. No pain," he said softly and pulled her in just as she burst into tears.

A few minutes later, thankful she hadn't bothered with mascara after all, she shuddered out a sigh, still within the warm safety of Spence's arms. Damn, crying was exhausting. She needed to get it together and call Carrie to see how she could help. She needed to get to work. She needed to do a lot of things. That's when her gaze fell to the window and the man standing on the corner outside, his eyes locked on her.

Keane.

In the next beat, the shop door opened and there he was, bigger than life, looking a little tense, a frown on his lips, his eyes on Spence's arms still around her.

"What's wrong?" he asked.

"A client's dog passed away this morning," Spence told him. "Willa and Macaroni were really tight."

Was it her imagination or did he relax slightly?

"Aw, hell," he said, voice warm and genuine now. "That sucks."

"Yeah." Spence ruffled Willa's hair. "It does."

Willa took some tissues from the box on her counter and mopped herself up, aware of Keane watching her. He'd been thrown by finding her in Spence's arms but he'd recovered quick, which was a point in his favor, she could admit. He'd also been running. He was in black basketball shorts, with compression shorts peeking out beneath, and a long-sleeve dry-fit shirt that clung to his broad shoulders and chest, revealing every line of sinew on him.

And there were many.

His black baseball cap sat backward on his head and reflective aviator sunglasses covered his eyes. He shoved the glasses to the top of his head over his baseball cap, revealing his dark eyes filled with concern.

She felt a little dizzy just looking at him, a fact she attributed to the lack of breakfast and the weight of grief.

"I'm sorry," he said quietly and she thought maybe he wasn't just talking about Macaroni. "What can I do?"

She was unprepared for the warmth that spread inside her at that. Unprepared and ill-equipped to handle. For weeks, inner alarms had been going off every time she got too close to him, blaring warnings at her, pummeling her with the memory of being stood up by him, and the even worse blow of him not remembering her.

But now that she'd told him about it and heard his reaction and explanation, something had happened to her mad. It was as if someone had reached out and turned the volume down. *Way* down.

Off, actually.

Or maybe it'd been the kiss. It was incredibly hard to hold on to resentment for someone when you'd had your tongue down their throat. Plus, he kissed like magic.

Spence pointed to the coffee on the counter. "Make sure she caffeinates before you attempt conversation," he warned Keane and then kissed Willa on the cheek. "I'm leaving you in good hands," he said to her.

She stared up into his warm eyes. "How do you know?" She really hoped he had some wisdom to depart here. She needed it, bad.

Spence's smile was crooked and just a little sad. "Because you know as well as I do, people change."

He was referring to himself. He'd changed a lot— he'd had to in order to survive. Or maybe he'd meant the rest of them. Elle and Haley and Finn, even the far more closed-off Archer, they'd all had big changes in their lives, things that irrevocably affected them.

But actually, she thought maybe he'd meant her, because they both knew how much she'd grown since she'd opened South Bark. Through her work and the love of her friends, she'd found a direction. That had given her confidence and anchored her in a way she'd never been before.

Spence held her gaze for a minute, silently remind-ing her that she was no longer that meek wallflower she'd been in high school, that she knew more than anyone else things weren't always what they seemed, that people weren't always what they seemed, and also . . . some deserved a second chance.

Aware that Keane was soaking up this conversation, both spoken and unspoken, she blew out a breath and nodded.

"You know where to find me if you need me," Spence said. He nodded at Keane and then was gone.

Willa realized she was staring blindly after him when the to-go cup of coffee got waved back and forth beneath her nose. She latched on to it like it was the last air in the room.

"Jesus, your fingers are frozen," Keane said and wrapped his much warmer hands around hers on the cup, sandwiching her in his heat.

She could feel the roughness of the calluses on his hands and she liked that. He was real, very real. She took a sip of the coffee, and then another, and then fi-nally just gulped it down, feeling the caffeine sink into her system with a soft, relieved sigh.

"Better?" Keane asked, dipping down a little to look into her eyes. "Yeah," he said, a slice of amusement in his gaze as he answered his own question. "There you are. You don't open for another hour, right?"

She glanced at her clock. "No, but—"

He pulled off her apron. "Love this one, by the way," he said, smiling at the printed words *I Don't Have to Be Good—I'm CUTE!* "And it's true," he said, grabbing her jacket from the hook by the door and wrapping her up in it. He went so far as to zip it up for her and pull her hood up over her head, tucking loose strands of her hair back out of her face.

The feel of his fingers on her temple and jaw, as rough and callused as his palms had been, should've felt intrusive.

Which was just about the opposite of how they felt. "Keane—"

"Shh," he said and took her hand. "I know I've given you absolutely zero reason to trust me but I'm going to ask you to anyway."

Yeah, she wasn't really all that good with trust.

He must have seen that in her gaze because he laughed softly, not at all insulted. "Reading you loud and clear but let's try this," he said. "How about you forget the asshole punk I was in high school for a minute, the one who'd say or do anything to get out of practice without having to talk to anyone, okay? Go off the guy I am today, standing here in front of you. Can you trust that guy?"

This time she hesitated on the other side of the fence, and apparently not above taking advantage of that, Keane said, "Close enough," and tugged her out the door.

Chapter 9

#NoSoupForYou

Willa couldn't believe she was doing this but apparently her feet had seceded from the States of Willa.

"Lock up," Keane told her and waited while she did just that. Then he took her hand again like maybe she was a flight risk.

And she was. "I don't want to talk about it," she said.

He laughed roughly. "Which *it?*"

"Any of the its. *All* of the its." Feeling like a shrew, she sighed and turned to face him. "But as for the one it in particular, the one where you stood me up—"

He opened his mouth to say something and she put her fingers over his mouth. "I'm moving on from that," she said softly. "I'm not a grudge holder—never have been, never will be—so it's silly for me to hang on to my mad over something that you honestly don't even remember—"

Wrapping his fingers around her wrist, he kissed her

fingertips before pulling them from his mouth. "Or intended," he said. "Because, Willa, I can promise you, I *never* intended to hurt you."

Staring into his eyes, she slowly nodded. "I know."

He held her gaze and nodded back, and then he walked her through the courtyard of her building, where he tugged her into Tina's Coffee Bar.

The six-foot-tall mahogany-skinned barista was serving and she winked at Willa. "Been a while since you were in here with a man, honey. Didn't like your last one, but I sure do like this one." She gave Keane a big white smile. "And good morning to you too, sugar. Haven't seen you much this week. How's the Vallejo Street renovation coming?"

"Almost done," Keane said.

Tina gave a big, deep laugh. "You've been saying that for months. Maybe you've grown too attached."

Keane just smiled. "How are the muffins this morning?"

"Out of this world, don't you doubt that for a single second."

Keane grinned at her. "I'll take half a dozen of your finest."

Two minutes later, Willa and Keane were outside. The morning was still gray but their way was lit by the strings of twinkling white lights, casting the cobblestones in black and white bold relief.

She watched Keane take in the two newest Christmas trees, one in front of O'Riley's Pub, the other in front of Reclaimed Woods, both decorated in simple red and gold balls. The only sound around them was the soft trickle of the water flowing from the fountain and some lovelorn crickets mourning the dawn's lack of warmth.

"Legend states that if you make a wish with a true heart, true love will find you," she said.

He met her gaze. "Legend also states that if you put your tooth under your pillow the Tooth Fairy will leave you cash."

She slowed, as always the fountain calling to her to make a wish. Keane slowed too, looking at her with a question.

She searched her pockets for change, but could only come up with a dog treat. "Damn." It was the swear jar's fault, all her spare change always ended up in there.

"What?"

"I wanted to make a wish," she said.

A small smile crossed his face. "You want to make a wish? You've lived here for how long and you've never made one?"

"Oh, I have." She paused. "I like to."

This garnered her a raised brow. "How many times have you wished?"

She bit her lower lip.

"More than once?"

Well, crap. How had they gotten on this subject? "Um . . ."

"More than . . . five?"

"Gee, would you look at the time?" she asked and tried to go but he caught her and brought her back around, his smile now a broad grin.

"Fine," she said. "If you must know, I toss a coin in every time I walk by."

He lost the battle with his laughter and she stared at him. Seriously, he had the best laugh. "It worked for Pru, I'll have you know," she told him. "She wished for true love to find Finn, and then he fell in love with her."

And Willa had been wishing ever since, even knowing how ridiculous and silly it was.

"So . . . you've been wishing for true love for who exactly?" he asked.

She stared at him in dismay. How had she not thought this through? "Me," she admitted, slapping her pockets because surely she had even a penny. "But I intend to fix that right now. I'll just wish for love for someone else."

"Who?" he asked warily.

She narrowed her eyes at his fear. "You. Got any change?"

He laughed. "Absolutely not." Then he pulled a dime from his pocket and held it up. "But how about this. *I'll* wish for you." And on that, he tossed the coin into the water.

Plop.

"There," he said. "Done. Hope it works out for you." He sounded fairly certain that it would and equally certain that it wouldn't be with him.

Which was good to know. Except it was also a little bit not good at all. "So you've never made a wish on true love before?" she asked.

He laughed. "No. That was a first."

"Because . . . you don't believe in true love?"

To his credit, he didn't brush off the question or try to tease his way out of answering. Seeming to understand how much it meant to her, he shrugged. "For some people, yes."

She nodded even as she felt a small slash of disappointment go through her. How silly was that? It wasn't as if love had worked out for her either. But she knew what the real problem was. It was that Keane had been clear about not wanting or needing anything serious in his life and yet here she was, finally feeling ready for just that in hers.

"And you?" he asked.

She stared at the water because it was far easier to talk to the fountain than hold Keane's too-honest gaze. "I've seen bits and pieces of it here and there. I know love's out there."

His eyes were solemn, intense, as he turned her to face him. "But?" he asked quietly. "I'm sensing a pretty big *but* here."

"But sometimes I'm not quite sure it's out there for *me*."

His gaze searched hers. "That seems pretty jaded for someone who wants everyone to believe in the magic of the holidays."

"Christmas has a happy connotation that brings joy and warmth. It comes every year, rain or shine. You can count on it."

"But not on love," he finished for her. His hand came up and he brushed a strand of hair from her temple, his fingers lingering. "I don't think it's always like that,

Willa. For some people, love's real and long-lasting. Forever."

"For some people," she repeated. "But not you? If you believe in love, why don't you believe in it for yourself?"

He shook his head. "I don't feel things deeply. I never have."

She stared at him, dismayed. "You don't really believe that."

"I do."

"But . . . I've seen you with Petunia."

He laughed. "Exactly. You've seen me dump her on you. I'm willing to pay a cat-sitter rather than deal with her."

"When you're at work, yes," she said. "But you've never once asked me to board her overnight when you were home."

"You board overnight?" he asked hopefully.

She laughed and smacked him lightly on the chest. "You know what I mean. You're frustrated by her and yet you still spend the money and time to make sure she gets good care when you're busy."

"Because she's my aunt's cat," he pointed out.

"Which is yet more proof. You're not close to your aunt but you took on her cat for her, without question or qualm."

"Oh, there was qualm," he said. "Buckets and buckets of qualm."

"You bought me muffins," she said softly, undeterred. "You wanted to cheer me up because I was upset."

"No, that was a sheer male knee-jerk attempt to make sure you didn't cry again. As a whole, we'll pretty much do anything to get a woman to stop crying."

"So what are we doing here, if you don't, or can't, feel things, if you don't ever want to find The One. What do you want from me?"

He flashed a wicked grin that made her body quiver hopefully but she snorted. "Right," she said. "'Animal magnetism.'"

"Just because I don't plan on finding The One doesn't mean I'm not interested in The One For Now."

She rolled her eyes. "Whatever. But I still think you're not giving yourself enough credit and you can't change my mind about that."

"What a shock," he murmured beneath his breath but his eyes were amused. Then that amusement faded. "From the outside looking in, I had a very traditional upbringing compared to you. Two parents, two older sisters, all college professors of science, their lives tightly run, everything entered into a planner, put in a neat little compartmentalized box." His smile was short. "But then along came me. I didn't fit in the box. I was wild, noisy, and destructive as hell. I was rough on the entire family and usually got left behind with a caretaker. My own doing," he said with a head shake. "It's not so much that I don't get attached, as I'm not easy to get attached *to*."

Willa's heart gave a hard squeeze. He'd learned too young that even the people who were supposed to un-conditionally love you didn't always—something she knew all too well. Only she'd compensated by going in the opposite direction and loving everything and everyone. "You didn't get a lot of affection," she said softly. "You weren't shown much emotion. That's why you think you don't know how to feel or give it."

"I don't think it," he said. "I know it."

Back in high school, she'd not been aware of any of this. She'd simply set her sights on inviting him to the dance, knowing only that he'd been a solid athlete and also an equally solid student, and that kids and teachers alike had flocked to him.

He'd had an easy smile and a natural confidence that had made him seem impenetrable at the time. Now, looking back on it, she could see that he'd used his charisma as a personal shield and she'd not looked past it.

Which made her just as guilty as everyone else in his life.

He nodded for her to sit on the stone bench she'd personally lined with boughs of holly and little jingle bells weeks ago now. It was early enough that few people came through the courtyard. There was the occasional runner or dog walker, but mostly they had the place to themselves. With the low-lying fog, it felt like they were all alone.

It was incredibly intimate.

They ate muffins in companionable silence for as long as she could stand it, but silence had never been her strong suit. Eventually her curiosity got the best of her. "When Tina said maybe you've grown attached to your place, why did you say not likely?"

"I told you." He shrugged. "I always sell them when I'm finished."

"Because you don't get attached."

"Right."

"But we decided that isn't exactly strictly true," she pointed out.

"No, *you* decided."

She blew out an annoyed sigh.

He didn't ask her to translate the sigh. Clearly it wasn't necessary. Instead, he turned his head and met her gaze. "You say more with silence than any woman I've ever met. Spit it out, Willa, before you choke on it."

Where did she start with alphas . . . "It's your home."

"It won't be a home until someone's living in it."

"You're living in it!"

He smiled at her exasperated tone and ran a finger down her nose. "I annoy you."

"In so, so, *so* many ways," she said on a laugh. "Seriously, you have no idea."

"I have some."

"Is that right?" she asked. "Because I'd think that annoyance is one of those messy emotions you don't bother with."

His eyes darkened. "I bother with some emotions."

"Yeah? Which ones?"

He calmly took the half-eaten muffin out of her hand and dropped it back into the bag.

"I wanted that," she said.

"And I want this." He moved faster than she imagined anyone as big as he was could move. Before she could so much as draw another breath of air, he pulled her hard against him, his hands fisting in her hair, his mouth seeking hers.

The kiss started out gentle, but quickly got serious and not so gentle. His lips parted hers, their tongues touched, and she heard herself moan. His hot mouth left hers and made its way along her jaw, her throat, where he planted openmouthed kisses that made her shiver for more. If she hadn't been sitting, her knees wouldn't have held her up, because he kissed away her annoyance, her good sense, any ability to think, *everything*.

Except her ability to feel.

And oh God, what she felt. She could barely even hold on, she was so dizzy with the hunger ripping through her, but then he pulled back and stared at her, his hair crazy from her fingers, those chocolate eyes fierce and hot, his breathing no more steady than hers.

She pressed her palms to his chest to try and ground herself but she still felt like she was floating on air. "Wha . . . ?" It was all she could manage. Clearly, their chemistry had exploded her brain cells. She shook her head to clear it. "Okay, I stand corrected. There are some emotions you do exceptionally well. Like lust." She paused. He'd been upfront with her, and brutally honest to boot. They weren't going to be each other's The One, but they could have this. He was game.

And in spite of herself, so was she. "Why did you stop?"

He looked at her for a long moment, at first in surprise and then with a slow smile. He knew he'd coaxed her over to the dark side. "We're in the middle of the courtyard," he said.

"We don't have to be." She couldn't believe she said

it but, well, she meant it. She was still plastered up against his big, hard body, emphasis on *hard,* and all she could think about was what he'd feel like without the barriers of their clothing.

But Keane wasn't making a move to take her back to his place.

Or hers.

Instead, he had his hands on her shoulders, holding her away from him. Embarrassed, she started to get up but he held on. "No," she said, "I get it. You're . . . feeling things and you don't like to. Not for your house, not for Petunia, and certainly not for me—"

She broke off with a gasp as he hauled her back into him, right onto his lap this time. One of his big hands palmed her ass to hold her still against an unmistakable bulge of a rock-hard erection.

"See, you're feeling *something,*" she said breathlessly. "So *why* aren't we running for one of our places?"

"Because by the time I got you there, you'll have changed your mind," he said. "You've had a rough morning. I don't want this to be a spur-of-the-moment decision I push you into because of the crazy heat between us. And then there's the work factor. We're both on the clock in a few minutes and, Willa"—he held her gaze—"when we go there, we're going to need more than a few minutes."

At that low, gruff tone, she went damp.

"So," he said firmly. "We're going to sit here enjoying the morning and each other's company."

"But . . ." She lowered her voice to a mere whisper. "We could be doing that naked."

He groaned and dropped his head to her shoulder as part of his anatomy seemed to swell beneath her. "It's not nice to tease."

Who was teasing?

Reading her mind, he laughed soft in his throat and it was sexy as hell. "Talk," he said. "We're going to talk until we both have to go to work."

She blew out a sigh and her gaze snagged on the nearest Christmas tree. "Did you have Christmas trees growing up?"

"Yeah. My parents always hosted the holiday party for their entire department and the decorations had to be perfect. Which meant I could look but not touch."

She turned her head and met his gaze. "Why am I getting the feeling you didn't always do as you were told?"

He laughed again and she felt like she'd won the lottery. "I never did what I was told," he said. "One year I sneaked downstairs in the middle of the night and tried to climb the tree."

"What happened?"

"It fell over on me. Broke all the ornaments and I cut open my chin." He rubbed his jaw, smiling ruefully. "I was a total miscreant. My parents told me I was going to get coal for Christmas that year."

"Did you?"

"No, I got a one-way ticket to my dad's brother's ranch in Texas for the entire winter break, where I shoveled horseshit for three long weeks."

She searched his expression, which was calm and easy. In direct opposition to the erection nudging her butt. "You don't look particularly scarred by that experience," she said.

"My uncle loved to build things. He had all these amazing tools and machinery." He leaned back, one arm along the back of the bench, his fingers playing with the ends of her hair. She wasn't even sure he was aware of doing it.

"It was the first time I'd seen anything like it," he said. "The first time I got to watch someone work with their hands. He had an entire barn filled with antique tools." He smiled. "He gave me one, a vintage level. I still have it. Someday I'll collect others to go with it. I definitely got bitten by the builder bug that winter. Looking back, it's actually one of my best childhood memories." He nudged her shoulder with his. "Now you. Tell me something from one of your past Christmases."

She searched her brain for a happy memory to match his. "My mom gave me a necklace when I was little once," she said. "It had a charm with the letter *W* engraved in gold, with all these little rhinestones outlining the *W*. I loved it." She smiled. "I wore it to school and some mean girl named Britney said it was fake and from a bubble-gum machine. She grabbed it and it broke."

"I hope you punched her in the nose," Keane said.

She bit her lower lip. "I stomped on her foot and made her cry, even though she was right. The necklace was fake. It turned my neck green."

He grinned and she felt the breath catch in her throat as she watched the early-morning light magnify his beautiful smile. "Atta girl," he said.

She laughed a little, finding humor in the bittersweet memory for the first time.

When their coffee and muffins were gone, he stood and pulled her up with him. Her phone was going off and so was his.

"Real life's calling," he said reluctantly.

Right. She had a business to open and he had God knew what to build today, and they both had people depending on them to do their jobs. "Thanks for the muffins," she said and started to walk off.

He caught her.

"We still have unfinished business," he said in that sexy voice with the smile that made her stupid.

"That's nothing new."

He tightened his grip on her hand when she would have pulled free. "I didn't thank you for trusting me enough to tell me about high school."

"I wouldn't take it quite as far as trusting you," she said. "I haven't signed on the dotted line for the trust-you program yet."

"A wise woman." He gave her fingers a meaningful squeeze as he reeled her in and planted a soft but scorching-hot kiss on her mouth. "But I might surprise you."

She watched him walk away and then sank back to the bough-lined bench so hard that the little bells tacked to either side jangled as loudly as her nerves.

"That was interesting."

Willa looked up at Elle. She was wearing form-fitting black trousers, FMP's, and a power-red fitted blazer over a white lace tee, all of which emphasized her curves and general badassery.

"You look amazing," Willa said. "How do you walk in those shoes without killing yourself?"

"No changing the subject. I went to grab a coffee and saw you two pressed up against each other like there'd been some sort of superglue incident."

Well, crap. "Are you sure?" Willa asked. "Because it's pretty foggy this morning and—"

Elle pointed at her. "You know who might buy that? No one. Because that was one smoking-hot kiss. I mean I get it, the man is sex on stilts. But you keep trying to tell us you don't like him like that so imagine my surprise to find you two out here attempting to exchange tonsils."

Oh God. It *had* been smoking hot, incredibly so. In fact, she could still feel the hard, rippling muscles beneath his shirt, the slow and reassuringly steady beat of his heart under the palm of her hand. The way it'd sped up when his mouth had covered hers.

"Not that anyone believes you about not liking him, by the way," Elle said. "When he showed up in Archer's office this morning looking all hot and edgy, needing to kick some serious Ethan ass, I—"

"Wait, what?" Willa asked, sitting up straight. "Keane went to Archer's office?"

Elle went brows up. "He didn't tell you."

"Do I look like he did?"

"No," Elle murmured thoughtfully, tapping a perfectly manicured fingernail to her chin. "Which actually makes him even hotter now."

"For keeping secrets?"

"For caring so much about your safety. That, or he already knows how stubborn and obstinate you are."

Willa shook her head. She couldn't go there right now. "Did anyone else see the kiss?"

Just then, Rory stuck her head out the back door of South Bark. "Okay, not that I'm judging or anything," she called out, "but are you going to stand around all day kissing hot guys who you pretend not to like, or are we going to get some work done?"

"I think it's safe to say someone else saw," Elle said dryly.

Chapter 10

#AllThatAndABagOfChips

Keane went back to Vallejo Street for what should've been a hot shower but he decided cold would be best under the circumstances. He was pretty certain a guy couldn't die from a bad case of needing to be buried balls deep inside a certain strawberry blonde, green-eyed pixie, but he figured the icy shower might ensure it.

It didn't help.

After, he didn't go to either North Beach or the Mission District project, both of which needed his attention. Nor did he hit his desk to unbury himself from paperwork. Instead he got busy on the finish work at the Vallejo Street house—the trim, the floorboards, the hardware for the windows and doors . . . the last of what had to be done before the place could be put on the market.

At first, Pita watched him suspiciously from the open doorway. Then she slowly and deliberately worked her way into the room to bat at a few wood shavings. When she got too close to his planer, he stopped. "Back up, cat. Nothing to see here."

Instead, she sat and stared at him, her tail twitching.

"Suit yourself." When he looked up an hour later, she'd curled up on the wood floor in the sole sunspot and had fallen asleep. He heard the sound of Sass's heels coming down the hallway and looked up as she appeared.

"Bad news," she said.

"We didn't get the permits for the Mission project?"

"Worse," she said.

"There's not really a Santa Claus?"

She didn't laugh. Didn't snort. Didn't ream him out for being an insensitive dumbass. Shit. "What is it?" he asked. "Just tell me."

"It's your great-aunt Sally," she said quietly. "Her doctor's admin called here because you're listed as her next of kin."

This was news to him. "What's wrong?"

"Apparently she needs to go into an assisted-living facility."

"Why, what's wrong with her?" Answers to this question bombarded him. Heart failure. Cancer . . .

"Rheumatoid arthritis," Sass said. "It's acting up and she can't get around like she used to, taking care of an apartment or herself without help. They've got a facility lined up—it's the one she wants, but there's a problem."

"Killing me, Sass," he said, pressing a thumb and a finger into his eye sockets.

"She doesn't have the money, Keane. She needs five grand up front for the first month."

"Tell them they'll have it today," he said.

"You know how many zeroes that is, right? And her insurance won't kick in until month three, so—"

"Tell them they'll have whatever they need, Sass."

"Okay." Her voice was softer now, more gentle. "I realize you're all alpha and manly and won't want to hear this, but I have to say it anyway—this is incredibly generous of you—"

"Is there anything else?"

"Actually, yes," she said, "and for you this is going to be the worst part, so girdle your loins, pull up your big-girl panties, and anything else you have to do to face the music."

"I swear to God, Sass, just tell me all of it or—"

"She can't have a pet at this place," she said quickly. "Not even a goldfish."

Keane turned around and stared at Pita, still sleeping calmly, even sweetly, in that sunspot. He might've been warmed by the sight if it hadn't been for the wrecked box of finishing nails that she'd pulled apart, which lay all around her like the fallen dead.

"Keane?"

Shit. He blew out a breath, dropped his tool belt, and headed to the door. "Text me the address for the place."

"Only if you promise me you're not going over there guns blazing to dump that sweet little cat on them. You'll get Sally kicked out before she's even in there."

Not that he would love nothing more than to dump the antichrist on someone, *anyone,* but even he wasn't that much of a bastard. "Just get me the damn info, including their phone number."

"Why don't you let me handle the transfer," she started, sounding worried. "I'll get someone to help her pack and—"

"I want to see the place and check up on it, okay? She doesn't have any other family who'll give a shit."

She stared at him, eyes suspiciously shiny, and Keane stilled. "What are you doing?"

She tilted her head up and stared at the ceiling, blinking rapidly. "Nothing." But she sniffed and waved a hand back and forth in front of her face.

Oh, Jesus. "You're . . . crying?"

"Well, it's all your fault!" she burst out with. "You're being sweet and it's my time of the month!"

He wasn't equipped for this. "First of all, I'm not even close to sweet. And second, I bought you stuff for that, it's in the hall bathroom."

"See?" she sobbed and tossed up her hands. *"Sweet."*

He tried calling his aunt's cell but she didn't answer. He drove to the facility and checked it out. It was a nice, clean, surprisingly cheerful place. After, he went to his aunt's and found her stressing over the arrangements, so he helped her pack and took her to the facility himself.

He felt like shit leaving her there but she seemed relieved to have it done and clearly wanted him out of her hair, so he went back to work.

At the end of the day his body was demanding food, so he found himself at O'Riley's Pub seeking their famous wings.

And maybe also a Willa sighting.

The pub was one half bar, one half seated dining. The walls were dark wood that gave an old-world feel to the place. Brass lanterns hung from the rafters, and old fence baseboards finished the look, which said antique charm and friendly warmth. And much like the rest of the building, there was holiday décor everywhere. Boughs of holly, strings of twinkling lights, tinsel, and a huge Christmas tree sitting right in the middle of the place.

He wondered if Finn had let Willa loose in here. Seemed likely. Music drifted out of invisible speakers. One wall was all windows that opened to the courtyard. The street view came via a rack of accordion wood-and-glass doors revealing a nice glimpse of Fort Mason Park and the Marina Green down the hill, and the Golden Gate Bridge behind that.

But he paid no attention to any of it. Instead, his gaze went straight to the end of the bar where the O'Riley brothers and their close-knit gang could usually be found.

Willa was in the middle of a huddle with Elle, Pru, Haley, Finn, Archer, and Spence. As he moved closer, he could hear them arguing over several tree toppers sitting on the bar in front of them.

"It's my turn to decide and I think that one's the best," Haley said, her attention on what looked like an intricately woven angel. "Last year was Spence's turn, and I go after Spence."

"No, last year was *Finn's* turn," Spence said, pointing to a ceramic star. "And I go after Finn."

"But it's got to be the dog," Willa said, stroking a stuffed Saint Bernard with holly around his neck. "He's a rescue dog." She caught sight of Keane and gave a quick, genuine smile. "Hey," she said. "What are you doing here?"

Apparently looking for you, he thought, his day suddenly not seeming so shitty.

"We'll have a dart-off," Archer said, back to the topic at hand. "Three teams of two. Haley, Spence, and Willa will each pick one of the rest of us to be on their team. Best team wins choice of tree topper for their captain. Get your asses to the back."

When Archer gave people an order, they obeyed. Everyone got up and headed to the back room where the darts were played.

Elle was right on Archer's heels until he put up a hand to stop her.

Elle went hands on hips. "What have we said about using your words?" she asked him.

"You're not playing," Archer said.

Elle looked around her like she couldn't believe he'd said such a thing. "And since when are you the boss of me?"

Archer pointed to her impossibly high heels. They were black and strappy and revealed her sky blue toenail polish and a silver toe ring. "No one plays darts in sandals," he said.

"Sandals?" She laughed. "Honey, these are *Gucci.*"

"I don't care if they're flip-flops, it's safety before beauty. You need to lose them to play, because I'm not risking your toes, even if you're willing to do so."

"Let me be crystal clear," she said. "*Not* losing the heels."

"Then you're not playing."

"Fine." Elle stuck a finger in his face. "I hope your team gets its ass kicked."

Archer looked unaffected. "Never going to happen."

"You're down a player now," Elle said.

Archer turned to Keane. "You play?"

Yeah, he played. He'd been a champion in his bar crawl days, but he gave a slight shrug. "A little."

Willa stopped in front of Keane, eyes narrowed. "A little or a lot?" she demanded. "Do I want you or Finn?"

"Hey," Finn said. "Standing right here."

Keane never took his gaze off Willa. "You want me," he said with quiet steel.

She flushed to her roots, and he grinned at her.

"I beat all of you just last week," Finn grumbled. "Even Archer."

There were pool tables and two dartboards in the back room. Everyone lined up at the dartboards. Archer and Haley, Spence and Finn, and . . . him and Willa.

Haley was good, and no surprise, Archer was great.

Spence and Finn were both off the charts.

"See?" Finn said to the room.

Willa . . . sucked. There was no other word for it.

"Dammit," she griped when her dart fell off the board.

"I've got you," Keane said and hit a bull's-eye.

Willa pumped a triumphant fist in the air. "Yes!" She threw herself at Keane and when he caught her, she gave him a smacking kiss right on the lips. Grinning, she stepped back. "The Saint Bernard topper it is!"

"There's going to be no living with her now," Finn said. "You all know that, right?"

Archer looked at Keane. "You can aim, you're tough under pressure, and even better yet, you can lie. Tell me you can shoot and you're hired—*Shit*," he muttered, his attention going to the dance floor. Elle was out there, her heels still firmly in place on her feet, dancing with some guy Keane had never seen before. Dirty dancing.

Archer moved toward them and cut in. Elle looked pissed but allowed it. Sparks flew between them and Keane turned to Willa. "Is that something new?"

"Those two?" Willa laughed. "They fight like that whenever they're together."

"Yeah, that's not what I mean."

She looked confused and he grinned. "Never mind," he said. "I'll explain when you're older."

She eyed Archer and Elle again. "They both insist there's nothing going on."

He didn't buy it but it wasn't his business.

Willa inhaled a deep breath. "It's getting late. I should go."

"Dance with me first."

She laughed.

"I'm serious."

Her eyes widened and she sent a startled look to the dance floor. "If you think I suck at darts, you should see me on the dance floor. I'm a really bad dancer."

"So am I."

She rolled her eyes. "Like I'm supposed to believe you're bad at anything."

He flashed a smile. "How will you know unless you give me a shot?"

"That's one thing I really shouldn't do."

"Chicken?" he asked softly.

She narrowed her eyes. "Never." And then she stomped off to the dance floor.

He caught up with her just as the music changed, slowed. Slipping an arm around her waist, he pulled her in, tucking that wayward lock of hair behind her ear.

She shivered.

"Cold?" he asked, running his free hand along her arm, urging it up to slip around his neck.

"No." Her warm breath brushed his jaw as she stepped into him. "I'm starting to think you're a little like that chocolate bar I keep in my fridge for emergencies."

"Irresistible?"

"Bad for me."

He laughed and let the music drift over them, enjoying the feel of her warm, soft body against his, the way she gripped him tight, one hand at the back of his neck, the other at the small of his back, fisted in his shirt. He could feel her heart pounding against his but it wasn't until she trembled that he tipped her head up.

She shook her head at his unasked question. "Okay, maybe you're also a *little* irresistible," she murmured. "It's just that you're always so . . ."

"What?"

"Everything."

He turned his palm up and entwined their fingers together, bringing their joined hands to his mouth as they swayed in sync to the music, her steps unsure and too fast. He matched her steps to his, slowing her down, looking into her eyes.

"You're scared," he realized, not talking about dancing anymore.

"Terrified," she confessed. She wasn't talking about dancing either. "Join me, won't you?"

"There's nothing to fear here, Willa."

"Because we're just two consenting adults who are hugely attracted to one another, and we both know the score. No falling. Just some good, old-fashioned fun." Her huge eyes blinked up at his. "Right?"

"Right," he murmured against her lips. "But you forgot something."

"What's that?"

"You do make me laugh, and I dig that. So yes to the fun, but, Willa, nothing I feel about you is old-fashioned." He ran the tips of his fingers lightly down her back until they came to a stop at the low waistband of her jeans, stroking the bare skin between the hem of her sweater and the denim. Another shudder wracked her and he pulled her even closer to him, their bodies forming an unbroken line from chest to toe.

Closing her eyes, she sighed softly and tipped her face up to his. As he lowered his mouth to hers, she parted her lips for his eagerly. He swallowed her soft moan, rocking her in tune to the music as they kissed. "You do so know how to dance," she accused softly.

His hands traveled up her slim spine. "I know other things too. Like how much I want to touch you."

She laughed nervously. "Keane—"

"Shh," he whispered into her hair. "Later."

Both the street and courtyard doors of the pub were closed to the winter air, but every time someone came in or out, a breeze whisked through, brushing over their heated skin.

When the song ended, Keane tipped Willa's face up to meet his, rasping his thumb over her lower lip. "Thanks for showing me how to dance."

She sank her teeth into the pad of his thumb just hard enough to sting, making him laugh.

She was as dangerous as Pita.

The air around them crackled, much the way it had around Archer and Elle earlier, the heat between them pulsing and ebbing in the crowded pub. But unlike Archer and Elle, Keane knew exactly what it was.

"I really do have to go," Willa said.

"I'll walk you up."

"That's . . ." Her gaze fell to his mouth. "Probably a bad idea."

He had to smile. "There's no doubt." If she wanted him to push her on this issue, she was going to be disappointed. It wasn't his style to push. When they slept together—and God, he really hoped that was going to happen—it would be because she wanted him and she was ready, and not because he talked her into it. So he took her hand and they walked out into the courtyard.

There really was a *whole* lot of Christmas going on out here. The fountain misted softly in the evening chill, lit red and green from the lights.

Old Man Eddie was out here, manning the fire pit. He pulled a sprig of mistletoe from his pocket and tossed it to Willa.

In return, she handed him her leftovers. "Wings," she said. "Extra sauce."

"Thanks, darlin'. I love my lights. Meant a lot that you'd do that for me."

"Anything," Willa said.

And Keane knew she meant it. It was part of what made her special, and different from just about anyone he'd ever known. She really would give a stranger the shirt off her back.

In the stairwell, Keane met her gaze. "You have plans for that mistletoe?"

She smiled but waited until she was at the top of the stairs, turning to walk backward toward her apartment as she flashed him a grin. "Some things a man should find out for himself."

He caught her at her door and pushed her up against it. He had no idea if they were going to push their limits or what, but he wanted her to think of him after he walked away. To that end, he wrapped his fingers around her wrist, the one still holding the sprig of mistletoe, and raised it slowly up the wall until it was above her head, held to the wall by both of them.

Then he lowered his head and brushed her mouth with his. And then—to torture them both—again.

Moaning, she dropped the mistletoe and tugged her hand free to grip the front of his shirt with two fists. She was still holding tight when he lifted his head.

"It's the damn mistletoe," she whispered.

He let out a low laugh. "Babe, it's not the mistletoe."

Chapter 11

#SillyRabbit

Willa dropped her head to Keane's chest and *thunked* it a few times, hoping it would clear her thoughts. Instead, since his chest was hard as concrete, she gave herself a mini concussion. "What am I going to do with you?" she asked.

"I've got a few suggestions."

She lifted her head and took in the heated amusement in his dark gaze. And something else too, something that stole her breath and made it all but impossible to look away. "Keane," she whispered and shifted in closer.

His hands went to her hips and he lowered his head slowly. A sigh shuddered out of her and she closed her eyes as his lips fell on hers. Dropping the mistletoe, she wrapped her arms around his neck, the silky strands of his hair slipping through her fingers.

With a rough sound that came from deep in his chest

he pulled her closer, his hands threading through her hair to change the angle of the kiss, taking it deeper. With one tug he bared her throat and dragged his mouth from hers only to scrape his teeth along her skin.

She gasped in pleasure and need and probably would have slid to the floor in a boneless heap if his muscled thigh hadn't been thrust between hers, both holding her up and creating a heat at her core that made her forget why she wasn't ready for him.

Her body couldn't be *more* ready.

But then he gentled his touch and nuzzled his face in the crook of her neck. Sweet. Tender. And with what sounded like a low chuckle, he pulled back.

She struggled to open her eyes. "Wow," she whispered.

With a soft laugh that turned her on even more, he brushed one last kiss to her temple. "Lock up, Willa. Dream of me."

And she knew she would.

Keane woke up on Sunday to a clanking, clattering that sounded like a flock of birds had gotten into his bedroom and were beating their wings against the window trying to get out.

Sitting straight up in bed, he whipped his head to the window, expecting to see a blood bath.

Instead he saw his shades all out of whack with a suspicious cat-size bulge behind them. Then a black face and searing blue eyes peeked from between two slats. And then four paws.

"Mew."

"So you're stuck," he said.

"Mew."

Shaking his head, he got up and attempted to separate her from the shades. She wasn't having it. In fact, she lost her collective shit.

"This would be a lot easier if you stopped hissing and spitting at me," he said.

Her ears went back and she tried to bite him.

"Do that again and I'll leave you here," he warned.

She switched to a low, continuous growl. When he finally got her loose, she stalked off, head high, tail switching back and forth, pissy to her very core.

Shaking his head, he turned to the shades.

Destroyed.

He searched out his cell phone and called Sass. She didn't pick up so he left a message. "I know it's Sunday, but if you're around, I could use some help. Call me back."

He disconnected and met Pita's still pissy gaze. She'd come back in, probably to remind him that she was an inch from starving to death. "She's not going to call me back," he said.

He tried Mason next. Also went to voice mail. Shit. He fed the heathen and hit the shower. He was halfway through when he felt like he was being watched. He opened his eyes after rinsing off his shampoo and found Pita sitting on the tile just outside the shower, staring him down.

It wasn't often he felt vulnerable, but he had the urge to cup himself. "Problem?" he asked her.

She gave one slow-as-an-owl blink. "Mew."

She didn't sound angry. In fact, she sounded . . . lonely. Seeming to prove that point, she actually took a step into the walk-in shower.

"Watch out," he warned her. "You're not going to like it."

And indeed, when the water hit her square in the face, she slitted her eyes and glared at him as she retreated back to the safety zone. Lifting a paw she began to meticulously wash her face free of the evil water that had dared land on her.

"I told you so," he said and stilled.

I told you so.

It'd been a common refrain of his parents whenever he'd done something they'd considered stupid. And admittedly, he'd done a lot of stupid. Such as when he'd broken his leg in his sophomore year of college and lost his football scholarship.

"Smarts never fail you," his father had said. *"Science never fails you. Being a professor is a job that won't fail you. I told you that you needed a backup plan."*

"Holy shit," Keane muttered, shaking my head. "I just opened my mouth and my father came out."

Pita sneezed but it sounded like a derisive snort.

A little traumatized, Keane got dressed and then stood there in his foyer, staring down at Pita, who'd followed him to the door. "I have to go to the North Beach job to check on yesterday's progress," he said. "Wait here and don't destroy anything."

She gave him one blink, slow as an owl.

"Shit." She was totally going to destroy something.

Maybe several somethings. "Listen . . ." He crouched low to look her in the eyes. "I can't take you to kitty day care today; it's closed. And Sass and Mason are ignoring me because it's Sunday."

She just kept staring at him. Didn't even blink.

"Shit," he said again and pointed to the carrier. "Your only other option is to come with me but that's a bad idea—"

Before he'd finished the sentence, Pita had walked right into her carrier without fuss or a single hiss.

Shocked, he zipped up the bright pink bedazzled case and met the blue eyes through the mesh. "Look, I know you're unhappy about all of this, but we're stuck with each other for now."

She did more of that no-blinking thing.

"How about this," he said. "I promise to do the best I can, and in return you promise to stop taking a dump in my shoes."

Pita turned her back on him.

"Okay then. Good talk." He carried her out the door and to the truck, driving her to North Beach. When he parked on the street in front of a café two doors down from his building, a group of women stood on the sidewalk talking to each other at ninety miles an hour.

". . . Just wait until you bite into their warm cinnamon buns . . ."

". . . Couldn't have found a better place to have your thirtieth-birthday girls' bash . . ."

". . . Ohmigod don't turn around, but there's a hot guy at your six and he's carrying his cat in a pink bedazzled carrier—I said *don't turn around!*"

But they'd all turned around. Six of them, smiling at him.

Nodding at them set off an avalanche of waves and more smiles as he walked to his place.

"Now those are buns I could sink my teeth into," one of them murmured.

Keane resisted running up the stairs. Entering the house, he came to a shocked stop as Mason and Sass jumped apart, looking tousled and guilty.

They all stared at each other for an awkward beat and then Mason got very busy with his nail gun while Sass began thumbing through her work iPad as if it were on fire.

"What the fuck," Keane said.

Mason accidentally discharged a nail into the floor.

Sass went hands on hips and took the Defensive Highway. "Hey, what we do behind your back is *our* business."

"True," Keane said.

"And we never let it affect work," she said. "Never."

"Okay," he said.

"I wouldn't," Sass added, softer now. "I love this job."

"Sass," Keane said on a low laugh. "I don't care what the two of you do on your off hours, as long as I don't have to see it. What I meant by what the fuck is . . . what the fuck are you two doing here working but not picking up your phones?"

"You said last week all hands on deck until we finish," Mason said, apparently finding his voice. "Whelp, all hands are on deck."

"Yes, but I called you," Keane said with what he thought was remarkable patience. "Both of you. No one answered."

"Because you wanted a cat-sitter," Sass said. "And much as I do love this job, evil-cat sitting is not in my job description."

"Or mine," Mason said.

Keane stared at them. "You didn't know that's what I wanted."

Sass shifted her gaze pointedly at the cat carrier he was still carrying. "You don't hire stupid people."

He blew out a breath and set the cat carrier down.

"What are you doing?" Mason asked, eyes wide with horror. "Don't let it out."

"It's a she."

"*It* will attack me," Mason said.

Sass rolled her eyes. "Mas here thinks the cat is Evil Incarnate."

"*It is,*" Mason said.

"She rubs against his legs," Sass said. "He's convinced that the cat is trying to establish that she's the dominant in their relationship."

"She left me *half* a field mouse," Mason said.

"She's noticed your lack of hunting skills and inability to feed yourself," Sass told him. "She's trying to show you how to hunt. It's a compliment."

"*Half* a field mouse," Mason repeated.

Keane shook his head and unzipped the carrier. "No one leave any doors open," he directed. Then he got Pita a bowl of water and food, and finally did his walk-through.

Then he left Mason a list of things he wanted done and he and Pita headed back to Vallejo Street, where he strapped on his tool belt. The favorite part of any of the jobs he took on was always the woodwork. Carpentry had been his first love and it was still the thing that fulfilled him the most. On this job, he'd really gone old-school in the traditional Victorian sense, bringing back the original oak plank flooring and ornate wood trim, which was what he was working on today. Sanding and varnishing. The trim would go next.

An hour into it, he paused to pull out his vibrating phone. It was Sally finally calling him back with a FaceTime call. He answered and was treated to . . . a huge mouth. The skin around the mouth was puckered with age. The lips had been painted in red lipstick.

"Hello?" the mouth said. "Keane? Goddamn new-fangled phone," she muttered. "Can't hear a damn thing."

"Aunt Sally, I'm here," he told her. "You settled in okay?"

"*What?*"

"You don't have to hold the phone up to your mouth like that. You can just talk normal—"

"Huh? What's that? *Speak up, boy.*"

Keane sighed. "I said you can just talk normal."

"I am talking normal," she yelled, still holding the phone so close to her face that only her mouth showed. "I'm calling to talk to Petunia. Put her on the line."

"You want to talk to the cat."

"Do you have hearing problems? That's what I said. Now put her on for me."

"Sure." Keane moved into the kitchen, because that's where Pita hung out most, near her food bowl. The food bowl was empty.

No sign of Pita.

"Hang on," he said into the phone and then pressed it against his thigh to block video and sound. "Pita," he called. "Pita, come." He felt ridiculous. Cats didn't "come." Neither did the antichrist. "Cat," he said. "Petunia?"

Still nothing. He strode through the house and stilled in the dining room. Oh fuck, he thought, staring down at the hole in the floor. The air duct, without its grate, because it was on a sawhorse with some trim drying after being lacquered.

He dropped to his knees and peered down the open vent, but couldn't see a thing. "Pita?"

There was a loaded silence, then a rustling, followed by a miserable-sounding "mew."

His heart stopped. "Okay, not funny. Get your fuzzy, furry ass back up here," he demanded, still holding the phone tight to his thigh.

This time the "mew" sounded fainter, like she'd moved further into the vent. He brought the phone back up. "Hey, Aunt Sally, I've got another call I have to take. I'll call you right back, okay?"

"Is there something wrong?" the red, wrinkled lips asked.

"No worries," Keane assured her and hung up. He retrieved Pita's food bowl, refilled it, and then jangled the bowl above the open vent. "Hear that?" he called down the hole. "That's your food. Come and get it."

Nothing. Not even a rustle this time.

"Christ." Keane got to his feet and strode into the next room, where he knew the venting system led to. He tore off that grate, flicked on the flashlight app from his phone and peered into the hole. "Pita?"

More nothing.

"Dammit, cat." He turned off the flashlight and rubbed his temples. At a complete loss, he did the first thing that came to mind. He called the only person he knew that the cat actually liked.

"Hello?" Willa answered, sounding soft and sleepy.

"I woke you. I'm sorry."

"Keane?"

"Yeah," he said. "I've got a problem."

"Still?" She yawned. "Aren't you supposed to call a doctor if that conditions persists for more than four hours?"

He froze for a beat and then laughed. Pinching the bridge of his nose, he shook his head. "Not that kind of problem." He paused. "And I'm pretty sure there's no guy on earth who'd actually go to a doctor for that."

"Yet another reason why men die younger than women. What's the problem, Keane?"

"Pita."

"You have her today too?"

"Yeah. My aunt had to go into a rehab facility with assisted living. While I was working, Pita went down a vent and either joined a rat compound or she's just enjoying fucking with me like every other female I know, but I can no longer see or hear her."

Silence.

"Willa?"

"Your aunt had to go into a home?"

Hadn't he just said so? "Yes, and—"

"And you're holding on to Pita for her? Indefinitely?"

"Well I *was*," he said. "Now I'm pretty sure I've accidentally killed her."

"I'll be right there."

Chapter 12

#WheresTheBeef

After Keane's call, Willa slipped out of bed for the second time that morning. The first had been an hour ago at the desperate knock at her door.

That had been Kylie. "Remember Vinnie?" her friend had asked, pulling the tiny puppy from her pocket. "My so-called pal never came back for him, can you believe it?" She kissed the top of the puppy's head, which was bigger than his body. "I think she abandoned him, *and* me . . ."

Oh boy. Willa looked into Vinnie's warm puppy eyes and felt herself melt. "So what's your plan?"

"I'm keeping him," Kylie said firmly. "He'll be a Christmas present to myself. My problem is that I have to go to work. Is there any way you can help me today?"

Which was how Willa had ended up back in bed cuddling a three-week-old puppy until Keane had called.

Now she scooped Vinnie up, cuddling the tiny handful close. "We've got a search-and-rescue situation, buddy. You up for it?"

Vinnie yawned bigger than his entire body, which wasn't all that hard. Juggling the little guy, Willa ran around handling her morning routine as quickly as possible. She had to set Vinnie down to brush her teeth, which turned out to be a mistake because when she turned back around, she found him sitting proudly next to what looked like a pile of fresh Play-Doh. Except it wasn't so much fresh as incredibly stinky.

He was looking at her as if to say, *It wasn't me, nor was it me who just chewed the shoelace off your shoes. I have no idea who'd do something like that, especially given the poo situation; that'd just be mean.*

With a sigh, she cleaned up the mess and then pulled sweats on over her pj's. She grabbed the baby bottle Kylie had left with her for Vinnie, who got very excited at the sight of it and began panting happily, short little legs bicycling in the air as if he could fly to the bottle.

"In a sec," she promised. She grabbed her bag and a jacket and ran out the door, ordering an Uber on her cell as she waited for the elevator.

The car ride was a luxury she couldn't quite afford but it was pouring rain and she had Vinnie, and Keane had sounded . . .

Vulnerable.

She'd have gone for that alone because . . . well, curiosity had killed the cat and all. But it wasn't just nosiness that had her hurrying.

She cared about Petunia, and more than that, she cared about him.

"Not good," she told the puppy as he finished his bottle, tucking him into her sweatshirt beneath her jacket to keep him warm. "Not good at all."

Sticking his head out the collar of her sweatshirt, Vinnie licked her chin. His eyes, bigger than his head, were warm and happy as he stared up at her in adoration.

"Okay, so here's how we're going to play this," she said. "When we get there, we're not, repeat *not,* going to get attached to the hot, sexy guy that lives there, okay? It's no use getting attached to someone who isn't going to get attached back."

"Then why go to his house this early if you're not going to get attached?" the Uber driver asked. "Didn't your mother teach you better than that?"

"Hey, no eavesdropping," she said. "Or judging."

"How much you like this guy?" he asked, his gaze scanning her clothes from his rearview mirror. "Because maybe you want to dress nicer."

Said the guy in a grungy gray T-shirt and hair so wild and crazy it touched the roof of his car. "These are my favorite sweats," she said.

"But they're not getting-laid sweats. They're more like . . . birth control sweats."

She looked down at herself as they stopped in front of Keane's building. Good thing she wasn't worried about getting laid.

Wait . . . was she? Well, too late to worry about it now.

"Leave me a good review?" the driver asked as she got out.

Willa sighed. "Sure."

Keane had barely refrained from tearing down the wall—the *new* wall—between the living room and the dining room to get to Pita when he heard Willa's knock.

She stood there in the pouring rain, hood on her parka up.

"Hey," she said, clearly just out of bed and looking sexy adorable. "S&R at your service."

He knew how hard she worked, and that today was probably a rare day off for her, and yet she'd come when he'd called. Okay, so she was there for the cat and not him, but still, he felt pretty wowed by that.

By her.

It didn't happen often in his world, help freely given like this with nothing expected in return, nothing to be held over his head later. And that meant a lot.

He pulled her inside, getting her out of the rain, which was dripping off her.

"You're in a tool belt," she said, staring at it.

"Yeah." Was he mistaken or had her eyes dilated. "Why?"

She wet her lips and stared at the tool belt some more. "No reason."

He laughed softly. "You like the tool belt?"

She flushed. "Well, it's a cliché for a damn reason. They're sort of . . . sexy."

"Good to know," he said, biting back his smile. "And thanks for coming."

Willa pushed her hood back and met his gaze, her eyes heavy-lidded from what he assumed was sleep. Her silky hair was more than a little wild, flopping into her eyes, clinging to her jaw. He slid the jacket off of her in the hopes of keeping her dry. This left her in sweat bottoms that said *SWAT* up one thigh, rain boots, and a snug long-sleeved hoodie that clung to her curves and told him she wasn't wearing a bra.

His mouth went dry.

From the hoodie pocket a little puppy head poked out. *"Ruff!"* he squeaked out so hard that his huge ears quivered.

"Vinnie's back," she said of the palm-sized dog. "I'm babysitting." She looked around. "Wow. This place is seriously just . . . *wow*." She turned in a slow circle. "I meant to ask you, the molding—is that original woodwork?"

"Original and restored."

"Gorgeous," she said, walking through, her voice low and reverent. "Seriously, if this was my home, I'd never leave it."

Uncomfortable with the praise and yet feeling his chest swell with pride, he didn't say anything. But it was his fantasy home too.

"And you're really going to flip it?" she asked, meeting his gaze.

He shrugged. "That's the plan. I sell everything I renovate. It's my income."

"Right." She nodded. "You don't get attached to things, I get it. So where can I put Vinnie while we search for Petunia?"

He drew a deep breath and walked her into the kitchen, the leather of his tool belt creaking as he moved, although he was pretty sure she wasn't finding that so sexy at the moment.

She set Vinnie up in the deep laundry sink, layering it with a soft blanket and then setting his special dog bed in there—a tissue box—with his water and a few toys. "Stay here and be a good boy," she said. "And I'll give you a treat."

"Does that apply to all the males in the room?" Keane asked.

She sent him a long look.

Okay, so no. Shaking his head at himself for even wishing for things that weren't for him, he turned and walked into the dining room. "Here," he said, crouching low at the vent. "She went in here."

Willa eyed the air duct. "Where does it lead?"

"The den. I pulled the vent cover from that one too but she wouldn't come out." He wasn't a guy who panicked. Ever. But he felt a knot in the center of his chest and was pretty sure he was pretty close to panic now.

"Chances are that she can't back out," Willa said. "She's a little . . . *husky*." She whispered this last word, as if Pita could not only hear them but also understand English. "Which direction does the vent go?"

He pointed to the left. "The next room over."

Willa moved to the wall between them and put her ear to it. "Petunia!" she called out and stilled, listening.

There came a very faint "mew."

"Shit," Keane said. "That's it." He rose to his feet and left the room, grabbing his hatchet from his large job tool box. He moved back to where he'd left Willa. "Stand back."

She turned and looked at him, her eyes going wide. "What the hell are you going to do with that?"

Wasn't it obvious? "Tear the wall down."

"Wow," she said, and this time she *definitely* wasn't impressed. "Hold off a second there, Paul Bunyan." She went back to the second vent. Down on her hands and knees, she once again called out to Pita. "Petunia? I know you can't turn around and go back, and that you're in the dark and probably very unhappy about all of that, but you have to push forward, okay? You've got to come to me or the Big Bad Wolf here is going to huff and puff and chop this whole place down. And you should know, he's going to rip into some beautiful molding and break my heart."

"Mew."

"That's it," she cooed, still on her hands and knees, her pert ass up in the air, her sweats stretched tight across her cheeks. "Come to me, baby."

He groaned. "Killing me."

Still in position, in fact one of his very favorite positions, she craned her neck and looked at him. "I'm trying to save your wall here."

"Carry on," he said, his voice an octave lower than before.

She stared at his mouth for a beat, swallowed hard, and then turned back to her task. "Petunia?"

Nothing.

Keane shifted closer and Willa pointed at him. "Don't you even think about touching that wall."

His sexy tyrant.

"I mean it," she said.

He had to laugh. "I hate to break this to you, Willa, but you've finally met someone as stubborn and obstinate as you. Pita's not coming out of there, not even for your sweet nothings because—"

Because nothing. There was a rustling and then the saddest looking lump of filthy fur stuck her head out of the duct, and Keane nearly dropped to his knees in relief. "I can't believe she came out of there at just the sound of your voice."

"I'm good but not that good," Willa said as Pita snatched something from her palm and ate it like she'd been gone for five days without food instead of an hour. "It's a pupperoni treat. Works every time. Aw," she said to the dirty cat. "You poor baby. That must have been so traumatic for you."

"Hugely," Keane said, swiping his brow. "You should hold me."

She laughed and he found himself smiling at her like an idiot. "You always carry pupperoni treats in your pocket?"

"Always," she said and sat on the floor with Pita, not looking at all bothered by the fact that she was now filthy too. From another pocket she pulled out a comb and proceeded to use it to get most of the dirt and dust off the cat.

"I'm not even going to ask what else you carry on you at all times," he said, moving close, crouching at her side to stare into the cat's half-closed-in-ecstasy eyes. "You've put her in a trance."

"Most cats get a little hypnotized with pleasure when you comb them," she said and smiled. "Actually most females."

"Huh. Now that's one thing about your kind that I didn't know."

"You think that's the only thing?" she asked with just enough irony in her voice to have him taking a longer look at her.

"You have something you want me to know?" he asked.

"Absolutely not." But she blushed a gorgeous color of red and he had to admit to being more than a little curious.

Apparently having had enough of the pampering, Pita climbed out of Willa's lap.

"Hold up," he said to the cat. He called Sally back and pointed the FaceTime call toward Pita.

Sally talked baby talk and the cat stopped and stared unblinking into the camera, listening intently.

After, Sally thanked Keane and disconnected. Pita stalked off, tail and head high.

"That was sweet of you," Willa said.

"That's me, a real sweetheart. And you're welcome, princess," he called to Pita's retreating figure. Grabbing Willa's hand, he pulled her upright.

Her hands went to his chest, but instead of using him to straighten herself, she held on, sliding her hands up and around his neck, rocking against him in the process.

"That thing is happening again," she whispered.

Yeah. It most definitely was. "That 'thing' likes you," he said. "A lot."

She snorted. "I didn't mean that. Although"—she pressed into him some more, wriggling her hips not so subtly against his erection—"I definitely noticed."

"Hard not to."

She snorted again at that but curious as hell, he had to ask. "So what *did* you mean?"

She bit her lower lip and got very busy staring at his shirt. He slid a hand up her back and into her hair, tugging until she looked up at him.

Her gaze locked on his mouth.

"I meant that thing where I want to do things to you," she said.

He smiled. "Not seeing the problem here, babe."

She shook her head and went to pull away. "I can't stay. Big day. It's the Santa Extravaganza at the shop."

"I thought you weren't working today."

"I'm not. My employees handle this event for me; they always do. I'm just setting up and making sure everything looks good."

He caught her and when she tensed, he very gently pulled her back in, giving her plenty of room to escape if she really wanted. "So I do scare you."

"No." She shook her head. "The only things I'm scared of are creepy crawlies and Santa Claus. Which is why I have my girls handle Santa Extravaganza for me."

He paused. "Okay, we're going to circle back to that," he said, "but first, if you're not scared of me, why are we . . . 'not ready' again?"

She gave a small smile that held more than a few secrets. "Maybe I'm just . . . cautious."

Smart woman, he had to admit. "And the Santa Claus fear?"

"How are we supposed to trust a full-grown man who wants little kids to sit on his lap and whisper their deepest secrets?" she quipped.

"But you love Christmas."

"Christmas, yes. Santa, not so much."

"So why do the Santa Extravaganza then?" he asked.

She shrugged as if uncomfortable with this subject. "It's a huge moneymaker and I give half the profits to the SPCA. They need the dough." She headed to the door, scooping up Vinnie on her way out. She gave the tiniest dog on the planet a kiss on his face that made Keane feel envious as hell, and walked out the door.

Chapter 13

#KeepCalmAndBeMerry

At the end of the day, Keane found Pita napping . . . on his pillow. He started to remove her but she flattened herself, becoming five-hundred-plus pounds, and he blew out a breath because they both knew arguing with her was a waste of time. And in any case, she'd had a rough day and he understood rough days. "I'm going out for a little bit," he told her. "And while I'm gone you're not going to destroy a damn thing, right?"

She yawned, stood, plumped up his pillow with her two front paws like she was making biscuits, and then plopped back down and closed her eyes.

"Behave," he said firmly.

She met his gaze, her own serene, and he was pretty sure he'd just made a deal with the devil.

Thinking *fuck it,* he headed toward O'Riley's. Sure, there were fifty places to get dinner between his place and the pub, maybe even more than fifty, but there was never any question of where he'd end up after work.

He wanted to see Willa.

From the beginning he'd known he was fascinated by her, but he hadn't realized it would become so much more than a physical attraction.

He still had absolutely zero idea how to process that.

It was no longer raining, but the air was frigid. Shoving his hands in his jacket pockets, he lowered his head against the wind. Entering the building through the courtyard, he stopped by the fountain when Old Man Eddie stepped out of the alley.

Eddie was at least eighty, and that was being kind—something time hadn't been to him. He had Wild Man of Borneo shock white hair and in spite of the cold air, wore board shorts and a Grateful Dead sweatshirt that looked as if he'd been wearing it since the seventies.

"So you're Willa's now," the guy said. "Right?"

Keane gave him a closer look. "Not sure how that's any of your business."

The guy beamed. "Good answer, man. And I like that you didn't deny it. Our Willa, she's had a rough go of things. But she's picked herself up by the bootstraps and made something of herself, so she deserves only the best. Are you the best?"

"Rough *how?*"

Eddie simply smiled and patted him on the arm. "Yeah. You'll do." And then he turned and walked away.

"Rough how?" Keane asked again.

But Eddie had vanished.

Keane let out a long, slow breath. As he knew all too well, the past was the past, but it still killed him to think about Willa as a young kid, on her own.

At the fountain, a woman was searching her pockets for something. She was early twenties and looked distressed as she whirled around, eyes narrowed.

He realized it was Haley, Willa's optometrist friend.

"Lose something?" he asked.

"No. Well, yes," she corrected. "I wanted to make a stupid wish on the stupid legend but I can't find any stupid coins . . ." She sat on the stone ledge and pulled off her shoe, shaking it. When nothing came out, she sighed. "Damn. I always have a least a penny in there."

He pulled a quarter from his pocket. "Here."

"Oh, no, I couldn't—"

"Take it," he said, dropping it in her hand. "For your 'stupid' wish on the 'stupid' legend."

She laughed. "You're making fun but it really is stupid. And yet here I am . . ." She tossed up her hands. "It's just that it worked for Pru and it appears to have worked for Willa." She gave him a long look making him realize she meant him.

He shook his head. "We're not—"

"Oh no." She pointed at him. "Don't ruin my hope! I mean it's Willa. She pours herself into taking care of everyone, the kids she employs, the animals, her friends." She smiled a little. "Well I don't have to tell you; you know firsthand."

He absolutely did. Willa had taken on Pita for him when she had less than zero reason to like him. She'd taken him on as a friend when he wasn't sure he deserved it.

"She deserves love," Haley said. "She gives one hundred percent to everyone and everything but herself so we all knew it was going to be something big when she fell. Someone who really knocked her off her feet." She smiled. "You've got the big down anyway."

"I'm not sure it's what you think," he said quietly.

"Yeah, well, nothing ever is." She turned back to the water. "If you'll excuse me."

"Sure," he said and left her to her privacy.

The pub was packed. Lights twinkled above all the laughter and voices and "Santa Looked a Lot Like Daddy" was busting out of hidden speakers.

And speaking of Santa, he was sitting at the bar calm as you please, tossing back a shot of something.

Keane made his way to the far right end of the bar, where Willa sat with Elle, Spence, and Archer. There was a row of empty glasses and a pitcher of eggnog in front of them. Elle and Spence were deep in discussion about Spence's workout routine.

"You have to eat healthy more than once to get in shape," he said to Elle.

"Cruel and unfair," she answered and jabbed a finger at Archer, who was shoving some chili fries into his mouth. "Then explain *him*."

Archer swiveled his gaze Elle's way and swallowed a huge bite. "What?"

Elle made a noise of disgust. "You eat like you're afraid it's going out of style and yet you never gain a single ounce of fat."

Archer gave a slow smile. "Genetics, babe. I was born this way."

Elle rolled her eyes so hard that Keane was surprised they didn't fall right out of her head. Shifting past all of them, he headed toward Willa. No longer in sweats, she wore a black skirt, tights, boots, and the brightest red Christmas sweater he'd ever seen. Her gaze was glued to Santa in the middle of the bar and Keane would've sworn she was twitching. He purposely maneuvered to block her view of the guy. "Hey."

"Hey." Her smile didn't quite meet her eyes. "Be right back," she said and, slipping off her stool, headed into the back.

Keane looked at Elle, who was also watching Willa go, her eyes solemn and concerned. "I know she's not a Santa fan," he said. "But what am I missing?"

"A lot," Elle said but didn't further enlighten him.

And he knew she wouldn't. Elle could keep state secrets safe. He looked at Spence, who seemed sympathetic but he shook his head. Archer might as well have been a brick wall, so Keane turned to Haley, who'd just come in, apparently having made her wish.

She grimaced.

"Tell me," he said.

"Her mom dated a drunk Santa who chased her around the house wanting her to sit on his lap. Back then they called it funny for a grown-ass man to terrorize a little girl."

"And now they call it a fucking felony," Keane said grimly.

Elle and Archer both turned to look at him with a new appraisal—and approval—in their gazes. But they still weren't talking.

And he got that. Good friends stood at each other's backs unfailingly. He was grateful Willa had that. After how her childhood had gone, she needed that.

But he wanted in her inner circle and he wanted that shockingly badly. He made his way down the bar. "Hey," he said, tapping Santa on the shoulder.

Santa turned to face him with the slow care of the very inebriated. "Whadda want?"

"There's free drinks down on Second Street for Santas," Keane said.

The guy's eyes brightened. "Yeah?" He got to his feet, weaving a little. "Thanks, man."

When Santa headed for the door, Keane followed the path Willa had taken. The hallway ended at the kitchen. There were a couple of other doors as well. Offices, he assumed. The bathroom door was shut so he waited there, holding up the wall and contemplating the utter silence on the other side of the door. After another few minutes went by, he pushed off the wall and knocked. "Willa."

Nothing.

It wasn't the first time today that one of the females in his life has refused to speak to him but something didn't feel right. "I'm coming in," he warned and opened the door.

The bathroom had two stalls, a sink, and was pleasantly clean.

And empty.

The window was wide open to the night, the cold air rushing in.

She'd gone out the window.

He strode across the room and stuck his head and shoulders out, taking in the corner of the courtyard and the fire escape only a few feet away. Craning his neck, he looked up and saw a quick glimpse of a slim foot as it vanished over the edge of the roof.

Five stories up.

"Shit," he said, his vision wavering. "Why is it always something high up?" Muttering some more, he pushed himself through the window, bashing his shoulders against the casing as he squeezed through. *Squeeze* being the operative word.

Also he hadn't thought ahead to the landing problem coming out headfirst, so there was an awkward moment when he nearly took a dive out face-first before he managed to right himself.

He stared at the damn fire escape and then rattled it. It held and he blew out a breath. "You've fucking lost it," he told himself as he began to climb.

He passed the second floor and began to sweat. He was outright shaking as he counted each story off to himself to keep his sanity. "Three." He held his breath and kept going. "Four."

Finally, level with the roof, he made the mistake of looking down. "Fuck. Five. *Fuck.*" He had to force himself up and over the ledge, and flopped gracelessly to the rooftop.

Chapter 14

#HoHoHo

Willa turned her head at the sound of a body hitting the rooftop, wide-eyed at the sight of Keane flat on his back like the bones in his legs had just dissolved.

"Keane?" she asked in disbelief.

He didn't move, just lay there with his eyes closed, breathing erratically. "Yeah?"

She'd been sitting here alone contemplating her life and watching the occasional glimpses of the moon through the slivers of clouds streaking across the midnight black sky. The moonlight did strange things to the world, leeching out the color so that everything seemed like nothing more than a web of shadows cast in silver. Maybe she'd hit her head when she'd taken a header out of the bathroom window.

Stupid panic.

But then again, she'd rarely thought clearly while

operating under high stress. And it seemed at the moment, she wasn't the only one.

Keane finally spoke again. "What the hell?"

"What the hell what?"

"What the hell are we doing on the damn rooftop?"

"I come up here when I want to be alone," she said, emphasis on *alone*. But then she took in the sheen of perspiration on his face, the way his chest was rising and falling like he'd just run a marathon. "Are you afraid of heights?"

"No," he said, still not moving a single inch.

"No?" Her gaze was glued to his lips, the ones she wanted hers on again now that she was thinking about it.

"No, I'm not afraid of heights." He paused. "I'm terrified of them."

This ripped a laugh right out of her. Her own troubles momentarily forgotten, she leaned over his big, long, tough body, the one she dreamed about at night. Every night. "And you still came all the way up here to save me?"

"At the moment, I'm the one that needs saving. Pretty sure I'm going to die of lack of oxygen."

Still leaning over him, she lowered herself until she nearly-but-not-quite touched him from head to toe. "Don't worry, I know CPR."

He kept his eyes closed but his mouth curved. "You're teasing me. And I'd make you pay for that but I can't because seriously, *dying* here."

Keane both felt and heard her laugh at him as she kissed one corner of his mouth.

"Take it from me," she whispered. "When facing your worst fears, all you need is something else to concentrate on." Then she kissed the other side of his mouth.

He liked where this was going. "Like a distraction," he said.

"Exactly."

He opened his eyes. "I like the sound of that," he said, knowing the logic was more than a little faulty but unable to concentrate with all sorts of dirty, wicked scenarios of how they might "distract" each other playing through his mind. "Maybe I've already died and gone to heaven."

She lifted her head with a smile. "You think this is heaven?"

"You're touching and kissing me," he said. "So yeah. I think this is heaven."

He felt the brush of her hair on his face and then her teeth sank into his earlobe, making him groan. The dilemma—let her continue, or stop her before they took this where she hadn't intended to go . . . ? Before he could decide, her hot, sexy mouth made its way back to his and her hands slipped under his shirt, landing on his abs, her fingers spreading wide.

"You're hard," she whispered against his lips. "Everywhere."

True story.

Her fingers danced up, up, up, teasing his nipples for a beat before heading southward, and he stopped breathing.

She shifted and then jumpstarted his heart by straddling him.

"Willa," he said but she was kissing her way down his throat and he was having trouble drawing air into his lungs. Fisting his hands in her hair, he tugged her face up so he could look into her eyes. "Willa—"

"That's my name," she agreed and bit his lower lip, tugging a little bit so that he mindlessly rocked his hips up into hers.

Jesus. He sat up and caught ahold of her hips, tightening his grip to keep her still. "What are we doing?"

"Oh, sorry, I thought you knew." She took his hands in hers and brought them up to her breasts. "Any further questions?"

She filled his palms perfectly, her nipples pressing through layers of clothing for his attention. Yeah. He was most definitely in heaven.

"I'm ready now," she said softly.

She had his full attention and he searched her gaze. For the first time he could see her expression clearly and it was filled with heat and need and banked anger.

She was looking to defuse that anger, on him. And he was okay with that. More than. She needed him and God knew he needed her. "Come here," he said, nudging her even closer, his hands taking over, cupping her breasts, his thumbs rasping over her tight nipples as she let her head fall back, a gasp escaping her.

"More," she demanded.

"We're outside, Willa, on the roof. Anyone could come up—"

"No," she said against his mouth, "that fire escape's nearly a hundred years old. No one'll use that rackety old thing but me and the gang, and they're all in the pub."

His life flashed before his eyes again. "You mean I could've died on that thing? Is that what you're telling me?"

"You're in heaven, remember?" Her hands were on the buttons of his Levi's, popping them open one at a time.

And he was rapidly losing the ability to think rationally. "What if someone uses the inside stairs access?" he asked.

She shoved his jeans and knit boxers out of her way and wrapped her fingers around him so that his eyes crossed with lust.

"Those stairs are noisy as hell," she murmured. "We'll hear anyone coming a mile away." She tipped her head down to watch what she was doing to him.

He looked too and at the sight of her hands on him, he groaned, not recognizing his own guttural voice when he spoke. "Willa, be sure—"

"Oh, I'm sure." Her own voice was soft and husky, sounding more than a little breathless now too. "But if you're worried, you could work faster."

He let out a low laugh—which was a first, laughing with his personal favorite body part in a woman's hands. "Fast isn't my style."

"It probably should be tonight—" She broke off on a breathy gasp when he unzipped her bright red sweater and nudged it off her shoulders, letting it catch on her elbows, pinning her arms to her sides. While she became preoccupied with freeing herself, he happily realized she wore only a bra beneath, a sexy, lacy, mouthwateringly sheer number. He tugged the cups down, and not wanting her to get cold, cupped one bared breast while he sucked the other into his mouth.

A shuddery sigh escaped her and she cupped his head, holding him to her like she was afraid he might try to escape.

Not a chance. "How much did you have to drink tonight?" he asked.

She thought about that for a minute. "Enough to know I want this, but not too much that I'll have to kill you in the morning."

He stared back but who was he kidding, that totally worked for him. Sliding his hands up her skirt, he palmed her ass. "You're wearing too many clothes."

She laughed breathlessly as fingers wriggled their way beneath her tights and panties, where he found her hot and wet, very wet. He spent a glorious moment teasing panting little whimpers out of her while her hips oscillated against his touch and her nails dug into his biceps. "You like this."

She moaned something inaudible but he got the gist. *More.*

With one arm banded low on her back, his mouth busy at her breasts, his fingers stroked her in the rhythm she wanted. Using her body as his compass, he rose up and swallowed her cries as she came for him, her body shuddering in his arms.

Brushing his lips over her sweaty temple, he held on to her, stroking her back until she finally lifted her head. "Not exactly how I saw my evening going," she said, still a little breathless as she slumped against him.

"Not sure who could've foreseen an orgasm on the roof."

"I meant you." She put a finger to his chest. "I didn't see *you* coming."

"That's because I haven't."

She laughed, and loving the sound, he pulled her in by the nape of her neck and kissed her. "Ditto," he said against her mouth. He hadn't seen her coming either, not until she'd hit him over the head, knocking him out with her vibrant, sexy, adorable self.

She flashed a smile at him, warm and also filled with trouble—which he really hoped boded well for him.

She went to work, wrestling off one of her boots. By the time she wriggled a leg out of her tights, he'd lent his hands to the cause. Then she wrapped her fingers around him and was guiding him home when he barely managed to catch her.

"Condom," he managed.

She stilled, eyes wide on his. "Oh my God, I can't believe I almost forgot," she whispered and fisted her hands in his shirt, going nose to nose with him. "Tell me you were a Boy Scout, that you're prepared, that you have a damn condom."

The thing was, he hadn't expected to need one and he still wasn't exactly one-hundred-percent sure he should even go there now. He met her gaze. "I wasn't a Boy Scout."

She groaned and dropped her head to his chest. "But."

She jerked her head up, face hopeful. "Yeah?"

Sitting on the roof with her straddling his lap, he

somehow managed to pull his wallet from his back pocket, thinking *please have been smart enough to leave a condom in there . . .*

"Yes!" she burst out with when he came up with one.

Laughing, he tore the thing open and started to roll it down his length, but she pushed his hands away.

"Me," she said. "I want to . . ."

By the time she got him halfway covered, he was back to sweating and trembling like he was a seventeen-year-old kid with zero control. "I've got it," he said, putting his hands over hers to finish the job.

"Because we're in a hurry?"

"Because I'm about to lose it in your hands."

She snorted but the laughter seemed to back up in her throat with the sexiest little gasp when he pulled her closer so that the insides of her thighs snugged tight to the outsides of his.

"You're going to let me drive?" she teased.

"This rooftop's too rough for you to be on your back," he said, cupping her bare ass. "Up on your knees, Willa." And then before she could move, he lifted her himself, urging her to sink slowly onto him.

They both gasped, mouths locked on each other's, kissing deep and wet, hands clutching whatever they could reach, moving slowly at first, then faster and harder, until Keane completely lost himself. Winding his fist in her hair, he forced her head back, suckling on her exposed throat, marking her.

She came first, digging her fingernails into him, the combination of pleasure and sweet pain sending him skittering into the void right along with her.

Chapter 15

#HitMeBabyOneMoreTime

It was a very long time before Willa managed to catch her breath and her world stopped spinning out of control. Or started spinning again. She couldn't figure out which. In either case, she was completely dazed as she realized something shocking.

Several somethings, actually.

One, she was sitting on Keane, wrapped up tight in his warm, strong arms, arms that still quaked with the seismic rockings that came after some really great sex.

Really, *really* great.

And two, she felt both wildly alive and . . . *safe,* two things she'd most definitely never felt at the same time in her entire life.

Since that invoked some worrisome emotions, all of which tried to encroach on her momentary blissful haze, she shoved them all back and lifted her head.

Keane's dark eyes were on her, intense and yet

steady. God, she loved that. Her axis was tilted and she was in danger of losing her grip, but he had her. And just looking at him, she calmed. "So, that was . . . something."

His low chuckle reverberated from his chest to hers.

She smiled. "Was that a good enough distraction for you?"

His answering smile was slow and lazy and incredibly sexy. "If I say no, will you try to distract me again?"

"Maybe."

"I thought I'd seen and done it all," he said, "but this was a first for me."

She let out a low laugh and tried to right her clothing. "I can bring out the best or the worst in just about anyone."

"What would you call this?"

She didn't need to even think about it. "The best." She was failing at putting herself back together. Keane took over while she sat on his lap like a limp rag doll. Since she couldn't resist his delicious mouth, she leaned in, lingering—just for another moment, she told herself—kissing him one last time. But before she could break it off and get up, he banded his arms around her tightly and took over, kissing her long and deep and hard until she was back to a panting, needy mess.

When he slowly pulled back, she let out an unhappy moan of protest and her mouth chased after his.

This had him letting out a low laugh. The warm look in his eyes made her remember that she wanted things for herself. Things she'd never wanted before. Things she'd set aside because she knew he didn't want them. Suddenly more confused than ever, about the night, the holiday season, her damn life, everything, she crawled off of him and went back to her original pose, sitting, hugging her knees close to her chest.

He seemed happy to hold the silence as well, there in the dark beneath the half-ass moon.

"I could use some popcorn," he finally said.

She laughed a little and met his gaze. "That was some animal magnetism."

"Yeah," he agreed, tucking a lock of her hair behind her ear. "It was." He pressed a single soft kiss along her jaw. His breath was warm against her skin, sending a shiver through her, and she found herself leaning into him, closer to that calm aura that always surrounded him. "So. You kicked Santa out of the bar for me."

"How did you know?"

She smiled wryly and patted the phone tucked into her pocket. "A text came in from Elle before you got up here." Turning her head, she met his gaze. "You're a good guy, you know that?"

"Just don't let it get out." He took her hand and brought it up to his mouth, brushing his lips over her knuckles. "I'm not really much of a talker," he said quietly. "But you are."

She snorted. "Tell me something everyone doesn't already know."

"Exactly what I was hoping you'd say. So talk to me, Willa. Tell me about the Santa thing."

Well, she'd walked right into that one. She tried to pull her hand free of his but he held on, doing the same with her gaze. "Look," she said. "Just because we . . . did *that,*" she said with a vague wave of her hand to the rooftop behind them, "doesn't mean we have make to small talk."

"What I want to talk about has nothing to do with *that*." He gave her a small smile. "Also known as the hottest rooftop sex I've ever had. Not to mention, the *only* rooftop sex I've ever had."

She let out a low laugh, but looked away.

With a hand to her jaw, he brought her face back to his.

"Okay," she said. "I agree the rooftop sex was very hot. But as per our previous agreement, we don't have to do this. I mean there's a me, and there's a you. And sometimes there's this crazy, stupid"—she waved her hand vaguely again—"thing. But it was just a one-time thing. And it's probably out of our systems now." She met his gaze with difficulty. "So really, you don't have to do the whole awkward-after with me."

"Maybe I'm a sucker for the awkward-after."

With a laugh, she dropped her head to her knees. "I'm trying to give you an out here, Keane." Hell, she was trying to give *herself* an out. Her heart needed it, bad.

Because she got it: he didn't get attached. But she sure did, and hard. And she was going to have to be very careful to protect herself.

"Humor me," Keane said. "Pretend I'm irritable to talk to."

Not much pretending required there . . .

"Tell me what happened tonight," he said.

"Well," she quipped in a last-ditch effort to lighten up this conversation. "It's about the birds and the bees—"

"You know what I want to know, smartass."

She sighed. Yeah, she did. He wanted to know why, if she was afraid of Santa, she celebrated Christmas like she was still five years old, and he wasn't going to accept the nonanswer she'd already given him.

But she rarely allowed herself to think about it, much less talk about it.

After a long beat of silence, he spoke. "When I was little, I was sent to a Catholic military boarding school one year, run by nuns and ex-marines."

She looked at him. "You were? How old were you?"

"Five. Actually, not quite five. But by the time I turned ten, I was back at home in the public school system. Let's just say, I didn't fit in at the private school."

She gasped, almost unable to fathom this, even though she'd gone into the childcare system at the same young age. "Your parents sent a four-year-old away? And then left you there until you were ten?"

He shrugged. "I was a pain in the ass. I did pay for that though."

"The school punished the kids?" she asked in horror.

"Only if you were an asshole punk." He tipped his face up to the dark night, a small smile on his lips. "I still twitch if I see a nun."

She fell quiet, mulling over the reason he'd shared the story. He'd wanted to be open so she would. Dammit. "I didn't twitch when I saw Santa," she said.

"No," he agreed. "You didn't twitch. You had a full-on seizure."

Keane watched as Willa fidgeted. He knew she wanted to move on from this subject, and she wanted that badly too. But he felt like they were on the precipice of something, something deeper than even their sheer physical animal attraction. He also knew that this was the point where he should be running for the hills, but he didn't want to end this here.

She still hadn't said a word and he resigned himself to that being it, this was as far as they went, when she finally spoke.

"I was sent away for the first time right about the same age as you," she said softly.

He turned and met her gaze. "What happened?"

"I was in the foster system on and off for most of the next fourteen years." She paused. "My mom's an alcoholic. She'd get it together for a little bit here and there, but not for long. Usually she'd fall for some guy, break up and fall off the wagon at the same time, and then go a little crazy, and I'd end up back in the system."

Christ, how he hated that for her. "Any of those 'some guys' dress up like Santa?"

"Just the first one," she said with a shudder. "After a few encounters, I finally got my nerve up and spilled his coffee on his lap. And that was that."

"Tell me it was fucking boiling hot," he said.

She smiled proudly. "Yep."

He hoped like hell she'd melted the guy's dick off but either way she'd been left with a scar too. Shocking how violent he could feel for something that had happened to her twenty years ago, but violent was exactly how he felt at the moment.

People had disappointed her. Hurt her. And damn if he hadn't put himself in position to do the same by making it clear that what they shared was in the moment only.

He'd never felt like a bigger dick.

Reaching out, she squeezed his hand. *Comforting him,* he realized and he actually felt his throat go tight as he held on to her fingers. "How many times did you go into the system?" he asked.

"At least once a year until I turned eighteen and was let loose."

His gut clenched thinking about how rough that must have been for her. "Not a great way to grow up."

She shrugged. "I got good at the revolving door. I'm still good at it."

"What do you mean?"

"You don't attach," she said. "And I don't tend to lock in. At my shop, customers come and go. The animals too. Even my employees. And men. The only constants have been my friends." She shifted as if uncomfortable that she'd revealed so much. "I should go—"

He tightened his hold on her because no way in hell was he crawling back over the edge of this building after her. "I'm going to call bullshit on the not-locking-in thing," he said gently. Oh yes, she was a flight risk now; he could feel her body tensing up. "You're smart as hell, Willa. You're self-made. You never give up, and the depth of your heart is endless. If you wanted to lock in, as you call it, you would."

She looked away. "Maybe you're giving me too much credit."

"I doubt that."

He couldn't even imagine what her early years had been like for someone like her, with her heart so full and sweet and tender. And then the foster care system, which must've been a nightmare. "Are you still in contact with your mom?" he asked.

"Yes. She lives in Texas now, and we text every other week or so. It took us a while to come to the understanding that twice a month is the right amount of time for us—halfway between missing the connection and wanting to murder each other in our sleep." She smiled, but he didn't.

Couldn't.

She pulled out her phone. "No really, mostly it's good now, or at least much better than it ever was in the past anyway. See?"

> Mom:
> Hi honey, just checking in. You're probably busy tonight . . . ?

"Translation," Willa said. "She's sober and also fishing." She tried to take the phone back but he'd gotten a look at her return text and smiled.

He read it out loud, still smiling.

> Willa:
> The daughter you're trying to reach will neither confirm nor deny that she has plans tonight since you're clearly trying to find out if she's seeing someone. This violates the terms of our relationship. If you continue to harass your daughter in this fashion, she'll start dating girls again.

Keane stopped and looked at her, and when he managed to speak, his voice sounded low and rough to his own ears. "Again?"

She squirmed a little bit and dropped eye contact. "It was a one-time thing," she said. "A phase. And I got over it real fast when I realized girls are crazy."

"Guys aren't much better," he said.

"No kidding."

He smiled as he rasped his thumb over her jaw, letting his fingers sink into her hair.

"Keane," she said softly. "Thanks for tonight." She rose. "For no strings, it was pretty damn amazing."

He didn't say anything to this. Couldn't. Because he was suddenly feeling uneasy and unsure, two things he didn't do well. Not that he said anything. No reason to reveal his own pathetic insecurities.

She moved to the edge of the roof and turned back. "Do you need help down?"

"Over my dead body."

She laughed. And with that, she vanished over the ledge.

Keane moved over there and looked over the edge, and then had to sit down hard while life passed before his eyes. "Fuck." It took him a moment to get his shit together, and by then Willa was long gone.

Perfect.

He moved in the opposite direction, toward the door that led to the inside stairwell, consoling himself with the fact that at least there was no one to see him taking the easy way down.

Chapter 16

#Legendary

The next morning Willa stood in the back of her shop shoving down a breakfast sandwich with Cara and Rory. It was midmorning and they'd been swamped since before opening.

Although not too swamped that she couldn't relive the night before, the way Keane's voice had been a rough whisper against her ear, the heat in his eyes as he'd taken control and moved knowingly inside her, his hands both protective and possessive on her body.

When a text came in, she was tempted to ignore it, but in the end her curiosity won. It was from Elle.

> HeadOfAllTheThings:
> I'm going to need a detailed report of what went down last night.

"Dammit," she muttered, and Cara and Rory both pointed in unison to the swear jar.

Willa pulled a buck from her pocket, shoved it into the jar, and moved to the dubious privacy of her office to stare blankly at Elle's text.

No one had seen her and Keane last night, she was certain of it. But when she'd climbed down the fire escape, she'd run smack into Pru in the courtyard.

Willa sighed and put her thumbs to good use.

> Willa:
> Going to have to kill her.
> HeadOfAllTheThings:
> Wear gloves, keep the fingerprints off the murder weapon.

Willa had to laugh as she responded.

> My favorite part of this is that you don't even question who I have to kill.
> HeadOfAllTheThings:
> The less I know, the less I can say during the interrogation.
> HeadOfAllTheThings:
> But seriously, where are my deets?

When Willa ignored, and in fact deleted, the texts, Elle simply called her.

"Houston, I have so many problems," Willa said miserably.

Elle laughed. "If you think having a hot guy want you is a problem, we need to talk. I'm at work right now and swamped, so I mean this in the most loving fashion I can deliver given how many idiots I've dealt with since dawn—did Keane screw your brains out on the rooftop last night, and if so, was he amazeballs or do I have to hurt him?"

Willa dropped her head to her desk and thunked it a few times. Because here was the thing about Keane. He was smart. Sexy. Incredibly handsome and virile. And when he looked at her, he sent a quiver through her body in all the best possible places . . . every time.

Being with him so intimately last night had been incredible—but in retrospect, it was a bit scary too because now her heart was invested.

And then there was the fact that Keane didn't intend to get invested at all.

At least she'd set the ground rules by saying out loud that it'd been a one-time thing. That helped.

Okay, it hadn't helped at all but she'd been the one to instigate what'd happened up on that roof, and she had no regrets.

"Well?" Elle demanded.

"It was a one-time thing."

"Great," Elle said. "Got no problem with that. But it isn't what I asked you."

Willa blew out a sigh. "Yes and yes."

There was a beat of silence. "If it was so great, why won't there be round two?"

"He's not round-two material," Willa said and had to bite her tongue because she immediately wanted to take the statement back. Keane was smart and funny and sexy, and well worthy of a round two. Which meant she'd just lied to one of her closest friends in the whole entire world.

But the truth was too hard to say out loud. The truth

hurt. The truth was . . . she wasn't sure *she* was round-two material.

"Honey," Elle said after another long beat of knowing silence. "Let me tell you something about yourself that you don't know. When you lie, you speak in an octave reserved for dogs."

"I can't do this." Dammit, her voice was so high that probably Elle was right, only dogs could hear her. She cleared her throat. "Not now."

"Fine," Elle said agreeably. "Girls' night. Does tomorrow sound good? Pizza and wine and a little chit-chat about believing in yourself, since you're one of the very best human beings I know and love."

"You hate most human beings," Willa said.

"Proof that I mean it then. Shit, I'm looking at my calendar. Can't tomorrow night, Archer needs my help on a job."

"Maybe we should have girls' night to discuss why you and Archer haven't—in your own words—screwed each other's brains out," Willa said. "Everyone knows it's going to happen sooner or later."

"Well then, 'everyone' should be watching their backs," Elle said grumpily. "It's not going to happen. Ever. I'm clearing my schedule for tonight. Pizza and wine and a heart-to-heart."

"I'm on a diet."

"Me too," Elle said. "It's a *fuel* diet. I eat whatever's going to fuel my soul, and tonight that's going to be pizza."

Willa opened her mouth to claim that she was busy but Elle had disconnected. "Dammit, I hate when she gets the last word," she muttered.

Keane was halfway through his morning laying out wood floor at the North Beach house, while playing last night repeatedly in his brain. The good parts, not the part where somehow he'd let Willa put them into the one-night-stand category.

No, he'd shoved that aside. Instead he kept going back to when Willa had come all over him, shuddering gorgeously in his arms, his name on her lips—

Someone knocked on the front door for the second time. He had a crew of ten today but no one stopped working.

"Sass," he called out.

Nothing.

"Sass!"

Looking irritated as all hell, she stuck her head in from the hallway, jabbing a finger to the phone glued to her ear, reminding him with a scathing look that she was here ordering the window treatments.

He blew out a sigh, dropped his tool belt, and moved toward the door himself. It couldn't be a subcontractor; they would've just let themselves in. He hoped it wasn't a neighbor complaining about the noise. He tried to keep it quiet but some things couldn't be helped.

Like the nail gun he'd been using on the flooring.

He pulled open the door, prepared to politely apologize and then continue doing exactly what he'd been doing. Instead he stared in shock at his Aunt Sally.

She was hands on hips. "I've had to chase you all over town. Do you have any idea how much I just paid in cab fares?"

He stuck his head out the door, looking past her for the cab. "I'll pay—"

"Already done." She sniffed with irritation. "You don't answer your phone. Which is rude, by the way. Your entire generation is rude with this whole twittering and texting ridiculousness. No manners whatsoever."

Keane pulled his phone from his pocket and saw the missed call. With a grimace, he shook his head. "I was using power tools and couldn't hear—"

"Don't give me excuses, boy. I've got one hour left before I have to be back. Where's Petunia? Where is my sweet baby girl? That thing is scared of her own shadow. All these people and the racket must be terrifying her."

If Petunia was a "sweet, little thing" or "scared of her own shadow," Keane would eat his own shorts. As for where she was, well that was going to be complicated. Knowing today would be loud as hell, he'd dropped Pita off at South Bark this morning.

And okay, so he'd been hoping to lay eyes—and maybe his mouth as well—on Willa. Yeah, he'd gotten her message last night loud and clear.

It'd been a one-time thing.

He got it. And actually, one-time things were his specialty. It was all he ever did these days. So the smart thing was to get on board and agree with her.

But he wasn't feeling all that agreeable, not that he wanted to think about *that*.

And in the end, it hadn't mattered. Willa hadn't been in the shop yet and he'd dealt with Rory, who'd been closed-mouthed on where her boss might be.

Worried that he might've had something to do with her absence, Keane had both texted and called Willa's cell, but hadn't gotten through. He could admit to feeling uneasy. Either she'd decided last night had been a huge mistake on top of a one-time thing, or . . . well, he couldn't think of an alternative.

But the thought of her regretting what had been the best night in his recent and ancient history didn't sit well with him. His big plan had been to rush through the day and get back to South Bark before closing so he could see what the hell was going on.

"Well?" Aunt Sally demanded.

He joined her on the porch and shut the door behind him, closing off the noisy racket from inside. Plus if she was going to yell at him, he'd rather she didn't do it in front of his crew and undermine his authority. "What do you mean you only have an hour left?" he asked. "Did you run away from the home? What's going on?"

"Oh no," she said, shaking a bony finger in his face. "You first. Where's my baby?"

"She's not here. I knew the noise would upset her so I—"

"What have you done with her? Oh, my God." She wrung her hands. "You did it, you sold her."

"No," he said. "She's with a friend."

"She's delicate, Keane. And I don't even think she knows she's an animal, much less a cat! I know that's what your parents did to you when you caused some ruckus, shipped you off, but that's not how to handle things." She sounded worried sick, which made him feel like a first-class jerk.

And a little shell-shocked. That's exactly what he'd done. He'd shipped the cat off rather than deal with her, just like his parents had always done to him. Jesus. *Was he like them?* "She's fine," he promised. "My . . . friend loves cats." Look at him trip over the word *friend.*

"Your friend?"

"Yes," he said and really hoped that was true, that at the very least he and Willa were still friends, that he hadn't blown that last night.

"Where is this person?" Aunt Sally demanded. "Take me to her right now."

Okay then. He stuck his head back inside and came face-to-face with an obviously eavesdropping and also obviously amused Sass. *"Chicken,"* he whispered.

"You don't pay me enough to lie to sweet old ladies," she whispered back.

In fact, yes he did pay her enough to lie to old ladies. He paid her enough to run a third-world country. But now wasn't a good time to point that out. "I'll be back," he said.

Sass smiled. "Want me to call ahead and warn Willa that you've lied to your sweet old great-aunt and ask her to lie for you as well?"

"Not lie," he said. "I merely omitted a few facts."

"Such as you pawned off her cat to day care."

"Just hold down the damn fort," he said and shut the door on her nosy nose.

He turned back to his aunt and took her hand. "I'll drive."

Ten minutes later he parked outside the Pacific Pier Building, right in front of South Bark Mutt Shop.

Sally eyeballed the shop and then turned and glared daggers at him. "If there's one little hair on Petunia's sweet little head harmed . . ."

"Death and dismemberment," he said. "I know." Just as he also knew that if anyone had been harmed, it wouldn't be that cat. She could slay anyone at a hundred paces.

Working her way through some dreaded bookkeeping on a break, Willa stopped and stared sightlessly out the window. Over the last few weeks there'd been a pattern of her cash drawer being short forty bucks.

Even more concerning, it only happened when one of her employees closed up. She hated the implication but she was now down one hundred and twenty precious dollars and she couldn't ignore it any longer.

Rory poked her head in. "Everything okay?"

Rory had been with Willa the longest. Willa didn't want her thief to be Rory, but she couldn't be sure so she said, "Yep."

"Okay," Rory said, clearly not buying it but not pushing either. "I'm going to groom Buddy. Can you listen for customers?"

"Of course." Buddy was a twelve-year-old cat who hated baths. But he did love being combed, so they had an ongoing love/hate relationship, though he was partial to Rory.

A few minutes later, the bell above the front door rang. Willa was heading out there when from the back came a startled scream, a growl, a yelp, and then a crash.

She raced back there and found Rory on her hands

and knees peering under their storage shelves, and Lyndie standing in the center of the room wringing her hands.

"What happened?" Willa asked.

"Something startled me and Buddy." Rory muttered this with a scathing glance in Lyndie's direction, and Willa knew there was a lot more to this story.

"Something?" she asked.

"Yeah, and then he bit me and I let go of him. He's under the shelves cowering. Come here, Buddy," Rory said in a singsong voice. "I'm not mad at you, I'd have bitten me too. I didn't mean to startle you."

Willa dropped to her hands and knees next to Rory and peered under the shelving to find two huge, terrified eyes staring back at her. "Aw, baby, it's okay. Come on out now . . ." She pulled a pupperoni treat from her pocket and waggled it enticingly. "We'll go right to the combing part, okay? You love that."

Buddy, always unable to resist food of any kind, crab-crawled his way out from beneath the shelf and very cautiously took the treat.

Willa gently pulled him into her body and cuddled him close, kissing him on top of his bony head. "You poor, silly baby." She craned her neck and eyed Rory's finger, which was bleeding profusely. "How bad?"

"I'm fine," she said and headed to the sink.

Willa had to believe that, at least for the moment while she dealt with Lyndie and the suspicions that had been churning in her own gut. "When did you get here?"

Lyndie sucked on her lower lip and exchanged a glance with Rory.

Willa bit back a sigh. She'd thought they were past this. "Lyndie," she said quietly, gently. "I know you slept here last night. I know you sleep here when you need to."

"No," she said, the denial instantly defensive. "I—"

"Stop," Willa said in that same calm voice. No judgment. No censure. Because she, more than anyone, understood the need to get out of a bad situation and yet have no safe place to go. "I want you to feel safe here. But on the nights you need a place to sleep, you just have to let me know. I've got a couch four flights up that's far better than the floor of this wash room. Ask Rory, she slept there on and off her entire first year with me."

Rory nodded. "She makes cinnamon toast late at night when you can't sleep and we watch Netflix."

Lyndie stared at Willa for a long beat and then swallowed hard. "You'd let me sleep in your apartment?"

"Yes," Willa said. "But there's something that I *won't* let you do. And that's steal from the till."

Lyndie's eyes shuttered. "I didn't steal anything." She backed up to the door. "You can call the cops but you can't keep me here to wait for them—"

"I'm not calling the cops," Willa said and rose to her feet. "I need you to listen to me, Lyndie, and really hear what I'm saying, okay? I love having you as an employee, I love how you treat the animals, but no one's holding you against your will. More than that, I don't want anyone here who doesn't want to be here, and I won't allow anyone to take advantage of me. Rory, what's my policy on stealing?" she asked without taking her eyes off Lyndie.

Rory had washed out her finger and was wrapping it in a paper towel to stanch the bleeding. "Two strikes and you're out."

"And why isn't it three?" Willa asked.

"Because you were born early and without patience," Rory recited.

Willa nodded. "Do you get what I'm telling you?" she asked Lyndie.

The girl swallowed hard. "I've had my first strike."

"You've had your first strike," Willa agreed. She was firm on that, always. Boundaries mattered with the animals and boundaries mattered with the kids as well.

"I'm sorry," Lyndie whispered.

"Thank you, and I know. But we both deserve better, okay?"

Lyndie nodded and Willa moved to the grooming station with Buddy. "You two go out front and take care of customers. I've got Buddy."

When they were gone, she cooed to the scared cat, "And you, you adorable little beast. Let's make some magic together."

"How about me, want to make some magic with me too?" asked an unbearably familiar, low, and sexy voice from behind her.

Keane, of course, because who else could make her heart leap into her throat and her nipples go hard while everything inside her went soft at the same time?

Chapter 17

#ReadMyLips

Keane was amused that he'd rendered Willa speechless. For once.

But there was no getting around the fact that she didn't exactly look happy to see him. Moving toward her, he picked up the comb she'd dropped and handed it to her, holding on to it until she met his gaze. "Hey."

"Hey," she said back. At first, she'd looked a little bit like a deer in the headlights, but now she was closing herself off, right before his very eyes.

"You okay?" he asked.

"Yes, just busy, so—"

"Not so busy at all!" Rory had stuck her head in the door and was grinning like a loon. "Lyndie and I've got it all handled out here so you two just"—she smiled guilelessly—"make magic or something."

And then she was gone.

"She's match-making," Willa muttered. "I was very

busy having a moment with them and now they're match-making."

"Want to talk about that moment you were having?" he asked. "Seemed serious."

"I've got it handled."

She always did. She was good at that, handling whatever came her way. "Okay, then let's talk about how even your employees can see how much you like me," he said.

She rolled her eyes at that, which made him laugh. He moved in and let his mouth brush her ear. "You telling me that you didn't have a good time last night?"

As close as he was, he felt the tremor go through her but before he could pull her in, she stepped free and glared at him. "Stop using your sex voice," she said, hugging herself. "And you know I had a good time." She hesitated, looking around like maybe she was making sure no one could hear them. "Twice," she whispered.

He burst out laughing. "You mean three times."

She stared at him. "You were counting?" she asked in disbelief.

"Of course not. Didn't have to." He leaned in. "And anyway, we both know it was four."

She pointed at him. "And that. *That's* why we're not doing it again. Because you want to talk about it. And I don't."

He caught her when she would've moved away. "We really not going to do that again?"

"One night," she said softly, holding his gaze. "You agreed. No strings attached. You agreed to that too."

"Yeah." He shook his head. "I might've been premature."

She choked out a laugh. "Now that's one thing you weren't . . ." She shook her head when he snorted. "I think we both know that we're better off as friends, Keane."

"Friends," he repeated, still unsure how he was feeling about this.

"Yes," she said. "Friends stick." She lifted a shoulder, as if a little embarrassed. "I guess I wouldn't mind if you . . . stuck."

He looked at her for a long beat, picturing the novelty of that, being friends with a woman he wanted naked and writhing beneath him. "I like the sticky part."

She pushed him but he caught her hand and got serious. "I'm in," he said.

Her mouth curved. "In as friends, or was that another sexual innuendo?"

"Both," he said just to see her smile go bright again.

When it did, his chest got all tight. It told him that this was something much more than the still sizzling chemistry between them, but given the look on her face, he didn't have to point that out. She already knew.

"So," she said after an awkward pause. "What brings you here? You done working for the day?"

"No, my great-aunt wants to see Pita."

Willa processed Keane's words and felt her spine snap straight as she rushed for the door.

Keane was right on her heels and she sent him a

glare over her shoulder. "You should've told me right away she was here!"

"I told you as soon as you stopped talking about magic and sticky."

"Oh my God." She was going to have to kill him. He was keeping up with her, his broad shoulders pushing the boundaries of his work T-shirt, jeans emphasizing his long legs, scuffed work boots on his feet, all combining to make her heart take a hard leap against her ribs.

Or maybe that was just *him* doing all of that to her.

She took another peek and their gazes locked and held. During that long beat, Willa forgot her problems with Lyndie, forgot the shop . . . hell, she forgot her own name because images from last night were flashing through her head again. The way his big, work-roughened hands had felt on her, the deep growl from his throat as he'd moved deep inside her, touching something no one else ever had. He'd taken her outside of herself and it'd been shockingly easy for him to do so, as if he'd known her all his life.

Then there'd been the sheer, unadulterated, driving need and hunger he'd caused. And fulfilled . . . And she'd put them in the friend zone.

She was an idiot, a scared, vulnerable idiot . . .

An older woman was making her way around the shop, walking slowly, maybe a little painfully, her face pinched with anxiety and concern.

"Aunt Sally, this is Willa Davis," Keane said, introducing them. "She owns and runs South Bark."

"Lovely to meet you," Willa said.

The woman narrowed her eyes. "You're the *friend* who has my Petunia?"

She slid a look Keane's way. "Yes. She's safe and sound, as always when she's here."

"As always?"

Ruh-roh, Willa thought, but before she could speak, Sally beat her to it.

"I want her back." Keane's aunt's white hair was in a bun and that bun quivered with indignity. "Right now."

"Aunt Sally," Keane said quietly, putting his hand over the older woman's. "Pita—er, Petunia really is very happy here, I promise you."

"Who's Pita?" Sally asked.

Willa laughed but when Keane sent her a pained look, she turned it into a cough.

"She wasn't meant to be crated all day," Sally said. "She hates being contained—"

"Oh, I don't keep the fur babies in a crate," Willa said. "I only take on a very select few in the first place and they stay with me or one of my employees all day. Petunia is one of those select few. And she's really wonderful, by the way. So sweet and loving."

This time it was Keane to choke on a laugh and then tried to cough it off.

Willa ignored him. "Petunia really enjoys being high up and viewing the world from a safe perch."

"Yes," Sally said with great relief, losing a lot of her tension. "She does."

Willa turned and gestured to the other end of the store, where she had a built-in shelving unit lining the wall with an assortment of animal beds for sale, ranging from Saint Bernard–size down to small enough for the tiniest of kittens.

Petunia was on the highest shelf in the smallest of beds, half of her body overlapping on either side— which didn't appear to be bothering her one bit, as she was fast asleep.

"Oh my," Sally breathed, cupping her own face, which had softened with pleasure. "She looks . . . ridiculous."

Willa laughed. "She chose the perch, and she's perfectly content. She just came back from a walk—"

"A walk!" Sally exclaimed. "Outside?"

"On a leash," Willa said. "One of my friends took her and two golden retrievers out together this morning. They all had a great time."

Sally whirled to Keane, eyes bright as she reached up and smacked him in the chest. "You're brilliant."

Keane looked surprised. And wary. "I am?"

"And here I've been thinking how sad it is that you never recovered from losing Blue enough to get another pet. Blue was his childhood dog," she said to Willa before looking back at Keane. "I thought when your mother and father gave that dog away without talking to you about it first that the loss had irrevocably destroyed your ability to love another animal."

Keane's expression went blank. "They didn't give him away," he said. "I left the back door open and he escaped. It was my fault."

Sally shook her head. "I always wondered what hokey-pokey bologna they fed you. Keane, you loved that dog beyond reason, you'd never have carelessly left the back door open knowing your yard wasn't fenced in."

"How do you know this?" he asked. "You weren't around."

"My sister and I share a best friend. And let's just say that Betty didn't turn her back on me like everyone else. She keeps me updated."

Keane still wore that blank expression, but there was something happening behind his eyes now that tugged hard at Willa's heart.

She'd bought his party line that maybe he was a guy who didn't feel deeply, who didn't have a sensitivity chip. A guy who couldn't attach. But she was starting to suspect it was the actual opposite, that he had incredible heart, he'd just been hurt. Badly.

"Petunia," Sally called softly, her voice cracking with age. "Baby, come to Mama."

Petunia immediately lifted her head with a surprised chirp. She leapt with grace to the counter and jogged straight to Sally, right into the woman's open arms.

Sally bent her head low, and cat and woman had a long moment together, the only sounds being the raspy purr from Petunia and the soft murmurs from Sally. "I have to go, Petunia," she whispered softly. "You might not see me for a while. You be a good girl for Keane, okay? He's male so he might not know much, but he's got a big heart, even if he doesn't know that either."

Willa's heart squeezed hard. She turned to Keane with worry and he gave her a very small smile, reaching for her hand. She gently squeezed his fingers.

His eyes were warm as they slid over her features.

Warm and grateful, she realized. Because she'd taken good care of Petunia? Or that she'd been kind to his aunt? Or maybe it was simply because she was there.

Sally lifted her head. Her eyes were dry but devastated as she turned away. "I need a ride back now," she said and snapped her fingers in the air.

Keane smiled grimly at Willa. "I've been summoned." Leaning down, he brushed a kiss across her mouth before looking into her eyes.

For what she had no idea. But wanting to give comfort however she could, she pressed into him and felt him let out a low breath, like maybe he was relaxing for the first time all day.

Pulling back, he kissed her once more, and then he was gone.

Chapter 18

#NoChill

Keane was good at burying emotions, real good. He was also good at compartmentalizing. But when he'd walked Sally inside her rehab center and she'd hugged him, whispering, "Be better than the rest of the family," and then patted his cheek and walked away, he'd had a funny feeling that he couldn't place.

That evening, just as he was leaving work to pick up Pita, his architect and engineer showed up for an impromptu meeting on the Mission job. Worried about making Willa work late, he quickly called South Bark. Willa was with a customer but Rory told him no worries, they'd take care of Petunia as late as he needed. Someone would just take her home if need be.

Relieved, he went into his meeting and when it was over an hour later, he realized with a hit to his solar plexus what the niggling feeling about Sally had been.

She'd been trying to tell him goodbye.

He left the jobsite and stopped to see his aunt on his way to South Bark—only to be told that Sally had been taken to the hospital.

When he got there, they wouldn't tell him a damn thing because she hadn't listed any contacts. Luckily Keane knew the nurse and in spite of the fact that they'd slept together twice before he'd backed off when he'd seen wedding bells and white picket fences in her pretty eyes, Jenny seemed genuinely happy to see him. They exchanged pleasantries and then he asked about Sally.

She shook her head. "I can't tell you anything about her condition—I could lose my job for that. You're hot, Keane, and great in bed . . ." She smiled. "Really, *really* great, but even I have my limits."

She did, however, let him sit in Sally's room.

Exhausted, he stretched out his legs and leaned his head back. He was half asleep when his aunt's cranky voice came from the bed. "You paid my rehab center bill."

And he'd pay her hospital bill too, if she needed. "Don't worry about it," he said.

"Worrying is what I do."

"Just get better."

"Huh," she said. "Is that out of concern for me or concern for you that you might get stuck with Petunia?"

"Both."

She cackled at that. "I might have to write you into my will."

He found a smile. "Look at you being all sweet. I knew you had it in you, deep, deep down."

"Just don't tell anyone," she said. "They'll think I have no chill."

He blinked. "What?"

"It's a term used when you act specifically uncool about something."

He laughed. "I know what it means, I'm just wondering how you know."

Sally shrugged. "My nurse keeps saying it about the doctors. Now stop stalling and explain to me what the hell you're doing here. I know I didn't have anyone call you."

He shook his head. "And why is that?" he asked, apparently still butt-hurt over it.

She closed her eyes. "You should be home with your girl right now."

Keane scrubbed a hand over his face. "Willa's not mine."

"Spoken just like a man who's never had to work for a woman in his life."

This wrenched another laugh from him. He stared at his clenched hands and then lifted his head. "I want to know what's going on with you. I want you to put me on as your next of kin and contact, and I'd like to have your power of attorney as well."

"Circling the inheritance already?"

"I want to be able to make sure you're being cared for," he said.

She stared at him, her rheumy eyes fierce and proud and stubborn as . . . well, as he imagined his own were. Finally, she blew out a rough breath. "I lived the past three extra decades without any family at all."

"Yeah and how has that worked out for you?" he asked.

She huffed and leaned back, closing her eyes. "It doesn't matter now. What matters is that you go."

"Not happening."

Her mouth went tight, her eyes stayed tightly closed.

He blew out a sigh. "Aunt Sally—"

"I'm dying," she said flatly.

He stopped breathing. "No." He stood up and moved to her bedside, covering her hand with his. "No," he said again.

She looked up at him. "You can stand as tall as a tree and scowl down at me all you want. I'm eighty-five years old. It's going to be God's truth."

"When?"

She shrugged.

"Soon?"

"Only if you keep drilling me."

He let out a low laugh and scrubbed a hand over his face. "Christ."

"Look, I could choke on my Metamucil tomorrow morning and go toes up just like that, you never know."

"And I could die from slipping and falling in warm cat yak getting out of bed," he said.

She laughed. "It's the warm that always gets me." She sobered. "I just want you forewarned. Since you seem so fragile and all."

"Yeah," he said dryly. "I'm as fragile as a peach."

"I want you to listen to me," she said, squeezing his fingers with surprising strength.

So he bent low, thinking she was going to tell him something important in regard to her wishes.

"If you take my cat to the pound after I'm gone," she said, "I will haunt you for the rest of your life, and then I'll follow you to hell and haunt you for all of eternity."

Chapter 19

#MischiefManaged

Keane drove straight to South Bark. It was past seven and he felt like a dick that he'd left Willa to deal with one of his problems. He could only hope Pita had been . . . well, *not* a PITA.

The shop was closed, locked up tight as a drum, and dark, except for the twinkle of the holiday lights strung across the glass window front. He took it as a good sign that there wasn't a note posted for him.

He pressed his face up against the glass but no one was inside. Turning, he strode across the cobblestone courtyard, lit by more strings of lights. The water fell from the fountain, the sound muted by the music tumbling out of the pub, which was still going strong.

Near the alley, Old Man Eddie was talking to two gray-bunned ladies. "Some beauty for the beauties," he said, handing them each a little spring of green held together by a red ribbon.

The ladies handed him some cash and smiled broadly. "Thanks for the . . . *mistletoe.*"

Mistletoe his ass, Keane thought with a reluctant smile. That was weed. He entered the pub and moved to the end of the bar. Rory was there, seemingly in a standoff with Max, who was minus his sidekick, Carl.

"No," she said.

"Look, you want a ride home to Tahoe for Christmas," Max said. "And I happen to be going that way. Why take two buses and a damn train when I could drive you?"

"Maybe I already have my tickets."

"Do you?"

She rolled her eyes.

Max just stood there, arms folded across his chest.

"What's your problem?" she snapped.

"You know what my problem is," he said. "It's you."

She pointed a finger at him. "You know what you are, Max? You're a hypocrite." And she whirled away from the bar, nearly plowing Keane over.

He put his hands on her arms to steady her.

She backed away from him, a scowl still on her face. "Sorry."

"No worries," he said. "You okay?"

"If one more person asks me that, I'm going to start kicking asses and taking names."

"Fair enough," Keane said, lifting his hands in surrender. "I'm just looking to relieve whoever is on Pita duty."

A small smile crossed her face. "I offered to be, but Willa insisted. She was here with her friends, it was girls' night, but I lost track of her."

"Try the back," Sean suggested from where he was serving behind the bar. "Pool table."

Archer and Spence were playing pool back there, and arguing while they were at it.

Seemed like it was the night for it.

"It's getting too cold. You've got to get him off the streets," Archer was saying as he shot the four ball and bounced it off the corner pocket.

Spence stood and pointed at the nine ball. "Bottom pocket," he said and made his shot before pointing at Archer. "And I've gotten him off the damn streets. Multiple times. Have you ever tried arguing with someone who literally fried their brain at Woodstock?"

"Man, that guy is *still* frying his brain," Archer said. "And speaking of, he hung some of his clippings in the alley entrance and is telling any woman who walks by that it's mistletoe."

"You talking about Old Man Eddie?" Keane asked.

Archer and Spence exchanged a look. "Yeah," Spence finally said. "We're trying to figure a way to keep him warm and healthy for the winter months that he'll agree to. So far all he agrees to is living in the fucking alley."

Keane nodded. "He's out there right now, selling some of that 'mistletoe' to a couple of older ladies."

Archer jabbed a finger at Spence. "Deal with him tonight or I will."

"Thought you gave up being a cop," Spence said.

Archer narrowed his eyes and the testosterone level in the back room spiked to off-the-chart. "Was that supposed to be funny?"

"A little bit, yeah." Spence turned to Keane. "You play?"

Keane eyed the pool table. "Some."

Archer's bad 'tude never wavered as he reset the balls.

"Never mind him," Spence said. "He's just pouting because he's a big, fat loser tonight. I'm already up fifty bucks."

"You whined so much when you lost last week that I felt sorry for you," Archer said. "I'm letting you win."

Spence shook his head. "Lying to make yourself look good is just sad. Especially since girls' night ended and Elle isn't even here anymore for you to show off."

Archer shoulder-checked Spence hard as he moved around the table to shoot.

Spence practically bounced across the room but he didn't look bothered in the least. In fact, he looked smug.

Archer slid him a hard look. "You know why I want Eddie cleaned up or gone. You fucking damn well know why."

Spence's easy smile slipped. "Okay, yeah. I do know." He waited quietly while Archer shot again, and then again, each time sinking multiple balls into the pockets. "I'll deal with it. I promised Willa the same thing because she doesn't want her kids tempted."

Keane choked on his beer. "Her kids?"

Archer looked up from the pool table and actually smiled. "She didn't tell you?"

Spence gave Archer a shove. "You're an asshole." He turned to Keane. "Not *her* kids. Her employees, the ones she so carefully collects to save, since there was no one to save her."

Keane prided himself on being cool, calm, logical. Emotions didn't have a place in his everyday life. But ever since he'd walked into Willa's shop that first time, he'd been having emotions. Deep ones.

Spence's words evoked a picture in his mind of what it had been like for Willa, leaving the foster-care system at age eighteen without anyone to take care of her. "She's got someone now," Keane said, surprising himself.

Archer shot again and sank the last of his balls. "Big loser, my ass." He pointed at Spencer. "You owe me fifty bucks. And also, if you keep opening your trap about Willa, she's going to kick your ass." He turned to Keane. "You mean what you just said? About Willa having someone now?"

Keane opened his mouth but nothing came out. Until this very moment he'd truly believed that a no-commitment policy was the best thing for him. No, wait. That wasn't exactly true. He'd been doubting his policy for a while now. Since Willa had plowed her way into his life.

He just had no idea what to do with that realization.

Spence laughed quietly at the look on Keane's face. "Give him a sec, man. I think he just shocked himself more than us."

Truer words . . . "I've gotta go," Keane said.

"Nice job," Archer muttered to Spence. "You scared him off."

"Nah, that guy can't be scared off. He's as bull-headed stubborn as you are. And hell, you still can't even admit what you feel for Elle, so . . ."

Keane didn't hear the rest of that thought because he walked out of the pub into the chilly night. He hit the stairwell and climbed to the fourth floor, not stopping until he was in front of Willa's door.

With absolutely zero idea of what he thought he was doing.

She opened after his knock wearing a tiny pair of flannel plaid PJ shorts just barely peeking out from beneath a huge hoodie. "Hey," she said and then frowned. "What's wrong?"

Not wanting to get into his aunt being in the hospital or his epiphany about Willa herself, he shook his head. "Nothing. Is it still girls' night? Are you guys having a pillow fight?"

"No," she laughed. "Pru wasn't feeling good. We cut it short before we even got to dinner."

Keane had learned to tell her mood by her hair. The wilder the strands, the wilder her emotions, but tonight her hood was up, falling over her forehead with the words *I Solemnly Swear That I Am Up to No Good* across it. "Sorry you got stuck with Petunia," he said.

"Oh, I didn't mind." She turned from him to look for the cat, or so he assumed, and saw the words *Mischief Managed* written across her sweet ass, making him realize the sweatshirt and shorts were a matched set. Nudging her aside, he let himself in.

Her place didn't surprise him. He'd seen her shop and he'd had an idea that her home would somehow look the same, cutesy and colorful.

"Mischief managed?" he asked.

She blinked like he'd surprised her. "You know Harry Potter?"

"Well, not personally," he said and smiled. "But I read the books."

"You mean you saw the movies?"

"No, I mean I read the books."

She didn't look happy about this. Color him completely lost. "And that makes me . . . ?"

She moaned and closed her eyes. "Bad for me. Oh so bad for me!"

Yeah, still lost. "Can I be bad for you over dinner?" he asked. "Because I'm starving."

Her eyes flew open and she stared at him.

He had no idea what she was thinking. "Are you hungry?" he asked.

"I'm always hungry. But it's getting late."

"And?"

"And . . ." She looked boggled. "Lots of reasons."

"Name one."

"Okay . . . Well, it's nearly Christmas. And Christmastime is usually for dear friends and family."

He just looked at her, not buying any of that.

"Keane," she said softly.

Was he going to tell her about his epiphany about wanting more from her? Hell no. One, he had no idea what that more was. And two, assuming he could figure that out, he then had to convince her to feel the same. No wonder he'd lain low on love. This shit was hard. "You told me family is where you make it," he said. "You told me your friends are your family. You told me we're friends. Was any of that a lie?"

"No, but . . ." She looked at him beseechingly. "I'm trying to resist you here, okay? I'm trying to tell myself we have nothing in common except this weird and extremely annoying chemistry that won't go away, not even when we . . ."

He went brows up, really wanting to hear her finish that sentence.

"Okay, when *I* jumped your bones on the roof," she finished, eyes narrowed, daring him to laugh. "But then you show up at my door, clearly exhausted and rumpled and looking . . . well, hungry, and it makes me want to do things."

"Things like . . . ?"

"Take my clothes off. Okay? You make me want to take my clothes off."

He started to smile but she poked him again. "Don't say it," she warned. "Don't you dare say that me stripping works for you."

"But, Willa, it does work for me. You stripping will always work for me."

This earned him an eyeroll. "Shock," she said. "But *friends* don't do that. They don't, Keane," she said when he opened his mouth. "And I was going to be okay with that. But then you went ahead and told me you've read Harry Potter." She hesitated and considered him. "Which one?"

"All of them."

She covered her face and moaned miserably. "All of them," she muttered. "I'm a dead woman. You've just killed me dead."

"I read a lot," he said, trying to improve his odds. "Not just Harry Potter."

"Making it worse . . ." She dropped her hands from her face. "Why are you here again?"

"To pick up Pita."

"Oh yeah."

"And to thank you for watching her." He paused. "With a meal because I'm starving and I want to buy you dinner. You look like the very best thing I've seen all day long, Willa. Can I tell you that without a disagreement?"

She eyeballed him for a long beat. "Dinner where?"

He bit back his victory smile. "Your choice."

"Sushi?"

He manfully held in his wince. He hated sushi. "Your choice," he said again.

"But you hate sushi."

"How do you know?" he asked.

"Because your eyes grimaced. Why would you agree to sushi if you hate it?"

He was starting to get a headache. "Because when I said your choice, I meant it. Are we going to argue about that too? And if so, can it wait until I get some food?"

"Sure. How about Thai?" she asked and studied his face carefully.

He gave her his best blank face. He wasn't crazy about Thai either but now his eye was full-out twitching. "Thai it is," he said. "You ready?"

She went hands on hips. "You don't like Thai either? What's wrong with you?"

"Many, many things," he said, wondering when

she'd come to be able to read him so damn clearly that he couldn't hide a thing from her. "Can we go now?"

"Italian. Indian. Taco Bell."

A laugh escaped him. "Yes."

"Which?"

"Willa, if you get your sweet little ass on the move, I'll take you to *all* of them."

She bit her lower lip and stared at him, her eyes bright.

Not moving.

"Babe," he said. *"What?"*

"I want to go somewhere *you* want to go," she said. "Can we make it your choice?"

What he wanted was to go to her bed. Directly and without passing Go. He wanted to strip her out of every stitch of clothing and feast on her.

For a week.

Some of that must have shown on his face because she blushed to her roots. "Pizza," she said quickly. "Pizza work for you?"

"Thank Christ, yes," he said.

She nodded and then hesitated.

"What now?" he asked.

"You ever going to tell me what's wrong?"

"I'm getting pizza and beer." *And you,* he thought. "What could be wrong? Come on." He reached for her hand, but she evaded with a low laugh.

"I can't go like this," she said. "I have to change first."

"I like what you're wearing."

She looked at him as if he'd lost his marbles.

"Okay, fine," he said. "Throw on sweats and call it good."

"Did you come through the pub?"

"Yes. Why?"

"Because then people saw you. People like Spence and Archer. Maybe Elle too, if she was still there. And trust me, they watched you leave and saw that you weren't leaving at all, that you came upstairs. They're going to gossip about it, and then tomorrow I'll be interrogated by the girls. Did I let you in? Did you stay? And what was I wearing? And I'll be damned, Keane, if I tell them that I was wearing sweats."

He blinked. He didn't quite follow. In fact, he needed to buy a vowel but he nodded gamely, willing to agree to anything to get food. "Okay."

"Okay." She vanished into her bedroom.

Chapter 20

#WithASideOfCrazy

Willa ran into her bedroom and startled Petunia, who was sleeping on her bed. "Sorry, don't mind me," she said to the cat and yanked off her clothes. She pulled on a pair of jeans that weren't comfortable but they gave her a good butt, and a soft green Christmas sweater that had a reindeer on the front, and fell to her thighs.

Which made the good-butt jeans unnecessary.

She peeled them off and tried a pair of black leggings instead.

Now she just looked a little lazy.

"Shit." She stripped again and started over.

And then over again.

Ten minutes later she'd tried on everything in her closet—which was now in a pile on her bed in front of Petunia—and she was in her bra and panties and starting to panic.

Nothing worked.

She swore a bunch more and started pawing through everything she'd already discarded on her bed, telling herself it was silly to be hung up on this. Silly and ridiculous and asinine and stupid—

"Willa," Keane called out, his voice shockingly close, like maybe he was heading down the hall toward her bedroom. "What are you doing, sewing a brand-new outfit?" His voice was right outside her door now.

With a squeak, she grabbed up her huge sweatshirt and held it in front of her. "Don't rush me!"

He poked his head into the room, eyes half amused, half male frustration. There was at least a day of scruff on his jaw and it was sexy as hell, damn him.

A fact that only served to annoy her.

He rubbed his belly like it was hollow. And hell, with those ridged muscles and not an ounce of fat anywhere on him, it probably was hollow.

"I've been waiting for hours," he said, petting Petunia when she meandered over to him for a scratch.

"It's been ten minutes," Willa said.

"Feels like hours." Keane pressed his thumb and forefinger to his eyes like he was trying to hold them into the sockets. "You ready?"

She tore her gaze off his lifted arms and the way his biceps and broad shoulders and back muscles strained the material of his shirt. "Almost," she said a little thickly.

Or not even close.

Reading her expression, he groaned and then looked around her room. "Did a bomb go off in here?"

She eyed the mess. "Maybe."

"You've got a lot of clothes and"—his gaze locked and snagged on a lacy bra and undies—"stuff." Then he saw the secondary pile on the club chair in the corner. "Holy shit," he said. "How many clothes have you tried on?"

"All of them!" she said. Maybe yelled. And then glared at him to see if he so much as dared to crack a smile. "I've got nothing to wear."

He once again took in the huge piles of clothing all over the place. "Okaaaaaay . . ."

She sighed.

He cut his eyes to hers, rubbing his jaw. The sound of his callused fingers against the scruff gave her a zing straight to her good parts.

And she'd had no idea she had so many.

"It's just pizza," he said.

"And here I'm scrambling to look hot enough to ruin you."

He smiled at that. "Willa, I fantasize about you. A lot. And I'm good at it too. You should know that you and your daily hotness have already ruined me."

And in turn, he was ruining her as she stood and breathed, not that she was about to admit it. "So you're saying I look hot to you right now," she said.

His gaze slid slowly over her. She was covered—mostly—by the sweatshirt she was holding to her front, but by the flash of heat in his gaze, he had X-ray vision. His expression softened. "You look batshit crazy and frustrated and hot as hell," he said. "Never doubt it."

She felt a reluctant smile pull at her mouth. "Turn around."

"I've already seen it all."

"Only once, and it was dark."

He smiled. "I have good night vision."

"Do you want to eat?" she asked and he turned around. She pulled back on her good-ass jeans and picked up a white sweater that was a little tight and gave her some impressionable assets, if she said so herself. "And you usually do too," she told him. "Look hot as hell."

He had his back to her, hands on his hips. He had a really great build, and if she was being honest he also had the best ass she'd ever seen, and she spent a few seconds taking in the sight. "Usually?" he asked.

"Well . . ." She eyeballed her room, which looked like a survivor of a category five hurricane. "Sometimes you look hotter than hot," she admitted. *Like now, with those jeans stretched across his buns . . .*

He turned to face her, taking in her outfit in a way that told her he appreciated the white sweater very much. "When?" he asked.

"I'm not telling you. It'll go to your big head."

"Already did," he said and looked down at himself.

Her eyes followed suit, landing on his crotch, and at the obvious hard-on there, she snorted. "I meant your other big head, you pervert."

He grinned at her, charming her effortlessly, damn him. "Now you're just throwing out the compliments left and right," he said. "Let's talk about the *big* part."

She laughed. "You know exactly how big you are . . . *everywhere.* You almost didn't fit. And why are we even having this conversation?"

"Because I like to talk about sex," he said.

"See, *pervert.*"

"Well, you should know . . ." His smile dared her to remember exactly how it'd been between them last night.

But here was the thing—she didn't have to drum up the memories; they were burned in her brain. *Combustible.* They'd been—and were—combustible together.

He smiled cockily at her and that was it. She pointed to the door. "Out!"

"Okay, okay!" Laughing, he told Petunia he'd be back for her and left the room, his stomach growling, the sound reaching her across the room.

"Have you really not eaten all day?" she asked.

"It was a crazy-busy day."

Taking pity on him, she shoved her feet into boots with a three-inch heel so she could pretend to be tall and took a quick peek in the mirror.

Her eyes were bright, her cheeks were flushed.

All thanks to her mad dash, she told herself, and absolutely not the man waiting in her living room.

As to why her heart was racing, she decided it was best not to speculate.

"Mischief managed?" he asked hopefully when she came out, like maybe she was a live hand grenade.

"Mischief managed," she assured him, and hoped that was true.

They walked. The night was chilly but clear. They headed into the Marina. With the streets lined with restaurants, bars, galleries, and shops, there were a lot of people out walking, threading their way into the eclectic mix of mom-and-pop places mixed in with high-end stores. In a single square city block, you could eat any kind of food from just about anywhere in the world, not to mention buy anything you wanted.

They got pizza and she told him how a customer had walked into the shop earlier with his parrot on his shoulder. The bird had taken one look at Petunia and fallen in instant love. He'd flown to the edge of the bed Petunia had been snoozing on and begun to garble his love song to her but the cranky cat had smacked him in the face with her paw.

The parrot had left brokenhearted.

They talked about his day too. How Mason had stapled his own hand to the ceiling and then superglued the ensuing slice in his hand rather than go to the doctor.

"Oh my God," Willa said. "And you were okay with that?"

"Cheaper than an ER trip," he said and laughed at the horror on her face. "It's actually what we do. A lot." He showed her a couple of scars on his hands and arms that had been "treated" by superglue.

She shook her head. "Boys are weird."

"I'll give you that," he said.

She laughed and so did he. And the shadows in his eyes faded away a little bit and she felt about ten feet tall.

After dinner, they walked some more. They stopped to watch through the window of a candy shop as a woman pulled her dough through a complicated machine, turning the red and white lines into candy canes.

A crowd had gathered and Willa wound her way to the front, practically pressing her nose to the window in awe. Smiling, she stood there mesmerized when Keane pressed up close behind her, giving her a different kind of yearning altogether.

"Hey, little girl, want some candy?" he whispered in her ear.

"Ha-ha, but yes," she said, not looking away from the window. "I really do."

She felt him smile against her jaw. "Wait here," he said. "I'll be right back."

Not ten seconds later, she felt him brush up behind her again and she laughed. "That was fast."

"Oh, sorry. I got jostled."

Not recognizing the male voice, Willa's smile froze in her throat. She whipped around and faced a guy about her age. Same height, he wore glasses that kept slipping down his nose and an awkward smile.

"Hi," he said. "You should watch on the nights they make chocolate candy canes. Have you ever had one? They're better than *anything*."

"Sounds delicious," she said, but couldn't help thinking *I bet it's not better than sex with Keane Winters . . .*

"They're using chocolate tomorrow night," he said. "I'll be here." He paused and looked at her with a hopefulness that made her want to give him the pupperoni treat in her pocket and pat him on the head. She'd just opened her mouth to let him down gently when she felt a presence at her back. A tall, built, warm, strong presence with testosterone and pheromones pouring off of him, and since her nipples went hard she didn't have to turn this time.

Keane settled in close, not saying anything, just being a silent, badass presence. Craning her neck, she found him giving the Chocolate Candy Cane Guy a death stare that would've made most people pee their pants.

Chocolate Candy Cane Guy gave a little start, cleared his throat and looked at Willa again, an apology in his eyes. "I'm sorry," he said. "I didn't realize you were . . . on a date."

"No worries—" she started but he spun on a heel and vanished into the crowd. She turned to face Keane. "Seriously?"

"What?" he asked innocently.

"Oh no, you don't get to 'what' me like that," she said, saying the word *what* in an imitation of his own much lower timbre. "What the hell was that?"

"Me getting you candy." He held up the bag.

"No, you just peed on me in public."

His mouth twitched.

"You did!" she said, tossing up her hands. "You totally intimidated that poor guy and all he was doing was talking to me."

Keane looked after him. "You think I was intimidating?"

"Enough to make him go crying for his mama." She jabbed him in a rock-solid pec. "You can't dominate me like that. I don't like it at all."

He smiled, but it was a little bit like the Big Bad

Wolf's smile as his hands went to her hips. And right there, surrounded by a crowd of people, none of whom were paying them the slightest bit of attention, he hauled her into him.

"I'm not done being mad," she said.

"I know. It's okay." His hands slid up her arms and cupped her jaw, warm and strong. "You just tell me when you're done." And then his eyes went dark and heated as he lowered his head. "I'll wait . . ." And then he kissed her.

The air around them crackled and in spite of the cold night, the heat between them pulsed and ebbed. Willa felt the rumble of his rough groan as he palmed the back of her head to hold her to him. And just like that, everything around them faded away to nothing more than a dull murmur in the background. There was nothing past the feel of Keane's strong arms around her, the steady beat of his heart thudding against the erratic pace of her own.

Eyes closed, she felt herself melt into him, their bodies seeking each other as if they'd been together for years. It actually scared her and she clutched at him.

In response, he slowed the kiss down, soothing her until they stilled entirely, mouths a breath apart but sharing air. The night breeze caressed her face along with his fingers and she opened her eyes.

His face was shadowed but she wasn't afraid anymore. Feeling almost like she was in a dream, she went back up on tiptoe and lifted her hands to the nape of his neck, the silky strands of his hair slipping through her fingers as she pulled his face back to hers. "When," she murmured against his mouth.

The last thing she saw before her eyes drifted shut again was his smile.

She parted her lips for him eagerly, desperate for another taste, and felt a heat wash over as his hand fisted in her hair. Unable to get close enough, she paused, moaning at the feel of him hard against her.

When he finally lifted his head, she was breathing like a woman who needed an orgasm.

Bad.

She did her best to look unaffected, but he laughed at her. *Laughed.* And then he took her hand and they walked back to her place.

As they got off the elevator, Keane felt Willa squeeze his hand and look at him as she unlocked her door. "What?" he murmured.

"You okay? You seemed a little off when you first came over, and it's back now."

He was a stone wall when he wanted to be, or so he thought. But apparently not with her, because she put a hand on his chest. "Tell me what's wrong?" she asked softly.

It'd been a damn long time since someone had asked him that question and meant it. But he didn't do this, he didn't unload. Ever. She didn't need the burden of his aunt's illness, or the odd sense of limbo his life had become as he sat in his big Vallejo Street house night after night making up reasons not to sell it and move on, so he shook his head.

Her hand slid up his chest, her palm once again

settling on the nape of his neck, her fingers sinking into his hair.

Clearly she also knew just how much he loved it when she touched him like that.

"Keane, when you ask me if I'm okay, you expect honesty, right?"

His brain was more than a little scrambled by her touch, which was arousing as all hell and took away his power of speech, but he did manage a nod.

She nodded back, as if to say *good boy,* as her guileless eyes met his. And then she moved in for the kill.

"So why would I expect anything less from you?" she asked softly. "Tell me what's wrong."

"You first," he said.

"Me? What about me?"

"You could tell me about this morning, when I walked in on you and your employees having what seemed like a pretty serious confrontation."

"Lyndie screwed up," she said. "She then 'fessed up, the end."

"Not the end. What you did, letting her off the hook like that, it was really generous. Incredibly so. Anywhere else, anyone else, would have fired her, and you know it."

"Everyone deserves a second chance," she said. "Now you."

Letting out a low laugh, he pressed his forehead to hers, stepping into her so that they were toe to toe, letting his hand come up to cup her face. Knowing her better now, knowing the incredible woman she was, she truly amazed him. She'd overcome a rough and dark past, and yet she was an incredible light.

One that drew him in.

Neither of them had been given much love, but she hadn't been stymied by that. Instead she'd turned it around, giving it back wherever and however she could.

And what had he done? He'd blocked himself off. Yes, he'd made a life for himself too, and a damn decent good living while he was at it, but he was still closed off. It was hard for him to open up but he wanted to try, friend zone or not. "Now me," he repeated softly.

She nodded. "Now you. Tell me what's wrong, and what I can do to help."

"What's wrong is that I need you," he murmured, dropping his head to kiss the underside of her jaw. "What you can do to help is let me in."

She was ego-strokingly breathless from his touch. "You're already in," she panted.

Was he? Testing that theory, he nudged her inside her apartment, kicked her front door shut, and gently pushed her up against it.

She stared up at him as he lowered his head, not closing her eyes until the last second, but when his mouth covered hers, she moaned and wrapped her arms around him tight enough to hurt in the very best possible way.

Chapter 21

#TurnDownForWhat

Willa lost herself in Keane's words . . . *"I need you,"* in the feel of his hard, heated body up against hers, in the taste of him as he kissed her in the way only he could. He made her ache and yearn and burn. She'd told him that he was in, and she meant it.

Like it or not, he was definitely in her heart. What she wasn't sure was what it meant, to either of them. She'd said they weren't going to do this again, and she'd said that out of self-preservation, but now with his hands on her, she couldn't remember why exactly.

"I'm not usually this easy," she said out loud, hoping to make him laugh and relieve some of this tension, because she didn't know about him but *she* felt strung tighter than a bow.

"Willa." He did indeed laugh, sexy low and gruff as he pressed his face into her hair. "Babe, you're many, many things. But easy isn't one of them."

When she tried to shove him away, he tightened his grip and lifted his head to meet her annoyed eyes with his laughing ones. Then his smile faded. They watched each other for a beat, his gaze suddenly heated and unwavering. "I know you said one night was all you wanted," he said. "But I'm thinking two is better than one."

She nodded, happy to be on the same page. "Two is always better than one, right?"

Letting out a very sexy, very male sound of agreement, he kissed her again, his hands both rough and arousing as they slid up to fist in her hair, holding her still for his kiss. With one tug he bared her throat, scraping his teeth along her skin, making her shudder and press even closer if that was possible. Then his hands skimmed beneath her shirt. She managed to get hers into the back of his jeans and—

"Mew."

Breathless, they broke apart and turned in unison to find Petunia, head low, butt raised in the air and wriggling.

"Watch out," Keane said. "Attack mode initiated."

"Petunia," Willa said softly and the cat lifted her head. Ice blue eyes were narrowed in disapproval.

"I didn't know that she's a kiss blocker," she said on a laugh.

"In two more minutes she'd have been a cock block—"

Still laughing, Willa put her fingers over Keane's lips. "No swearing in front of the children."

He nipped at her fingers and heat slashed through her from her roots to her toes, setting fire to some special spots along the way. "So," she whispered, staring at his mouth. "Where were we?"

He slid his hands up her arms and back into her hair. "Right here." And he kissed her again, a slow, melting nuzzle of lips; warm, comforting.

Tempting.

Her body moved of its own volition, shifting closer, seeking his heat. With a groan, he pulled her in, those wide shoulders blocking out the light, everything but him. One of his big, warm hands settled at the nape of her neck, holding her steady as he continued to kiss the ever-loving daylights out of her.

She cupped his strong jaw, stroking the two-day stubble that she wanted to feel scrape over her body. When her jacket fell from her, she startled. He'd un-zipped and nudged it off her shoulders and she hadn't even noticed.

"Shh," he whispered, his mouth on her throat. "I've got you."

And he did. Supported between the wall and his big, delicious body, it was okay that her legs felt wobbly.

Because he had her.

They had to break the kiss for a single beat when he lifted her shirt over her head and then his warm hands were on her bare breasts.

He'd unhooked her bra, letting that fall away as well.

Lifting his head, he looked down at her and let out a long, slow exhale, like he was struggling with control. He watched as she arched into his touch, begging with-out words for his mouth, for him to find her irresistible, pretty.

"I can't take my eyes off you," he murmured, lips at her ear. "You're so beautiful, Willa."

"Mew!"

"Quiet," they both said at the same time, holding each other's laughing gaze.

"I thought it was kids that were supposed to act like birth control," he said.

Petunia actually sighed and stalked off, legs stiff, tail twitching.

"Don't go away mad," Keane told her. "Just go away."

"Keane."

"Only for a few minutes," he called after the cat. And then he lifted Willa into his arms, the muscles of his shoulders and back rippling smoothly under his shirt. Mmm. Pressing her mouth to his jaw, she wrapped her legs around his waist as he carried her down the hall to her bed.

Where he tossed her.

A surprised squeak escaped her but before she'd bounced more than once he was on her, pressing her down into the mattress, covering her body with his.

"What did I say about dominating me?" she asked with a laugh.

He raised his head, his eyes as dark as the night. "I was hoping that didn't apply to sex." His mouth left her lips, heading toward her ear, taking little love bites as he went. "Cuz I'm feeling a little dominant here, Willa."

Each nibble, each scrape of his teeth seemed to melt her bones away. "That's okay," she panted. "Maybe we could take turns."

"Maybe." His movements over her were sensual,

slow, and dreamlike, and so erotic she writhed for more. He worked his way south from her neck to her collarbone—who knew that was an erogenous zone?— making her gasp when he got to her breast. His tongue worked her nipple over, teasing and tormenting along with his talented, knowing hands, and the sensations drove her right to the edge of a cliff and left her hanging there. *"Keane."*

"I know." He slid further down her body, divesting her of the sweats as he went. Then he made himself at home between her legs, spread wide by his broad-as-a-mountain shoulders.

"Um," she said. "I—"

He scraped her panties to the side, pressed a kiss to the hot, wet flesh he exposed, and she promptly forgot what she'd been about to say. She heard a shuddery moan and was shocked to realize it was her. "Off," she demanded, pushing his shirt up his ridged abs, not wanting to be the only half-naked one, but also wanting to see his gorgeous bod.

Without skipping a beat or taking his mouth off of her, he reached one hand up and tugged his shirt over his head. This did momentarily rip his mouth from her heated skin, but the moment he was free of the shirt, he went back to loving her with his mouth.

She could feel him now, *all* of him. "When did you lose the rest of your clothes—Oh my God," she cried out, eyes crossing with lust when he did something in combination with his teeth, his tongue, and his fingers. "Don't stop doing that."

"Never," he promised as he played with her, teasing

her to the very edge. But just as she felt her toes start to curl, he stopped and she cried out.

He only flashed a wicked smile, not at all concerned that he was a fraction of an inch from certain death for leaving her hanging like that. Leaning up over her, he gave her one hard kiss and then hooked his long fingers in the sides of her panties, tugging them down her legs, sending them sailing over his shoulder without taking his eyes off of her.

And what he'd exposed.

"Oh, Willa. Christ." His big hands held her thighs open. "You're so gorgeous." Surging up, he kissed her mouth, his hands still tormenting her, the sensations skittering down her every nerve ending with a little *zing,* driving her back to the edge she'd never really left. She dug her fingers into his biceps.

"If you stop again—"

"I won't." And true to his word, he continued the assault, the sexy bastard, slowly kissing his way south, stopping at her belly button to take a little nibble out of her, making her squirm.

Laughing softly against her, he tightened his grip on her hips, holding her still so he could drive her crazy. This involved his mouth taking the scenic route, where he alternately dragged his tongue along her heated skin and stopped once every other breath or so to take a little love bite.

"Keane!"

He lifted his head, his eyes dark, so dark she nearly drowned in them. "Last time we did this your way," he said. "It's my turn now. My way, Willa."

She swallowed hard at the heat and fierce intensity of his low voice. "And your way is to torture me?"

He flashed another wicked grin. "To start."

With a groan, she flopped back to the bed, arms over her head.

"Yeah, I like that," Keane said and reached up, stroking his hands along her arms to her fingers, which he wrapped around the bottom rung of the headboard. "Don't let go." Then he held her open, groaned at the visual, and licked the length of her center.

Willa got a little fuzzy on the details after that but they involved her moaning his name nonstop and fisting her hands in his hair, and after a shockingly short time, coming apart for him.

Completely.

His body was hard and muscular and felt amazing against hers and she forced her eyes to open to take in as much as possible because this was absolutely going to have to be it. She couldn't do this again with him and not hopelessly fall. In fact, she was only half convinced that she could resist doing so *this* time.

Braced on his forearms on either side of her head, he looked down at her. A lock of hair fell over his forehead, his eyes dark with heat and sexy concentration, his mouth still wet. The sight of him took her breath.

God, *he* was the beautiful one, she thought dazedly. Simply beautiful. Reaching up, she traced his bottom lip with a fingertip and then tugged him closer so she could suck that lower lip into her mouth.

He gave a half groan, half growl as she slid her tongue into his mouth, sliding it along his.

"Love the taste of you," he said and thrust inside of her.

She cried out and arched up to meet him, unable to figure out when he'd put on a condom, but grateful one of them was thinking with something other than their pleasure buttons.

Above her, Keane's eyes drifted shut, his expression uninhibited pleasure.

He took her breath.

He had one arm beneath her shoulders to anchor her, the other gripping her ass as if he needed to be as close as possible. When he began to move, it was in a slow, lazy grind, like he had all the time in the world to love her.

But he didn't. Given the lump in her throat, they were on a time crunch now, before panic hit. So she shoved him, rolling him to his back. To his credit, he went easily, flashing a wolf smile.

"Your turn?" he asked huskily, his voice pure sex.

Not wasting her breath with words, she rocked her hips, fast and hard.

"Yeah," he murmured, filling his hands with her breasts. "Your turn."

Then he became the backseat driver, reaching between them, touching her intimately, knowingly, causing her to explode all over him.

While she was still dazed, she felt his hands shift her, snugging her inner thighs tighter to the outsides of his, causing him to fill her even more, taking her on an out-of-body experience. And this time when she began to convulse around him, he followed her over the edge.

Early the next morning, Willa came awake all warm and toasty, her face smooshed into the crook of Keane's neck. He was flat on his back, out cold, and she . . . well, she was all over him.

Petunia was no better, having made herself at home on his feet.

Willa put a finger to her lips and very carefully eased away and dashed into her bathroom. She caught a look at herself in the mirror and blinked at the flushed, dazed expression on her face. Was she . . . smiling? Damn, she was. She tried to turn it into a frown but couldn't. She literally couldn't.

That's when she noticed the duffel bag on the floor. Keane must've brought it in last night when he'd run out to his truck to get his phone charger somewhere around midnight.

The bag was unzipped and she accidentally-on-purpose took a peek inside. Extra clothes. A tooth-brush. Deodorant.

In her hand, her phone beeped and scared her half into an early grave. "Hello?" she whispered.

"Hey," Elle said. "I—"

"He's got a one-night-stand kit!" she whispered.

Elle paused. "Who has a what?"

Willa shut the bathroom door, leaned back against it, and let her weak legs collapse, sliding down the door until she was sitting on the floor. "Keane," she said. "He showed up here last night to pick up Petunia and now I'm in the bathroom looking at a duffel bag full of his stuff that—"

"Whoa. You can't just go from last night to this morning without more details than that! What's the matter with you? I want the good stuff. You slept with him again?"

Well, technically, there'd been very little actual sleep involved both on the roof *or* last night, which had been one round after another of torrid, erotic, sensual sex such as she'd never known.

"You're holding out on me," Elle said.

"Forget that!" Willa whispered. "He has a *one-night-stand* kit!" Okay, technically last night made night two, so it was really a two-night-stand kit.

"Honey, that just makes him a smart man."

Willa rolled her eyes so hard they nearly fell out of her head and she disconnected. Things were fine. She was fine. She could do this. One-night stands turned into two-night stands all the time. In fact, she stared at Keane's stuff and could admit that maybe Elle was right. Not that she was about to admit it because Elle already knew she was right.

Elle was always right.

Willa slipped into the only clothes she had in the bathroom—yesterday's work clothes. She did this because she could think better when she wasn't naked. A quick peek in the mirror confirmed she was still smiling like an idiot. She took a deep breath and opened the door.

Keane stood there propping up the doorjamb with a beefy shoulder, expression slightly wary. "Hey."

"Hey."

He gave her a half smile. "Gotta be honest. I figured you'd be long gone when I woke up."

"It's my place."

"You know what I mean," he said. He wasn't playing this morning.

So she wouldn't either. "I'm working hard at being a grown-up," she said. "And that would have been rude anyway."

His smile spread and sent warmth skittering through her. "God forbid you be rude." He tugged her into him and nuzzled at her neck. "Mornin'."

Since her knees wobbled, she clutched at him. "Mornin'. Um, Keane?"

"Mmm?" His mouth was busy at her throat and he was big and warm and shirtless, and her eyes nearly rolled back in her head.

"I really do have to get to work," she managed. "It's later than I usually get started. You can stay, of course, use my shower, whatever. Just lock up when you go."

He lifted his head and met her gaze. Searched it. And then apparently decided she was indeed to be trusted being a grown-up because he nodded.

Relief that they were handling this without hurt or hard feelings, and even better yet, a discussion that she wasn't ready to have, she leaned in and kissed him, going for short and sweet.

But he tightened his grip, changed the angle of her kiss and took over in Keane fashion. By the time he let her go, she had to search her brain for what her game plan had been.

"Work," he said with a smile. "We both have to get to work."

"Right." She blinked. "Um . . ."

With a low laugh, he put his hands on her hips and turned her toward the living room, adding a light smack on her ass to get her moving. "Have a good one."

She'd had so many orgasms the night before that she couldn't count them. She was wearing a perma-smile. What could go wrong?

Chapter 22

#ThrowingShade

When Willa was gone, Keane looked down at Pita, sitting calmly near his bare feet.

She regarded him from down the length of her nose and gave a little sniff.

"Yeah, yeah," he said. "You're stuck with me again."

His phone was having a seizure on the nightstand, full of texts and emails from Sass and Mason. He scrubbed a hand down over his face and swore when the phone went off again, this time a call from Sass. He hit ignore.

"Mew," Pita said, going for pathetic.

"I know. Food. Pronto." He pulled on his jeans and searched out his shirt, finding it hanging from a lampshade.

Normally this would've given him a smile because it meant the night had been suitably down and dirty and sexy hot.

And it had been those things.

It'd also been a helluva lot more. Which he figured was the real reason Willa had taken off so early for work. She was feeling it.

But she didn't want to.

Not the best feeling in the world. Pulling the shirt over his head, he turned in a circle looking for his shoes.

Petunia was sitting in front of them looking very smug and happy with herself.

"Move, cat."

For once in her life, she did as he asked. She moved—revealing that she'd once again used his shoes as her own personal kitty litter.

Willa sat on the counter of her own shop in yesterday's clothes, stuffing her face with Tina's out-of-this-world muffins.

The muffins didn't fix anything that was wrong with her life, but they did make her feel better.

It was still early, way before opening time, a fact for which she was grateful. At some point she'd have to figure out how to eke an extra hour out of her day in order to get upstairs to her apartment and out of yesterday's clothes. She'd also have to figure out how to lose the ridiculously sated, just-laid expression still all over her face, but so far it was refusing to go away.

Damn orgasms.

Rory and Cara showed up and took one look at her and smiled. "Are you making the walk of shame in your own shop?" Cara asked.

Yes. "Of course not."

Rory eyeballed Willa up one side and down the other. "Actually," the girl said, "the true walk of shame is when you take all the mugs and plates you've been hoarding from your nightstand to your kitchen."

They both laughed.

Willa ignored them and popped the last muffin into her mouth. She took a moment to close her eyes and moan as the delicious pumpkin spice burst onto her tongue.

"She's not talking," Cara said to Rory. "That's weird. I've never seen her not talk."

"As soon as the caffeine kicks in she'll come back to life." Rory nudged Willa's coffee closer to her and then backed away like Willa might be a cocked and loaded shotgun.

"But she doesn't look tired," Cara said, staring at Willa. "She looks like how my sister looks when her boyfriend's on leave from the Army and they boink all night long."

Willa choked on her muffin.

Rory pounded her on the back, flashing a rare grin as Elle and Haley and Pru knocked on the back door.

Willa came to life with sudden panic. "Don't let them in!"

So of course Rory let them in. "Watch out," her soon-to-be-dead employee said to her best friends. "She's not fully caffeinated and I think she's also had a lot of sex."

Willa choked again. She glared at everyone, but her best friends were in possession of more muffins and coffee, so she held out her hands. "Gimme."

Pru handed everything over. "Sorry I had to bail on girls' night, but I'm feeling much better." She studied Willa's face, head cocked. "Hmm. Keane's good. He even got rid of the stress wrinkle between her eyes."

"Wow," Haley said, peering in close to see for herself. "You're right. Sex works better than that ninety-buck wrinkle lotion we all bought that doesn't work worth shit."

Willa glanced at Elle, who was standing there quietly assessing the situation. "I'm going to need you to say something here, Elle. You know, be your usual voice of reason so I don't murder anyone."

"There's no Netflix in prison," Elle said.

"Okay, that'll do it, thanks."

Elle tipped her coffee to Willa's in a toast of solidarity.

Willa drank her coffee and let out her biggest fear. "Am I being stupid? Letting another guy in? Is this a mistake?"

"Is he as good a guy as he seems?" Pru asked.

Willa thought about it. "He doesn't like cats and yet he's taking care of Petunia. He's financially taking care of his sick aunt even though he barely knows her. He's got an incredibly demanding career going but he always makes time for me. And . . ."

"What?" Elle pressed quietly when Willa broke off.

"He makes me feel good," she said. "Special." She felt a little ridiculous even saying it and her face heated.

But Elle smiled and it was the kind of smile that reached all the way to her eyes. Rare and beautiful. "Well then," she said, squeezing Willa's hands. "There's your answer."

"But I think I blew it," Willa said. "He stayed over last night and I woke up and . . ."

"Panicked," Elle said helpfully.

Willa blew out a sigh and held up her finger and thumb about an inch apart. "Maybe just a very little bit."

Elle held up her own two hands, two feet apart. "Or a lot." She looked at Willa. "I still don't get why you can't just enjoy a hot man and hot sex. You can always bail when and if it fizzles out."

"But what if it doesn't fizzle?" Willa asked. "What then?"

"You enjoy it," Elle said gently.

Right. Why hadn't she thought of that?

"What did you do?" Haley asked. "Kick him out?"

"Worse," Elle said, looking amused.

Willa put her hands to her hot cheeks. "I ran out of my own place like the hounds of hell were on my heels."

Haley bit her lower lip.

Pru didn't have the same decorum. She didn't bother to try to keep her laugh in; she let it out and in fact almost fell over she was laughing so hard.

Elle shook her head. "I tried to tell her—*never* leave a hot man alone in your bed."

Well, technically he hadn't been still in bed when she'd left but why had she left again? Willa honestly couldn't remember her justifications for that, which left the only possible answer.

She was running scared and that just plain pissed her off about herself. Since when was she a scaredy-cat?

She hopped off the counter, pointing at Pru. "You're off today?"

"Yes."

"You're officially an employee. Rory will tell you what to do. We're having a big sale and she'll need extra hands on deck. I'll be back!"

"But why me?" Pru called after her.

"Because you laughed the hardest."

"Well, shit," Pru said.

It was still early when Keane got out of his truck, jogged up the stairs to the Vallejo Street house, and quietly shut the door behind him. Coast clear. All he had to do now was get up the stairs to his shower without being seen and—

"Whoa," Sass said from behind him.

Fuck.

"Mas!" she yelled. "Come look at this."

Keane turned to face her, eyes narrowed.

She smiled sweetly as she looked at her watch. "How nice of you to show up for work today. We've been calling you."

"I've been busy."

She ran her gaze down the length of him and came to a stop at his bare feet. "Where are your shoes? Under her bed?"

Actually, they were in the Dumpster, not that he was about to tell Sass that. He thrust out Petunia's carrier. "Take this," he said. "I'm going to shower. I'll meet you in the office for the morning meeting in ten—"

Someone knocked on the door and grateful for the interruption, Keane hauled it open.

Willa stood there chewing on her lower lip, looking a little bit unsettled that he'd opened the door so quickly.

He didn't know why he was so surprised. She'd been surprising him continuously from the moment she'd let him into her shop that first morning three weeks ago now and saved his ass by taking Pita.

"Hey," she said quietly. "I—" She broke off and looked beyond him.

Keane turned and realized that Sass was watching avidly. Mason walked into the foyer as well, eyes on his phone as he spoke. "It's about damn time, boss. You ignored my calls all morning—which is a huge infraction of the rules, as you like to remind us every other second—" He raised his head from his phone and eyed the situation. He winced, turned on his heel, and walked back out.

Not Sass. She stood there smiling wide. "Hi," she said, reaching out a hand to Willa. "I'm Sass, Keane's admin. And you're Willa, or as we like to say around here, The Amazing Person Who Makes the Boss Smile. We love you, by the way."

"Thanks," Willa said. "I think."

"I've seen you before," Sass said. "At O'Riley's Pub. You were up onstage doing karaoke with two of your friends, singing Wilson Phillips's 'Hold On' like it was your job."

Willa grimaced. "Oh boy."

Sass smiled. "Yeah, you guys were a lot of fun. If you ever get Keane up there to sing, I'm going to need it recorded."

"Okay," Keane said, pulling Willa inside before turning to Sass. "I'm sure you have to go back to work now."

Sass smiled. "Yes, with you. We're not done with our morning meeting. We were just getting to the why you've been ignoring phone calls, texts, and emails, but I'm guessing the reason just showed up."

Keane pointed down the hall. "I'll be there in a minute."

"Oh, don't postpone a meeting for my sake," Willa said hurriedly. "You're busy. I'm just going to go—"

Keane grabbed her hand. "Wait. It'll only take me a minute to kill Sass—"

"If I had a dime for every time he said that," Sass quipped.

Keane didn't take his eyes off Willa. "Please?" he added quietly and was relieved when she nodded. He then turned to Sass. She was still smiling at him, the kind of smile that said she was getting a lot of mileage out of this. Reluctantly letting go of Willa, he nodded at Sass to follow him.

"Don't start," he warned as they moved down the hall, hopefully out of hearing range. "I know damn well that if it'd been an emergency, you'd have let me know. You were snooping just now because I'm never late. I don't pay you to snoop, Sass, so get your ass to work."

She kept grinning.

"Don't pay you to grin at me either."

"Well, honestly," a woman said. "That's no way to talk to the people you care about."

Keane glanced over into what would eventually be the dining room but at the moment was a blueprint room. Meaning there were several pairs of sawhorses set up with large planks of plywood as makeshift tables. Covering these tables were the blueprints of the building.

The woman was standing amongst the sawhorses, glaring at him.

He blew out a sigh. "Mom, it's called sarcasm. That's how we show we care."

"Well, it's hurtful," she said. "I taught you better than that."

No, actually, what she'd taught him was to show no feelings at all. He looked at Sass, who'd clearly let his mom in.

Sass smiled. "Meet the emergency."

Keane turned back to his mom. She'd not stopped by any of his jobs for a long time, and in fact, they'd talked just last month, so . . . "What's wrong?"

His mom straightened and came toward him. If she noticed his bare feet or the fact that he was still carrying a cat carrier because Sass hadn't taken it from him, she gave no indication.

"I wanted to tell you that we're all done with the rental," she said. "Which I assume you know because you deposited money into our account. We don't want money from you, Keane. That wasn't part of the deal."

His parents had both retired two years ago. And

because they'd assumed they were the smartest people they knew, they refused his advice for years regarding getting a financial planner. So when they'd invested their funds with a "friend who knows what he's doing" and that friend took off with all their money, they hadn't wanted to admit it.

In fact, Keane had only found all this out when he'd inadvertently learned from a mutual acquaintance that they'd gotten an eviction notice. They'd finally admitted that they were broke and because of that might soon be homeless, but they still refused to take money from him.

So he'd been forced to let them "work" for him instead. He'd put them up in an apartment building he owned in South Beach. In return they insisted on helping him renovate the place in lieu of paying rent. Just until they got on their feet.

It'd been a serious pain in his ass because he and his mom had butted heads on every single renovation the building had required.

But at least they weren't in the streets. "You could have just called me," he said.

His mother nodded. "I did. Your admin said you weren't taking calls and suggested I stop by."

Sass slid him a . . . well, sassy look. He returned the volley with a "you're fired" look but she just smiled at him serenely.

She knew as well as he did that she was the glue. His glue. It would be comforting if he didn't want to strangle her more than half the time.

"Anyway . . ." His mother made a big show of holding out a set of keys. "Wanted to give these back to you."

He didn't take them. "Mom, you can stay there. You don't have to go."

"But we're done with the work."

"Stay there," he repeated. He didn't want them out on the streets. He didn't want to have to worry about them. "It's no big deal."

"No big deal?" she asked, looking as if he'd just suggested she murdered kittens for a living. "You giving us a handout is *no big deal?* Well, I'm glad to know we mean so little to you then."

"You know that's not what I meant."

"I'll have you know we have plenty of other options," she said stiffly. "Your sisters, for one. Janine wants us in her house with her. With her child, so that we could be a *part* of their lives. Rachel would have us as well."

Okay, so he stood corrected. She absolutely *could* make this more difficult. And he knew firsthand that his sisters were just making noise with the offer to host them. Janine's husband would probably run for the hills if that happened. James was a decent enough guy but he was smart enough to have hard limits, and living with the elder Winterses was definitely a hard limit.

"By all means," Keane said. "If that's what would make you happy. But the offer to stay in my apartment building stands."

Her lips tightened.

And because he wasn't a complete asshole, he

sighed. "Listen, I really could use someone to manage the place, to keep up with the building and the renters' needs."

She stared at him for a beat, clearly torn between choking on her own pride or calling his bluff calling hers. Finally she snatched the keys back from his held-out palm and shoved them in her pocket.

"We'll keep a careful accounting of our work, crediting it back for rent," she said.

"Mom, I trust you."

"Expect monthly reports," she said.

The equivalent of a hug and kiss and an "I love you, son."

She turned to the door and then stopped. Still facing the door, she said, "And I know that's Sally's cat. You're helping her too."

"She's family," he said and then he lied out his ass. "And the cat's no problem."

"You're doing more than just taking care of her cat," his mom said. "Sally called me yesterday and told me everything."

Keane let out a low breath. "Then you know that me helping her is the least I can do."

She didn't say anything for a long beat, did nothing but take a small sniff that struck terror in his heart.

Was she . . . crying? He'd never seen her lose it and truthfully, he'd rather someone ripped out his fingernails one by one than see it now. "Mom—"

"I'm fine." She sniffed again and then still talking to the door softly said, "I was the teacher, for twenty-five years. But sometimes you teach me things I didn't expect."

He stared at her, stunned.

"Well," she said with a nod. "I'm off. I'll call you, keep you updated."

"You don't have to—"

"I'll call you," she repeated and he realized that she was trying, in the only way she knew how, to stay in his life.

"That would be nice," he said. "I'll call you too, okay?"

Her voice was soft and there was an unmistakable sense of relief in her voice. "Okay."

And then she was gone.

He turned and caught the flash of someone ducking behind a doorway. A petite, insatiably curious redheaded someone. Slowly she peeked back out and winced when her eyes locked on him.

She was cautious of getting in too deep with him and besides the fact that he'd come right out and told her he didn't do deep, she was right to be wary. Giving in to this thing between them would be insanity, and having his mother remind him of the way he was wired, how the entire family was wired—with an utter lack of the giving-someone-your-heart gene—had been a wake-up call. Willa was dodging a bullet here and she didn't even know it.

"You okay?" she asked quietly.

Was he? He had no idea, not that he was about to admit it. "Yeah." He thought maybe he could see some pity in her gaze and he pretty much hated everything about that so he gave a vague wave at the place around him. "I've really got to get to work."

She nodded, but didn't move. Instead she clasped her hands tight together and held his gaze. "I wanted to explain my abrupt departure this morning. It's just that when I woke up wrapped around you like one of those amazingly delicious warm pretzels at AT&T Park, I . . ."

"Panicked?"

"No," she said. "Well, okay, yes, but only for a few minutes. I don't regret last night, Keane. I just wanted you to know that. I'm sorry—"

"Willa, stop," he said, interrupting her. Both this morning with her on top of the visit with his mom had left him feeling a little hollow and far too raw to deal with any more heavy emotions. "Forget it, okay? It was nothing."

She looked a little stunned at that and it took him a second to realize she thought he was saying what they'd shared was nothing. "Not what I meant," he said, but since he didn't know what he *did* mean, he fell silent.

She nodded like she knew though, which he was glad about. Someone should know what the fuck was going on here. His tool belt was lying on one of the sawhorses and he put it on, hopefully signaling he was good with no further conversation.

She took a deep breath. "If this is about me hearing that conversation with your mom—"

"It's not."

"Because it's not your fault how she treats you," she said.

"Yes, it is. I was a rotten kid, Willa. I was," he said firmly when she opened her mouth. "I get that some of it was because I didn't get a lot of positive attention, but that's no excuse."

She was arms crossed now, defensive for him, clearly not willing to believe the worst of him, all of which did something painful and also a little wonderful inside his chest.

"What could you possibly have done that was so bad?"

"For one, I was a complete shit. Even after I graduated high school. They gave me tuition money to complement a partial football scholarship for two years, until I got injured and blew the scholarship. I hated every second of school, by the way. So when they gave me tuition for year three, I quit and used the money for the down payment for my first renovation project."

"I take it they didn't approve."

"I didn't tell them for several years," he admitted.

Her eyes widened.

"See?" he asked. "A complete shit. I paid them back with interest, but the point is that as a result of my own actions, they don't trust me very much."

"Not everyone is made for the academic life."

He shook his head. "Don't make excuses for me, Willa."

"Well someone has to give you a break," she said, tossing up her hands. "You've worked pretty hard to help your aunt and your family. You've worked hard to make something of yourself and—" She broke off and looked at him as if she'd never seen him before.

"What?"

"Oh my God," she whispered. "I just realized something. I accused you of not being able to attach. But clearly you can, and deeply."

He started to shake his head but stopped because given his growing attachment to her, not to mention some extraordinarily deep emotions on the same subject, she was right.

"And not only can you obviously love and love deeply," she said slowly, putting a hand to her chest like it hurt. "You can even hold on to it. Maybe even better than me. Hell, *definitely* better than me."

His chest got tight at the thought of her believing that about herself. "Willa—"

"I know, right? Not a super comfortable feeling." She paused when from inside his pocket, his phone went off.

It'd been doing so for the past half hour. Subcontractors, clients . . . probably Sass as well. And even as he thought it, a well-dressed couple parked out front.

Clients with whom he had a meeting with in . . . he looked at his watch. Shit. Right now.

"The real world calls," Willa said and took a step back.

"This is my real world," he said. "They can wait."

"Keane," Marco Delgado, a longtime client, called out with a smile. "Good to see you, my man."

"It's okay," Willa said as she moved farther away.

Kind of the story of his life really.

"You understood this morning when I needed to get to work," she said, "and I understand this."

And then she was gone.

Shit. Whelp, he was happy to know she understood. He just wished he knew exactly what she understood and if she would explain it to him.

Chapter 23

#SquadGoals

Willa went to the shop. The shop had always been her escape, her joy, her first and only love.

But as she walked in with all the Christmas lights sparkling and a customer's dog barking at her stuffed Rudolf the Red-Nosed Reindeer sitting on the kitty-litter display, and Rory smiling and handling customers from two different corners of the place, she didn't feel the usual calm wash over her.

She hadn't felt calm since she'd woken up that morning but especially not after overhearing the conversation between Keane and his mom. Because now she knew an uncomfortable truth about herself. She'd been cruising along with Keane, secure in the knowledge that he wasn't interested in love, but there was a fatal flaw with that.

It was all on her. *She* was the one with the issues.

She hadn't seen that coming.

Luckily her day was long, not allowing her much time to think or dwell. And at the end of it, she looked around for more to do but there wasn't anything. And yet she didn't want to go home. Going home alone would remind her that she was . . .

Well, alone.

So she went to the pub, where Finn immediately caught her eye and gestured her over. "Try this," he said, handing her a mug. "Homemade whipped cream over the best, most amazing hot chocolate ever invented."

"How many ways are there to make hot chocolate?"

"Only one way," he said. "My way." He gestured to the mug. "It's a new recipe, a surprise for Pru. Tell me what you think."

She sipped and he was right. It was the most amazing hot chocolate ever invented. "Oh my God."

He smiled. "Yeah?"

"Oh yeah. It's orgasmic."

He grimaced and took the mug away from her. "Not in my pub."

She could see Spence and Archer in the back arguing over the darts and knew she could go back there and join them. Knew too that Finn would make her his famous chicken wings if she wanted. But for the first time in as long as she could remember, she didn't want to be here either.

Finn's smile vanished. "Hey. What's wrong?"

"Nothing."

"Willa." He leaned in. "Don't bullshit a bullshitter. I know you better than just about anyone. Something's wrong." He studied her a minute. "Is it Keane? Do I need to beat the shit out of him?"

She choked out a laugh. "You think you could?"

"No, but I could get Archer to do it. Archer could make him disappear and no one'd ever be the wiser. Just say the word."

"No!" She laughed again, but it faded fast. "No," she repeated firmly and shook her head. "This one's on me."

"Fine. We'll help you bury the body. Just name the time and place."

"You're not even going to ask me why?"

"I don't need to know why."

That was the thing about Finn, and the others as well. They loved her like family should. Unconditionally. Without question. No doubt. No hesitation.

No qualifiers.

And even though Finn was just teasing, she knew if she ever needed something, anything at all, he'd be there for her.

Always.

Her throat tightened because she loved knowing that, but at the moment it wasn't what she needed.

He caught her hand as she slid off the barstool. "Seriously, what can I do?" he asked quietly.

"You've already done it." She brushed a kiss over his jaw. "Thanks."

She took herself to the rooftop. She climbed the fire escape and then stilled as she was bombarded with flashes of the last time she'd been here. Keane's hands holding her over him, his mouth at her ear whispering dirty sweet nothings, his hard body driving hers . . .

The breath escaped her lungs and her knees wobbled.

She'd come here to be alone to wallow, but now all she could do was ache . . .

When the stairwell door opened and a pair of obviously women's heels clicked their way across the rubber composite, she sighed. "Unless you have food with you, go away."

"Who do you think I am?" Elle, of course. "I've got food *and* wine," she said. Always prepared, she stopped next to where Willa sat right on the rooftop without anything to protect her clothing and shook her head. "Clothes deserve respect, honey. Serious respect."

"I'm in Levi's," Willa pointed out.

"Levi's deserve respect right along with Tory Burch." Elle searched her bag and came up with a *Cosmo* magazine. She tossed this to the ground and then carefully sat on it. "This is how much I love you. I'm sitting on the ground in a dress and heels." She handed over a box of Finn's wings.

"What's this?" Willa asked.

"A bribe."

And that's when Pru popped her head up over the ledge from the fire escape. "Is the coast clear?"

Elle waved her over. Willa knew Elle hadn't used the fire escape herself because one, climbing it in heels was a death sentence, and two, she only did things where she could look cool and gorgeous, and no one looked cool or gorgeous climbing the fire escape.

Pru climbed over the ledge, followed by Haley.

"I'm not in the mood to talk," Willa warned them.

"I remember a time when I said the exact same thing to you," Pru said and sat on Willa's other side.

"And I respected your wishes and left you alone."

Pru laughed good and long over that. "Hell, no, you didn't. You sat right next to me and held my hand while we marathoned *Say Yes to The Dress*. Elle got drunk."

"I did not," Elle said.

"Right," Pru said. "That was me. My point is, we're not leaving you alone."

Haley was beaming at them. "You know what this is right here? It's squad goals."

Elle pointed at her. "You need to cut back on Instagram."

Willa took the box of wings and dug in. "You guys don't have to stay. I'm not sharing the wings and there's nothing to watch."

"Well now that's just an insult to the universe," Haley said and pointed to the sky.

Which was a glorious blanket of black velvet littered with diamonds as far as the eye could see.

It was gorgeous, Willa could admit. "I'm pretty sure the universe is feminine. A male would've messed that all up."

Haley snorted in agreement.

"So men suck," Elle said. "What's new about that?"

Pru, the only one of them in a sturdy, stable, loving relationship, shook her head in disagreement. "Men are just flawed, is all. And that's a good thing."

"How?" Willa asked. "How in the world is that a good thing?"

"Hello, have you never heard of makeup sex?"

Willa thought about sex with Keane and sighed. It was pretty amazing. Off-the-charts amazing. She could only imagine what makeup sex would be like . . .

"They don't mean to be dumbasses," Pru said. "But sometimes they just can't help it. That's just how they're wired. But I've gotta say, Willa, Keane seems like a really good guy."

"You're certainly glowing like I've never seen you glow," Haley said.

Everyone looked Willa over closely and she swallowed a bite of delicious chicken wing and rolled her eyes. "If I'm glowing, it's from sweating in the shop all day."

"You haven't done anything for yourself in far too long," Haley said. "You should do Keane."

Everyone burst out laughing and Haley shook her head. "Okay, not what I meant. But hey, whatever works."

"I think I need a moment from . . . doing Keane," Willa said.

"Why?" Pru asked.

Wasn't that just the question? She knew she was giving off wishy-washy vibes but she wasn't being wishy-washy so much as she was going after one desire while protecting the other.

Meaning she wanted Keane in her bed. Oh how she wanted that . . . while somehow also keeping her heart protected.

The ship might have sailed there, she thought . . .

Yeah, it was too late. And if she'd been smart, she would have cut her losses before now. But she so loved being intimate with Keane, loved everything about it, and she'd had this fantasy that she could somehow keep the goodness of that separate from her growing emotions for him.

That ship had sailed too.

"It's a new development," she admitted. "See, in the beginning it was him who didn't want anything too serious, while I was ready to find a partner."

"And now?" Elle asked.

"And now . . ." Willa closed her eyes. "I want to keep sleeping with him but I don't want to call it a relationship. What does that make me?"

"A man," Elle said.

"Honey, I don't see the problem," Pru said over their laughter. "He's not going to get attached, you just said so. Go for it. But I have to warn you that sometimes really great sex turns into really great intimacy, which can then turn into a really great relationship before you even realize it."

Willa shook her head. She'd never been in a really great relationship; no need to start believing in that now. "I don't think we can move forward without a conversation. I think he wants to define things. We were on the brink of that this morning but luckily his work got in the way."

"Hey, I've got an idea," Haley said. "Call him over and then take off your top and distract him from talking. What?" she said when everyone just stared at her. "Willa has great boobs."

Elle eyed Willa's boobs critically. "It's true. Woman pay big bucks for a rack like that."

Willa looked down at herself. She was short. A more polite word was *petite*. But in height only because everywhere else she wasn't dainty. She had curves. Hips. The aforementioned boobs. Even her stomach was a little too curvy to suit her but no amount of sit-ups or exercising seemed to help that.

Or at least she was pretty sure sit-ups and exercise wouldn't help. "He's too smart to fall for that. He'll see right through the distraction technique." She dropped her head to her knees. "Damn. I was so sure this wasn't in danger of going anywhere, that *he* wasn't relationship material . . ."

"And now?" Elle asked.

"And now . . . I'm realizing *I'm* the one who isn't relationship material." There. She said it. Admitted her biggest failing out loud.

Her friends gasped in instant denial, but Willa knew she was right and her heart felt heavy with it. "I'm not sure what to do here," she said softly. "I think I'm . . . broken."

"No," Elle said adamantly and everyone else piped in with equally emphatic *no*s.

"Please," Willa said. "Let's just move on to another topic, okay? How about those Niners, right?"

"You can't just ignore this," Pru said. "At least go back to having great sex!"

Haley nodded vehemently.

Willa had to laugh. "Just tell him right out that all I want is sex?"

"*Great* sex," Pru corrected.

"Agreed," Elle said. "Men do it all the time so why not?"

Willa looked at them. "So you honestly think I should just show him my boobs."

"Always works for me," Pru said. "When Finn and I get in a fight, I flash him and he forgets what we're fighting about. Boobs are magic."

Willa shook her head. "Nothing's ever that easy." At least not for her.

"Hang mistletoe and lure him in," Haley said. "Put it up in a convenient place, but not *too* convenient because you don't want to have to kiss any toads by accident."

"Oh, and lose your bra," Pru said. "He'll be so preoccupied, he'll never know what hit him. Guaranteed."

Haley was nodding. "So see, you have your plan. One, shave all the way up past the knee. Two, hang some mistletoe. Three, lose the bra. Four, call him over and let the good times begin. And then after the good times, when he doesn't quite have all the blood back to his brain, tell him you're okay with being just friends with benefits. It's every guy's dream come true. Just make sure to spell out what exactly the benefits are so he doesn't think you mean a threesome or anal. Tell him preapproved benefits only."

Pru choked on her wine and Elle had to beat her over the back.

Haley smiled. "I think it's perfect. Honestly, he'll never know what hit him. *Wait!*" She wore a small backpack as a purse and pulled it off to paw through it. "And these, take these!" She held up a set of spiked handcuffs.

This time they all stared at her, agog. Well, except for Elle, who took them and looked them over. "Nice."

"They were a Christmas gag gift," Haley said. "Office holiday party last night."

"From that pretty brunette temp receptionist?" Elle asked.

Haley blushed. "I wish. No, which is why I'm willing to give them up to Willa for the cause."

"Thanks," Willa said dryly. "Your sacrifice is duly noted, but not necessary. I do *not* need handcuffs."

"Oh, I don't need handcuffs to enslave a man either," Elle said, slipping them into her purse. "But it never hurts. The key?" she asked Haley. "Because it's all fun and games until someone loses the key . . ."

Haley handed over a small key.

Pru snorted wine out her nose again, and it was mayhem after that but somehow, after another few glasses of wine, The Plan suddenly seemed totally and completely feasible.

Friends with benefits . . .

What could go wrong?

Chapter 24

#ThatsWhatSheSaid

The next day Keane ran from jobsite to jobsite putting out fires. By the time he got back to his office and dropped into his chair at his desk to catch up on paperwork, he was done in.

Which was a good thing. Being this tired made it difficult to think about what had happened between him and Willa.

Or more accurately, what wasn't going to happen between him and Willa.

Shit. Opening his laptop, he froze when something brushed against his legs.

Pita was winding herself in and around his calves, rubbing herself all over his jeans and leaving a trail of hair as she did so.

"You must be desperate if you're willing to be friendly to me," he said.

At that, she leapt into his lap, turned in a circle, and then plopped with zero grace to lie all over him.

"Okay," he said, awkwardly patting her on the head. "We're doing this then."

A rumbly purr filled the room and she began to knead with her paws. When one of her needle-sharp claws caught on his crotch, he yelped and jumped to his feet, unceremoniously dumping her to the floor.

Paws spread wide, hunkered low to the floor, she looked up at him from slitted eyes.

"Well then, watch the damn claws, Jesus."

She turned away, tail straight up in the air, quivering with temper. And he knew—she was *so* going to take a shit in his shoes tonight. "Dammit, wait." He caught up with her and scooped her back up, sitting in the chair again, setting her next to him. "Stay," he said.

She shot him a look that spoke volumes on her opinion of being commanded to do anything, but she did indeed stay.

He was knee-deep into the engineering notes on the Mission project when he got a text.

Willa:
Can you come over after work? Need your help with something.

He stared at the words and felt an onslaught of emotions that he wasn't equipped to deal with. Hunger. Desire. Aching desire. How was it possible that a month ago he'd thought his life was just fine, but now he had this person in it who added color and laughter, one he had an amazing connection with, such as he'd never felt before, and he couldn't remember what he did without her?

He couldn't imagine what the woman who never asked for help could need, but it didn't matter. He'd do anything she needed. He got up and looked at Pita. "Behave."

She gave him a look that was a firm "maybe but probably not."

Shaking his head, he moved to the door.

"Whoa," Sass called from her desk in the next room over. "Whatcha doing?"

"Gotta go."

"There's a stack of stuff here for you to go over and—"

"Gotta go," he repeated.

She searched his gaze a moment. "So it's like that, is it?" She shook her head. "You poor bastard."

He drove to the Pacific Pier Building, parked, and walked through the courtyard.

Eddie was standing by the fountain, watching the water. Someone had given him a down parka with fur hood and he looked warm and happy.

"Found my cheer," he said to Keane.

Keane noted the flask in the guy's hand and smiled. "Good."

"You find yours? Cuz I got some mistletoe if you need."

"I'm good," Keane said. "But thanks."

"Understood." Eddie nodded. "There can be a lot of trouble with mistletoe . . ." He paused. "Or women."

Amen to that . . .

Keane took the stairs to Willa's door—which was ajar.

"Come in," she yelled from inside.

Frowning that she'd left her door not only unlocked but open, he walked in. Willa was high on a ladder next to the biggest tree he'd ever seen stuffed inside an apartment this size. She was looking festive and gorgeous in a short black skirt, black knee-high boots, and a bright red hoodie sweater snug to her every curve.

He looked his fill, loving the way the skirt clung to the sweet curves of her ass, enjoying the look at her legs. He loved them best wrapped around him but this was a good view too.

"I made a special holiday drink and I needed a taster," she said, backlit by the strings of lights across her faux mantel. When she turned to face him, he got the full impact of her front view. The strings on her hoodie sweater were weighted by tassels that bounced around right at breast height, drawing his gaze there. Four words were embroidered across her chest—*Dear Santa, Define "Naughty."*

And Keane realized something else he loved about the sweater—she was braless.

"What's going on?" he asked.

"I was hoping to bribe you into helping me hang some decorations."

He laughed. "You're putting up *more* decorations?"

"You know, I can sense the sarcasm there but I'm going to ignore it." Twisting, she met his gaze. "I've got some mistletoe."

This took his brain down Dirty Alley and he had to clear his throat to speak. "Your tree is different than the one you had before."

"That one's in my bedroom now."

"How did you get this one up here?"

"Archer helped me stuff it into the dumbwaiter." She smiled down at him. "Thanks for coming."

"Anytime," he said and realized he absolutely meant it. No matter that what was best for him seemed to be some distance, he still wanted in her life. He'd take whatever he could.

They stared at each other some more and then started to speak at the same time. He had absolutely zero idea of what he'd been about to say, but Willa looked like she had no idea either so there was a beat of awkward silence. Then they both started again.

Shaking his head, he pointed at her. "You first," he said at the exact second she said the same thing.

She started to laugh and shifted her weight and he had no idea how it happened, but in the next beat she was in free fall. He managed to catch her but they both went down.

He landed flat on his back with her over the top of him, an elbow in his sternum, a knee uncomfortably close to his nuts.

"Oh! Oh my God," she cried, all aflutter as she pushed upright—using his gut for leverage. "Are you okay?"

He wasn't sure, a feeling he was starting to get used to when it came to her. Wrapping his hand around her leg, he cautiously moved it from the danger zone.

Hoping to avoid any other damage, he caught her wrists and rolled, pinning her beneath him.

There. His body was safe, she was safe, and maybe, just maybe, he was going to manage to keep his heart safe as well.

But then she let out a throaty little "mmm" and spread her legs to make room for him between them.

"*Oh,*" she breathed and then wriggled a little bit, making his eyes cross with lust. With a low laugh, he dropped his forehead to her shoulder.

She was killing him.

"Keane?"

"Yeah?"

She gave him a little push.

Thinking she'd come to her senses he shifted off of her but before he could get up she pushed again so that he fell to his back.

And then she claimed the top for herself. "Mmm," she said again.

Stunned, he put his hands on her hips, his fingers digging in a little bit in a desperate attempt to get reined in. "You did that on purpose?"

"No. Well not totally anyway." And then her mouth swooped down and covered his in a kiss meant to annihilate every single operating brain cell.

And it did.

When they broke apart for air, she was sprawled over the top of him, her pretty breasts smashed into his chest, her forearms flat to the floor on either side of his head, her legs straddling his hips so that not even a sheet of paper could have fit between them.

With a groan, he thunked his head onto the floor.

She slid her hands under the back of his head to protect it and he slid his gaze to hers. "Willa, what are we doing?"

She stared at him for a beat, chewing on her lower lip. "I was hoping it was obvious."

"Nothing with you is ever obvious."

"How about this—does this help?" She wriggled right over his erection and he groaned.

"You don't seem opposed," she murmured.

Hell no, he wasn't opposed. But there was something in her eyes behind the hunger and desire, something just out of his reach, something she wasn't saying. But before he could try to figure it out, she kissed him again, deeper, wetter, her sweet tongue chasing his. And either he'd just given himself a concussion or she was that good because he got lost in her. Given the breathy little pants and how her hands fought his for purchase on each other's bodies, he wasn't alone. She was just as lost as he.

They rolled several more times, jockeying for the driver's seat, but finally he pinned her to the floor, his hands once again capturing hers, a thigh spreading her legs, making himself at home as all his confusion about his feelings for her vanished. They always did when they were together like this.

He wanted to believe that she felt the same, that maybe that was what she hadn't been able to say, and he told himself she'd get there.

"Keane," she whispered throatily, arching to him. "Please . . ."

Yeah. He intended to please. He'd please her until she cried out his name in the way she did when she came. It took less than two seconds to discover that she was indeed not wearing a bra and that her sweater was soft and stretchy, so much so that one tug exposed her perfect breasts.

Another discovery—he was incapable of logic when he had her panting and writhing beneath him like this. He had a sweet, hard nipple trapped between the roof of his mouth and his tongue, and a hand inside her panties—where he discovered with a heartfelt groan just how into him she was—when one of their phones went off with the Muppets version of "Jingle Bell Rock."

"Ignore it," he murmured into her mouth, his fingers slowly caressing her hot folds.

She moaned out some wordless agreement and tightened her grip on his hair, doing her best to make him bald before his next birthday, and he could care less. Her panties were cutting into the back of his hand so he gave a quick tug and accidentally ripped them right off her. He stilled. "I'll buy you more," he said in apology. "I—"

"I liked it," she whispered.

Oh Christ, he was such a dead man. Rearing up, he kissed her hard and then slid down her body, pushing her skirt up as he went, groaning at what he'd exposed.

On the coffee table near his head, her phone buzzed again. He glanced over at it automatically, not meaning to invade her privacy. But then he saw the first line of the incoming text.

Haley:
Did the no-bra thing work on Keane?

"What is it?" Willa murmured.

He pushed off of her and came up on his knees. "You tell me."

She accessed the text and grimaced. "Well, crap." She sighed and sat up. "Okay, so I realized that I wanted to see you but not to talk, and—"

"And instead of being the promised grown-up about it and just telling me you were horny, you went back to high school and told your friends?" he asked.

"Worse," she said with a guilty wince. "I took advice from them on what to do."

He stood and stared down at her.

"I know!" she said. "I'm sorry! But they're deceptively sweet and really nosy, and very bossy and convincing!"

He tried to take it all in. "So the sexy sweater, the mistletoe, the text . . . all of it was some sort of plan to seduce me?"

"And the no-bra thing," she said. "Don't forget that part."

He pulled her up to her feet. "I really liked that part," he admitted. "But Jesus, Willa, I'm an easy lay when it comes to you. You could've just told me."

"I'm sorry," she whispered again and stepped into him, her eyes on his, warm and worried. "But for all my big talk, I'm not very good at . . . well, talking."

Her phone went off again. "Oh my God," she said. "Give it to me so I can tell them to knock it off." She stretched to reach it and Keane tried to not enjoy the mouthwatering view of her bent over the table. He wanted to reach out and push the skirt up, biting back a groan at the thought of the view *that* would give him.

And then he realized that she'd taken a call, not a text, and her voice was off. Scared, and urgent.

"Rory, where are you—" She broke off, her body unnaturally still and filled with tension. "Are you hurt?"

Keane went to her bedroom and grabbed her new undies from her dresser.

"On my way," she was saying in her phone. "Text me with the exact address. I'm coming for you." She disconnected and whirled in a circle, clearly looking for her things.

Keane held out the undies and then picked up her purse and keys for her.

"Always one step ahead of me," she murmured, stepping into the panties. "I'm sorry, but I've got to—"

"I'll drive."

"No, Keane, I'm not going to ask you to—"

"You didn't ask," he said and nudged her out the door.

Thirty-eight agonizing minutes later, Willa glued her face to the passenger window. "This one," she said, rereading the address she'd gotten from Rory. "Dammit."

"What?"

"This is her ex-boyfriend Andy's house." The pit of anxiety in her gut grew. "The one who put that bruise on her face all those weeks ago now."

Keane turned down the street. It was narrow, lined with apartment buildings that had seen their heyday decades ago.

There were no spots available on the street.

"Just stop here," Willa said, unhooking her seatbelt, leaping out before Keane could get the truck into park. She heard him swear behind her. "I've got this," she said over her shoulder. "I've got her. We'll be right back out."

"No, Willa. Wait—"

But she couldn't wait, not another second. She ran up the walk and into the building. She'd never been here before but she knew from the text that Andy lived in apartment 10.

With her phone in hand and the knot of fear in her gut growing, she knocked on the door.

It swung open, revealing a dark, cavernous room she couldn't see into. "Rory?" she whispered.

A soft whimper was the only reply. Anxiety and worry drove Willa forward, hand out to combat the fact that she couldn't see. *"Rory?"*

A light came on further inside the place, illuminating a kitchen. Rory appeared in the doorway, giving Willa a frantic "come here" gesture.

Willa rushed toward her through the still dark living room, her relief short-lived when she tripped over something on the carpet and went sprawling.

Rory gasped and ran forward, helping her to her feet. "Hurry! Move away from him!"

The anxiety and worry had turned into bone-melting fear. Ignoring the burning in her hands and knees, Willa let Rory pull her into the kitchen. "Please tell me I didn't just trip over a dead body."

"Not dead." Rory paused. "I'm pretty sure."

Willa gripped Rory's arms and looked her over. There were no noticeable injuries. "Are you okay?"

"I think so."

"What happened?"

Rory bit into her lower lip. "Andy got a job and said he was making bank. He said his boss had offered me a part-time job too and that he'd pay cash, a lot of it. All I had to do was show up and be, like, the receptionist or something. Only when I showed up, there was no office. Turned out it wasn't an office job at all. The boss takes people out for bungee jumps off the bridges and Andy assists. I was supposed to greet the 'clients' and take their money. But that's illegal, I know it is, and when I said so, the boss fired both me and Andy on the spot. And then Andy took me here instead of home and we got in a big fight about it."

"Still waiting on the part that explains his prone body on the living room floor," Willa said.

"It turned out we disagreed about other stuff too," Rory said, averting her gaze. "Like on the definition of the word *no,* so . . . I showed rather than told." She paused. "With a knee to his balls."

Willa's heart stopped. "Did he touch you?"

"Only a little," Rory said. "And that's when I dropped him to the floor. But he hit his head on the corner of the coffee table going down." Her face fell. "Which is my fault, right? Am I going to go to jail?"

"No," Willa said firmly, grabbing Rory's hand. "It was self-defense—" She broke off when Rory let out a startled scream but before Willa could react, a hand wrapped around her ankle and tugged.

For the second time in as many minutes, she went down and then blinked up into Andy's menacing, pissed-off face.

Damn, those spiked cuffs would have come in handy about now . . .

"You," he grated out, staring down at her with a frown like maybe his head hurt. And given the wicked slash across his eyebrow, it probably did.

"Let me go, Andy." Willa said this with a forced calm that she absolutely did not feel. In fact, it took real effort to speak at all with her heart thundering in her throat. "The police are on their way."

"I didn't do anything wrong."

Willa struggled, but it was futile so she went with Plan B and jammed her knee up between his legs.

Andy's eyes widened as he let out a squeak and slowly fell off her, curling into a fetal position.

"Well if I didn't break his nuts, that sure did," Rory whispered.

Willa rolled to her hands and knees, but before she could stagger upright she was yanked to her feet by a large shadow of a man who moved with the silent lethalness of a cat.

Keane.

He had a dangerous, edgy air to him as the harsh kitchen light hit his taut, tense features, his eyes filled with temper and concern.

"I'm okay," she said.

He didn't speak until he'd made sure for himself, looking over both her and Rory before hauling Willa in close to his side and reaching for Rory's hand.

The girl grabbed on to it like it was her lifeline and Willa knew the feeling.

Because he was her lifeline too.

"What happened?" he asked.

Willa gave him the short version and after hearing it, Keane called the police.

Behind them, Andy stirred and groaned. Keane let go of Willa and Rory and moved over him. "Get up."

"Fuck you."

Keane shook his head, like he couldn't quite believe what an idiot this guy was. Then he hauled Andy to his feet and pinned him against the wall so that they were nose to nose.

Andy closed his eyes.

Keane gave him a little shake until he opened them again. Keane didn't raise his voice or give any indication of being furious, but the air fairly crackled around him. "Let's get something straight."

"Fuck you," Andy said, repeating himself.

Keane put a forearm across his throat and leaned in a little, which appeared to get Andy's full attention. "So, a couple of things," Keane said calmly. "You're not going to touch Rory ever again. You're not going to talk to her, see her, or even think of her."

Andy hesitated and Keane pressed harder, which had Andy suddenly nodding like a bobblehead.

"Same for Willa," Keane said, still quiet. Deadly calm. "In fact, you're not going to get within a hundred feet of either of them. Do we need to go over what will happen if you do?"

Andy shook his head.

"Sure?" Keane asked.

More wild nodding.

"Keane," Willa said softly, setting a hand on his biceps, which felt like solid granite.

Keane let him go and Andy slid to the floor, hands protectively cupping his goods.

That's when the police showed up.

Two hours later, Keane finally led Willa and Rory into his truck. They'd had a few tense moments when the police had first arrived before getting everything sorted out.

Meaning keeping Rory out of having to take a ride to the station.

"I'm such a screwup," Rory said quietly from the backseat. "I have no idea what I'm doing with my life."

Before Keane could say a word, Willa twisted from the front seat and reached for Rory's hand. "Honey, no one knows what they're doing with their life."

"They seem like they do," Rory mumbled. "On Instagram everyone has normal pics of family and boy-friends and . . . really great-looking food."

"Trust me," Willa said. "Even your most perfect Instagram friend has an asshole ex and eats chocolate cereal for dinner once in a while, okay? You're not alone and you're not any more screwed up than the rest of us."

Rory choked out a laugh. "Was that supposed to be comforting?"

Willa gave her a small smile that tugged at Keane's heart. "Yes." She glanced over at him. "Right?"

"Right," he said. "But for the record, I don't like chocolate cereal. My jam is Frosted Flakes."

At this, Rory managed a second laugh and so did Willa, both of which warmed him. He didn't know how and he didn't know when, but the walls guarding his heart had fallen and he'd been conquered. Hard.

Chapter 25

#DontStopBelievin

Willa's brain was on overdrive as Keane walked them upstairs to her apartment. At the front door, Rory gave Keane a hug and vanished inside.

Willa quietly shut the door to give them privacy and looked up at the man quiet at her side. "I'll keep her here with me tonight. It won't be the first time she's slept on the couch." She paused. "I wanted to thank you," she said softly. "For tonight."

He smiled. "You mean when you lured me here under false pretenses pretending to need help with the mistletoe when really you wanted to take advantage of my body?"

She felt herself blush. "I meant with Rory. I wish I hadn't needed to be rescued by my . . ." She broke off.

He arched his brow, clearly waiting to hear how she intended to finish that sentence, but she'd talked herself right into a damn corner.

"By your what, Willa?" he asked softly. "The guy you're just fucking? Your friend? Someone you care about maybe too much? What?"

Overwhelmed, and also short of air because there was a big ball of panic in her throat, she looked away.

She heard Keane draw in a deep breath. "I'm going to give you a pass on that right now," he said. "Because we both know you have some shit to figure out. But I want you to know something and I need you to really hear it." He tipped her face up to his. His expression was serious and just about as intense as she'd ever seen it, including when he'd had Andy pinned against the wall.

"This thing between us?" he asked. "There's no price. I needed a cat search and rescue and you came running. You need a ride and maybe a little muscle backup to deal with some asshole, I'm going to come running. You following me?"

She chewed on the inside of her cheek, trying to figure out if the math really worked out. "I'm pretty sure I get more out of this than you do."

He shook his head. "Has anyone ever told you that you're stubborn?"

"Don't forget obstinate," she said. "And yeah, I've heard it a time or two." Or hundred . . .

"I'm not looking to rescue you," he said with quiet steel. "This, between us, has nothing to do with anything like that."

"What does it have to do with?"

He looked at her for a long beat, clearly weighing his words. "You let people in," he finally said. "I've seen you."

She wasn't sure where this was headed but she could tell she wasn't going to like it. "Okay . . ."

"Your friends, you'd give them the shirt off your back. Same with the kids you hire and keep safe." He stepped even closer so that they were sharing air. "You give them a safe haven, you let them into your life. You do the same with all the animals that come your way." He planted his big palms on the wall on either side of her head and let out a low laugh like he was more than a little surprised at himself. "I'm saying I've changed my stance on relationships and commitment. I want in your damn life, Willa."

While she was still reeling from that, he pulled something from his pocket.

A key.

"What's that?" she asked, her heart starting a heavy beat.

"A key to the Vallejo house."

"Why—why would you give me a key?"

He shrugged. "For the next time you and any of the girls need to all crash together since I have extra beds. Or if there's a leaky sink . . . or hell, say you buy a pizza and need someone to eat half of it." He smiled. "I'd be happy to be that someone."

She stared at him. "I can't just let myself into your house," she said.

"Why not?"

Yeah, her body said. *Why not?* "Because that's a big step," she said carefully.

"It doesn't have to be." His expression was leaning toward frustration. "It's just a damn key, Willa."

She stared down at it and nodded. And then shook her head. "It feels like a lot more."

"What it is, is up to you."

She stared at it some more, shocked at how much one little key could weigh. And then a low oath came from Keane and suddenly the key was gone from her palm as fast as it had appeared.

"You know what?" he said, jamming it back into his pocket. "Never mind—"

"No, you just took me off guard—"

He shook his head. "Forget it. Another time maybe."

Chest tight, unsure of what the hell had just happened and which one of them was to blame for the sudden chasm that had opened so wide between them that she couldn't possibly cross it, she hesitated. She had no idea what to say. "'Night," she finally whispered.

"'Night."

Well, she'd walked herself right into a corner now, hadn't she, leaving her no choice but to go inside and shut the door. She immediately turned to it, palms on the wood. Her heart felt heavy, and scared.

She didn't want to end the night like this.

She hauled the door open again, Keane's name on her lips, and there he still stood, hands braced up above him on the doorjamb, head bowed.

He lifted his head, his expression dialed to frustrated male.

"Um," she said. "I think I might have overreacted about the key."

He just looked at her. Not speaking.

She had that effect on men.

"I really am all sorts of messed up," she admitted in a soft whisper.

His eyes warmed a little but his mouth stayed serious. "Well, you're not alone there."

She didn't want to, she really didn't, but she let out a small laugh. And then she tipped her head down and stared at her feet and felt her eyes sting.

For so long she had been just that. Alone. Yes, she had friends, dear friends who were more like her family than . . . well, than any of her blood family had ever been.

But friends didn't sleep in her bed and keep her warm and make her heart and soul soar. Friends didn't give her the best orgasms of her life, even better than her handheld shower massager.

Now she had this guy standing right here in front of her, a smart, loyal, sexy-as-hell guy whose smile took her places she'd never been before. He wasn't into messy emotions but even so, and even knowing she was, he was still standing there. Baffled. Irritated. Frustrated.

But still standing there.

For her.

"You're thinking so hard your hair is smoking," he said.

She was surprised she hadn't gone up in flames. All she could do was stare at him, more than a little shocked at the intensity shining from his eyes.

He really did want more.

And if it was true, if he really wanted in her damn life as he'd so eloquently said, then . . . well, then there wasn't anything holding them back. Not a single thing.

Except, of course, herself.

Her heart had started a dull thudding, echoing in her ears. "You're not ready for this," she whispered.

He smiled, but it was filled with grim understanding and not humor. "You don't get to tell me what I am or am not ready for, Willa. And in any case, what you really mean is that you're not ready, isn't that right?"

She sucked in some air, but she shouldn't have been surprised that he called her out on this. He wasn't one to hide from a damn thing. "I want to be—does that count?"

"For a lot, actually," he said. "You know where to find me." He brushed a warm, sweet kiss across her mouth and then he was gone.

Keane walked down the stairs of Willa's building, not sure how to feel. This wasn't how he'd seen the evening going. If things had gone his way, he'd be stripping Willa out of her clothes right now.

He thought about how they'd taken each other to places he'd sure as hell never been, and he wanted to go there again. He'd thought, hoped, Willa was coming to feel the same way.

Crazy, considering that until a few weeks ago he could never have imagined that he'd want a relationship. The irony of the fact that he and Willa had mentally changed positions didn't escape him.

Damn. He'd known better than to get attached but he'd gotten sidetracked by a pair of sweet green eyes and a smile that always, *always,* put one on his lips as well.

Willa made him feel things and he'd gotten swept

away by that. But her entire life had been one big Temporary Situation; foster care as a kid, working at the pet shop where animals came in and out of her life but didn't stay, men—when and if she let them in, that was.

And for a little while at least, he'd been in, but was starting to realize that had all been an illusion, just hopeful thinking on his part. Because though it was true he'd not done permanent any more than she had, he at least wasn't fundamentally opposed to trying. Apparently, it only took the right person.

Problem was, that person had to want it back.

With a gnawing hole in his chest, he went home to Vallejo Street. Yeah, dammit, home. He'd gotten attached to this place every bit as much as he had Willa.

Both had been bad ideas.

He looked around at the big, old, beautiful house that reflected back at him some of the best work he'd ever done. He could sell it in a heartbeat and make enough of a profit from the sale to slow his life way the fuck down. He'd have time for the things that he'd never had time for.

Playing pool.

Sitting on rooftops star-gazing.

A woman in his bed every night, the *same* woman.

Things he'd never wanted before, but wanted now. *Craved* now, the way he used to crave only work. In fact, for long years in his life, the physical aggression of his job had kept him calm. Pounding nails. Carting hundreds of pounds of drywall up and down flights of stairs.

That was no longer the case.

He was a guy who prided himself on staying true to himself. He'd always known that he wasn't the guy who wanted a white picket fence, a woman wearing his diamond, and two point five kids. He'd never seen himself craving any of that.

But there was no longer any solace in the thought of being on his own for the rest of his life. And if he was being honest with himself, he could also admit he'd changed his mind about love and commitment as well.

Shitty timing on that . . .

Restless, determined to go back to his original plans, he strode through the rooms and headed into his office, where he called Sass.

"Somebody better be dead," she answered sleepily.

"I need you to get Vallejo on the market."

This got him a load of silence.

"Sass?"

"You're calling me at"—there was a rustling, like she was sitting up in bed—"midnight to tell me you want to sell your house?"

"I was always going to sell this place," he said. "You know that."

"Noooooo, you weren't. I mean yes, you *pretended* you would," she said, sounding far more awake now. "But we all knew . . ."

"What?"

"That you'd finally found yourself a home you wanted to keep instead of living like a vagabond. Especially now that you and Willa are a thing. She loves the place too—"

"You're wrong," he said flatly. "On all counts. Get the place on the market."

This time the beat of silence was shorter. "It's your life," she said and disconnected on him.

"It is," he said to the cat who was sitting at the foot of his bed, eyes sharp and on his face, tail switching about. "My life."

Pita stopped twitching her tail, said her piece with a simple but short and succinct "mew," and stalked up the bed toward him.

"We've discussed this. I don't share my bed with cats."

Not giving a single shit, she walked up his legs and then leapt to his chest, where she sat, calm as you please.

"No," he said. "Absolutely not."

She lifted a paw and began to wash her face.

"Cat, I'm serious."

She changed things up, washing behind her ears now.

"If you start going at your lady town, it's all over," he warned.

Still on his chest, she lowered her paw, turned in a circle, daintily curled up in a ball, and closed her eyes.

"Not happening," he said.

She didn't move.

And neither did he.

Chapter 26

#MagicallyDelicious

The next morning Willa lay in bed staring at the ceiling feeling the entire weight of her heart sitting heavily in her gut.

No regrets, she told herself. She'd done the right thing being honest with Keane, for both of them.

Trying to believe that, she got up and realized with some shock that it was the day before Christmas Eve. Normally this was her favorite time of the year. She loved the renewed sense of energy and anticipation the city of San Francisco put off, loved the smiles on the faces of everyone who came into her shop, loved the magic of the holiday, loved everything about it.

But her cheer was definitely missing as she quickly and quietly got ready for work.

Rory was still asleep on the couch. After Willa had entered her apartment last night to find Rory waiting up for her, she'd had to set aside the feeling of devastation about pushing Keane away and paste a smile on her face.

Rory had needed that of her. They'd sat together and talked. Rory'd had a little meltdown, admitting she missed her family, that she wished she hadn't so completely messed it up with them.

Willa had asked her to pretty please consider going home for Christmas and make peace with them. When Rory said she couldn't get a ride to Tahoe on this short of notice, Willa had once again promised to work it out for her. The girl didn't have much in the way of family, but there was a lot of love and forgiveness there if she would only reach out.

Her own heart had squeezed hard at that, almost as if the poor organ was desperately trying to tell her that there was something in there for *her* to think about as well.

Now in the light of day, she knew she wasn't caffeinated enough to go there. She tiptoed past the couch, thinking she'd handle the morning shop rush on her own today.

An early Christmas present to Rory.

Her first grooming client was a feisty little pug named Monster who had terrible asthma. He whistled on the inhale and snorted on the exhale, making him sound like an eighty-year-old man smoking and climbing stairs at the same time.

As soon as she got Monster in the tub, Elle and Haley showed up with coffee and muffins.

"Whoa," Haley said, stopping short, eyes on the pug. "That's the homeliest dog I've ever seen."

Monster tipped his head up, his huge black eyes on Willa as he snorted for air. She kissed him on the top of his wrinkly head. "Don't listen to her. You're adorable. And don't ask me how last night went," she warned the girls.

"Don't have to ask," Elle said. "You're not wearing your just-got-laid smile."

"It's because you didn't take the handcuffs," Haley said. "Isn't it?"

Willa lifted her hands off Monster, his signal to shake. Water flew all over them. Well, all over herself and Haley. No water dared to hit Elle.

Haley squealed and Monster seemed to grin with pride as he shook again.

"You're only egging him on," Willa warned, laughing.

"Dogs can't be egged on like that."

"He's a male," Elle said, still completely dry. "He was *born* to be egged on. Now talk to us," she said to Willa.

Willa sighed, and leaving out the part where she'd let Keane walk away, told them about the Andy portion of the previous evening.

Both Elle and Haley were suitably horrified, but when Rory walked in they pretended they'd been discussing the weather.

Looking surprisingly well slept, Rory stared at them suspiciously. "Willa told you about last night, didn't she?"

Elle and Haley 'fessed up and fussed all over Rory. The girl pretended to hate every minute of it but no one was fooled; she soaked up every drop of love and warmth that came her way.

When the door in the front of the shop rang, Willa left her friends to continue spoiling Rory and, holding a towel-wrapped Monster tucked in the crook of her arm, headed out there.

And then nearly tripped over her own two feet at the sight of Keane, looking deadly sexy in a pair of dark jeans, an aviator jacket, and sunglasses.

He smiled at Monster. "Cute."

Just looking at him made Willa ache so she very carefully didn't look right at him. "You need me to watch Pita?" she asked.

"No."

When he didn't say anything else she finally met his gaze. A huge mistake, in the same way looking directly into the sun was a huge mistake. It was painful. Even more painful was the apology she owed him. "Keane?"

"Yeah?"

"I'm sorry I had a little freak-out about your key."

"Key?" came a low whisper from behind them. Pru. "Holy cow, what did we miss?"

When Willa turned to look, Pru was indeed there; she must've come in the back door. Now all three of her friends plus Rory were crowded in the doorway, eavesdropping like a bunch of little boys.

"Whoops," Haley said, wincing when she caught Willa's gaze. "Excuse us, we're just . . ." Looking a little panicked, she turned to the others, eyes wide. "What are we just?"

"Um . . ." Pru said.

Elle shook her head in disgust at them. "Amateurs. We're eavesdropping, and shamelessly. And it'd be helpful if one of you would actually repeat whatever happened last night so we know what's going on."

Willa stared at them. "Are you kidding me?"

"Honey, you know I don't kid," Elle said.

Rory was looking horrified. "Ohmigod. I think they're fighting because of me. I ruined their night."

Willa's mad turned to guilt. "No, honey, that's not it. It has nothing to do with you."

"No, but it must," Rory insisted. "Because everything was fine between you two—until I got stupid and needed you, needed you both because Andy would've hurt you, Willa, I know it, and . . ." Her voice cracked. "That would have been my fault."

Elle wrapped an arm around Rory and hugged her close, but her eyes never left Willa and Keane. "Not your fault," Elle said firmly. "Not last night, and not whatever's happening here. In fact, these two silly kids are going to take their little discussion to Willa's office and not come back out until everything's fine and everyone's smiling because it's Christmas Eve Eve, dammit."

"Will you?" Rory asked Willa, looking heartbreakingly unsure. "Will you two go work it out?"

She was asking because nothing in her life had ever worked out before. Willa knew this and felt the air leave her lungs in one big whoosh. No way was she going to let Rory give up on emotions. On love. No way would she be the one to make her lose faith. "Of course," she said, knowing she could pretend with the best of them, and she'd make Keane do the same. Then she'd also make him promise to give her some space until her heart didn't threaten to burst at the sight of him. With that plan in mind, she handed Monster off to Pru and gave Keane a nudge toward her tiny office.

But Keane, of course, couldn't be nudged anywhere. He was big and strong and as hardheaded as . . . well, as her. He slid her a gaze that was partial amusement that she thought she could push him, and part challenge.

He wanted to be asked.

God save her from annoying, big, badass alphas. She blew out a breath and, very aware of Rory's concerned gaze on her, smiled through her gritted teeth. "Will you please come into my office so we can"—she glanced at Rory, even sent her another smile—"work things out?"

"Would love to," Keane said easily. He even took her hand and led the way.

She allowed it, but the moment they crossed the threshold over her office door, she shut it and opened her mouth. "Look, I know I don't have the right to ask but I'm going to need you to pretend for Rory that we're fine—"

Keane didn't answer. Instead, moving with the speed and agility of a caged leopard, he pressed her up against her desk. Then he sank his hand into her hair, tilted her face up, and crushed his lips to hers.

And damn. All the swirling, boiling emotions abruptly shifted, turning into something else altogether. With a moan, she threw herself against him, almost knocking him right off his feet.

He simply readjusted his stance and yanked her harder up against him. Somehow that worked for her and she continued to mindlessly climb him like a tree, desperate to get him even closer, her hands splaying across his strong, wide back. Which was how she felt the tremor wrack his body. She felt other things too, like how he was pressed up between her legs, hard and insistent.

There wasn't air for words, not then and not when he cupped and squeezed her ass in his big, callused palms.

So hot. So perfect. So—

The door opened.

"Oh, sorry," Cara said as she stuck her head in. "I just wanted to tell you I'm subbing for Lyndie today and . . ." She broke off at the look Willa gave her. "Okay, so they sent me back here to find out if you guys are fighting," she admitted. "Rory wants to know."

Shit. "No one's fighting," Willa said, trying to be casual. "We're just . . . discussing cat care," she said, trying not to sound breathless or look as if she'd just had the daylights kissed out of her. "For Petunia."

Cara nodded. "Kitty care," she repeated. "Got it. I'll tell Rory."

When she was gone, Willa turned to Keane. "So about pretending to be fine for Rory . . ."

He hit the lock on the door with one hand and hauled her back into him with the other, covering her mouth with his. He grabbed the string on the blinds to the courtyard window and lowered them, all without letting her mouth free. It was quite the feat really. She might have suggested they turn the light off too because there was plenty of light filtering in through the shades, but she knew that request would be futile.

Keane liked the visuals.

She broke the kiss. "You need to stimulate her," she managed. "That's important in kitty care."

Keane arched a brow.

She gave a head jerk to the door, signaling that they were probably being eavesdropped on.

He looked at her for a long beat, his eyes dark and unreadable. "Kitty care," he repeated and before she could blink, he'd lifted her up and plopped her ass onto her desk and then stepped between her legs. His mouth was at her ear now, his voice so soft as to be almost inaudible. "You want me to stimulate your pussy."

She choked out a laugh and tried to shove free, but he tightened his grip. "You know that's not what I meant!" she whispered. "Rory's fragile right now and we have to make her feel safe."

"She is safe," he said in her ear. "And so are you." And then he smiled again, a very naughty smile as he raised his voice a little, to a conversational pitch. "Okay, so talk me through this . . . stimulation." He pressed his mouth to her ear again, using his bad-boy voice in a barely audible whisper. "Tell me slowly, and in great detail."

She shoved him again but he still didn't budge.

"I miss your body wrapped around mine," he said softly, serious now. "I need you wrapped around me again."

Her heart softened. There was a problem with this, she knew it way in the back of her head, but God help her, she couldn't articulate anything with his hands on her to save her life. Tightening her fingers in his shirt, she tugged.

He fell into her and his big body shook with laughter as he set a warm palm on either side of her hips and lowered his face to hers.

"Keane—"

"I know the rules now. This doesn't mean anything, it's just a one-time turned three-time thing, etc., etc. . . ."

She snorted and he smiled. "Hush now, Willa," he murmured, setting a finger over her lips. "Not a sound." His hands slid into the back of her jeans to cup and squeeze her ass. She started to moan and Keane bit her lower lip.

Right. Not a sound.

But the brutal strength in his embrace had her breathless as she twined her arms around his neck, pressing her breasts against his chest, because if they didn't get skin to skin in the next few seconds, she was going to spontaneously combust.

Somehow he managed to wrestle her boots off. And then popped open her jeans. When he slid a hand between her legs and stroked her over her panties, she had a moment's panic.

"What?" he asked when she froze.

"You have to promise not to look. I'm not in cute undies. In fact . . ." She grimaced. This was going to be embarrassing. "I'm wearing my ugliest ones. They're my willpower panties. I wear them so I won't show them to anyone. In this case, you. You're the anyone."

He stared at her and then tossed his head back and laughed. He looked so utterly sexy she lowered her guard, which was how he got her jeans halfway down.

"I know I'm totally sending mixed signals," she managed. "But it's not like I stopped wanting you—"

"Good."

"But . . ."

He groaned. "It's always the *but* that gets you."

"But," she continued, needing to get this out. "I'm . . . a little mixed up—"

He slid her a wry look. "A little?"

She tried to close her legs, not easy with a hundred and eighty pounds of muscle standing between them.

"Shh," he said again, somehow both gentle and badass at the same time. "I've got you, Willa. I get you. For now, this works. You always work for me, however I can have you."

And on that emotionally stunning statement, he dropped to his knees, tugged her jeans the rest of the way off, and looked. And he took his sweet-ass time about it too. He was grinning when he rose to his full height again. "I like them."

"You're a sick man," she managed.

"There's no doubt," he agreed and kissed her some more, until she was back to squirming, in the very best way now.

"Hurry," she murmured breathlessly against his mouth and together they freed each other's essentials.

And good God, there was nothing like Keane's essentials . . . She was very busy filling her hands with him when his stubbly cheek rasped across her bare nipples and she nearly came on the spot. His mouth was everywhere, wild, fast, and she kissed him back as best as she could while still trying to get him inside her.

He laughed low in his throat but before she could kill him for that, he managed to drop to his knees again and get his mouth on her.

A minute ago he'd been in a huge rush and *she* still was, but now he held her down and took his time driving her insane with his tongue, and when she lost it, when she began to come, he rose up and covered his mouth with hers, swallowing her cry as he protected them both and then thrust inside her.

Their pace was frantic, desperate. Hungry. It didn't matter how many times they were together like this, Keane never failed to steal the very air from her lungs. She felt herself come again, or still . . . she had no idea. With Keane it was always one endless and erotic beat in time.

When she could finally see and hear again, she realized his face was snuggled into the curve of her neck, his breath puffing against her skin like a soft caress. One hand was drifting up and down her back, slowly, gently, helping her to calm, his other hand cupping her jaw, his thumb on her lips reminding her to be quiet.

Oh, God. Had she been quiet? She couldn't remember!

He grinned and she bit his finger. Hard.

Laughing softly, he straightened and then helped her off the desk. Her damn knees wobbled and he tightened his grip, pulling her into him, cuddling her into him.

She felt his lips brush her temple, and his hand stroked the hair from her eyes. Then that hand took hers and brought it to his mouth. She could feel the warmth of his breath on her skin and the gesture felt so . . . intimate, even more so than having him buried deep inside her. "That was . . ." She paused, searching for the right word.

"Kitty care at its finest?"

She tried not to laugh and failed. "Keane," she said softly. "What the hell are we doing?"

He slowly shook his head. He didn't know either. "I just needed to see you," he said simply.

"And I needed to see you," she said. "But what does it mean?"

"That you needed me bad."

She choked on another laugh.

"You don't think so?" He turned and lifted up his shirt. He hadn't refastened his jeans so they were sagging a little, enough to reveal the ten fingernail indentions, five on each perfect butt cheek.

She slapped her hands over her eyes in tune to his soft laugh.

Great. He was invigorated by sex and she . . . well, she'd lost another chunk of her heart. She straightened her clothes, swearing when she couldn't find her panties. Being a sex fiend was getting expensive.

Keane came close and buttoned up her top for her, his hands lingering to cup her face, gently tilting it up to his for a soft kiss. "Okay," he said. "Tell me. Tell me what you want me to know. Do you still need space? Because I'm thinking eight to nine inches should do it."

She huffed out a soft laugh and rubbed her temples.

"It's just that when we do this"—she gestured vaguely at her desk—"it makes me feel things. More each time."

"Good."

She tipped her head back and stared at the ceiling as she let out another low laugh. She felt his hands slide up and down her arms.

"Willa, look at me."

She hesitated because she knew damn well she got lost in his eyes every time, but she did meet his gaze.

"You get that you're not alone in this, right? I'm right here in this with you, and just as unnerved by what's going on."

She shook her head. "Are you? Because you seem so at ease with it. You move in and out of the intimacy without even blinking an eye, like it's not hitting you."

He studied her for a long beat. "You think I don't have emotions?"

"I think you're better at managing them than I am."

"You've got to have faith," he said. "In me. In us."

"That's hard for me."

"So are you ending this then?"

"No." Her stomach quivered at just the thought. "No," she said again more firmly and actually clutched at him.

"Okay," he murmured, pulling her in, holding her tight. "Okay, I'm not going anywhere."

She was too choked up to do anything more than nod as she sought comfort in his embrace for a long moment before pulling back, making sure they were both decent.

"I'm not going to pretend anything," he warned her

when she turned to the door. "Not even for Rory. Don't ask me to."

She shook her head. "I won't."

Her entire crew was hanging close by, clearly trying to eavesdrop. When they saw her, they all scattered wildly.

Except for Elle, who studied Willa for a long beat and then Keane.

Willa ignored her the best she could and gestured for Keane to make his escape. Instead, he came close to her and kissed her. Not a deep kiss but not a light one either. It was the kiss of a man staking his claim. When he lifted his head, the barest hint of a smile crossed his lips. "Still your ball and your court," he said.

And then he walked away from her without looking back.

When Willa finally got home that night, she had a raging headache from the thoughts she'd managed to block all day. A raging headache and some deep gouges courtesy of an extremely pissed-off cat who'd been brought in for grooming after a run-in with a rose bush.

The cat had been so wild that Willa had refused to let Rory or anyone else work on her, which meant she'd handled the situation alone.

And had paid the price.

Rory had wanted to treat Willa's deep scratches but Willa had told her she was fine.

But really, she was as far from fine as she could get.

Feeling much more alone than she could remember

feeling, she strode through her dark apartment without bothering with lights. Outside, rain was battering the building and inside, all she wanted was a PB&J sandwich—triple-deckered—and her bed. She was halfway through making the sandwich when she was driven crazy by her leaky kitchen faucet. "Shut up," she told it.

Drip. Drip. Drip.

Dammit. She used to love being alone. When had she stopped loving it?

Drip. Drip. Drip . . .

"Fine. I'll shut you up myself," she muttered and crawled under the sink with a wrench. She gave the loose bolt a twist and then screeched in shock and surprise when icy water burst all over her.

Sputtering indignantly, she sat on her kitchen floor and stared down at herself.

She was a mess.

Fitting, given her day. Refusing to cave to it and lose her collective shit, she was back at spreading peanut butter when she heard a knock at her door. Because it was past midnight and that kind of a night, she brought the knife with her to look out the peephole. Her good parts tingled and she told them to shut up too.

Keane stood on her doorstep looking dark as the wet, cold night and just as dangerous.

Chapter 27

#WhatYouSeeIsWhatYouGet

Keane hadn't been able to fall asleep to save his life. Feeling oddly weighted down, he'd gotten up to run, figuring pushing himself to exhaustion should straighten his shit out.

As he pounded the sidewalks, he ticked off the positives in his life. One, his great-aunt Sally was back in her rehab facility and doing well. She'd even left *him* a message for a change, telling him that an old friend had offered to take Pita off his hands. Two, his real estate agent was officially accepting bids for the Vallejo Street home over the next week.

He was in a good place. Hell, he was in a great place, so he should be over the moon.

He wasn't. None of it felt right.

Not giving up Pita. Not selling the Vallejo Street home. Not giving Willa space to figure her shit out, none of it worked for him on any level.

He ran harder, until his muscles quivered with exhaustion. And that's when he'd realized he'd ended up in front of Willa's building.

The simple truth was that he'd been drawn here like a moth to the flame. He loved her smile, loved her laugh, loved the way she made him do both of those things with shocking regularity. He loved the way she brought him out of himself, not letting him take himself too seriously. He loved . . . everything. Absolutely everything about her.

She opened to his quiet knock and he drank in the sight of her; hair wild, eyes flashing bad temper, her shirt drenched and just sheer enough that she could have won any wet T-shirt contest the world over.

She looked him over as well. "A water pipe spray you too?" she asked.

"No, I've been running."

"On purpose?"

He was surprised to hear himself laugh. "Can I come in?"

"Sure," she said so agreeably that he was suddenly suspicious.

"So what do you know about plumbing?" she asked.

"Everything."

"Then you're my man," she said. "I've got a leaky faucet you can fix."

He was so tired he could hardly hold himself up. "Now?"

"I tried to fix it myself and nearly drowned." She waved at herself with a knife that looked like it'd been dipped in peanut butter. "I had a shitty afternoon and evening, and all I wanted was a PB&J and some sleep, but the drip-drip-dripping is killing me . . ."

Since she sounded far too close to tears for his liking, he wrapped his hand around her wrist to stop her from waving her knife around. "I've got it," he said quietly and then took her knife because he might be a sucker when it came to her, but he wasn't stupid.

He shut and locked the door and moved past her into the kitchen. The makings of a peanut butter and jelly sandwich sat on the counter. There was water all over the floor and the cabinet beneath the sink was open. "You could have called me," he said.

"I know how to fix a damn leaky sink for myself."

He might have argued that she didn't or they wouldn't be having this conversation but he'd had a long day too, extremely long, and he wasn't that far behind her in the bad-mood department. Eyes gritty with exhaustion, he grabbed the wrench and went to work.

It took him two minutes. He set the wrench aside and still flat on his back, took a look at Willa.

She was sitting on the counter licking peanut butter off her thumb with a suction sound that went straight to his favorite appendage. "Done," he said, voice a little thick as he got to his feet and moved to stand in front of her.

"So it's not going to drip all night, forcing me to kill it?" she asked.

"There's no killing on your to-do list tonight."

She sighed deeply. "Thanks," she said softly. "Really."

"You're welcome. Really." He stepped in closer so that her knees pressed against his thighs.

She fisted her hands in his shirt and tried to tug him closer but he resisted.

"I want my eight to nine inches," she whispered.

Somehow he managed to resist. "I need a shower, Willa."

She tugged harder. "Not for me you don't."

"I ran over here, so yes I do."

She choked out a laugh. "And they call me stubborn and obstinate." She stared at him and her smile faded as she slowly dragged her teeth over her bottom lip. "I can't sleep," she murmured.

Her hair was in her eyes. Her mascara was smudged. Her shirt was still wet and she shivered as she pressed close, and again he had to hold her off. "Careful, I'm all sweaty."

"Don't care." She snuggled into his chest and when she tilted her face to his, it was the most natural thing in the world to kiss her. She tasted like peanut butter and heaven.

"Why can't you sleep?" he asked against her lips.

"I was grooming a geriatric cat and got complacent but she taught me. She got my back and shoulder pretty good trying to claw her way out of town and it's all burning like I'm on fire, which means I'll have to sleep on my left side or my stomach and I'm a right-side sleeper." She huffed out a sigh, then sucked in a sharp breath and flinched away from his hands as he tried to turn her away from him to get a look. "No, it's fine—"

Ignoring her protests, he put his hands on her hips and forced her to turn, and then began to peel her shirt gently upward.

"Seriously, I—"

He stopped short at the sight of the raw, red, angry gouges deep across her back and shoulder. "Willa, these have to be cleaned."

"I know, I will." She tried to pull her shirt back down, but he held firm and then finally just pulled the thing over her head, tossing it across the room.

"Keane!" she gasped, crossing her arms to cover herself, trying to turn to face him, but he held her in place while he surveyed the wounds.

"First aid kit?"

"Hall linen closet," she said.

He went to hunt down the supplies he needed and when he came back, she hadn't stayed. *Shock.*

He found her in her bathroom, holding a towel to her breasts, twisting, trying to see the gouges in the mirror.

The curve of her bare back was smooth and delicate, and so damn sexy to him. He wanted to run his hands down her spine to her ass, bend her over and—

The fantasy was cut short when she reached to touch one of the scratches and winced in pain.

"Hold still," he said and went to work.

She didn't speak while he cleaned the scratches. She didn't breathe either it seemed, but by the end her muscles were quivering, giving away her pain. Leaning forward, he placed his lips at the base of her neck.

A sigh shuddered out of her as she let her head fall forward, giving him better access, and he was a goner.

"Keane . . ."

"Tell me to go and I will," he whispered against her

beautiful skin and then it was him holding his breath, waiting on her response.

Willa turned to face Keane, and caught the same hunger and desire on his face that she knew was all over hers. Going up on tiptoe, she gently brushed her mouth over his. *"Don't go."*

With a rough groan rumbling from his chest, he carefully wrapped her up in his arms and took control of the kiss. And oh God, how he kissed her, like she was the sexiest woman on the planet. It was addicting.

He was addicting.

When they were both breathing like lunatics, he raised his head. Eyes dark on hers, he ran his fingers along her temple, tucking a strand of hair behind her ear, letting his thumb brush her jaw, her lower lip.

Melting into him she closed her eyes, but that only made it seem all the more intimate, the way their bodies had sought each other out, pressing close.

Around them, her apartment was still dark beyond the kitchen, the rain drumming against the side of the building the only sound.

Except for her accelerated breathing.

Because she had no idea if she'd fooled him even a tiny bit but she could no longer fool herself. This wasn't just sex.

"Willa."

She dragged her eyes open, raising her eyes to meet his, hoping he couldn't see the truth in her expression. Something dark and unreadable moved deep in his eyes but she didn't want to go there. Instead she took his hand to lead him to her bedroom.

But he stopped her. "Shower," he said firmly and turned on the hot water.

"But—"

"Don't worry, I give good shower."

He had them both stripped down to skin in a blink and nudged her into the hot, steamy water. Soaping up his hands and running them all over her body, he proved his statement.

He was good in the shower.

Twice.

When she was sated and shaking from the aftermath, he propped her up against the tile wall and quickly and efficiency washed himself up. Just watching him, she got hot and bothered all over again.

When he caught her staring at him like a voyeur, he smiled. "See something you like?"

"You know I do." She reached for him, but he turned off the water, dried her off first, and then finally allowed her to drag him off to her bed. She tried to push him down to the mattress but he took her with him so that they tumbled together in a tangle of limbs. Wordlessly he rolled her beneath him, his mouth on hers for a deep, bruising kiss.

She wasn't the only one feeling desperate tonight.

He had her stripped of her towel in a blink and she pressed herself close to all those hard, hot muscles she hadn't gotten enough of. Wasn't sure she *could* get enough of.

Slowing her down, Keane let his hands roam, heating every inch of her skin until she was begging for more. When he finally rose above her and thrust in deep, the world stopped.

He made her look at him and that was new for her. Eyes open. Heart open.

New and terrifying.

And in that moment, she knew the truth. She'd fallen irrevocably, irreversibly in love with him.

Closing her eyes against the onslaught of emotion, she tried to take it all in. His scent. The rough rumble of his sexy groan. The way his arms banded around her, one hand fisted in her hair, the other at her hip holding her, grounding her so that she could let go of everything but this. Because he had her.

He always had her.

Remember, she told herself desperately, remember how his body felt thrusting into hers, his muscles clenching, his skin hot under her hands. "Keane," she whispered, his name falling from her lips without permission.

He groaned, and knowing he was close she wrapped her legs around him and met his thrusts with an intensity of her own, forcing her eyes to meet his, reaching one hand to lay flat against his chest, needing to feel the beat of his heart.

Afterward, she lay pressed against him, feeling her pulse pounding, thinking that had been the most real, most erotic experience of her life. "Thanks for tonight," she whispered.

His huff of laughter brushed her temple. "No, thank *you.*"

"I meant for the plumbing rescue," she said. "I didn't want to need you to come in and wave your magic wand and fix my life."

"Babe, I didn't wave my magic wand until after I fixed the plumbing."

She lifted her head and stared at him in disbelief. "Did you really just say that?"

His mouth twitched. "Trying to avoid having a deep, meaningful conversation that probably won't end well for me. Thought charm might help."

"That wasn't charm, that was pure cheese."

He smiled. "But you laughed. I love your laugh, Willa."

She felt herself soften. "You're changing the subject."

"Trying," he said and rolled off the bed. Bending to his jeans, he began to pull on his clothes.

"Are you leaving?"

"Yes."

"Are you tiptoeing around my crazy and trying not to crowd me, or are you running away as fast as you can?"

He gave a low laugh and grabbed his phone off her nightstand.

He really was leaving. She got up and wrapped her arms around him from behind. "Keane."

Turning, he met her gaze. "I'll never run from you."

This stole her breath and she just stared up at him.

He stared back. Not exactly patient, but one hundred percent attentive and willing to hear whatever she said next.

"I'm just in deeper than I meant to be," she said softly.

"And again, you're not alone there."

Her heart squeezed. "I don't know what any of this means, what to feel."

"I know." He pressed his jaw against the side of hers. "I'm trusting you to figure it out and get back to me."

"Do *you* know?"

"I'm getting there," he said, as always brutally honest and unapologetic.

A part of her was deeply grateful for that. But another part of her was terrified because she was pretty sure she knew too.

It was just that her heart had two speeds: asleep or foot-to-the-metal. She'd been in relationships where she'd gone full throttle, feeling some of what she felt like when she was with Keane. Excited. Happy. *Alive.* Except that in each of those relationships, she'd been the only one all in. And then she'd stayed all in, past the warning signs. Past the recommendation of her friends. Past logic and common sense.

And she'd been burned.

Oh so burned.

"Willa." Keane's voice was as heartbreakingly gentle as his hands, which came up to her arms. "Don't rush yourself, not for anyone and especially not for me." That said, he kissed her, a devastatingly perfect kiss.

And then he was gone.

Chapter 28

#TheTribeHasSpoken

Willa woke up on Christmas Eve morning with her toes frozen. So was the rest of her. She thought about how much nicer it'd have been to be wrapped around Keane's big, warm body right about now.

And not just to climb him like a tree, but because she didn't like mornings. Because she thought that with him in bed with her, looking at her in that way he did that said she was the prettiest, smartest, funniest, sexiest thing he'd ever seen, she might learn to like waking up after all.

It was just that he had a way of making her feel special. Like she mattered. *Really* mattered. When she was with him, she felt like a better version of herself. So why the hell did she need space again? The answer was simple.

She didn't.

She blinked at the ceiling. Wow. She really was in

love with him. And damn, if she'd only figured that out last night, he might still be here.

With a sigh, she sat up in bed and checked her phone. Shockingly, there was nothing. No missed calls, no texts.

Nothing.

She set the phone in her lap as an odd emotion drummed through her, one she couldn't put words to.

Liar. She had words, several of them. She was feeling unnecessary because no one had needed her.

She swiped her finger over the screen of her phone and let her thumb hover over Keane's name. "Don't do it," she whispered to herself. "Don't . . ."

But then her finger swiped. "Whoops," she said to the room.

Keane answered her FaceTime call wearing sweatpants and nothing else, and her breath stuttered in her chest. His hair was wet and she could only imagine how delicious he smelled.

He took in the shirt she was wearing and his eyes darkened.

"You left your T-shirt here," she said and then bit her lower lip. "I slept in it."

His smile went hot. "Commando?"

"Yes," she admitted. "You owe me a trip to Victoria's Secret, by the way."

"I'll buy you whatever you want, and also thinking of you without panties is making me hot."

"Everything makes you hot," she said.

"True story." He cocked his head and studied her. "So whatcha doing up so early? Making a list, checking it twice? Tell me it's full of your deepest, darkest sexual fantasies."

She choked on a laugh. "No!" Then she bit her lower lip, but the question escaped anyway. "Do *you* have a list of fantasies?"

"Absolutely," he said, no hesitation.

She blinked. "About . . . me?"

He just looked at her, eyes molten-lava hot, and she felt herself go damp. "Written down?"

He tapped the side of his head. "All in here, babe." He smiled. "Unless you want me to write them down. We could mix our lists up and take turns picking out one at a time, and—"

"You want to act out our fantasies together?" she squeaked.

He just smiled and she nearly had an orgasm on the spot. "I . . . I don't know if I can write them down," she admitted.

"Sure you can. Close your eyes, think of something you've always wanted to try, and write it down." He waited expectantly.

She stared at him. *"Now?"*

"I will if you will."

Ten minutes later when her morning alarm went off, she had five fantasies written out. So did Keane.

"Time to get up," she said.

"Babe, I'm already up."

She rolled her eyes. "What's it called when you sext over FaceTime?"

He flashed a grin. "Sex-Time?"

She laughed. "You just made that up."

"No." He smiled. "Yeah. Show me under the shirt, Willa."

She wasn't going to admit that his soft demand gave her the very best kind of shiver. "Keane."

"Come on, show me yours and I'll show you mine."

"Is there anyone there with you?" she asked.

He turned his phone so she could see that he was in his bedroom at Vallejo Street, alone except for Pita sleeping on his pillow.

"I thought she wasn't allowed on your pillow."

"She's not," he said. "But apparently she's the ruler and I'm just her bitch." Then his face was back in the screen. "Show me," he said.

She lifted the hem of the shirt high, did a little shimmy, and then dropped the material back down.

Keane's eyes were so hot she was surprised her screen didn't melt. "That's going to get me through a very long day," he said, voice low and reverent.

She laughed. "You could get porn up on your phone anytime you want. Hell, you could probably get any woman in your contact list to send you nudie pics."

"I don't want any woman. I want you."

Her heart skipped a beat at that. "The feeling's mutual."

He smiled. "Have a good day, babe."

"You too." And with her heart lighter than she could remember feeling, a burgeoning hope blooming in her chest, she disconnected and went to work.

Willa did think of Keane, but not about the sexual fantasies.

Okay, she thought about those. A lot.

But mostly she thought about the man he'd grown into and how much that man had become such an integral part of her life in one short month.

When an older couple came into the shop to buy treats for their miniature schnauzer, finishing each other's sentences and holding hands like they were newlyweds, she had to ask. "How long have you been together?"

They grinned in unison. "Fifty years," the man said. "Fifty of the best years of my life."

"When you find the right one, honey," the woman said, her eyes on her hubby, "don't ever let go."

"Ever is a long time," Rory noted thoughtfully when the couple was gone.

Which was funny because ridiculously, Willa was suddenly thinking how much comfort was in the thought of forever . . .

She almost called Keane to tell him she thought maybe she'd figured some things out, namely that she realized she wanted in.

She wanted him.

But she didn't trust herself not to mess it all up over the phone so she sent a short text inviting him to the gang's private Christmas party at the pub that night, ending it with a *please come.*

By the time she closed up the shop and changed for the party, she hadn't gotten a response from him, and wasn't sure what that meant.

She walked into the pub a little off her game, but she'd made Keane wait for her to figure things out— she could certainly do the same for him.

The pub was closed to the public; tonight was just a family thing. Spence, Finn, Archer, Elle, and Haley, Pru, and Sean, Finn's younger brother, who was doing his best to adult these days now that he'd hit the ripe old age of twenty-two.

Finn poured Willa a glass of wine. The rest of the gang was at least a round ahead of her, everyone greeting her with hugs and cheer, and she felt her throat go tight with love. She was so damn lucky to have these people in her life.

"Where's Keane?" Pru asked. "You invited him, yeah?"

She nodded. "I left him a text."

"Does that mean you've decided to stop fighting yourself and your heart and go for it?" Pru asked.

Willa never thought the admission would be difficult but she was still surprised when her eyes filled as she nodded.

"Alcohol!" Elle called out. "Stat! Another one of us is about to go down the rabbit hole."

Finn and Pru, the first ones "down the rabbit hole," grinned wide.

Then Finn and Sean served them a feast that—no surprise given the fearless and competitive nature of the guys—turned into a chicken-wing-eating contest.

Spence won, though Willa had no idea how he did it. He was as tall as a tree with the lean muscled build of a runner, not a single ounce of extra meat on him.

And yet he put away twenty-five wings.

"Twenty-fucking-five," Archer said in awe as he counted the pile of bones on Spence's plate. "Ten more than your closest competitor." He looked at Finn. "That's you, man. You going to keep going, or forfeit so we can crown him?"

Finn looked down at his place and inhaled as if he was fortifying himself.

"Forfeit," Pru said for her man. "What," she asked at Finn's look. "None of *them* have to sleep with you tonight. As the lone person who does, I vote you're done, before you explode."

"Yes!" Spence thrust a fist in the air triumphantly and then let out an impressive burp. "'Scuse me."

Willa had been sneaking covert glances at the door, hoping to see Keane, but he was still MIA.

They moved on to their annual Christmas Karaoke Championship, first fortified by another round of heavenly spiked eggnog. And if Willa kept looking to the door every few minutes, no one called her on it—although she caught Elle and Archer exchanging more than one worried look, which she ignored.

The prize for karaoke was the same as for the wings—bragging rights for the entire next year.

And everyone wanted those bragging rights. Bad.

The girls got up and did "Moulin Rouge."

Spence and Finn did "Purple Rain."

But then Archer, seeming unaffected by the alcohol they'd consumed—although the Santa hat sitting askance on his head was clear evidence that he was very relaxed—sang "Man in the Mirror" and brought down the house.

Afterward, he came back to his seat, tipped back his chair, and gave them all a rare grin.

Elle was staring at him oddly. "How much have you had to drink?"

"He's drinking virgin," Finn said. "He said he's our DD tonight."

Elle's eyes widened. "So you're completely sober," she said to Archer. "And you can sing like that? How did I not know you can sing like that?"

"You don't know a lot about me."

He said this mildly but Elle blinked like he'd slapped her.

Ignoring this reaction, Archer reached past her to grab a handful of cookies that Haley had baked herself. "Are these as good as they look?"

"Better," Haley said while Willa rubbed the kink in her neck, the one she'd gotten by taking too many peeks at the damn door.

"We do karaoke all the time," Elle said to Archer, apparently unable to let it go. "You've never sang like that before."

"Sure I have."

"Never," she said adamantly. "You could go on any singing show in this country and win."

"No shit," he said easily. "But I don't want to sing for a living. I want to catch the idiots and asshats of the world for a living."

"Why would you choose such a dangerous job when you could literally stand there and look pretty and sing?" Haley asked.

Archer shrugged. "Because I'm *good* at catching the idiots and asshats of the world," he said. "I'm not all that good at looking pretty."

"You just like wearing at least three weapons at all times," Elle accused.

"That too," he agreed and went for more cookies. "Isn't it time for gifts yet?"

He was referring to their annual White Elephant/ Secret Santa gift exchange. The rule was simple—the gifts had to be under twenty bucks, not that this stopped them from competing like it was for a pot of gold.

It all started out very polite, with each of them setting their wrapped present in a pile. Then, like calm, civilized adults, they took turns choosing and unwrapping one.

But in ten minutes flat—a new record for them—it turned into a wrestling match when Haley jumped on Archer's back and bit his ear to keep him from getting the *Star Wars* shower curtain that she wanted so badly.

"Okay," she said ten minutes later, the shower curtain safe in her hands. "That didn't happen."

"Spence already put it on Instagram," Elle said.

"Dammit!"

There was another scuffle over some bacon toothpaste and then they all shared another round of eggnog.

Willa drank her third and took yet another glance at the pub doors.

"You okay?" Pru asked her.

"Yes." She shook her head. "Actually, no, I'm some distance from okay. I mean I thought I was fine, you know? I was alone and I was good at that. I'd given up men and that was working for me—until, of course, the sexiest of all the men in all the world named Keane made me forget my no-man decree, and now . . ."

She shook her head. "And now I'm not good at alone anymore."

"You could switch things up and come to bat for my team," Haley suggested. "But you should know, women are even harder to deal with than men, trust me."

"I don't want a team," Willa said. "No more sexy times, which really sucks because me and Keane were good at it, *really* good. Okay, so *he* is the one who's really, really, really, *really* good—"

"Uh, honey," Elle said and drew her finger across her throat signaling Willa that she should stop talking now.

But she wasn't done. "You know what? I think I'll be my *own* team. I've got a good shower massager, I'll take care of my own business."

Normally this would've gotten her a big laugh, but instead each of her dearest friends in the world was looking at her with varying winces and grimaces on her face. *Oh shit.* "He's right behind me, isn't he?" she whispered.

"Little bit," Spence said.

She didn't look. She couldn't; someone had glued her feet to the floor.

Finn topped off her drink and hugged her tight. "It's not as bad you think."

No. It was worse.

Elle leaned in. "Hey, guys *like* women who can take care of their own business."

Archer appeared to choke on his own tongue.

Pru smacked both him and Finn upside the back of their heads and pulled Finn away. *"Kitchen,"* she said firmly.

Haley quickly stood. "I'll go with you. Spence?"

"Yep." Spence's gaze slid past Willa for a beat and then he lowered his voice. "You let us love you, Willa. But maybe it's time to expand your horizons beyond the core group, you know?"

"But *you* haven't," she said desperately.

"Trying and failing isn't the same as not trying," he said. And then he walked away, nodding at the man behind her.

Willa could feel Keane, but she wasn't ready to look.

"Whatever you do," Elle said quietly, "do it from your gut and take no prisoners." She watched Spence walk away. "I'm going after him," she said. "You know this is a rough time for him. Unless you need me to stay and kick ass and take names . . . ?"

"I'll be okay," Willa said bravely.

The only one left, Archer set his beer down and looked at her. It was hard to take him seriously with the Santa hat. "Let me guess," she said miserably. "Follow your heart or something Hallmark-y like that, right?"

This had Archer letting out a rare laugh. "Fuck, no."

She let out a low laugh too in spite of the panic choking the air from her lungs. Of all her BFFs, Archer was the most closed off. King of his own island and no one had a set of the laws but him.

"I was going to say run like hell," he said, "but Keane looks like he can catch you with no problem at all." His smile faded and he ducked down a little. "But if you've changed your mind and don't want to be caught, you give me the bat signal and I'm there, okay?"

She looked into the eyes of the man who would do anything, and she meant anything, to keep his friends safe. "Okay."

And then she was alone in the bar with the only man who'd ever really snagged a piece of her heart. Slowly she turned and faced him.

He looked utterly exhausted. It must be raining again because his hair was wet, his long dark lashes spiky. He hadn't shaved that morning. And probably not the morning before either.

"I'm sorry," he said.

She blinked. "For what?"

"A lot of things but let's start with tonight. I wanted to be here earlier, I intended to be, but . . ." His eyes were dark, his expression was dark, and her heart immediately stopped.

"What's wrong?" she asked, thinking *please don't let it be Sally . . .*

"Pita's gone again, but this time I think she got out of the house."

She gasped. "What?"

"There were people going in and out all day and I was working in the attic and . . . shit." He shoved a hand through his wet hair, leaving it standing on end. "I fucking lost her."

"Why didn't you call me sooner?"

"I did. You didn't answer. I figured you were pissed that I hadn't shown up. I came here to beg you for help—"

"I didn't hear my phone—" She slapped her pockets.

Empty. She turned in a slow circle looking for her purse, which she'd left on the bar unattended. She ran over there and pulled out her phone and saw the missed calls. "I'm so sorry." She headed for the door. "Let's go."

Chapter 29

#MakingAListAndCheckingItTwice

Keane drove them to Vallejo Street, his mind filled with worry about Pita but still having enough room to enjoy the way Willa looked tonight, which was smokin' hot. "I'm sorry about taking you away from your Christmas party." He slid her a lingering look. "I like the dress."

She looked down at her little red dress. Emphasis on *little*. "I wore it for you."

He felt a knot loosen in his chest and met her deep green gaze. "The invite. Was that just to the party? Or into your life?"

She nibbled on her lower lip but held his eyes prisoner. "Both," she said.

The rest of the knots fell away as he pulled up in front of his house. Rain pelted the truck as he turned to her, one hand on the steering wheel, the other going to the nape of her neck.

She leaned across the console and kissed him, short

but not sweet. "Petunia first," she said quietly. "The rest later. We have time."

He cupped her jaw, his thumb stroking her soft skin. "I like the sound of that," he said. "I'll go check with the neighbors. See if anyone saw her."

"Can I use your office to make some posters?" she asked and, if he wasn't mistaken, shivered while she was at it.

"Posters?" he repeated in question, peeling out of his sweatshirt and pulling it over her head.

"Missing Cat posters." She hugged his sweatshirt to herself, inhaling deeply as if she liked his scent.

He reached into his pocket and held out the key he'd tried to give her the other day. He smiled. "You're going to need this to get inside."

Her fingers closed over his and their gazes met and held. "Thanks," she said. "For the key and the patience." Then she was gone, running up the steps, letting herself inside the house.

He watched her go and then grabbed his spare jacket from the backseat. A minute later he was going up and down the street asking about Pita while the woman he was pretty sure had just agreed to be his gave up her Christmas Eve helping him, simply because he'd asked.

Half an hour later, he had to admit defeat. No one had seen or heard the cat.

The streets were quiet, traffic was low to nonexistent, but that was because of the storm. Earlier, during rush hour, there'd been heavy traffic. For all he knew, Pita had gotten scared and run off, and then ended up lost. Or she'd been taken by someone.

Or worse, hit by a car.

He stood under a tree whose roots had cracked the sidewalk, only half protected from the rain, wet as hell, trying to figure out how he was going to ever face his aunt again when his phone vibrated.

"Well, finally," Sharon, his real estate agent said. "I called your office line first and your new girl answered."

"I don't have a new girl."

"Then your new girlfriend. She offered to take a message for me but after I told her the fabulous news—"

"What news?"

"Well now see, that's what I'm trying to tell you," Sharon said. "After I gave her the message, I realized I wanted to tell you myself so I tried your cell and hit pay dirt. You ready?"

"Just spit it out already."

"Okay, Mr. Grinch, you're not in a partying mood, I get it. But that's going to change because . . ."

"Sharon, I swear to God—"

"We not only have an offer, it's *The* Offer. Fifteen percent over our asking price! Merry fucking Christmas, Keane!"

He went shock still as conflicting emotions hit in a tidal wave. No, more like a tsunami. Over the past two days plenty of offers had come in, but nothing to write home about. He'd told himself the relief he'd felt was simple exhaustion.

But now that relief turned over in his gut because an offer for fifteen percent over his already inflated asking price was insane and more than he'd hoped for, way more. There was no reason not to jump on this offer, none. He'd told himself he wanted out, had wanted that badly enough to make it happen, and now here he was.

Wishes of his own making.

"Keane?"

"Yeah." Where was the elation? Or the sense that this was the right thing? "I'm here," he said, squinting as the wind kicked up, rain slapping him in the face.

"Tell me I'm accepting this offer," Sharon said.

If this was my home, I'd never leave it . . . Willa's words floated in his brain.

"Keane," Sharon said, suddenly serious. "I'm not going to lie, you're scaring me more than a little bit with the whole silent act here. Tell me we're selling. Say it out loud before I have the rest of this stroke you're giving me. I mean it, Keane. If I die from this, and it feels like I might, I want you to know I'm leaving my five cats to you. *Five.*"

"Yeah," he said. "I hear you."

"So can I accept this offer?"

He tipped his head up, looking through the branches of the tree at the wild, stormy sky. When he'd put the house on the market, he'd done so because he knew he wasn't cut out for the stability this house would provide. He couldn't even keep a damn cat. And yeah, things were looking good with Willa but there were no guarantees. There were never any guarantees. "Accept the offer," he said.

Sharon wooted and whooped it up in his ear and then disconnected, leaving him standing there in the storm, the icy rain slapping him in the face.

He should feel good. Instead, a pit in his stomach

warned him that maybe he wasn't thinking this all the way through, that maybe he was letting his lifelong, string-free existence rear its head and take over, ignoring how things had started to change deep within him.

Taking a deep breath, he turned back to the house, stopping in surprise when he found Willa on his porch. "Hey," he said. "Why are you out here in the rain?"

"I tried calling you," she said. She was hugging herself. And no longer wearing his sweatshirt. He started to take his jacket off to give it to her, but she held up her hand.

"I found Pita," she said.

"Seriously? Where?"

"You put a grate over the vent she went down last time, and then a chair over that, probably to dissuade her from another adventure." She held his gaze. "Or maybe it was for aesthetic value so that the room looked good when real estate agents paraded their clients through here."

Oh shit. He hadn't told her. Why hadn't he told her? *Because you hadn't really believed she could ever be yours* . . . He opened his mouth but she spoke quickly. "Petunia somehow squeezed herself under the chair, snagged the grate up with a claw, and down she went." She lifted a shoulder. "She was filthy so I cleaned her up in the bathroom sink. No worries, I cleaned up after, good as new for your new buyer." Her eyes were fathomless. Unreadable. "Congratulations, by the way."

"I was going to tell you about the offer," he said quietly.

She nodded, which was kind of her since they both

knew he hadn't even told her when he'd put the place up on the market. "Willa, I—"

"No," she said. "You don't owe me an explanation. Not for that, and not for the fact that you're giving Petunia away." Her mouth was grim. "I'm sorry, your phone was ringing off the hook, I thought maybe it was an emergency so I answered. Sally's friend's coming tomorrow morning to pick up Petunia."

Actually, Keane *did* owe her an explanation because it wasn't what she thought. It wasn't him trying to keep from getting attached, to the house or Pita. Or her. Because that ship had sailed. He *was* attached. He couldn't get *more* attached.

He hadn't told her about putting the house on the market because he'd been postponing doing that for so long he'd just assumed he could keep on postponing, never having to make the conscious decision to keep it.

As for Pita, he'd regretted that decision from the moment he'd so readily agreed. He'd thought being free of the cat and the house would simplify his life.

Turned out he didn't want simple. "Sally's friend wants to adopt Pita for her grandkids."

"So you're really giving her up?"

"Not me," he said. "Sally's friend wants her long-term."

"And you don't."

Recrimination and disappointment were all over her face.

"It wasn't my idea, Willa."

She stared at him for a long beat. "Well then," she finally said. "I'm glad for the chance to say goodbye."

He shifted in closer, reaching for her but she took a step back.

"Willa," he said quietly. "We all knew it was hopefully a temporary situation. There's no choice here."

She met his gaze. "There's always another choice."

Keane had thought admitting that he wanted her in his life was difficult but the joke was on him. The hardest part was still in front of him. How was he going to maintain a relationship when he had no idea how to even start? He'd never been successful at true intimacy.

But to be with Willa, he was most definitely up for the challenge. He started to tell her just that but a car came toward them, the lights shining through the downpour as it slowed and then stopped in front of the house.

Willa started down the steps but Keane caught her. "Willa—"

"I'm leaving, Keane. I called an Uber."

His other hand came up, holding her still as he stared down at her, his heart pounding uncomfortably. "Why?"

"You know why," she whispered. "This isn't going to work."

The Uber driver honked and Willa started to move but Keane held on to her, lifting a finger to the driver to signal they needed a minute. "Okay," he said, attempting to find his equilibrium here, not able to will his hands to let loose of her. "I fucked up but—"

"No, that's the thing," she said. "This isn't on you. It's all on me for thinking we could do this. The guy who doesn't need anyone or anything, and the girl who secretly dreams about love but doesn't know how to hold on to it." She put a hand to her chest like it hurt. "The mistake's mine, Keane. I let myself fall for the fantasy. Hell," she said on a short laugh. "I let myself fall period, even when I knew better."

The driver honked again and she turned that way but Keane blocked her. "I never meant to hurt you," he said, swiping a lone tear from her cheek with his thumb. "You believe in second chances, remember? Well give me one."

"It's not about second chances, Keane. It's that, as it turns out, we're *both* pretty damn good at being temporary specialists and leaving ourselves an escape clause."

Her shimmery smile broke his heart and he laughed mirthlessly. "I certainly didn't plan for an escape clause when I fell in love with you."

She stilled and stared up at him. "Wait—what?"

Jesus, had he really just said that, just opened a vein here when she had one foot out the door?

"Keane?"

Yep, he'd said it. Later he'd think it was like getting a brain freeze after gulping down a Slurpee too fast. There was nothing but the burn for a long beat as his mind went into a free fall. He loved her. Holy shit, *he loved her.*

But by the time he managed to gulp some air into his deprived lungs and kick-start himself again, Willa had given up on him and climbed into the Uber, leaving him alone in the cold, dark night.

Chapter 30

#TakesALickingAndKeepsOnTicking

Willa walked through the courtyard, soggy footsteps muted as she crossed to the fountain. It was as empty as her heart.

The water hitting the copper base was a familiar soothing sound and she stopped, hugging herself. She wished she'd kept Keane's sweatshirt, but his body heat had lingered in it along with his scent, and she was a junkie.

Time to go cold turkey.

"Hey," Rory said, coming around the fountain toward her.

"Hey. What are you doing out here this late, it's freezing."

"I'm fine," Rory said. "Just making a wish. World peace and all that."

Willa smiled. "When did you become the grown-up in our little twosome?"

"Since you dragged me into adulthood kicking and screaming." With a small smile, Rory pulled a little wrapped box from her pocket and held it out to Willa. "Merry Christmas."

Willa shook her head. "Oh, honey, you didn't have to—"

"You took me in off the streets. You gave me a job and force-fed me morals and honesty and trust." Rory's eyes went misty. "So yes, I'm giving you a present, small as it is."

Willa pulled her in for a hard hug. "I love you, you know."

Rory gave a small, embarrassed laugh. "Well, jeez, you haven't even opened it yet. Maybe you'll hate it."

Willa pulled off the paper and then let out a half laugh, half sob at the sight of the cute little key chain with a bunch of charms, each with a pic of some of her favorite customers' pets. "I love it."

"I'm going home," Rory said softly. "I'm nervous as hell and I might throw up if I think about it too long, but thanks for getting me the ride. Archer called me and said I'm leaving in half an hour. Should be in Tahoe by dawn."

"You'll call me, tell me how it goes?"

"Yes."

Willa gave her a long look.

"Okay, no, I won't call," Rory said. "I hate talking on the phone. But I'll text."

Good enough. Willa hugged her tight. "Still love you."

"Well, if you're going to get mushy . . ." Rory squeezed

her back, clinging for a moment. "Then I suppose I love you too." She pulled back and swiped her nose. "Thought you'd be with Keane tonight."

"Why?"

"Right. Because you're not a thing."

"Okay, fine, I might have been wrong about that before but we're back to not being a thing now. For good."

Rory rolled her eyes so hard that Willa was surprised they didn't fall out of her head. "Because while you love me, you looo-oooo-ooove him."

Willa didn't have the heart to tell her that sometimes love wasn't enough. "I'm not sure it's going to work out."

"Why not?"

"It's . . . complicated," Willa said.

"Complicated as in you got scared that he's not a dog or a cat or a wayward teen that needs taking care until it finds its final home?"

Willa blew out a breath. "Well why don't you tell me what you really think?"

"Sorry." Rory smiled gently. "But he's a good guy, Willa, we all think so. If you can't trust yourself, then maybe you can trust the collective certainty of the people who love and care about you. Don't find him a different permanent home than with you, Willa."

She choked out a laugh. "He's not a dog!"

"Exactly." And with that, Rory kissed her on the cheek and walked away.

Willa turned to the fountain. For months now she'd recklessly tossed coins into this very water, wishing for love. And then, apparently, she'd proceeded to panic when she'd actually gotten what she'd wished for.

"Dammit," she whispered. "Everyone's right."

"Well, of course we are, darlin'."

She nearly jumped out of her skin as she turned and faced Eddie, wearing board shorts and a really ugly Christmas sweater.

He smiled. "So what are we right about?"

"Sometimes I'm too stubborn and obstinate to see reason."

"Sometimes?"

She huffed out a sigh.

He grimaced at the look on her face. "Okay, now see, this is why I never managed to stay married. There's all these landmine discussions and I kept stepping on them and blowing myself up."

"It's not your fault. It's mine." Because of it, she'd walked away from Keane—not because he'd not told her about his house or Petunia, but because she was scared of everything she thought she wanted. Everything that had for once truly been within her grasp and standing right in front of her. "Oh my God." She looked at Eddie. "I've made a terrible mistake. I need a ride."

"Dudette," he said with a slow head shake. "I'd do anything for you, you know that, but they took my license away twenty years ago now."

"They" being the state of California, probably having something to do with the medical marijuana card he had laminated and hanging around his neck.

"It's okay." She slipped him all the cash she had in her pocket—twenty bucks—and a quick hug. "Merry

Christmas," she said before running to the stairs. She dashed into her apartment and grabbed her bag. Then she two-timed it back to the pub and banged on the door.

Sean answered and she pushed past him, rushing to the stage where her best friends in the world were currently fighting over who'd won a bonus round of karaoke—hip-hop style.

Archer was adamant that his rendition of "Ice Ice Baby" beat Spence and Finn's version of "Baby Got Back." Finn was laughing so hard he was on the floor. Elle was sitting on the bar filing her nails listening to something Pru was telling her and nodding in agreement.

They stopped and stared at her, making her realize that she was drenched from the rain and a complete and utter mess.

Inside *and* out.

"So it turns out that I really am too stubborn and obstinate to see reason. And also, I screwed everything up," she added breathlessly. "I need a ride."

They all kept staring at her.

"Now," she said. And then she whirled to the door, knowing she didn't have to wait. They had her back too. Just like she should've known that Keane would have her back. Pushing open the pub door she got to the street and then turned around to see who'd come to drive her so she would know which car or truck to go for.

They were all right there, every last one of them, pulling on jackets as they rushed out the door after her and her heart just about burst out of her chest. "Thanks," she whispered.

Spence pulled her in for a hard hug. "Anything for you," he said against her temple. "You know that."

"Even if I've been really stupid?"

"Especially if," Archer said and tugged on a wet strand of her hair. "Let's go."

"All of us?" For the first time she hesitated. "I'm not sure I need an audience for this."

"Tough," Elle said. "You're family. And family sticks together on Christmas."

Willa's eyes filled. "It's not Christmas yet," she managed.

Spence looked at his phone for the time. "Eleven thirty," he said. "Close enough."

They all piled into Archer's truck because he was the only actual sober one. "Where to?" he asked her.

"Keane's."

He smiled. "No shit. I meant I need an address."

Right. She started to rattle it off and then sat straight up. "We have to go to a tree lot first! He doesn't have a tree, I want to bring him a tree!"

Spence groaned, but Archer didn't blink an eye. And ten minutes later they were all standing in a tree lot, staring at the two trees that were left.

"That one," Pru said, pointing to a very short tree with three branches.

"No, this one," Elle said about a taller but equally sparse tree.

Archer looked at Willa. Then he turned to the guy running the lot. "You got anything else?"

The guy shrugged. "There's one in my trailer. It's slightly used, but it's the best tree on this lot."

"You don't want it?" Willa asked him.

The guy flashed a smile. "Got a hot date with the missus tonight. I'd rather have the fifty bucks."

"Forty," Archer said and paid the guy.

The tree went into the back of his truck and in ten more minutes they were at Keane's house.

Willa still had no idea exactly what she was going to say, only knowing that she had to say something, *anything,* to fix this.

Because she was done running.

When Archer pulled over in front of the house, they all looked at her.

She stared at the house, garnering courage. Thankfully her friends gave her the silence she so desperately needed. When she finally thought maybe she could get out of the truck and not have her legs collapse in anxiety, she opened the door. Turning back, she found the people she loved more than anything all squished in tight together, practically on top of each other, watching her with varying degrees of concern and worry. "I'm okay," she told them, struck anew by how lucky she was to have them in her life. To know she was loved. To believe in herself because they believed in her.

Keane hadn't had any of that and yet he was still one of the most incredible men she'd ever met. He'd never learned to love and yet he was able to feel it enough to tell her.

And she hadn't said anything back. In fact, she'd let

him believe he didn't deserve a second chance, when everyone deserved a second chance. And God, even though she didn't deserve it, she really, really hoped a second chance applied to her too. "Thanks for the ride. I'll talk to you guys tomorrow."

"Oh, we're not going anywhere," Elle said. "We're going to sit here quietly and well behaved—" She broke off to give the guys a long look. "And there will be *no* fart wars while we wait or someone will die."

"Hey, that wasn't my bad last time," Spence said. "I'm not the one who's dairy intolerant."

"Well excuse me," Finn grumbled. "How was I supposed to know the smoothie Pru bought me that night was milk based?"

"He hasn't had any dairy today," Pru told Elle. "He's dairy free."

"You don't have to stay," Willa repeated.

Archer shook his head. They were staying. "Until you tell us you're good," he said, and just like that it became law. "Wave when you're ready for the tree and we'll bring it up."

Okay, then. Willa ran up the steps and knocked. She wasn't sure what she expected but when Keane opened the door, she lost her tongue.

She could tell he was surprised too. His gaze tracked past her to the truck at the curb—and the five faces there, pressed up against a fogged-up window, watching.

"Don't mind them," she said. "There was nothing good on TV tonight."

He almost smiled at that, she could tell. Tucked

under one arm like a football was Petunia, lounging against his strong forearm like she'd been born to do so.

Keane wore only a T-shirt and sweat pants. No shoes. Hair looking like maybe he'd shoved his fingers through it. He seemed tired, wary, and distinctly not happy.

Her fault.

"How long are they going to stay out there?" he asked.

"Until I get my life together." She pulled the door from his grasp and shut it on her friends' collective faces.

"Do they know that might take a while?" Keane asked wryly.

She let out a low laugh and turned to face him, eyes on his face. "You love me?" she asked softly.

"So you *did* hear me." He took her hand with his free one and led her to the kitchen. He set the cat down on the floor near her bowl, and true to form, she waddled over to it and stuck her head into the thing like she'd been starved for the past five weeks.

Keane rolled his eyes, grabbed a clean dish towel, and turned back to Willa, running it over her dripping hair. "You're frozen through," he said, standing close, very close, affecting her breathing. He met her gaze and held it as he dried her off. "You need a hot shower and—"

She wrapped her fingers around his wrists and stilled his movements. "You love me."

He tossed the towel aside and cupped her face. "From the moment you let me into South Bark that first morning and gave me 'tude." He gave a little smile. "And then changed my life with your easy affection, huge heart, and the world's best smile."

"Oh," she breathed, completely undone. Her eyes filled and she snapped her mouth shut for a minute, swallowing hard. "I love you too, Keane." Oh God. She'd never said those words out loud before. She had to bend over for a second, hands on her knees, fighting the sudden dizziness.

Two strong hands lifted her. When she met his gaze, he was smiling a little. "How much did that hurt?" he asked.

She let out a breath. "Not nearly as much as this— I'm sorry I ran off like that. It was just like when you tried to give me your key, I . . . panicked."

"And?"

"And then I blamed you for holding back, but it was all me. I let you in and I fell hard. And then suddenly it was like that bad nightmare of going to school naked. I got scared."

"I know. Come here, Willa." And then instead of waiting for her to do so, he pulled her into his arms. "Are you scared now?"

"No," she said, holding on tight.

"Then have some faith in me to not hurt you."

"I've always have faith in you," she said. "It was the faith in me that took a while."

"This isn't all on you, Willa," he said. "It's on me too. I should've told you about putting the house up for sale. I should've told you about the offers that poured in. But the truth is that you were right all along. I didn't really want to sell."

She stilled and lifted her head to see his face. "So why are you?"

"I'm not." He shook his head. "I rescinded my acceptance of the offer."

She just stared up at him. "Because . . . ?"

"Because this house is no longer just a house to me," he said. "It's my home. And I want it to be yours too." He cupped her face and pressed his forehead to hers. "I'm hoping you want that too. Think you can handle it?"

She slipped her arms around his waist. "There's this incredible man I know. He let me watch him learn that being emotionally closed off didn't work, that it's worth the risk to let someone in."

He smiled. "He sounds smart as hell. Probably he's sexy as hell too, right?"

She laughed and pressed even closer, unable to believe this was really happening. "*So* damn sexy."

He looked deep into her eyes and let his smile fade. "I love you, Willa. I've spent years risking everything for my business, over and over. It's past time to risk my heart for you."

"Does risking that heart include letting me put up a tree?"

"It's a little late for that, I think."

"Actually, it's not." She ran to the front door. Yep, everyone was still curbside in Archer's truck. She waved.

Archer and Spence got out of the car, untied the tree from the truck bed and carried it up the front steps.

Keane blinked.

"Tree delivery service," Spence quipped. "Where do you want it?"

Keane looked at Willa. "Wherever she wants."

"Good answer," Archer murmured as they carted the tree in.

They deposited it in the large front living room. Spence walked out the front door first, Archer behind him. He turned and looked at Willa. "You good?"

She beamed at him.

"Yeah," he said with a barely there smile. "You're good."

And then they were gone.

Keane rubbed a hand over his jaw, staring at the tree, which was only slightly crooked. The topper was Archer's Santa hat.

"The holidays are going to be insane, aren't they?" he asked.

She smiled from the bottom of her heart and took his hand. "Yeah. Scared?"

"Bring it."

With a musical laugh, she leapt into his arms, wrapping herself around him. Then she snuggled in and smiled against his lips. "Mmm. You missed me." She wriggled against him. "Or at least a part of you did."

He entwined his fingers into her hair and kissed her, deep and serious. "All of me," he said. "All of me missed you. All of me needs you in my life. You are my life. We're doing this, Willa. And it's going to be good."

She got anticipatory chills. "Yes, please. We've done it in my kitchen, but not yours . . ."

With a rough laugh, he kissed her again. "You know damn well what I meant. But your idea works too. And after the kitchen, it's the upstairs bathroom. There's a handheld showerhead there that you're going to like." He flashed his wicked grin. "A *lot*."

She slid her hands to his jaw. "Are you sure?"

"Hell yeah. That showerhead's going to rock your world—"

Laughing, she went to kiss him but he stopped her. "I want you to be okay with all of this," he said. "With me."

"I know. And I am. So much. I'm completely yours, Keane."

Her words seemed to light him up from within. "And you'll tell me if it gets to be too much. I don't want you to run—"

She gently covered his mouth with her fingers. "I learned tonight when I thought I'd blown it with you that nothing is ever going to be too much. Now you. You'll let me know if I drive you crazy?"

He laughed. "I love your crazy. I love *you*, Willa. With everything that I am, I love you."

"Oh," she breathed softly. "You're good."

"Give me five minutes in that shower and you'll see how much better than good I really am."

She smiled against his lips. "I haven't given you your Christmas present yet."

"What is it?" he asked.

"Me."

The full-blown smile across his face was brighter than all the lights in the city. "Best present ever," he said and Willa knew that Christmas, not to mention the rest of her life, was never going to be the same again. It was in fact going to be better than her wildest dreams.

Epilogue

#GoodMorningSunshine

On Christmas morning, Keane woke up like he always did, slowly. He took a deep breath and smiled as the scent of Willa's shampoo filled his nostrils. This was because her hair was in his face. In fact, she had shifted in her sleep and was lying half on top of him, using him as her personal body pillow.

The day hadn't even started and already it was his favorite Christmas of all time. It'd only taken four little words—*I love you, Keane*—to make his world complete. But it was so much more than that. It was him realizing that the woman he loved more than anything loved him back every bit as much. It was her being okay with losing herself in him because she knew that she'd always find herself there too. It was her trusting him, believing in him, in *them*.

She was wearing his favorite pj's—absolutely nothing

but her birthday suit—and he slowly ran his hands over all that creamy warm skin he loved so much.

"Hmph," she murmured, not moving an inch.

He stilled, not wanting to wake her all the way, knowing she needed sleep since he'd kept her up most of the night checking off items on their "list."

He'd drawn the Bad Elf fantasy, and in a twist he'd made her the bad elf. The vision of her in nothing but an elf hat and tied to his headboard was going down in history as his all-time favorite, but he was open to topping it.

Still draped over him, Willa wriggled. "Why did you stop?" she asked, eyes still closed, voice groggy.

He went back to stroking her. Every time he stopped, she wriggled and made a noise of discontentment, making him laugh. "Merry Christmas," he murmured in her ear and took her lobe between his teeth.

She sat straight up. "It's Christmas!" she exclaimed as if she'd actually forgotten.

"Yeah," he said, hands on her ass, rocking her into him, loving the gasp that wrenched from her throat. On a mission now, he began to tug her even closer, his gaze locked on his target . . .

"Wait," she gasped, crawling off of him, running naked to her duffel bag on the floor. "I have another present for you."

"Mmm," he said watching as she bent over to rifle through the duffel. "You're giving me a gift right now—"

She grabbed his discarded shirt and pulled it over her head. Then she whirled and ran back to him, jumping on him like a kid on . . . well, Christmas morning. "Open!" she demanded.

The bag was bright red. He peeked inside and pulled out a pair of . . . boxers with eyeballs covered in glasses all over them.

"Interesting," he said.

"Crap!" She snatched back the boxers and stuffed them in the bag again. "Those are for Haley." She ran to her duffel again and came back with another bright red bag, same size as the other.

This time he pulled out a box of joke condoms that said *Size Matters! Think Big!* He laughed and reached for her. "This here's a present that needs to be shown how to use—"

"No, wait!" she said, laughing as she evaded him. "That's Pru's!" And she once again exchanged the bag. This time she peeked into it first and sighed. "Okay, *this* is it."

He took in her shaky smile and the way she was fiddling, and realized she was nervous. Setting the present aside, he sat all the way up, stuffed the pillows behind his back, and then pulled her into his lap. "Better," he said and reached for the present again.

When he pulled out the vintage tape measure, he let out a long breath. "Is this—"

"From the turn of the twentieth century," she said. "It's got a lightweight brass casing with a conversion table on the other side. After you told me about that time you spent working with your uncle and how much you liked his antique tools, this felt like something you might like."

"*Love,*" he said, marveling at it. It was amazing. "Where did you get it?"

"I found it at an antique store on Divisadero Street." She shifted uncomfortably, clearly embarrassed. "It's not much, and I'm not even sure it really works, I just—"

He leaned forward and kissed her to shut her up. Pulling back only a fraction, he held her gaze. "It's perfect. You're perfect."

She bit her lower lip and smiled. "Good. Let's get up. I've got something in my bag for Petunia before she gets picked up—"

"She's not getting picked up."

"She's not?"

"No," he said. "I called Sally and said the cat had to stay because I have a mouse problem."

She choked out a laugh. "You didn't."

"I didn't," he agreed. "I told Sally the cat had to stay because she belonged here in this house, that I'd fallen in love several times over and I needed both my girls here with me."

Willa let out a shaky breath. "I'm not going to get tired of hearing that anytime soon."

"Mew."

They both looked over at Pita sitting in the doorway. "She's demanding sustenance," Keane said.

Willa laughed and slid off him. "I'll go feed her. I'll be right back."

He heard her move into the kitchen. Heard her pad to the bin of cat food and stop.

He knew why. Knew exactly what she'd found. And two seconds later she came racing back into the room, a blur of red hair and soft, sweet skin as she jumped him for the second time that morning.

Straddling him, she beamed down at him, her eyes shimmering brilliantly.

"What?" he asked innocently.

She held out the robin egg blue box. *"Tiffany's?"*

"Are you going to quiz me or open it?"

She slipped the silver ribbon off the box and slowly lifted the lid. Gasped. "Oh my God," she whispered as she gaped at the platinum chain with a *W* encrusted in diamonds. "You remembered about the necklace my mom gave me when I was little." Tears gathered in her eyes as she let him put it around her neck.

This one was most certainly not going to turn her neck green.

"It's beautiful," she said, staring down at it. "It's the most thoughtful gift anyone's ever given me."

"Looks good on you." He pulled her over him and softly caressed her until she pulled back.

"Have you ever made love beneath a Christmas tree?" she murmured.

"No, but I'm in." Catching her against him he rose and then threw her over his shoulder in a fireman's hold, palming a sweet cheek. "I'm all about starting a new tradition."

She was laughing as he carried her to the still undecorated tree and together they crawled beneath it to lie on their backs. Her hand slipped in his as they stared up at the tangle of branches. "To new beginnings," she said.

He came up on an elbow and cupped her face. "Forever, Willa?"

She tugged him over the top of her. "Forever."

Want more warm, funny romance?
Look out for the next book in the
Heartbreaker Bay series

Accidentally On Purpose

Elle Wheaton's priorities are friends, career – and kick-ass shoes.
Then there's the muscular wall of stubbornness that's security
expert Archer Hunt – who actually comes before everything else.
Not that Elle's letting on. She's just seeing other men until she
gets over Archer . . . which should only take a lifetime . . .

Archer's wanted the best for Elle ever since he sacrificed his
law-enforcement career to save her. Their chemistry could start
the next San Francisco earthquake, but Archer doesn't want
to be responsible for the potential fall-out. Instead he's stuck
watching her go out with guys who aren't good enough for her.
Maybe it's time for a new mission – and for Archer to prove to
Elle that her perfect man has been here all along . . .

Coming soon from

headline
ETERNAL

Welcome to Cedar Ridge, Colorado, where the only thing more rugged than the glorious Rocky Mountains are the rough-and-tumble Kincaid brothers.

Meet Aidan, Hudson and Jacob in

 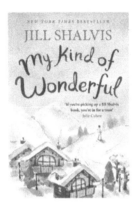 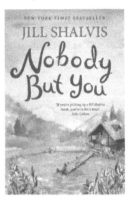

**'Humor, intrigue, and scintillating sex.
Jill Shalvis is a total original'**
Suzanne Forster

headline
ETERNAL

*W*hen Jill's neighbor decided to have an extension built, she was suddenly gifted with inspiration: a bunch of cute, young, sweaty guys hanging off the roof and the walls. Just the type of men who'd appeal to three estranged sisters forced together when they inherit a dilapidated beach resort . . .

Meet Maddie, Tara and Chloe in

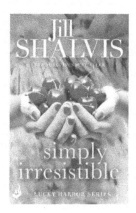 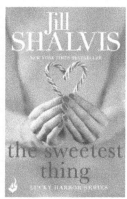 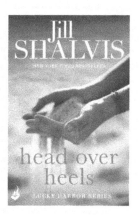

'Count on Jill Shalvis for a witty, steamy, unputdownable love story'

Robyn Carr

headline
ETERNAL

When the lights go out and you're 'stuck' in a café with potential Chocoholic-partners-in-crime and nothing else to do but eat cake and discuss the mysteries of life, it's surprising just what conclusions women will come to. But when they decide to kick things into gear, they'd better be prepared for what happens once they have the ball rolling . . .

Here come Mallory, Amy and Grace in

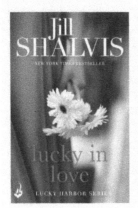 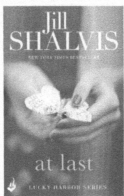 

'An abundance of chemistry, smoldering romance, and hilarious antics'

Publishers Weekly

headline
ETERNAL

The women of Lucky Harbor have been charming readers with their incredible love stories – now it's time for some very sexy men to take center stage. They're in for some *big* surprises – and from corners they'd least expect it.

Really get to know Luke, Jack and Ben in

 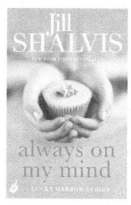 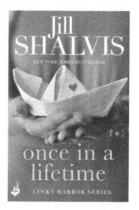

'Hot sex, some delightful humor and plenty of heartwarming emotion'

Romantic Times

headline
ETERNAL

$\mathcal{L}$ucky Harbor is the perfect place to escape to, whether that means a homecoming, getting away from the city or running from something a whole lot darker. Whatever the cause, Lucky Harbor has three more residents who are about to discover just how much this sleepy little town really has to offer.

Escape with Becca, Olivia and Callie in

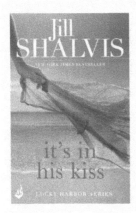 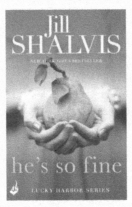 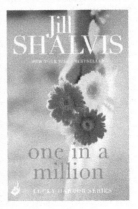

'Clever, steamy, and fun. Jill Shalvis will
make you laugh and fall in love'
Rachel Gibson

headline
ETERNAL

headline
ETERNAL

FIND YOUR HEART'S DESIRE...

VISIT OUR WEBSITE: www.headlineeternal.com
FIND US ON FACEBOOK: facebook.com/eternalromance
FOLLOW US ON TWITTER: @eternal_books
EMAIL US: eternalromance@headline.co.uk